ANONYMOUS
SOURCE

BREAKING NEWS MYSTERY #1

KRYSTEN BENNETT

Anonymous Source
Breaking News Mystery #1
by Krysten Bennett

Published by Krysten Bennett
www.krystenbennettwrites.com

This is a work of fiction. Names, characters, businesses, places, events, and incidents are either products of the author's imagination or are used fictitiously. Any resemblance to actual businesses, places, events, or incidents is purely coincidental.

First paperback edition January 2022

Cover design and interior formatting by KP CREATIVE LTD.

ISBN 9798779575089 (paperback)
ASIN B09MP3S1T5 (Kindle ebook)
ISBN 9798201652531 (ebook)
GGKEY WKLZ2RHXKTQ E (Google ebook)

For Ma.

You nurtured my imagination and instilled in me a lifelong passion for the written word. I am eternally grateful to you. Miss you. xoxo

SEVEN YEARS AGO
CHICAGO, ILLINOIS

THERE WAS NOTHING LIKE CHRISTMAS in Chicago to put him in a piss-poor mood. Traffic was a nightmare, holiday decorations taunted him with their good cheer, and people were so merry it made him want to stab them all in the face.

The only upside was the abundance of victims to choose from.

He caught sight of someone flagging him down at the corner of Michigan and Illinois and sidled up to the curb. Tacking on a friendly expression, he got out of the car and jogged around to the other side to help her with her oversized suitcase.

"Here," he said, using his pleasant voice, "let me get that for you." The damn thing was big enough to fit two bodies her size in there, if he cut them up just right.

"Oh, thank you," she said breathlessly, passing the luggage over to him. "If only I didn't have so many relatives, I wouldn't have to fly home with so much crap." Smiling, she rolled her eyes in a good-natured way. "Stupid people I love."

He flashed her a grin as he pulled open the trunk. "It's so much easier not to love people, isn't it?" he asked, heaving her bag inside.

She laughed, assuming he was kidding, and reached for the door handle. "Probably."

He slammed the trunk closed and rounded the car. By the time he was back behind the wheel, she had settled into the backseat. He shifted around to look at her, giving her his goofy, non-threatening smile. "Midway or O'Hare?"

"Midway, please," she said.

He glanced in his rearview mirror and shoved his way back into traffic, earning himself a sharp honk from the irate driver he'd cut off. "There's an L station not too far from here," he said. "You'd get there faster for a lot cheaper."

"Are you kidding?" She let out a sarcastic little laugh. "Not having to fight crowds of disoriented tourists and frenzied shoppers is more than worth it."

He smiled at her in the rearview mirror as the light turned green. If only she knew.

Today was the ten-year anniversary of his father's death, and he had plans to commemorate the occasion. First he'd pick up an attractive female passenger, preferably a tourist or one headed out of town who wouldn't be missed for a while.

Step one: Check.

In hindsight, he should've done this sooner. After all, the rat bastard had gotten exactly what he'd deserved. Why shouldn't he, too? He'd spent too long being the disappointing son of a narcissistic lowlife who beat his family and an alcoholic lunatic who suddenly snapped and went off in the deep end.

That was all about to change.

As soon as he'd turned eighteen, he'd gotten the hell out of Seattle and began making his way east, leapfrogging from town to town on a path toward greatness. It had all led him to this city, this day, this ride, this passenger.

At the next red light, he studied her in the rearview mirror as she looked out the window. She'd removed her hat and unfastened the top few buttons of her coat, confirming his original assessment that she was attractive. His fingers twitched in anticipation, and he gripped the steering wheel tighter.

Now for step two: Lull her into a false sense of security with his irresistible charm.

"So," he called over his shoulder, "where ya headed?"

She jerked to face him, surprised he'd broken the tacit rule. Upon seeing his easy smile, she relaxed. "Home for the holidays."

"Where's home?"

"Nowhere special," she said. "Colsboro, Ohio."

"Aw, c'mon," he chided. "Must be something special there." He winked at her. "Or at least there will be in a couple hours."

She let out an unexpected laugh. "I guess I can't argue with that."

The light turned green, and he eased the cab forward. "That's the spirit."

Step two: Check.

He was surprised to notice that his spirits had lifted, too. Today was the dawn of a new day, the beginning of a new him. Without his father's demons weighing him down and his mother's mistakes holding him back, he'd finally become the man he was meant to be. No one would ever underestimate him again.

Now for step three: Kill her. His favorite part.

The question now was, how would he do it? Being forced to devise the perfect course of action in less than an hour would be a challenge. This would be a memorable occasion he would reminisce about for years to come. Eventually, the whole world would know about it, too.

While she chattered away in the backseat—about her family in Ohio, about the summer internship she'd just gotten at the *Sun-Times*, about other insignificant things from her insignificant life—he nodded enthusiastically and pretended to care. Built a rapport. Gained her trust. Learned as much as he could about her.

As the meter ticked along and they neared her final destination, the itch in his fingers intensified and spread. He fought the urge to pull over and strangle her right there on the side of the highway out of sheer frustration. But he couldn't stifle the wildfire of anticipation taking over his body.

And then, without warning, he was ripped out of his fantasy by the sound of screeching tires and crunching metal.

"Shit," he hissed. Biting back a surge of anger, he shoved the gearshift into park, killed the engine, and twisted around to look at her. "Sorry about that. You okay?"

She nodded, eyes wide, and he saw for the first time they were a bright shade of emerald. "Don't apologize," she said, her voice wavering slightly. A shiver zipped down his back. "That was not your fault."

Before he could respond, someone pounded on his window, and they both swiveled toward the sound. The driver of the car in front of them had leapt out of his vehicle and charged toward the cab, leaving his door hanging wide open.

"Get out of the car!" he shouted, his voice muffled from behind the glass. He tacked on a few choice expletives, as if that would persuade him to obey.

"Christ," he grumbled, rolling his window down an inch. "Buddy, you really don't want me to do that."

He punched the window again. "I didn't want you to smash into my brand-new Mercedes, either, but here we are."

"Hey!" the woman called from behind him. He whirled around in surprise to find she'd slid across the backseat to the opposite window. "Chill out, slugger, it wasn't his fault—"

"Mind your own business, bitch!"

"Oh, no, he didn't," she muttered, reaching for the door handle.

"No, don't!" He fumbled for the central lock, but she shoved the door open and stepped out onto the pavement before he had a chance. He swore under his breath and reluctantly followed suit.

"Don't worry. This guy's not going to do anything to us." She eyed the man, who'd jolted backward a few feet now that there was no longer the protective barrier of the car between them. "We're all rational adults, right?"

"Lady, I'm the one who just got rear ended," Slugger snapped, pointing toward his Mercedes. "See?"

"Yeah, well, we got rear ended first." She pointed behind them, where a pickup truck had rammed into the cab's rear bumper, crumpled it like foil, and sent them slamming into the sedan in front of them. "See?" Slugger clamped his mouth shut and folded his arms over his chest. "So I think you owe my friend here an apology."

He glanced over at her in surprise. With the exception of his mother, no one had ever stood up for him.

"I don't think so," the man said defiantly. "I'm the victim here."

She took a step closer and made a show of sniffing the air. "Is that pot I smell?"

Slugger's cheeks reddened. "You don't know what you're talking about."

"I have two brothers who liked to push the boundaries in high school." She laughed. "I know what it smells like."

He snorted. "Good for you."

"The real question is what you know," she continued. "Under Illinois law, you're considered impaired if you drive under the influence of any drug or intoxicating compound that renders you incapable of driving safely."

"So what if I am high?" Slugger waved a dismissive hand. "I'm not the one who—"

"Stopped traffic by getting out of his car in the middle of the street to yell at two strangers?" She matched his cross-armed stance. "You're right, that definitely sounds like safe driving."

The man blinked at her. "You both got out, too."

"To see if you needed medical attention. Clearly you've sustained a head injury, but I suspect we can't attribute that to this accident." She smiled at his bewildered expression. "Now we're going to get back in our car. You probably should, too." She slid into the back seat, slammed the door, and gave him a little finger wave through the window. Slugger shifted his befuddled expression to him.

He smiled smugly. "I did warn you."

Slugger bobbed his head up and down. "Sorry."

"Not as sorry as you will be," he whispered. Before the guy could respond, he turned and sank back into the car, outwardly calm despite the red-hot rage filling his chest. He watched Slugger saunter back to his Mercedes, mind racing with possibilities.

But when he glanced up at the rearview mirror and saw her eyeing him with concern, the rage was tempered with something else—something he couldn't quite describe. Something he hadn't felt in a long time.

He cleared his throat and twisted around to face her. "That was kind of stupid," he said in a low voice. "But thanks for sticking up for me."

She smiled. "That guy was kind of an asshole who deserved to be put in his place," she replied. "But you're welcome."

By the time the police had come and gone, he'd regained his inner equilibrium, and she'd missed her flight. He could tell she was agitated and disappointed, but she didn't complain or place blame.

He was agitated and disappointed, too, but not nearly as kind as she. He'd make this up to her—and, more importantly, himself. He'd track down that bumbling fool and make him pay.

Then he would find her.

CHAPTER 1
PRESENT
COLSBORO, OHIO

THE WOMAN IN THE PHOTO wore a lacy white dress, satin stilettos, and a dramatic cathedral-length veil that framed her curly red hair in a soft halo. In her right hand, she clasped a bouquet of large-petaled scarlet flowers interspersed with baby's breath, their evergreen stems tied with a bright red ribbon. On her left hand, a vintage engagement ring sparkled in the warm light of the candles surrounding her.

But she wasn't a bride, and she never would be.

She was a murder victim.

The reporter sitting next to me shifted in his seat, bumping my elbow and jolting me back to the press conference. I snapped my folio closed and shoved it into my oversized purse, trying to refocus on the Colsboro chief of police—but I couldn't erase the memory of blood oozing from the woman's deeply slashed wrists.

At the podium, Pete Lockwood delivered a prepared statement about Stephanie Goodwin's death: Our detectives are hard at work, we won't rest until the killer is found, we're actively pursuing leads. Blah, blah, blah.

What he left out was that she wasn't her killer's first victim—nor would she be the last.

As soon as the chief opened the floor for questions, a reporter from the local NBC affiliate shot to his feet. "Have you identified any suspects?" he blurted, without waiting to be called on.

Lockwood's forefinger tapped against the podium, which I knew from experience signaled mild impatience. "We have a person of interest, but there's no one we're prepared to name at this time," he said curtly. "Next?"

"If this homicide occurred in Dover County, why are the Colsboro police involved?" a reporter from FOX asked.

"CPD has more resources at our disposal, so we're assisting Northville police with their investigation," Lockwood answered. "We hope that by pooling resources, we can identify the killer and close this case faster than working separately."

And there it was: The perfect segue. I raised a hand briefly to catch Lockwood's attention.

He let out a barely perceptible sigh. "Yes, Jennifer?"

"Are you working with the Corine and West Madison police departments as well?" I asked.

"On what?"

"The murders of Allison Donnelly and Gina Hadley," I said. "They were also raped and murdered in a similarly morbid fashion, and those crimes are yet unsolved. Same for Chelsea Quinn, who was, as you know, killed in CPD jurisdiction."

Lockwood nodded once. "True. However, we have no evidence suggesting all four homicides were committed by the same person. Aside from being women who were raped and murdered, there's nothing to tie them together, and no consistent *modus operandi*."

"Perhaps the fact that there's no consistent M.O. is the M.O.," I pressed. "In which case, you could be dealing with a serial killer."

"If you find compelling evidence," he said, "I'll be the first to consider it. However, until then, we're operating under the assumption they are not connected."

There was compelling evidence, and the chief knew it. But he also knew he could get away with brushing me off, as I wasn't about to mention that evidence at a press conference. The only reason I knew about the fingerprints found at the crime scenes was because they all belonged to people I was related to—a detail that neither one of us wanted to see the outside of a case file.

Which begged the question: Whose fingerprint had been left behind with Stephanie Goodwin?

Refusing to take any more questions, Lockwood turned the podium over to the department's communications director and strode down the aisle in the direction of the exit. Bolting to my feet, I snagged my bag and trench coat before following. The chief caught sight of me at the door and waved away the pair of lieutenants flanking him. He waited for me to catch up, then pushed through the door and held it for me.

"Ballsy questions," he said after the door clicked shut. "I doubt the Gibbs clan would want its connections to active homicide investigations to end up in the *Record* and all three major news networks."

"I knew you'd deny it." I kept my voice low as I increased my pace to keep up with his long stride. "But, Chief, the murders are *not* unrelated. You can't honestly tell me you don't think we're dealing with a serial killer."

"We are not dealing with a serial killer," he said gruffly as we neared the elevators. "I may or may not be, but you are not dealing with any killer, serial or otherwise."

"You sound like Mike," I grumbled.

"Imagine that." He jabbed the up button before turning to me, arms crossed over his chest. "We police really prefer to keep the law-abiding citizens alive, and you make that so much harder when you taunt criminals."

"It's not like I went looking for this guy." The elevator doors slid open, and I took a step back. "He initiated contact with me."

Lips pressed in a thin line, Lockwood nodded at a few uniforms who strode out of the car. "He still sending you photos?"

The image of Stephanie Goodwin in a bloodstained wedding dress flashed across my mind, and I hesitated before answering. "That's not the point."

He sighed and turned on his heel, stepping into the elevator. "What is the point, then?"

I followed him inside. "Serial killer, remember?" I said. "I've been telling you for months—"

"And I've been telling *you* for months," he interrupted, reaching out a finger to jab the button for the eighth floor. "This isn't the same guy you investigated in Chicago, Jennifer. Hell, even the one here in Colsboro three years ago is a stretch."

"They all sent me photos of their victims," I reminded him as the doors slid shut. "And for the record, this is the only time you'll hear me use the word 'they' as a singular pronoun."

His bushy salt-and-pepper eyebrows furrowed as he frowned. "The Chicago P.D. caught the first killer after you moved back home," he reminded me. "The second one probably stopped sending you photos because he got arrested, too. So, either this guy is referencing the same version of the murderer's handbook, or he's a copycat. Which sounds more likely to you?"

"It can't be a copycat. I never published anything about the photos."

"And you didn't tell a single person about them, right?"

"Well, yes, but—"

"Exactly." He looked down his nose at me. "Isn't it more likely that someone found out about the photos than the wrong guy went to prison?"

"The Innocence Project conservatively estimates one percent of inmates did not commit the crimes for which they were imprisoned," I said, "which means that somewhere in the ballpark of twenty thousand people currently incarcerated are innocent." I shrugged. "The guy in Chicago could be one of them."

The chief let out a short laugh. "That also means ninety-nine percent of inmates are guilty, and in all likelihood, so is he," he said. "Nice try, kid. Now drop it."

"I'll let it go if you tell me about your person of interest."

He scrubbed his face with his hands. "Despite the fact that I've known you since you were seven, you're still the media. We have a policy."

"I'll wear you down eventually."

"You know I was in the military." The corners of his mouth tipped upward. "I've withstood a fair amount of government-sanctioned torture. I can handle you unconscious and tied up."

"No biggie," I said casually as the elevator slowed to a stop. "I'm sure he's dying to tell me himself."

Lockwood's smile slid off his face. "Be careful, Jennifer." The doors opened and, before striding out, he paused on the threshold to meet my gaze. "I know you're no regular civvie, but you aren't invincible, either." He reached back into the elevator to press the button for the fifth floor. "Even Superman had a weakness."

Before I had a chance to respond, he stepped back, disappearing as the elevator doors slid shut. I leaned back against the wall with a sigh, unable to work up any annoyance at Lockwood's predictable resistance.

When the elevator stopped on five, the doors swished open to reveal Mike Demarco—arms crossed, stern expression tacked on his face, lecture no doubt waiting on the back of his tongue. He stepped in, shooting a glare over his shoulder at the uni behind him in a silent command to stay put.

"It's almost like you were waiting for me." I grinned as he tapped the button for the ground floor a few times more than necessary.

"I hear you're stirring the pot again."

"I like to keep things interesting." I wiggled my eyebrows up and down. "Want to find out how?"

Despite his admonishing expression, Mike laughed. "Nice red herring." He unfolded his arms and reached out to grab one of mine. "It's not going to work."

My smile widened as he pulled me closer. "But wouldn't you like to give it a try, Detective?" I said. "I'm notoriously persuasive—and creative."

He glanced to his left and pushed the emergency stop button. "Let's see what you've got."

I wrapped a hand around the back of his neck and pulled him closer so I could brush my lips against his. "I want to know about this person of interest," I said, my voice breathy. "Can I persuade you to tell me about him?"

His lips curved against mine. "I hope you don't use this tactic on everyone you try to weasel information out of."

"Well, I did try it once with Judge Hammond, but then she had me escorted out of the courthouse. I have a feeling it might work better on you."

"For the sake of argument, what would I get in return for sharing?"

"What do you want?" I looked up at him coquettishly from underneath my lashes.

"To move in with you." He slid his hands around my hips to the small of my back. "Or a Ferrari."

A few seconds ticked by while I recovered. "That is not a fair trade," I said, hoping my face hadn't betrayed the spurt of panic that zipped through my belly. "But if I happen to come into an inheritance—"

He smirked. "I think you're out of grandmothers who can leave you condos and trust funds."

"Astute observation."

"So that leaves option one."

"Moving in with me?" I leaned back to stare up at him. "Now I know you're not being serious."

Mike lifted a hand and pressed it to his chest theatrically. "It pains me that you don't take me seriously."

"Of course I do," I said, eyes wide to convey earnestness. "You know I count on you for answers to all the serious questions. Like, what's this guy's name?"

Rolling his eyes, he stepped back and pressed the button to restart the elevator. "Elvis Presley," he said. "There's a guy's name."

"Given the fact that he's most likely dead, I doubt Elvis Presley killed Stephanie Goodwin."

"I guess your question wasn't specific enough." He shifted closer to me as the elevator doors slid open and a few people from the third floor stepped on. "No wonder you haven't won a Pulitzer yet."

My mouth dropped open in mock dismay. "No wonder you haven't been promoted to sergeant yet."

His lips twitched. "Touché."

I waited until the elevator stopped at the ground floor and everyone had dispersed before resuming my interrogation. "At the presser, Lockwood said you were pursuing a person of interest. That's the name I want."

"Oh," he said, drawing out the syllable to indicate he'd had a revelation. "Yeah, I can't give you that particular name."

"Can't or won't?"

"Yes."

"Not even for a Ferrari?"

He let out a short laugh, slowing his pace so I could keep up. "I might get fired for accepting a bribe."

"It's not a bribe," I said. "It's just a woman stealing a few bucks from her trust fund, taking out several loans, and possibly selling a kidney to buy her boyfriend a Ferrari, followed by said boyfriend answering one simple question." We paused at the exit so I could shrug into my coat. "Two separate issues. No big deal."

He pushed through the door and paused on the other side until I rejoined him. "I'm afraid a jury of my peers might interpret it differently."

"What is the point of sleeping with a homicide detective if he won't give me classified information?"

Mike flashed me a grin and threaded his fingers through mine. "Um, the sleeping with a homicide detective part?" he suggested as we descended the steps toward the parking lot. "We have a lot of fun toys. And if you're talking about the one I think you are, I hear he's pretty amazing."

"Do you believe all the rumors you hear?" Scoffing, he nudged me with his shoulder, and I laughed. "Well, okay. If we're being honest here, I guess I'd have to confirm them." I sent him a sideways glance. "Off the record, of course."

He sighed . "Well, if we're talking off the record—"

"Mike, everything we talk about is off the record. You know that, right?"

He let out a short laugh. "Sure, except for Christine."

"Christine is not the record," I pointed out. "Christine is my best friend. The *Record* is the record. And this is not for the *Record*."

"Then what is it for?"

"Well, okay, it's for the *Record*," I admitted. "But I'm thinking more long term here."

We fell into silence as we made our way through the parking lot to my car—currently a crimson Honda Accord that was just waiting to be blown up, driven off a bridge, or flattened by a toppling skyscraper. My hope dwindling, I dug my keys out of my jacket pocket, clicked the doors unlocked, and reached for the handle.

"Wait." He grabbed my hand and spun me to face him. "I won't see it in tomorrow's newspaper, right?"

I mimed an X across my heart. "Cross my heart and hope to die."

"We found a fingerprint at the scene," he said. "Ran it through AFIS and found a match. We're currently arguing over how to handle it."

"Shouldn't you be picking him up yesterday?"

"Ordinarily, yes, but this is an unusual situation."

"Whose prints did you find?" I asked, curiosity piqued even more.

"The M.E.'s."

I frowned. "Dover County's medical examiner?"

He shook his head. "That's why it's so unusual. We could explain that as a careless mistake. But this guy wasn't even there—at least not officially."

"What M.E. was it, then?"

"Colsboro."

My pulse kicked up a notch. "Which one?"

"Gavin Baratti."

"Omigod." The exclamation slipped out before I could stop it.

His forehead wrinkled. "Is that significant for some reason?"

"Other than the obvious?" I said, too quickly.

"Fair enough," he said, unconvinced but unwilling to pursue it further. "Your place tonight?"

I nodded mechanically. "Sure." I leaned in and gave him a quick kiss before opening the car door. "See you then."

In the mean time, I hoped I'd be able to come up with a good explanation for my reaction. One that was believable.

But not the truth.

《》

BY THE TIME I RETURNED to the newsroom, it was nearly four-thirty—too late in the day to start any new projects. At least, that was my rationalization, because I desperately needed to tell my B.F.F. Christine Morgenstern what I'd learned. Or anybody, really. Finding the fingerprints of an M.E. at a murder scene in a neighboring county was interesting. The fact that those fingerprints belonged to Gavin Baratti made it stop-the-presses interesting.

"Gibbs!" Gus Simpson, my editor, shouted from the other side of the newsroom. A couple of staffers glanced up but were otherwise unperturbed; Gus yells a lot. "My office, now." Without waiting for a response, he turned on his heel and huffed off in the direction of his corner office overlooking the bullpen. I sighed inwardly and followed.

"Close the door," he barked, sinking into his swivel chair. "What'd Lockwood have to say about your theory?"

I dumped my purse and jacket on a chair and faced him, arms akimbo. "He refused to confirm it, but I think he's open to the possibility."

"Good. If he didn't announce it and doesn't plan to, that means we have the edge." I nodded distractedly, and Gus appraised my tight-lipped expression. "There's something else, isn't there?"

"Maybe."

He thought it over, the beginnings of a smile tugging on his lips. "More fingerprints?"

"Yes."

"Whose?"

I shrugged and glanced away.

"C'mon, Gibbs," he prodded. "You were on your way to Morgenstern's desk just now, so you're obviously dying to tell someone." When I hesitated, he lifted a bushy brow. "I sign your paychecks."

"Fine." I cleared my throat. "Gavin Baratti."

He let out a low whistle. "Oh, boy."

"What?" I demanded, crossing my arms over my chest. "I can handle this."

"Sure about that?" Ignoring my death glare, he leaned back and clasped his hands behind his head. "If not, tell me now, and I'll offer Peterson the crime desk instead."

I blinked. "What?"

"Well, before you dropped that bomb, I was going to offer you the crime desk," he said nonchalantly. "That is, if you're able to I.D. this killer and break the story before anyone else."

"Gus." Suspicious, I scrutinized him for signs he was messing with me. "Are you serious?"

"As serious as a nuclear missile." His hazel eyes sparkled. "Think you can do it? You will have to talk to your—"

"Hell, yes," I said without a second thought. I would've agreed to eat mud pie with an earthworm crust if it got me the crime desk.

"That's what I like to hear." Standing, he extended a hand toward me. "Shake on it to make it official?" A smile spread across my face as I grasped his hand and gave it a firm shake. Gus let out a gruff laugh at my expression before sinking back into his chair. "What am I paying you for, Gibbs? Get back to work."

"Yes, sir." I saluted him before gathering up my personal effects and zipping out of his office.

I dropped my stuff off at my desk, waved hello to my desk neighbor Tori, and weaved my way to the other side of the newsroom. I found Christine at her desk, squinting at the screen of her iMac. She leaned back and pushed her tortoiseshell glasses on top of her head as I pulled up a chair and plopped down next to her.

"So, what was Gus yelling about?" she asked without preamble.

"Nothing much," I said with a casual shrug. "Just wanted to give me the crime desk."

"Hot damn!"

"That is, after I identify this killer and break the story before anyone else." I leaned back and crossed one leg over the other. "In the entire universe."

She waved a hand. "Luckily, you're the only one in the universe the killer's got a hard-on for." When I didn't respond with an argument or grammatical correction, she frowned. "Okay, what am I missing? What's the catch?"

"Other than the fact that I have to beat out a thousand million other journalists to make it happen?"

Her gaze slid skyward. "You are so dramatic."

"There's been an interesting development," I said, and she raised a brow in silent question. "Turns out Dover P.D. found the M.E.'s prints in Goodwin's house."

Christine frowned. "Is that completely outside of the realm of possibility?"

"Not the Dover M.E." I paused for dramatic effect. "Our very own Dr. Gavin Baratti."

Her eyes widened into blue balloons. "Omigod."

"My reaction exactly."

"Oh, hell. That is quite an interesting development." She swiveled back and forth in her chair. "Let me get this straight. So far, Joey, Jason, and Kenny's prints have all been found at three separate murder scenes—and now, Gavin Baratti's at a fourth."

I blew out a breath. "Seems that way."

"What are you going to do?"

"Avoid him as long as possible."

"It's been, like, three years. Suck it up."

"Thanks for the support."

"Okay, then don't." She stopped swiveling and redirected her attention to her fingernails. "Meanwhile, Melanie Davenport sneaks in, figures it out before you do, and steals your promotion."

"That's mean."

"But possible." She tilted her head to one side, reconsidering. "Okay, Melanie might not be smart enough, but someone else might be."

"Fair enough," I conceded. "However, Mike only told me because I promised it wouldn't end up in the paper tomorrow."

"Mike told you this?" She let out a bark of laughter. "And I presume he still doesn't know who Gavin is?"

"Given the fact that he's a homicide detective and Baratti is a medical examiner, I suspect he's worked with him on a number of occasions," I said dryly. "So, yeah, he knows who he is."

"That's not what I meant."

"I know what you meant," I said, rising to my feet. "But that's another conversation I'm going to put off as long as possible."

She laughed again. "Let me know when and where that's going down. I'll bring the popcorn."

"Bite me."

She let out a low whistle as she watched me roll the chair back to its owner's desk. "You are going to be in so much trouble when this all comes out."

"Probably," I agreed, giving her a sweet smile. "But the promotion will make up for it."

《 》

WHEN I GOT HOME AROUND six-thirty, I found my younger cousin— who, for the past three months, had doubled as my roommate—in the kitchen preparing what smelled like spaghetti. It was one of approximately seven meals she could cook, and because she did most of the cooking and didn't pay rent, we'd eaten a lot of spaghetti since she'd moved in.

"Hey, cuz," she said cheerfully, tucking a strand of her chin-length auburn hair behind her ear. "Solve any murders today?"

"Not yet, but I still have a few hours." I dumped my bag and jacket on a barstool. "Want to help me? I could use a fresh perspective."

She looked up from the pot of sauce she was stirring. "Um, yeah," she said, as if it were obvious. "Selling stethoscopes every day isn't exactly fulfilling."

"And why do you do that, again?" I brushed past her to grab a wine glass from the cupboard and filled it with a generous pour from the open bottle of pinot noir on the counter. "You could've become something much more interesting, like a pilot or a unicorn whisperer."

Kellyn turned back to the stove. "Because Kenny convinced me I would be an incredible medical devices salesperson, and also that it would be fun to work for my husband." She sighed, annoyed. "He could sell a lifetime supply of condoms to a nun and make her think it was her idea."

I snorted. "And because you're a sucker?"

"That too." She placed the wooden spoon on the stove next to the spoon rest, making me cringe, and reached for the box of spaghetti. "Please, distract me from my pathetic life and tell me about these murders. Did Chief give you anything useful after the press conference?"

"That colossal waste of time made the news?" I rounded the bar, slid onto a barstool, and kicked my heels off. "He's resisting the serial killer theory, because there's no clear link among any of the four vics—except for being young women who were raped and murdered in central Ohio."

Kellyn opened the box of pasta and dumped its contents into a pot of boiling water. "He seems to be ignoring the fact that this guy has apparently made you his official spokesperson." She shifted around to face me, leaning a hip against the stove. "Which, by the way, is more than a little scary—and not just for you."

I gave her a pleasant smile. "If you're nervous, I'm sure you could go bunk with the boys."

She let out a short laugh. "Would *you* want to stay with your brothers if your marriage was falling apart?"

"Fair point."

"Besides," she said, turning back to the stove to stir the pasta, "Joey's tiny apartment is even smaller with Jason's bitterness taking up so much space."

My smile faded. "You two have a lot in common right now," I said. "Maybe it would help if you talked to each other."

She yanked the spaghetti server out of the pot and pointed it at me, flinging hot water and a couple of stiff noodles across the floor. "I am *not* getting divorced," she said. "No way am I going to be a twenty-two-year-old divorcee."

"Kenny cheated on you, Kell," I said. "Besides, there are worse things."

She bent to retrieve the spaghetti. "Like your auto insurance premiums every time you total a car?"

I groaned and rolled my head backward dramatically. "None of those were my fault!"

Kellyn smiled smugly. "Now, tell me about these murder victims."

Not willing to argue her deflection, I pulled my files out of my tote bag and placed them on the counter. "So, all the vics lived in a different county. Ages range from mid-twenties to early thirties. All Caucasian. Couple of brunettes, a blonde, and a redhead." I flipped through my notepad. "Professions include a clothing designer, teacher, bartender, and doctor."

"Mm," Kellyn said, her back to me as she stirred the pasta vigorously. "And which was the one my husband slept with?"

Wincing, I glanced at my notes. "Uh—Allison Donnelly. The twenty-nine-year-old brunette teacher from Heron County. Second victim." I let a few seconds pass before I asked, "Do you want to talk about it?"

"Sure." She dropped the spoon, leaving it swirling around the pot, and turned to face me. "How'd she die?"

"He slashed her femoral arteries," I said. "She bled out."

"How sad."

"Kell," I said sharpy. "That's messed up."

"You're right, no one deserves that. Except maybe Kenny." She smiled humorlessly at my scowl. "Please continue."

I cleared my throat loudly and turned back to my notes. "Chelsea Quinn was the first victim. She was stabbed in the chest with a sharp object. Cause of death was asphyxia from a pulmonary edema."

"Layman's terms?"

"She suffocated on her own blood."

Kellyn grimaced. "What else?"

"Gina Hadley, victim three, was found with a broken beer bottle jammed in her jugular," I continued. "She bled out. And our newest vic, Stephanie Goodwin, had her wrists slashed with a scalpel. Also bled out." I glanced up at her and reached for my wine. "Onto a beautiful wedding dress."

"Weird," Kellyn said, nose wrinkled. "What does that mean?"

I shrugged. "Hell if I know."

"It has to mean *something*."

"Kell, we're dealing with an insane killer." On the other side of the room, the lock on the front door clicked. "It could be a cryptic message about the aliens that brought him to Earth, or it could mean nothing at all."

The door burst open, and Mike's yellow Labrador retriever pranced proudly into the foyer, leash trailing behind him. While Mike closed and locked the door, Murphy bounded up to me for a quick sniff and a pat on the head before bouncing over to Kellyn.

Grinning, she bent to give Murphy a hearty pat on his rear end before turning to Mike, who strode across the living room with a giant rawhide bone in hand. "Back me up here, Mike," Kellyn said as Murphy danced excitedly at her feet.

"Happy to," he said, as he gave the dog the bone. "Just need a little more information first."

Teeth clamped firmly on his prize, Murphy trotted happily into the living room and curled up on his bed by the window, wasting no time getting to work on his treat.

"Jen doesn't believe the wedding dress means anything," Kellyn explained, turning back to the spaghetti.

"I didn't say that," I said.

"What wedding dress?" Mike leaned in to give me a hello kiss. "Something you want to share with me?"

I frowned up at him. "Stephanie Goodwin's wedding dress."

Mike snatched my wine glass and took a sip. "I have no idea what you're talking about," he said, "but it sounds like you got another photo today."

"Might have," I said vaguely, snatching the glass back.

His eyes narrowed slightly. "Thanks for keeping me in the loop."

"Sure thing."

He gave me a disapproving shake of his head before turning toward the kitchen. "Goodwin's case hasn't been assigned yet, but I think I would have heard about a vic decked out in a wedding dress."

My eyes followed him as he retrieved a wine glass and helped himself to the pinot. "Well, what do you make of the weird pattern stabbed into Chelsea Quinn's chest? She was yours."

Face expressionless, he eyed me over the rim of his wine glass for a few beats. "Chelsea Quinn had so many stab wounds in her chest, Baratti couldn't count them all."

I stared at him, feeling my forehead tighten as my brows drew together. "Can I see the crime scene photos?"

Letting out a humorless laugh, he sidestepped out of Kellyn's way as she lifted the pot of pasta from the stove and took it to the strainer waiting in the sink. "You've got to be kidding."

"I'll show you mine if you show me yours," I said, the corners of my mouth tilting upward.

"I think you're going to show me anyway." He set his glass down on the bar next to mine and seized the files sitting in front of me. Before I could protest, he put ten feet between us and began rifling through the contents. I slid off the barstool and joined him in the living room, watching his face darken as he flipped through.

"Well, shit," he said, staring down at the photo of Stephanie Goodwin. "I definitely should have heard about this."

"So maybe the Northville cops are being territorial."

Dropping down to the couch, he put the folder on his lap and flipped back to the front. He let out a quiet breath as he inspected the photo. "Hell."

"What is it?" I asked, sinking down next to him as he stared at the image of Chelsea Quinn—her head lolling uncomfortably to one side, bare chest speckled in a dozen raw red dots that oozed thick red blood.

"This isn't how she looked when we found her," he said in a low voice.

"What does that mean?"

"I'm not sure," he said, thumbing through my file until he got to Allison Donnelly's photo. She laid in a bathtub of shallow, red-tinged water; her left hand rested on the edge of the tub, clutching a cocktail napkin bearing a restaurant logo. "It would be tough for one person to pull off, but my gut reaction is he staged the scenes for these photographs, and then took all the extra props with him."

"Why go to all that trouble?"

"Maybe he wanted a souvenir."

"For himself, or for me?"

"Both." Jaw clenched, Mike flipped through the pages until he found Gina Hadley, who slumped against a brick wall with a broken beer bottle lodged in her neck. "Or maybe the difference between what the investigators see and what's in these photos is some kind of clue."

"About what?" I asked. "Surely not his identity."

"Might be." Mike's face was blank as he extracted the four photos from my file. "I'll take these to the precinct tomorrow and compare them to what we have."

I swallowed. "And what about the fingerprints?"

He closed the file and handed it back to me. "Seems like a stretch, but I wonder if he's planting them to make sure he gets your attention." He fell quiet for a few moments, forehead wrinkling. "The first three prints make sense, but I can't figure out why—"

"So he is sending you a message," Kellyn called from the kitchen. She whirled to face us, a smug smile played on her lips. "You're welcome."

Relieved at the interruption, I had to drum up some fake annoyance. "I don't know what you're so happy about."

"Absolutely nothing, so it might have something to do with this." She lifted her wine glass to her lips and drained it. Smiling, she sashayed back to the kitchen. "Dinner's ready."

Mike grabbed my hand as I stood and pulled me back down next to him. "This is worse than I thought," he said, his voice so quiet I could barely hear him over Murphy's exuberant bone chewing. "I thought he was just using you to get famous. But if I'm right, and he is leaving you clues…" He paused, carefully planning what to say next, and my stomach dipped. "It might be more than that."

"Like what?"

He shook his head slowly. "I don't know," he said. "But from now on, you need to show me every photo immediately, and you're not going anywhere alone. Understood?"

"This isn't just an elaborate plan to sneak your way into moving in with me, is it?"

His lips peeled back in a tight smile. "I'm serious, Jennifer. You need to be careful."

"I will be." I leaned in to give him a light kiss. "I'm always careful."

And I was. Like most things, though, it didn't always work out the way I intended.

CHAPTER 2

DESPITE MY BEST EFFORTS, THE next morning, Mike refused to share the official crime scene photos with me after he got them from the Corine, West Madison, and Northville police departments.

"I really enjoyed your arguments last night." He dumped hot coffee into his travel mug. "They were very effective."

"I'll say," Kellyn muttered from the foyer, where she was buttoning up her coat. "Well, I'm off to sell more medical devices to arrogant doctors with a God complex." She patted Murphy on the head and sent us a fake smile. "Don't wait up."

"Bye, cuz." I waited until the front door slammed shut before continuing. "I sense a 'but.'"

"But you've gone overboard, and now I'm annoyed," he said, filling my mug before replacing the carafe and jabbing the coffeemaker's power button. "Normally, I'd strongly encourage you to stay away from a case and trust you'd make the right decision, but now I will actively go out of my way to make sure you don't get involved."

"Too late," I said wryly. "I'd have to change my name and move to India for that to work. Either that, or let you move in with me." Sliding my eyes away from his, I screwed the lid onto my travel cup. "I'm not sure which option is worse."

When I turned to face him, his expression was pinched. "Okay, I get it," he said, annoyed. "You don't want to move in together."

"I didn't say that. I figured it was a tactic to persuade me to buy you a Ferrari." I retrieved my trench coat from the back of the barstool. "You know, if you worked with me instead of against me, we could accomplish great things together." I slid my arms into the sleeves, swung my purse over my shoulder, and accepted the mug he held out to me. "Just think about it."

He followed me to the door, putting a firm hand against it to prevent me from leaving. "I do," he said softly, tucking a strand of hair behind my ear. "We will accomplish great things together. But normal things, like making tiny humans. Not catching serial killers. That's my job, not yours."

"Aha!" I said triumphantly, choosing to focus on the last part of his statement rather than the sticky middle. "So you *do* think it's a serial killer."

"It was a hypothetical scenario." He snagged his jacket off the coat hook and shrugged into it. "Also, that wasn't the point."

I drew in a slow breath, watching him adjust his collar. "I know."

"Good," he said. "Then that's something *you* can think about."

FIRST THING I DID WHEN I got to the newsroom was put in a call to one of my informants. Orlando Drake was the bartender of the corporate world: His clients trusted him with their dirty laundry the same way alcoholics trusted the bartenders. Plus, as CEO of a security firm, he had a lot of neat spy toys.

"I don't have any contacts at Northville P.D.," I explained when he answered, "and Mike's not playing nice, so..."

"What's the point of dating a cop if he won't share classified police information with you?" Orlando asked.

"That's what I said. Apparently there are other benefits."

"I'll have to take your word for it," he said. "What do you want from Northville P.D.?"

"Crime scene photos."

"From what crime?"

I twirled the phone cord around my forefinger. "Stephanie Goodwin's murder."

"This isn't going to get you kidnapped, is it?"

"Of course not," I scoffed. "I almost never get kidnapped."

Orlando chuckled. "I'll do what I can and add it to your tab."

"What's this going to cost me?"

"More than a thank-you card and less than a kidney," he said before disconnecting.

From the desk across from mine, Tori tossed a mini basketball up in the air. "Days like this, I almost wish I did hard news," she said, catching the ball and volleying it to me. "No one ever tries to kidnap me."

I caught the ball and squished it in my hand a few times. "Is that something that interests you?" I asked, throwing it back to her.

She caught it one handed and flashed me her pearly whites. "Might be fun to try at least once. Find out if my kickboxing classes are worth thirty bucks a pop."

"If you're interested, I could talk to my lawyer about bequeathing you my job once I'm offed." I turned toward my computer and opened my email. "But make sure Gus ups your health insurance coverage first."

"I'll keep that in mind." Tori dropped the ball on her desk and bounded to her feet, sending the chair wheeling backward. "Want a coffee?"

I held up my travel mug. "I'm good."

While she was gone, I shoved some photo paper into my printer and reprinted the four images Mike had confiscated last night. Once my files were restored, I logged on to the *Record*'s search program and flipped to a fresh page in my notebook.

So far, I hadn't been able to find a connection among the victims, but there had to be something. With someone as organized as this killer—who had carefully planned not only the murders themselves but the clues he was supposedly sending me—there had to be a reason he chose these specific women.

Four hours later, I still hadn't found a link: No overlap in schools attended, no commonalities in their professions, no similarities in their birth dates, and no obvious links among their families. Frustrated, I threw my pen down on my desk and leaned back in my chair with a groan.

Tori pushed away from her computer and propped her feet up on her desk. "Still nothing?" she asked, and I shook my head. "Try taking a page out of the gravedigger's handbook and dig a little deeper."

"I'm open to suggestions."

"Have you talked to the victims' families?"

"Not the latest one." I blew out a breath. "I hate questioning victims' families. I feel like such an asshat."

"Maybe work on Mike some more first, and if he's being stubborn again, hit up your other police contacts," she suggested. "Find out if there are suspects in any of the previous cases—a disgruntled coworker, a jealous ex-boyfriend, or a suspicious husband. Anyone sketchy you could guiltlessly track down and cross-examine."

"A suspicious husband," I repeated, my mind taking off. "The killer sent me a photo of Goodwin dressed up like a bride."

"Creepy," Tori said, her forehead wrinkled. "That's got to mean something."

"Sure, but what?"

She dropped her feet back to the floor and raked a hand through her pixie cut. "I don't know, Gibbs," she said. "Maybe the flowers are symbolic. Maybe the ring is a copy of Princess Diana's. Or maybe the dress was sewn by the blind Mormon nuns who raised the killer."

"I don't think there is such a thing as Mormon nuns."

Her eyes slid north. "Whatever. You know what I mean."

"I do." I extracted Goodwin's photo from the mess on my desk. "Thanks, Phelps." She gave a little bow before I darted away in the direction of the photo lab, where I found Miguel Martinez behind his dual screens, intently scrutinizing an image of Mayor Ted Grant. He was so engrossed, he didn't hear me approach.

"Wow," I said from behind him, making him jump. "Grant really was not meant to be seen at a thousand percent magnification."

"Dios," he said, whirling around in his chair to glare at me. "Are you trying to give me a heart attack?"

"Why so jumpy?"

His coal-black eyes narrowed. "Maybe because hanging out with you is more dangerous than swimming with piranhas."

"Don't be so dramatic." I held up the photo and wiggled it in front of him. "So, listen, I need a favor."

Miguel perked up. "Gimmie." He seized the page from my fingers and studied it without flinching—though this was the least graphic of the four photos the killer had sent me, and he'd seen them all. "What do you want me to focus on?"

I gestured toward the middle, which contained the most information—the flowers and the ring. "I think there's a clue hidden in here," I said, "but it's too small to see clearly."

"Hmm." He squinted down at the image. "I can see the message."

"You can?" I asked excitedly. "What does it say?"

"It says stop chasing murderers before you end up getting murdered, too," he said, and I seized the photo in annoyance. "Send me the digital file, and I'll dig out my magic wand."

"Thanks, Miguel, you're the best," I said, beaming down at him. "And if you can make it happen today, the first round's on me the next time we do happy hour."

"Damn right." He waved a hand at me. "Now shoo."

《》

BY TWO-THIRTY, MIGUEL HAD DELIVERED on his promise, and Christine and I were examining the enlargements of Goodwin's photo under my desk lamp.

"The flowers might be lilies," I said. "Big red petals, yellow dots in the center."

Christine snatched the photo out of my hand and frowned down at it. "These petals are wide. Lily petals are narrower, plus they have those pollen things in the middle."

"Maybe they're a new variety of lilies," I suggested. "Maybe you can only buy them at one florist in the world, and it happens to be here in Colsboro, and they happen to keep thorough records of their customers."

"And maybe the Loch Ness monster is real." She scanned the image once more and passed it back. "They look like poinsettias to me."

I inspected them again. "You're right."

Christine straightened and folded her arms over her chest. "This time of year, you can find them everywhere."

I dropped the photo onto my desk and leaned back in my chair. "So that's a dead end."

"Unless poinsettias have some kind of mysterious meaning."

"I think the meaning is merry Christmas."

"Yes, I'm sure the psycho killer is just sending you holiday greetings." Christine picked up the second photo and held it close to her face. "I think there's something under her left hand." She pointed at a sliver of silver peeking out from beneath her fingers. "Looks like a craft knife or a box cutter."

"Or a scalpel," I said, frowning. "She was a surgeon."

"Think he murdered her with her own scalpel?"

I shrugged. "If he did, what's the significance? Besides, I doubt she stored her surgical instruments at home."

Christine blew out a frustrated sigh, flipping the photo back around. "Maybe the ring will be more helpful." A few seconds later, she let out a low whistle. "Diamond's two carets, easy. Cushion cut, surrounded by sapphires—and the band is inlaid with smaller diamonds." She glanced up at me. "Gotta admit, this guy's got good taste."

I shivered as a crazy thought tiptoed into my mind, and I grabbed the photo back from her to re-examine it under my lamp. The enlargements had caused the image to become somewhat pixelated, but even with the added blur, I knew exactly what I was looking at. Without thinking, I ran my thumb across the base of my left ring finger.

"Omigod," I whispered.

"What?" Christine asked eagerly.

"I know that ring." I tossed the photo down and shot to my feet so I could pace. "That ring used to be *my* ring."

Her jaw dropped, and she sank into my desk chair to inspect the photo under the lamp. "Okay, let's be logical here. Isn't it more likely that this is the same ring style, but not the exact same ring? Companies sometimes make more than one of a thing." She sent me a sideways glance. "Like, to make money."

I shook my head. "Family heirloom," I said in a clipped voice. "One of a kind."

"That does make the mass production theory a lot less likely," she muttered. "Could it be a replica?"

I crossed my arms over my chest. "In order to copy it, he'd need the actual ring to show a jeweler—in which case, it would be a hell of a lot easier just to use the real thing and skip the middleman." I stopped pacing and jerked around to face her. "Coupled with the fact that Northville P.D. identified Baratti's prints at the scene, the coincidence theory is looking a lot less likely."

Christine scrutinized me, as if gauging my mood. "There is another, simpler explanation."

I blinked at her. "What?"

She hesitated before answering. "He could have given it to her." When I frowned in confusion, she drew in a long breath and stood. "I mean, Gavin could have given the ring to Stephanie Goodwin." She let a few beats go by to let me consider the possibility, and when I didn't say anything, she continued. "Think about it, Jen. They're both doctors. They both went to med school in Chicago—"

"So did a thousand million other people."

She raised a brow at me. "Who all moved to Colsboro, Ohio?" I didn't respond, and she lifted a shoulder in a half-assed shrug. "They could've met in med school and reconnected years later, after—"

"Not possible." I darted toward my desk and sifted through the pile of papers until I found Goodwin's background information. "She was only thirty-two. Baratti would've been done with med school by the time she was there."

"That doesn't mean he didn't—"

"I know, Christine," I snapped, sharper than I'd intended. I closed my eyes and rubbed my temples, taking a few deep breaths. "I'm sorry."

When I opened my eyes, she was watching me with a sympathetic expression, which annoyed me further. "It's okay," she said, squeezing my shoulder before backing away. "I'll leave you alone."

Once she went back to her desk, I sank down into my chair and stared at the picture of the ring until my vision went blurry. What was I so upset about? We had broken up three years ago. I'd moved on, found someone else—so why should it bother me if Baratti had, too?

《》

I'D ZONED OUT BY THE time Orlando showed up with a beige envelope and a grim expression. I frowned up at him as he towered over my desk.

"You didn't need to hand deliver these," I told him.

"Yes, I did," he said gruffly. "I'm all too aware of how easy it is to track a digital paper trail." He glanced over at Tori, who watched us with rapt attention, and cleared his throat loudly.

"Oh!" she exclaimed, jumping out of her chair. "I just remembered I need to, uh—" She glanced at her watch. "Take my daily two forty-seven p.m. walk in the rain." She grabbed her coat from the back of her chair and bolted.

Orlando pulled her desk chair over and sat down in front of me, holding out the envelope. "Brace yourself. It's not pretty."

Mechanically, I opened the envelope and slid out its contents. The top photo showed a full-length view of Stephanie Goodwin's body, lying naked on the red-soaked sheets of her bed, wrists slashed open—but that was the extent of the similarities. Gone were the dress, shoes, and veil. No bouquet. No knife.

No ring.

"What the hell?" I muttered, unable to come up with anything more eloquent.

"M.E. was Nina Woods." Orlando crossed an ankle over his leg and leaned back as I flipped through the rest of the photos. "C.O.D. was exsanguination, sometime between ten Monday night and two Tuesday morning."

"When was she found?"

"Tuesday afternoon. A colleague from Dover General got worried when she didn't show up for rounds and went to her condo to check on her."

"Murder weapon?"

"None found at the scene. Likely a sharp object."

I lifted my gaze to him. "Suspects?"

"One." He steepled his fingers in front of his black button-down shirt and met my eyes. "Colsboro M.E. Gavin Baratti. His prints were ID'ed on a jewelry box in her bedroom." He leaned forward and sifted through the photos on my lap until he found the one he was looking for. "That one. Doesn't have any jewelry store logos or other identifying marks, so it'll be hard to trace."

I'd seen it before: Made of polished mahogany, it was intricately carved with a monogram of a B. I glanced down at it briefly to confirm, my stomach taking a sharp nosedive when it looked exactly as I remembered. The box was closed, but I knew if it were open, the inside would be lined in cushy blue velvet.

"One of a kind," I said quietly. Just like the ring.

Orlando studied me for a few beats. "Rumor has it detectives are bringing Baratti in for questioning this afternoon."

"Northville?"

He gave a minute shake of his head. "Evidently the Northville police have extended some kind of professional courtesy to the CPD, since Baratti's one of theirs."

I cleared my throat, sliding the photos back into the envelope. "I owe you for the personal delivery."

"Among other things." A hint of a smile played on his lips. "Shall I keep your tab open?"

"Might as well." I raked a hand through my hair. "I have a feeling I'll be calling you again before this is over."

The smile widened, and he didn't bother hiding it. "As you wish." He rose to his feet and returned Tori's chair to her desk, sending me a brief parting glance before he wove his way to the elevator.

I picked up the phone, pulled out my address book, and started making calls, mind racing faster than my fingers could dial. An hour later, I hadn't learned anything useful, but I was ninety-nine percent convinced my theory was correct—which meant I couldn't put it off much longer. Swallowing a wave of dread, I locked my computer, grabbed my purse, and stood. If I hurried, maybe I could get to the coroner's office before he was picked up. I draped my jacket over my arm and dashed to the elevator.

As I approached, the doors slid open, and Tori appeared on the other side. "Hey, I'm glad I caught you." She stepped off and handed me a padded envelope. "This was delivered for you. Told them I'd bring it up."

"Thanks." I took it distractedly and stepped onto the elevator. "Got a lead, so I'll see you tomorrow."

"*Ciao,*" she called over her shoulder.

Shoving the envelope into my purse without a second look, I jabbed the button for the ground floor in rapid succession, hoping the urgency would make doors close faster. As the elevator began its descent, my phone rang from inside my purse.

"Thanks for finally answering the phone," Joey said, skipping the pleasantries. "I've been trying to reach you for half an hour."

"Sorry, little bro," I said unapologetically. "What's up?"

"Don't know if this will mean anything to you, but Mike and Sardelis picked up Baratti." He paused, as if waiting for me to freak out. "They're questioning him in connection with Stephanie Goodwin's death."

I blew out an anxious sigh. "Does he have a lawyer?"

"They've been in there for awhile, but he hasn't lawyered up yet. He's not officially under arrest, so he probably doesn't see any harm in answering their questions."

That sounded like something Baratti would do. "Any chance you can pass him a note instructing him to shut his mouth until his lawyer arrives?"

"You know his lawyer?"

"I'm calling Pierce."

There was a brief silence on the other end of the line. "And will you be coming down to the precinct as well?"

"Yes."

"Hell," he said under his breath. "Text me when you're here so I can do my sworn duty and make sure no one gets murdered."

《》

WHILE I WAITED FOR PIERCE, I sat in the parking lot of the CPD and dug the padded envelope out of my purse, hoping whatever it contained would distract me for a few minutes.

It didn't.

Immediately after seeing its contents, I shoved it back into the envelope and then buried it at the bottom of my purse, ice running through my veins. Anxiety heightened, I drummed my fingers on the steering wheel until Pierce's Mercedes slid across my rearview mirror. Steeling myself, I grabbed my purse and got out of the car, slamming the door harder than necessary.

A light rain drizzled down as I crossed my arms over my chest and tapped my toe against the pavement. When Pierce appeared in my line of sight—striding toward me with the arrogance of a three-hundred-dollar-per-hour criminal defense attorney—I forced myself to hold my chin high. I couldn't, however, hold his piercing hazel gaze.

It had been almost a year since I'd seen my father, and ten since he'd had any parental hold over me—at least in a legal sense. But he could still make me wither like a dying flower with a single glance.

"Jennifer. Shall we?" He paused briefly in front of me before resuming his brisk pace. Letting out the air I'd been holding, I followed him up the steps of the CPD. "I presume you're going to your mother's for Thanksgiving dinner?"

I frowned at the unexpected question. "Yes."

"Then you'll come to my house for dessert in the evening," he said.

"Why?"

He stopped half a dozen steps from the portico, where Joey waited for us, and turned to face me. "Because I'm doing you a favor."

"Couldn't you just bill me?"

"No," he said brusquely. "You haven't seen Elle and the kids in quite a while. I remember how much you hate when family members are absent from one another's lives." He resumed his ascent before I could verbalize one of the sarcastic responses bouncing on the tip of my tongue. Swallowing a surge of anger, I trudged up the remaining steps.

Joey reached out to shake Pierce's extended hand. "Dad," he said. "Fifth floor, interview room two."

Pierce nodded, dropping his hand, and glanced at me. "When I return, I expect you'll have decided to accept my invitation." Without waiting for a response, he strode across the portico to the entrance, leaving me to grind my teeth together in suppressed fury.

Joey eyed me dubiously. "What invitation?"

"Not an invitation," I said flatly. "Quid pro quo—because Pierce can't do anything out of the goodness of his heart."

"Well, you did ask him to drop everything..."

I shot him a dark look, cutting him off. "And it's about time he did."

He ran his palm along the edge of his jaw. "You just asked your estranged father to bail your ex-fiancé out of an interview conducted by your current boyfriend," he pressed. I turned away, directing my glare at the doors. "What the hell's going on?"

"I don't know."

"I thought both Mike and the chief told you to back off."

"They did." I sent him a sideways glance. "But that was before they dragged Baratti in for an interrogation."

"Just an interview," he said. "Baratti's not under arrest."

I shrugged. "Whatever."

Joey was quiet for a few beats. "I hope you know what you're doing."

I let out a heavy breath. "I'll figure it out."

He threw an arm around my shoulders, squeezing me to his side. "You know I've got your back no matter what, right?"

I nodded distractedly and glued my eyes on the door. Fifteen long minutes passed before Pierce reappeared, and behind him, Baratti. It was the closest he'd been in three years, and my heart skipped a beat. The spin of the revolving door, the people coming and going—everything slowed to a sloth's pace. My mind went blank, my vision blurred along the edges, and I forgot to breathe.

Joey dropped his arm, startling me out of my stupor. "Hope you're ready for this."

Drawing in a shallow breath, I shoved my hands into my pockets to hide my clenched fists. "Me too," I murmured, forcing my face into a neutral expression.

As they approached, I studied him—same perfect posture, same carefully styled brown hair, same neat wardrobe. But as the distance between us shortened, I knew he wasn't the same. His expression was sadder, the warm chocolate eyes I remembered darker and more guarded as he appraised me silently.

Pierce cleared his throat, and I tore my eyes away from Baratti's to find him watching me with a bored expression. "They were forced to release Dr. Baratti," he said. "There wasn't enough evidence to arrest him."

I swallowed, trying to wet the desert in my mouth, and forced myself to speak. "Thank you."

"And?"

"And I'll be there on Thanksgiving," I said tightly.

"Eight o'clock," he said. "Any chance you can convince your older brother to join us?"

"I think Jason's been tortured enough over the last few months."

Pressing his lips together, Pierce glanced at Baratti. "Do you need a ride back to the hospital?"

Baratti opened his mouth, but I spoke before he was able to. "No," I said curtly. "I'll take care of it."

Pierce eyed me, one eyebrow hitched slightly above the other. "Are you sure?"

"Yes." I gave him a fake smile. "I'm emotionally bankrupt. I don't have anything else to trade you."

"Very well." He turned to Joey and clapped him lightly on the shoulder. "See you, son."

"Bye, Dad." Joey slid his hands into his pockets and shifted his gaze to me. "Good luck, sis." He pivoted and started to walk away.

"Hey, bro," I called, and he turned back to face me. "I was never here."

He gave me a wry smile. "Whatever you say."

I blew out a breath. "Buy me an hour."

"I'll try," he said, giving me one last look before turning around and striding back inside.

With nothing else to distract me, I shifted my attention back to Baratti. We stared at each other in silence for a few beats, neither one of us moving.

"Hello, Gavin," I said finally.

He swallowed, and I could almost see his defenses drop. "Hello, Jennifer," he said, his chocolate eyes wide and vulnerable. *Shit.*

I cleared my throat. "Can I buy you a cup of coffee and an hour of your time?"

He watched me for a few long seconds, unmoving. Inside my pockets, my palms began to sweat in anticipation of his polite but cool refusal. "Only if by coffee, you mean wine."

Relieved, I let out an unexpected laugh. "Oh, good. I've needed wine since about eight o'clock this morning."

His mouth twitched, an infinitesimal smile. "Me too."

SIX YEARS AGO
CHICAGO, ILLINOIS

IT WAS MY FIRST DAY at *The Chicago Sun-Times*, and I was covering a murder. As an intern. This was already the best job ever.

Technically, Nick Harvey was covering the murder. Harvey was a senior crime reporter who'd volunteered to become my mentor, teacher, and pseudo-partner for three months. At least that was what he'd said—with finger quotes around "volunteered"—when editor-in-chief Charlie Goodman had introduced us last month. More likely, he'd lost a bet. Either way, I was determined not to make him regret his volunteerism, forced as it might be.

During the cab ride to the coroner's office, Harvey and I reviewed the background information he'd pulled up for our victim: Hannah Percy. Caucasian brunette, age twenty-one. Studied marketing at the University of Chicago. Bartended on weekends to earn money for her tuition. Lived in an off-campus apartment in Hyde Park. No roommate. No boyfriend. No criminal record.

"Ever been to a morgue before, Gibbs?" Harvey asked as we walked down the sterile hallways of the Cook County medical examiner's office.

"No. Is this some sort of hazing ritual?"

"No comment." Harvey sent me a crooked smile as he held the door open for me. "This should be fun. Hope you have a strong stomach."

I smiled back at him and walked over the threshold. "I haven't been sick in thirteen years," I told him in a low voice.

He let out a hearty laugh, quickly smothering it when a white-coated man stuck his head out of a side office, dark eyes disapproving. "Sorry, Baratti, thought Graves was going to be here today." Harvey slid his eyes toward me, wincing dramatically, and stage-whispered, "Baratti doesn't like me. Apparently I'm disrespectful."

I stifled a snort, while he attempted to stifle a mischievous grin. "It's my fault," I said, turning back to the doctor and extending my hand. "Jennifer Gibbs. Lowly intern at the *Sun-Times* and punishment for something terrible Harvey probably did."

He gave me a firm handshake, the corners of his lips twitching. "Gavin Baratti. Forensic pathology fellow at the M.E.'s office and punishment for multiple somethings terrible Harvey definitely did."

Harvey rolled his eyes. "Can we see the girl's body, Doc?"

"Hannah Percy," Baratti and I said in unison.

Harvey glanced back and forth between us, brow wrinkled. "Right. 'Swhat I said."

Gesturing for us to follow him, Baratti led us deeper into the morgue and pulled out a cold chamber numbered forty-one. "Although I'm not done with my autopsy report yet," he said, lifting the white sheet to reveal Percy's head, shoulders, and neck, "I'm ruling it a homicide."

"Obviously," Harvey muttered, and we both turned to stare at him. He lifted his hands in mock surrender. "Sorry."

Lips pursed, Baratti returned his attention to the body. "He severed her carotid arteries with a serrated knife." He ran a finger above the angry jagged cut that tore apart her neck without touching it. "Cause of death was exsanguination. She bled out within minutes," he added for my benefit.

I slid my eyes up to Baratti's face for a moment's reprieve. "So she died quickly," I said quietly. "And she didn't suffer?"

He was quiet for a few beats. "After that, no, not for long," he said finally. "However, prior to that, he raped her with the same serrated knife, so..." He paused, scrutinizing me for a reaction. "I'm sure you know the answer to that."

Harvey cleared his throat. "You're not asking the right questions, Gibbs. You can't write about whether the victim suffered."

"I know that." I turned slowly to look at him. "I was thinking that raping and killing someone with a serrated knife is a very up-close-and-personal method that would require a helluva lot of rage—enough that the killer probably wanted to watch her suffer, and therefore may have known her." I forced a pleasant smile. "Which would narrow down the suspect pool considerably."

"Right," he said, eyes sliding skyward. "Forgot you were a criminal psych minor." He shifted to his other foot and crossed his arms over his chest. "Either way, it's better if you distance yourself from the vic. After seeing as many dead bodies as we've seen, you start to go a little numb."

My smile faded. "I hope not."

He blew out an annoyed breath and turned back to Baratti. "You got a T.O.D.?" He sent me a sideways glance. "That means time of—"

"I know what it means, Harvey," I said evenly, "but thank you."

"Based on rigor, body temp, and lividity when she was found yesterday," Baratti said before Harvey could summon a retort, "I'd place it at somewhere between ten P.M. Saturday and two A.M. Sunday."

"Does she have any defensive wounds?" I asked.

"No, but she does have ligature marks on her wrists and ankles." Baratii lifted the side of the sheet closest to me to reveal her right arm, which was purple and raw. "So she couldn't fight back."

"Maybe she didn't know him after all," I mused, almost to myself. "Maybe he just looked respectable enough not to be suspicious, or he took her completely by surprise."

"He hit her on the back of her head with a blunt object," Baratti said. "That would definitely have taken her by surprise—and given him time to restrain her so she couldn't fight back."

"Do you know if there were any prints identified at the scene other than hers?"

"Not yet," he said. "Hers were the only prints lifted from the knife, though."

I frowned as I thought it over. "So the knife was probably hers," I said. "It was a crime of opportunity." I blew out a breath, disappointed. "She almost definitely didn't know him."

"Aw, look at you," Harvey said, beaming at me. "Throwing around terminology like an old pro."

Annoyed, I pivoted toward him. "Are you always a condescending prick to people you've just met?" I said before I could stop myself.

Harvey let out a bark of laughter, and I blinked at him in surprise. "I like you, Gibbs," he said. "I think you're gonna do okay."

"Thanks," I said dryly. "Means a lot to me."

Baratti tried to hide his reaction—amused or annoyed, I couldn't tell—with a well-timed cough. "It doesn't necessarily mean that it was her knife," he said, and I shifted my attention back to him. "He could have brought it with him, wiped his prints off, and put hers on it."

"True," I said, nodding thoughtfully. "Wonder if there were any knives missing from her knife block."

"That's a question for Detective Fletcher," Harvey cut in, glancing down at his watch. "Speaking of which, we've got to run. I managed to persuade Fletch to meet with us."

"With your undeniable charm, I'm sure."

"You catch on quick, grasshopper." He turned on his heel and started for the door. "Come on."

I glanced from him to Percy's body and back again. "But I—"

Pausing at the door, Harvey turned back toward me with a disapproving expression. "He's only giving us five minutes, Gibbs, so we've got to go." Without waiting for a response, he pushed through the doors and disappeared into the hallway.

"He's like that with everyone," Baratti said from behind me, and I swiveled back around to face him. "A condescending prick, I mean."

"And here I was starting to feel slightly more important than a slug."

Smiling, he slid a hand into the pocket of his lab coat and produced a business card. "If you have any more questions," he said, holding it out to me, "feel free to give me a call."

I reached out and pinched the card between my forefinger and thumb, but didn't take it from him. "I can be a real pain in the ass. I ask a lot of stupid questions, because I'm just a lowly intern." I raised a brow at him. "Sure you want to make that offer?"

"Of course I'm sure." He released the card and dropped his hand. "Dead or alive." I tilted my head to one side, a quizzical expression on my face. "That's M.E. humor," he clarified. "It means one hundred percent certain."

"Clever," I said, sliding the card into my jacket pocket. "Thanks. I might take you up on that."

"By the way, I haven't heard any stupid questions yet." I tried to stifle a pleased smile as he nodded toward the door. "Now you'd better hurry. He'll abandon you here without a second thought."

I laughed and pivoted on my toes. "Thanks again," I called over my shoulder with a wave.

To my surprise, Harvey was waiting for me outside the double-door entrance to the building with a smirk on his face. Actually, the smirk wasn't much of a surprise.

"Now that you're done flirting with the M.E.," he said when I joined him, "can we get back to our investigation?"

"Sure thing, Harv. You're the boss." I slipped my sunglasses on. "Also, your definition of flirting is kind of disturbing."

He laughed, lifting an arm to hail a cab. "I'm disappointed in you, Gibbs. I would've won fifty bucks if you'd lost your lunch."

"Well, that's where you screwed up," I said. "It's only eleven o'clock. We haven't even had lunch yet."

"Maybe next time," he said with a crooked grin.

I slid my hands into the pockets of my blazer and felt the outline of Baratti's business card, the corners of my mouth turning up in a smile. "Yes," I agreed. "Maybe next time."

CHAPTER 3
PRESENT
COLSBORO, OHIO

"SO, WHY DID YOU ASK your estranged father to bail your ex-fiancé out of an interrogation?"

Baratti's question broke the awkward silence we'd been observing since leaving the CPD twenty minutes ago. After our initial ice breaker, I'd driven us to O'Malley's with the radio loud enough to discourage conversation but not so loud that it was obvious. Now that we sat face to face, the conversation I'd been avoiding had become unavoidable. But at least he'd waited until we'd gotten our wine.

I blinked at him. "Straight to the heart of the matter, I guess."

He shrugged. "Nothing to lose."

"Right." I shifted my eyes to my glass, gave my wine a swirl, and took a long sip to stall. A few beats later, I lifted my gaze to his. "I asked Pierce for his help because I know you didn't kill anyone. I know you're being set up."

Baratti's eyes widened, as if surprised by my declaration. "How?"

Taking in a deep breath, I pulled the thick file from my bag and set it on the table in front of me. "Because you're not the first person connected to me whose prints have been found at the scene of a murder."

His brows sank slightly. "You're referring to Joe's prints at Chelsea Quinn's apartment."

"Yes, but not just that. Kenny's were found at—"

"Kenny?"

"Kellyn's husband."

Baratti's eyes slid downward as he sifted through his memory. "That guy Kellyn brought to Joe's birthday dinner right before we—" He cut himself off and picked up his wine glass.

"They got married. Eloped, actually, about four months later." I cleared my throat to dislodge the lump that had formed. "Anyway, his were ID'ed at Allison Donnelly's house in Heron County in August. Then in October, Jason's prints were found at the scene of Gina Hadley's murder in McKinley County."

"And now me."

"You probably know they chalked Joey's up to rookie carelessness. Jason had become a regular at the bar where Gina Hadley worked." I drew in a shallow breath and blew it out. "And Kenny eventually admitted to having an affair with Allison Donnelly."

A thick silence fell between us. "Jen," he said finally, his voice tight, "I'm so sorry about—"

"Don't. It was a long time ago." He clamped his mouth shut and waited for me to continue. I stared at him, unblinking, as I worked up the courage for my next question. "I need to ask you something."

He nodded once. "Okay."

I tapped my finger on the table a few times before I was able to summon the words. "Were you in a relationship with Stephanie Goodwin?"

"No," he answered immediately. "I'd never even met her."

I ignored the strange feeling in my chest. "In that case, I have a follow-up question."

"Shoot."

"Have you had any break-ins recently, or noticed that anything was missing?"

"No."

"Sold or pawned any valuables?" I pressed.

The crease between his eyebrows deepened. "No."

Despite the implications of all these scenarios, any of them would have been a lot simpler than what we were apparently dealing with. Steeling myself, I opened my file.

"I've been receiving photos of the vics." I sifted through the contents until I found Stephanie Goodwin's. "Until today, though, I hadn't seen any of the official crime scene photos. I assumed they were more or less the same as mine, but I had a friend get me Goodwin's and found out I was wrong." I slid the photo Orlando had given me across the table toward Baratti, and his gaze drifted downward to examine it. "That's how Northville police found her. And this—" I extracted the second photo and placed it next to the first. "This is what he sent me."

As he scrutinized the photos, I took the opportunity to work on my wine. After a long minute, he finally asked, "Can I see the photo of Chelsea Quinn?"

I flipped to the front of the file and extracted the photo. "Rumor has it, she had so many stab wounds you had a hard time counting them all."

I passed it to him, and he let out a dry laugh. "That's not what she looked like when we got there." He brought the photo closer to his face and squinted at it. "It looks like these piercings on her chest are deliberately arranged this way."

I leaned forward to examine it upside down; from this angle, it looked like a lopsided Y formed from large, red dots. "You're probably right."

"Based on this new evidence," he said slowly, as if searching for the right words, "I think it's pretty clear he's trying to communicate with you." He lifted his chin and met my eyes. "Do you think this is connected to the murders you covered in Chicago?"

"I called Harvey today. He didn't get any photos addressed to me after I left, and to his knowledge, neither did anyone else."

"Has there been any movement in the case since then?"

"They convicted someone for the murders. If Harv's right, and the photos really did stop..." My voice trailed off.

"Then it would be logical to assume they caught the killer," Baratti finished, and I lifted a shoulder in a half-shrug. "But you're still getting photos." He ran a hand along his jaw, eyes unfocused as he considered. "Could it be a copycat?"

"Anything's possible."

"But you don't think so."

I sipped my wine. "Not many people know about the photos."

Baratti stared at me. "I'm one of them."

"True."

"And my prints were ID'ed at Goodwin's house."

"Also true."

"Is that why we're here?" He dropped his gaze to his wine glass. "You think I'm involved?"

"I already said I didn't."

He sighed heavily. "Either way, you didn't have to do this. They'd have figured it out eventually."

"Did they tell you where they found your prints?"

His eyes slid up to mine. "No." I drew the photo of the jewelry box out of my file and passed it across the table, studying him as his expression darkened. "My grandfather's ring box," he whispered. He grabbed the photo of Goodwin dressed up like a bride and squinted down at it. "It's too small. I can't tell if..."

As his voice trailed off, I slid the enlargement of Goodwin's toward him. As he studied it, the color drained out of his face as his eyes darted back and forth between photos.

"Maybe it's a lookalike," he said at last.

I dug the padded envelope out from the bottom of my purse and held it out to him. "This was delivered to me at work today."

Baratti hesitated, then took it from my fingertips and tilted it upside down so its contents fell to the table. He extracted the ring from the small plastic bag and examined it, running a finger along the tiny engraving inside the band.

"You looked at this, didn't you?" he asked quietly. "You know it's the real thing."

"Yes." My voice came out hoarse.

Baratti closed his fist around the ring, eyes flashing. "How the hell did he get this?"

"I don't know," I said evenly, "and I agree it's troubling—but the real question is why."

A muscle in his jaw twitched. "I suppose you have a theory for that?"

"At first I thought he was just using me for publicity, but now I think he's trying to send me a message." I gestured toward the photos. "The pictures he sends me are different from what the police see, the murders are committed in different jurisdictions, and there's no consistent M.O. He doesn't want the police to connect them. He wants me to be the only one to have all the clues."

He was quiet for a few beats as he stared at me, unblinking. "He wants you to know who he is."

"I didn't figure it out then." I swallowed against the lump in my throat. "Now he's making sure he has my attention and is forcing me to listen."

"You think he followed us—" Baratti cut himself off, dropping his gaze back to the ring sitting in his hand. He studied it for a few long seconds, his Adam's apple bobbing as he swallowed, before stowing it back in the plastic bag and tucking it into his inner jacket pocket. "You think he followed you here from Chicago?"

"It's a theory," I said noncommittally.

Baratti's face was blank. "Why are you telling me this?"

"At the very least, to warn you. He knows who you are and where you live." I tapped my index finger against the base of my wine glass. "And if my theory's right, he's also setting you up, for the same reason he tried to set up my brothers and Kenny: To get my attention."

"What does he want you to know?" He folded his hands together and placed them on the table. "What was the message hidden in the photos of Goodwin and the others?"

"Other than the fact that he's showing off how well he knows me, I have no idea." A shiver snaked its way down my spine, and my fingers tightened around the stem of my wine glass. "I need to get the official crime scene photos so I can compare them to what he sent. Otherwise, it's going to take longer to answer that question."

"I can get them."

I studied his expressionless face, trying to figure out what he was thinking and why he was offering to help me. It wasn't out of character for him; he had always gone out of his way to help other people, often to his own detriment. But I'd inadvertently turned his life sideways, and chances were, it was just going to get worse. It'd be safer—for both of us, in more ways than one—if he stayed out of it.

"No," I said finally.

His shoulders dropped. "Jennifer—"

"No," I repeated, more firmly this time. "It's my fault you got dragged into this in the first place, and I'm not going to wreck your life more by asking you for anything."

"It's not your fault, and I'm offering." When I didn't respond, he gave a minute shake of his head. "I wrecked your life three years ago. I've been looking for a way to make it up to you ever since. Let me do this."

I shook my head. "It's not negotiable."

"Good, I'm glad we agree." He gathered up the photos and slid the stack to me. "You can't stop me, and I know where you work. So you're just going to have to accept my contribution."

"Okay."

He blinked. "That's it?"

My eyes drifted downward, and I picked up my glass to keep my hands occupied. "When you've made up your mind—" I paused to finish off my wine. "There's nothing I can do to change it."

A thick silence descended upon us as we stared at each other from opposite sides of the table. Clearing his throat, Baratti reached for the bottle and gave us each another pour.

"How are you doing?" He tried to keep his voice light, but it came out strained. "Aside from attracting another homicidal lunatic."

I swirled my glass around in small circles, watching as the wine sparkled in the light. "Fine," I said. "How are you doing—aside from being a person of interest in a murder investigation?"

When he didn't respond, I lifted my eyes to his face, finding him watching me intently. I could almost see the thoughts churning around inside his brain, and I knew we were edging closer to dangerous territory.

"Before you say whatever you're thinking about saying," I said sternly, "don't say it." When he opened his mouth to respond, I shook my head definitively. "There's no reason to reopen old wounds. This is strictly professional."

"You made a deal with your father for me." His voice was barely audible above the bass of the overhead music. "That seems pretty personal."

"I'm a journalist. I operate on a quid-pro-quo basis with a lot of people." I waved a hand. "Not a big deal."

"So you would've done that for anyone."

I shifted uncomfortably. "I don't know if *anyone* is guilty or innocent. You, however—"

"You don't know that," he interrupted. "We haven't seen or spoken to each other in more than three years, and if you look at the facts objectively—"

"The logical conclusion is you've become a serial killing medical examiner?" I asked, brows arched skeptically. "Very Dexter of you."

Letting out a sigh, he scrubbed his face with his hands. "I don't know. I guess—" He dropped his hands back to the table and met my eyes. "I'm just surprised to see you, and even more surprised you helped me after everything that happened."

I kept my face carefully blank. "None of that warrants being framed for murder."

His head tilted to one side as he considered. "I guess I can't argue with that."

"No." I glanced around for our server, waving a hand to catch her attention, and dug my wallet out of my purse. "You can't, because it's true."

Baratti smiled politely at the waitress as she collected my payment and sealed the half-empty bottle of wine for transport. Once she had thanked us and darted off to an adjacent table, his smile slowly faded, and he turned back to me.

"Thank you." His fingers twitched, as if they wanted to reach out to mine, but he kept them to himself. "It would have been much easier not to call your father, not to see me, to find another way to give back the ring." He paused, and I wondered if the word *again* slithered through his mind, as it did mine. "I appreciate it."

I ignored the urge to tell him I hadn't thought twice about it, swallowing it down with the rest of my wine. "You're welcome," I said instead, and zipped up my wallet. "Listen, I'm on deadline, so we should probably get going."

His brow twitched. "Of course. I'm sure you have a big article to write."

I froze as I read between the lines, wondering if he was worried that I was about to destroy his career.

"I haven't reported on the fingerprints, and this is no exception." I met his eyes, expression sober. "I said I don't want to wreck your life, and I mean it."

He nodded, face blank. "I know. I trust you." Then he lowered his voice so I almost didn't hear him. "But maybe you shouldn't trust me."

«»

"SORRY I DIDN'T MAKE IT over last night," Mike told me Friday afternoon at lunch. "Nat and I stayed late at the precinct."

I tore open a packet of Splenda and dumped it into my iced tea. "Are you making progress?"

"Not much," he admitted. "We're re-interviewing Donnelly and Hadley's families and friends, but enough time has passed that people have forgotten a lot of details."

"Have you identified any suspects?"

"All persons of interest have been cleared, so we're starting from scratch." He took a sip of his coffee before lifting his eyes to mine. "Speaking of which, did you know your father is Baratti's attorney?"

"Why would I know that?" I asked, sounding defensive even to myself. "It's not like we're close anymore." I slid my hands under the table so they could fidget in private. "I mean, Pierce and I."

"Just thought it was odd." He gave me a lopsided smile. "And I knew who you meant."

A short hysterical laugh slipped out. "Of course you did."

"Anyway," he went on, "we have no persons of interest, let alone suspects."

"No boyfriends or husbands or jealous exes?"

Mike ran a hand over his short hair, shaking his head. "We can't even figure out how the victims are connected."

"Maybe they're not. Maybe that's the connection." He made a beckoning gesture with his hand, inviting me to elaborate. "We have four murders of four seemingly unconnected women, committed in four different counties with four different M.O.s. There's all kinds of jurisdictional red tape, not to mention the fact that you guys have a habit of being territorial and possessive."

His eyes narrowed slightly. "Okay."

"If there was even the slightest overlap, someone might get the idea that you're dealing with a serial," I said. "You might start talking to one another and comparing notes. Maybe even involve the FBI."

Mike rubbed his jaw thoughtfully. "All of which would mean more resources and a better chance of ID'ing him."

"Exactly." I paused to take a sip of my iced tea. "Which, for obvious reasons, he doesn't want."

His Adam's apple bobbed as he swallowed. "Because then it'd be game over, and he couldn't play psycho hide and seek with you anymore."

"On the other hand," I added quickly, "they can't be totally random, either, or he could lose control of the situation."

"True." Mike's brow scrunched, indicating deep thought. "And there is one thing they all had in common: They were all single."

"Which makes sense, right? No chance of being interrupted by a boyfriend or husband."

"Right." He crossed his arms over his black thermal henley. "So where do people go when they're single and ready to mingle?"

Despite the gravity of the situation, the corners of my lips twitched in the beginnings of a smile. "Speed dating? Blind dates? A good, old-fashioned classified ad in the personals section?"

"Too random." He shook his head. "If he wants to identify specific characteristics and vet them in advance, the easiest way would be—"

"Online dating," I finished, a full-fledged smile spreading across my face.

"Bingo." He considered it, finally giving in with a shrug. "It's a decent theory. Maybe you were right."

"About what?"

"Working together," he said. "Though it's a little disturbing how easily you slipped into the mind of a serial killer."

"I have a minor in criminal psychology," I reminded him, "not to mention a very active imagination."

We fell silent as the server dropped off our sandwiches and promised to return with drink refills. After a few minutes of eating in companionable silence, Mike put his sandwich down and looked at me.

"Don't let this go to your head," he said soberly. "I appreciate your input, but I still don't want you to be any more involved than this."

Swallowing the bite of roast beef and cheddar I was working on, I nodded. "I know."

"You can do all the research you want from the safety of the newsroom," he continued, "but no stakeouts, no amateur undercover operations, no Orlando hacking into police databases or helping you break into private property. Got it?"

Annoyed, I dropped my sandwich back into the red plastic basket. "You know I'm a grown-up, right?" I wiped my fingers on a napkin. "I wear suits and pay bills and stuff."

"And you have also made some bad judgement calls in the past—"

"Whereas you can walk on clouds."

"Of the two of us," he pointed out, "I'm the only one who's never gotten kidnapped in the line of duty."

I groaned. "Why are people so fixated on that?"

"Because normal people don't get kidnapped."

"Well, I'm not normal people."

"Asking you not to break the law is a normal request, so let's start there." He winked. "I like hanging out with you, and jail might get in the way of that."

"You may have a point." I wrinkled my nose. "Plus they probably don't have wine there."

"And that," he said, picking up his sandwich, "is as close to agreement I'm going to get."

《》

"HEY," I SAID TO TORI when I returned to the newsroom, "aren't you on an online dating site?"

Nonplussed, she watched me drape my jacket on the back of my chair. "Yes."

"Which one?" I plopped down into my chair and swiveled to face her. "I need a big selection of potential partners."

Tori's eyes widened. "Did you and Mike break up?"

I shrugged nonchalantly. "Just keeping my options open." I laughed at her startled expression. "Actually, I'm working on a new theory that the killer's hunting for his victims online."

"Via dating sites?" She smirked. "Good luck. There are about a zillion of them."

"And now we've come full circle." I grabbed a pen from my pencil cup and rolled it between my fingers. "So, what's the most popular one?"

"I'm on Passion Finder. There's no shortage of creeps to choose from."

"The same is true in the three-dimensional world, but that sounds like a good place to start."

"I was also on eConnections for awhile," she added. "You might also want to check out MeetUp and—"

"Okay, thanks," I cut her off, tossing the pen down on my desk in annoyance. "I think I'd have better luck nailing pudding to a concrete wall."

"We can divide and conquer. I already have an account on Passion Finder, so I can start looking there."

"If our killer did find them on a dating website, we can assume all his victims were heterosexual."

"Yeah, so?"

"So, I don't think that'll work," I said. "Your search results wouldn't include women."

"So we have to be men?" she asked thoughtfully. "That could be fun. I've always wanted to be able to pee standing up."

"I imagine that would come in handy at all the sporting events you attend."

"Girl, you have no idea."

《》

SHORTLY AFTER TORI LEFT FOR the Flyers hockey game, I called it a day and wandered over to Christine's desk to see if she wanted to grab a drink. Before I could get a word out, she swiveled away from her computer, a mischievous smile on her face.

"So I heard your father is Gavin's attorney. Care to comment?"

I rolled a nearby chair over to her desk and sat down. "How'd you hear about that?"

"The grapevine." She eyed me impatiently. "So?"

"So I called my father." I lifted a shoulder in a casual shrug. "No big deal."

"That alone is a big deal," she said, skeptical. "Calling him to save your ex-fiancé is an even bigger deal."

"Not if we don't make it one."

"What's your penance for requesting his services?"

"Thanksgiving dessert." I rolled my eyes. "Because I wouldn't want to be absent from every major holiday and make his new family think I don't care about them."

She winced. "And all the other days."

"Right."

"Was it worth it?"

I blew out a breath. "Ask me next week."

"Did you talk to Gavin?" she asked, and I nodded. "How'd that go?"

"About as fun as I expect Thanksgiving evening will be," I said dryly.

"I'm sure Mike feels the same way, though I suspect he'd prefer you hanging out with your father over your ex-fiancé."

I dropped my gaze to study my fingernails with feigned interest. "I suspect so, too."

"You didn't tell him, did you?" I didn't respond, and she let out a groan. "Jen."

"Well, what would you do?" I demanded, jerking my chin up to glare at her.

"Hard to say. I've never been in a relationship long enough to require a conversation like that, let alone get engaged and then break it off."

"Extrapolate."

Christine pushed away from the desk far enough to put her feet up. "I guess the right thing to do would be to tell him up front, so he doesn't find out about it from someone else."

I narrowed my eyes at her. "Oh, what do you know?"

She snorted. "You were aware of my credentials before you asked," she pointed out. "And anyway, I think you already knew the answer."

"Unfortunately, I missed my chance."

"It's only been twenty-four hours," she exclaimed. "How could you have missed your chance already?"

"Because Mike asked me at lunch if I knew Pierce was Baratti's attorney."

"And I suppose you said no."

"Not exactly," I said defensively. "I deflected."

Her blue eyes sparkled as she watched me squirm, amused by my distress. "How are you going to explain to him why you're having Thanksgiving dessert with Pierce?"

I grimaced and dropped my head to my chest in defeat. "I hadn't thought of that."

"Maybe you'll get kidnapped again and miss Thanksgiving," she suggested, too cheerfully. "Problem solved."

《》

AFTER I LEFT MIKE'S LATE Saturday morning, I called Orlando to ask for another favor, mentally wincing at how much my tab was about to go up.

"What's on the docket today?" he asked. "Need me to hack into the FBI? Plant a spy in the Russian government?"

"If I said yes, would you be able to?"

"The question isn't whether I'd be able to, but what you'd be willing to give me in compensation for risking being charged with extortion and espionage."

"That sounds pretty pricy."

"It would be—so I hope for your sake that's not what you wanted."

"I need to know if all my murder victims had online dating profiles and any overlap in their contacts." I drummed my fingers against my thigh. "Doable?"

"Might be, if you helped me on a job."

"Would that count as payment on my outstanding invoice?"

"Partial payment."

"Would I be doing anything illegal?"

"Not illegal,'" he said. "Morally gray, maybe, but not illegal." He cleared his throat. "Though you have no problem asking me to commit felonies for you."

I blew out a sigh. "Fine. You have a deal."

"I'll pick you up at seven-thirty," he said, and I could picture the smug smile on his face. "Wear something to attract a fair amount of attention to yourself."

"Like a Big Bird costume or a wedding dress?"

He laughed. "Do you have a Big Bird costume?"

"Well, no," I admitted. "But I do have a wedding dress."

He fell silent while he pondered my admission. "I'm not going to ask, but don't wear that, either."

"Those were my best attention-attracting ideas, so could you be more specific?"

"Sexy, babe. Something sexy."

"I'm beginning to see what you mean about this being morally gray."

"You agreed," he said cheerfully. "No take-backsies."

CHAPTER 4

"THAT SHOULD ATTRACT SOME ATTENTION," Orlando said, appraising my low-cut red dress and nude stilettos when I opened the front door to him that evening. "Glad it's not made out of bright yellow feathers."

"Hey, I can follow directions if they're too specific to have a loophole." I gave him a wry smile, reaching into the closet for my coat. "You look like a fancy ninja. I almost didn't see you out there in the dark."

He wore his usual all-black garb: Black leather jacket, black shirt and pants, and black tie with gunmetal tie clip. If he weren't standing under my floodlight, the only thing I'd have been able to see would've been the moonlight glinting off his freshly shaven head.

Orlando winked. "That's the idea."

"So what did you find out?" I asked once we were settled in his Range Rover.

He reached into the backseat to retrieve a file folder, which he passed to me before starting the SUV. "Me first."

Stifling my disappointment, I opened the folder and squinted down at the photo on top. "Who's this?"

"The evil Malcolm Wolf." He shifted into reverse and swung out of my driveway as if he were a professional driver. "Your mark for the evening."

I clicked on my overhead light and studied Wolf. Even in the dim light I could tell he was attractive: Artfully messy light brown hair, thick eyebrows on an otherwise smooth face, angled jaw, straight nose. His eyes were warm and smile genuine, despite the fact that he was posing for a BMV photo.

I let out a low whistle. "He doesn't look evil to me."

"You of all people know looks can be deceiving." Orlando rolled to a stop at a red light. "Wolf is a private investigator. He has in his possession some detrimental information on one of my innocent clients, which he discovered in the course of an investigation for one of his equally evil clients. Naturally, my innocent client doesn't want said detrimental information to be made public."

"Well, that is quite a pickle your allegedly innocent client is in." I scanned through the rest of the file's contents. "What would you like me to do about it?"

"Convince the evil Wolf to destroy the evidence." He sent me a sideways glance as the traffic light switched to green. "Easy peasy."

"Are you giving me unlimited resources to make it happen?"

"Babe. If that were the case, I'd do it myself."

"Point taken."

Orlando flicked on his turn signal and shifted into the left turn lane. "That said, I am not unwilling to pay him. I'd just like to exhaust other available options first."

"Do these options have anything to do with wearing a dress I'd be embarrassed if my parents saw me in?"

"Wolf's got a soft spot for the fairer sex."

"Ah." I clicked off the overhead light, closed the folder, and tossed it into the backseat. "In that case, I feel the need to clarify what I'm willing to do in exchange for a couple of user names from a dating site."

"Fair enough."

"I will not, under any circumstances, consume white zinfandel," I said, "nor will I do anything that ever appeared on *Survivor.*"

"Duly noted, but I doubt it'll come to anything that compromising." Though his features were obscured by the darkness, his somber voice assured me that he took my unspoken concern seriously. "Don't worry. I wouldn't ask you to do anything you're not comfortable with."

"Appreciate that," I said. "Just so you're aware, I am completely comfortable with spending your money. Also, I will need a stun gun and a Range Rover of my own."

Shaking his head in a what-am-I-going-to-do-with-you kind of way, Orlando zipped under another green light. "Although Wolf appreciates beautiful women, he lives up to his name in business—whether his opponent is male or female," he added. "Depends solely on how you play it."

"Guess it's a good thing we didn't go for the Big Bird costume."

"True. The dress will only enhance your skills of persuasion."

"So long as your innocent client hasn't done anything illegal."

"The information is of a personal nature and holds no interest to law enforcement."

"Excellent. I think I'll wing it."

Orlando blew out a breath. "Great plan."

I glanced over at him as we passed under a streetlight. "Hey, you wouldn't have asked me if I didn't have some obscure skill that could possibly be helpful in this situation."

"That, and Bullet doesn't look as good in a low-cut dress," he said, referring to his right-hand man and second in command. "He's at the restaurant already, saving you a seat at the bar."

"Is he also going to make Wolf sit at the bar with his powers of telekinesis?"

Orlando snorted. "The seat he's saving you is next to Wolf."

"How'd you know where Wolf would be?" I asked. "Were you born psychic, or is it a skill you've developed over the years?"

"What I do is more like stacking the deck than predicting the future." His lips twitched in amusement as he pulled into the parking lot of Viva Vino restaurant. "And a lot of surveillance."

"I'm disappointed. I wouldn't mind having a psychic on my side."

"You have a deck stacker on your side. That's better."

«»

HALF AN HOUR LATER, I'D used every tool in my she-shed in an attempt to persuade Wolf to relinquish what he knew about Orlando's client. Growing increasingly frustrated while Wolf leaned back in his chair and grinned smugly at me, I availed myself of the last-resort option.

"All right, Malcolm," I said, throwing my hands skyward. "Everyone's got a price. What's yours?"

He rubbed his chin in mock thought. "This is something I'm going to have to consider very carefully."

I narrowed my eyes. "I'll give you ninety seconds."

While Wolf thought it over, I turned away and nonchalantly sipped my wine. Shock rippled through me when my eyes landed on Kenny Shawe, sitting on the opposite side of the bar with his arm around a woman who was not my cousin. As if sensing he was being watched, he dropped his arm and glanced around until his eyes met mine. After a brief staring contest, he raised his beer bottle in a gesture of recognition, expression unreadable.

"Make me an offer," Wolf said, pulling me back to my assignment.

I tore my glare away from Kenny and plastered a pleasant smile on my face. "Is steady employment something you'd be interested in?"

His lips twitched in the beginnings of a smirk. "You offering me a job at Drake Security?" he asked, amused.

I smiled at him like the Cheshire cat. "Would you accept a job at Drake Security in exchange for the information in your possession?"

"Can you even do that?"

I signaled for Orlando. "I have a lot of power, but not that much."

After Orlando whisked him away, I scanned the packed bar for Kenny, intending to give him a piece of my mind and potentially pour my red wine down his crisp white shirt. Unfortunately, someone else had taken possession of his chair on the opposite side of the bar. I settled back to wait for Orlando and Bullet and contemplated how to get away with ramming Kenny's head into the side of the bar should he reappear.

And then he did.

"Looking for me?" Kenny asked, brushing up against my bare arm as he slid onto Wolf's vacated chair. Startled, I jerked toward him, finding his pale blue eyes sparkling in amusement.

"Kenny," I said stiffly. "What an unpleasant surprise." I glanced around, simultaneously trying to inch my barstool away from him. "Where's your date—or have you abandoned her already, like you did Kellyn?"

He mock pouted. "Why so cold?" he asked. "It almost feels like we haven't known each other for three years."

I stared at him blankly. "Well, that's what happens when you hurt a member of my family."

"But doesn't that include me?"

"Only legally."

Kenny studied me for a few beats. "I see what's going on here. You're mad at me for being on a date with another woman."

"I've been mad at you for several months, so I don't think that's it."

"Oh, but I think it is." He lowered his voice conspiratorially. "Are you going to tell Kellyn?"

I scrutinized him over the rim of my glass. "Are you asking me to do your dirty work for you?"

"I realize it's a lot to ask," he said dryly. "I'm sure you get no pleasure from defaming me."

"For some reason, Kellyn is reluctant to admit your marriage is over, and I've been looking for ways to convince her otherwise."

My lips curved up in a smile that didn't reach my eyes. "This should help, though."

"Don't be so quick to discount her feelings." Kenny lifted his palms in an exaggerated shrug. "Maybe there is a glimmer of hope."

"Says the man who's on a date with a woman who isn't his wife."

He matched my smile. "Says the woman who's on a date with someone who isn't her boyfriend."

"I'm not on a date." The denial slipped out before I could stop myself. "I'm working."

Kenny grinned as his eyes slid up and down, taking in my attire. "Change of career?" I narrowed my eyes slightly but otherwise didn't respond. "I suppose Mike knows you're here?"

"Of course," I lied.

He brought the bottle to his lips and took a long draw, and I stifled the urge to squirm. "Good. Nothing like dishonesty and infidelity to ruin a happy relationship, right?"

"Speaking from experience?"

His shoulders sank. "Look, I know you hate me because of what I did to your cousin—"

"Ah, something we agree on."

"But it takes two people to ruin a relationship."

"You're right," I said. "You and Allison Donnelly."

"Touché." Kenny smiled tightly. "But it was ruined before that—which is the point I'm trying to make."

I snorted. "Are you saying Kellyn did something to drive you to have an affair?"

He lifted his hands as if defending himself from a physical attack. "I know you'll always take her side over mine—and rightfully so," he added, quashing my protest before it materialized. "Despite what you think of me, I don't want to muddy your opinion of her. So, for the sake of your relationship, I'll take full responsibility."

"How magnanimous of you."

"My pleasure." Kenny polished off his beer and leaned closer, resting the bottle on the back of my chair. "Thank you for noticing."

I resisted the compulsion to shift away from him. "Don't you have a date to be getting back to?"

A muscle in his jaw pulsed, and he quickly turned it into a crooked smile. "As much as you do." He slid off the stool, straightened to his full height, and dropped his empty bottle on the bar, all while keeping his eyes locked on me. "Enjoy your night, Jennifer."

I held my breath and remained still until he vacated my personal space. Once his back was to me, I let my eyes follow him as he strode out of the bar. Just as I was about to relax, he halted, spun around to face me, and smirked, as if he'd known all along I'd been watching him. Refusing to give in, I let him hold my gaze until he finally turned and disappeared.

I drained my wine glass and all but slammed it down on the bar, clenching my teeth as I gathered my coat and purse. I had to leave before I broke his empty bottle on the side of the bar, charged into the dining room, and jammed it into his jugular.

«»

THE NIGHT WAS STILL EARLY by Saturday standards when I got home, but my encounter with Kenny had quashed my motivation to open the fat envelope Orlando left with me. Instead, I changed into sweats, poured another glass of wine, and flopped onto the couch to find out what mysteries Investigation Discovery had to offer.

The next morning, I woke to sunlight leaking in past the blinds and the beginnings of a headache. I dragged myself out of bed and found Kellyn in the kitchen pouring herself some coffee.

She gave me a once-over and offered me her cup. "Looks like somebody had too much fun last night," she said, opening the cupboard for another mug. "What kind of trouble did you get into?"

"A bottle of wine." I retrieved the creamer from the refrigerator and dumped some into my coffee. "After I did a quick job with Orlando in exchange for some information."

"Ooh, did you rappel down the side of a building or hunt for criminals in a helicopter?"

"Nothing that exciting." Luckily for her, I'd managed to resist the urge to decapitate or otherwise harm her husband. Not long after I'd stormed out of the bar, Orlando and Bullet had found me in the parking lot, pacing next to the Range Rover in a huff.

"What are you doing?" Orlando asked.

I spared him a brief glance. "Trying not to commit murder."

"Maybe you should reconsider," Bullet suggested. "Might make you feel better about whatever it is you're upset about."

"Upset? I'm not upset. What makes you think I'm upset?"

He let out a dry laugh. "Just a ridiculous thought I had."

I whirled to face them, hands on my hips. "You know what's ridiculous?" I asked, barreling on before either of them could answer. "My stupid cousin's stupid husband and his stupid smug face."

Orlando's brow hitched upward. "Want me to shoot him?"

Of course, I had declined, despite what my id was shouting from deep inside my lizard brain. And now, standing in the kitchen with Kellyn, I was starting to regret my super ego's restraint.

"That's disappointing," Kellyn said. "That would have been so cool."

"Maybe next time." I slurped some liquid from my too-full mug before taking it with me to the couch. "What about you?"

"No rappelling or helicoptering for me, either." She sat down on the love seat and folded her legs underneath her, wrapping her hands around her own cup. "What kind of information did Orlando dig up for you?"

I nodded toward the yellow envelope sitting on the coffee table. "That."

She eyed it dubiously. "Looks like enough information to solve your case."

"If it's the right information." I slid open the end table drawer and fished around inside for a pen. "And even if it is, it's going to take about seven fortnights to go through it all."

Smiling, Kellyn put her mug down on the coffee table and reached for the file. "I'm feeling generous today," she said, extracting the pages from the folder. "Give me a pen and tell me what we're looking for."

"As you wish." I found another pen and passed it to her before she could change her mind. "Just note any duplicate user names you find. Bonus points if they're all the same."

She let out a short laugh. "That sounds like a lofty goal."

"You know I've always been an overachiever."

《》

LATE THAT AFTERNOON, MIKE'S INVITATION to come over for dinner and a movie was a well-timed reprieve from the monotonous task that I had determined was minimally more worthwhile than mining for gold in the Ohio River. But then, my secret rendezvous from the previous night had come out over dinner, leading to a heated discussion focusing on my life choices that continued late into the night.

"Don't forget what we talked about," Mike told me the next morning as he adjusted his tie. "No more asking Orlando illegal favors."

Annoyed, I slid my feet into a pair of red heels. "What about sexual ones?"

"Jennifer, this is serious."

I rolled my eyes dramatically. "You make it sound like we met in a dark alley, and I bought heroin from him."

"You have no idea the information he wanted to bury wasn't evidence of a crime," he pointed out, sliding his suit jacket off its hanger. "He could have been covering up clandestine negotiations with North Korea to nuke Napa Valley. You wouldn't want Napa Valley to get nuked, would you?"

"You're right." Despite my irritation, the corners of my mouth twitched. "I definitely can't ask North Korea for any favors if they're planning to destroy all that wine."

Grinning, he shrugged into his jacket. "Or Orlando."

"Especially not him." I laid the back of my hand lightly against my forehead. "Oh, the betrayal."

"I knew you'd come around." He closed the distance between us and slid his hands around my waist. "If you had a compelling enough reason."

I softened as I tilted my head back to look at him. "You play dirty."

"Anything to keep the wine safe." He pulled me closer and gave me a light kiss. "And you."

I ran my fingers down his tie and changed the subject. "Why so dressed up today?"

"Court." He gave me another kiss before releasing me and turning away. "I have to testify in the Rollins case."

"Ah," I said, following him out to the kitchen. "Well, I like it. If you don't work late, I might let you make up for being a controlling jerk last night."

Lips twitching in the beginning of a smile, he pulled a pair of travel mugs out of the cabinet. "And if you behave yourself, I might let you make up for being an impulsive risk taker."

I snorted, reaching into his fridge for the sugar-free French vanilla creamer he kept on hand for me. "I sat at a bar and had a brief conversation with a pleasant stranger. It's astonishing I survived."

"Don't joke about that." He filled the mugs and handed one to me. "You've come close on more than one occasion."

I sloshed some cream in and screwed on the lid. "I know," I said, returning the bottle to the refrigerator. "I'm sorry. I'll be good."

"I have spies everywhere," he said, striding to the closet to grab our coats. "So I'll know if you do anything out of line."

"Stalker," I muttered.

"I prefer the term 'close-range people watching,'" he said, holding up my trench coat so I could slide my arms into the sleeves.

"Either way," I said, "it's kinda creepy."

He grasped my arm firmly and spun me around, pressing his lips to mine. A few beats later, he pulled back and gave me a mischievous smile. "Think of it as my way of showing affection."

Skeptical, I eyed him as he shrugged into his own jacket. "I can think of more fun ways to do that."

"One of the ways," he amended, grabbing a dog biscuit from the jar on the counter. En route to the front door, he tossed it to Murphy, who caught it without moving from his spot on the couch. We let ourselves out, locked the door, and descended the stairs to the parking lot, where my car was parked next to his truck.

"Love you," he called over his shoulder.

Twenty minutes and a three-block walk through the rain later, I plopped down into my desk chair and began scrolling through emails while Tori and I chatted about our respective weekends.

And procrastinating. Yesterday Kellyn and I had found twenty-seven duplicate users among the four victims, which I now had to track down and compare. By the time I'd consumed enough caffeine to feel somewhat equipped to take on the task, my computer pinged to announce a new email. My breath caught when I saw the subject line.

Number Five.

I stared at the message for a long sixty seconds before I worked up the nerve to reach for my mouse. Taking a deep breath, I opened the email and clicked on the attached image. My heart jumped when I saw her.

She was still alive—and I knew who she was.

CHAPTER 5

A BRUNETTE WOMAN SAT AT a green felt-topped table wearing a white button-down shirt and black vest. In one hand, she held a deck of playing cards; the other hand hovered above it as if about to deal the next round. The background was dark and frame cropped close, giving no hint to her surroundings. A pair of black-rimmed glasses rested on her nose, magnifying the palpable fear in her eyes, but she stared directly at the camera.

Directly at her killer.

Jolted out of my trance by the thought, I sent the image to my printer and fished my cellphone out of my purse, hoping I was wrong about her identity.

"Hi, honey," my mother said when she answered my call. "Now's not a good time. Laura's a no call, no show—"

My stomach dropped. "Laura?"

"Yes. Laura Garrett." Paper rustled in the background. "You've met her."

"Right. Remind me, which one is she?"

"Tall, brown hair, glasses." She sighed. "Ordinarily very responsible."

"Maybe something happened to her."

The line went silent for a couple of long seconds. "What makes you say that?"

I shrugged, then realized she couldn't see it. "What you just said. Does she live nearby? Maybe someone should check on her."

"That's what I was thinking—especially now that you've got me all worried." She paused, and more papers shuffled across her desk. "Ah, here it is. Emerald Gardens apartments in Shannon."

"Which one?"

"Jennifer, what's going on?"

I plucked the photo off the print tray and slid it into my purse. "I'll meet you there," I offered, trying for nonchalant. "I've got to make a trip to Shannon anyway."

"For what?"

"Gotta see a guy about a thing," I said vaguely. "So, what apartment?"

She hesitated before answering. "Two fifty-six."

"Okay." I shot to my feet, grabbed my jacket, and looped my purse over my shoulder. "I'll be there in twenty."

"Sweetie, that's really not necessary."

Swallowing my argument, I waved goodbye to Tori and bolted for the elevator. "Maybe not, but I'll feel better if you don't go alone."

"You watch too much Investigation Discovery."

"True." I hoped I was just being paranoid, but I had a sinking feeling that wasn't the case. "I'm getting in the elevator now. See you soon."

I disconnected before she could argue and immediately dialed Mike.

THE RAIN HAD SLOWED TO a drizzle when I parked crookedly in front of Laura Garrett's apartment building. I cut the engine, tucked my cellphone and keys into my jacket pockets, and shoved my purse under the seat. When I made it up to Laura's second-floor apartment, I found my mother beating against the door—so loudly, in fact, she didn't hear me as I pounded up the stairs.

"Mom?"

She spun toward me. "No one's answering."

"How long have you been knocking?"

"A few minutes." Her eyes darted around. "Maybe her neighbor—" Without finishing the sentence, she turned on her heel and rapped her fist on the door across from Laura's until its occupant opened it.

A short elderly woman ogled us from behind thick glasses. "My, my. Someone's had her Wheaties today."

"Have you seen your neighbor this morning?" my mother asked. "Laura Garrett in two fifty-six."

She shook her head. "Not since yesterday," she said. "Nice young girl. She helps me carry my groceries inside from my car. It's getting harder for me to climb the—"

"Do you have a key to her apartment?" I interrupted.

"As a matter of fact, I do." She toddled back into her apartment, leaving the door ajar. A long minute later, she returned and held out a gold key. Before my mother could seize it from her, she jerked it back with surprising speed. "How do I know you're not just asking for her key so you can rob her and leave her tied up in the bathroom?"

"Because we could have done the same thing to you when your back was turned," I pointed out, "but we didn't."

She considered. "That's true." She glanced back and forth between me and my mother. "Who are you? How do you know Laura?"

"I'm her boss," my mother said. "Kathryn Mallaghan."

The old woman nodded, then shifted her attention to me. "How about you?"

"I'm her boss's daughter." When she raised her eyebrows at me, I added, "Jennifer Gibbs."

"Nice to meet you." She patted her chest. "Donna Gould. I'm Laura's neigh—"

"Laura didn't show up for work today, and she didn't call," my mother cut in. "She always calls, even if she's only ten minutes late. We just want to check on her."

Donna pulled her sweater tighter and nodded again. "Laura is very conscientious," she agreed. "After my Henry died, she—"

I held up a hand. "I'm sorry, but can we save the story for later? We're really worried about Laura."

The wrinkles on her forehead deepened as she frowned in disapproval. "Very well," she relented, "but I'm coming with you."

"I don't think that's a good idea—" I began.

"I have the key." She shuffled outside, her pink slippers swishing across the threshold, and pulled the door closed behind her. "Follow me."

My mother and I exchanged a glance before trailing behind her obediently. We reached the door about five weeks later, and Donna tried to shove the key into the lock with a trembling hand. After three attempts, my mother snatched it away from her.

"Let me try," she said, reaching around Donna.

"Hold it right there!" All three of us whirled around to find Joey jaunting up the stairs two at a time. When I'd been unable to get a hold of Mike, who I'd belatedly realized was probably in court, I'd redirected my calls to Joey. "What do you think you're doing?"

My mother parked her hands on her hips. "You don't get to interrogate me. I gave birth to you."

"Sorry, Mom." He reached the landing and directed his glare at me. "I was talking to Jennifer."

My eyes widened. "She's the one who's got the key!"

"Which, had you not called her first to confirm, *you* would have."

My mother blinked. "Confirm what?"

Ignoring her, Joey softened his expression and shifted toward the old woman. "Ma'am, why don't you go back inside? It's damp and chilly out here."

Donna beamed up at him, eyes huge behind her thick glasses. "Yes, sir, Officer," she said. "Please let me know if I can assist."

"I certainly will." Joey watched her as she wobbled back into her apartment and we stared at him impatiently. Once she'd closed the door, he looked down at me. "Did you call it in?"

"You're here, aren't you?"

"Call what in?" my mother asked, her face pale despite the chilly air.

Joey lifted a brow in silent question, and I shook my head. "I didn't tell her. I didn't want to freak her out."

"Freak me out about what?" she demanded.

"Mission accomplished," Joey said wryly, pulling a pair of latex gloves out of his pocket and wrestling his fingers into them. He held out his hand expectantly. "Give it."

My mom reluctantly handed him the key, exchanging another unreadable glance with me as he pounded on the door a few times, calling Laura's name and identifying himself as the police. He waited ten seconds, then repeated the process with the same results.

Satisfied he had fulfilled his legal duty, he inserted the key into the lock and shoved the door open. "You two wait out here." He disappeared inside and pulled the door closed behind him.

A few seconds later, my mother blew out a short breath. "Nope, not happening." She turned the knob, pushed the door open, and grabbed my hand. "Let's go."

The apartment was dark, curtains drawn tightly and all lights off but for the chandelier above the table in the dining room, straight ahead of us. I blinked at the scene in front of me; it took a few long seconds for my brain to register what my eyes saw.

Underneath the bright lights, Laura laid spread-eagle on a rectangular dining room table, her arms, legs, and head duct taped in place. A long, thin object stuck out of her head at a ninety-degree angle. From this distance, I couldn't tell what it was, but I definitely knew what the dark liquid pouring down the side of her face was.

My mother let out a strangled gasp, and Joey whirled around.

"Get out," he said firmly, then shepherded us outside, arms held wide. He closed the door behind us, expression grim. "Do. Not. Move." We nodded mutely, and he turned away, pulling his cellphone out of his inner jacket pocket.

I surveyed my mother. "Are you okay?"

"You knew." She shook her head, her green eyes round with shock. "How?"

I didn't answer right away. Aside from a handful of people, most of whom had badges, no one knew about my anonymous pen pal—my mother included. "The killer sent me a photo," I said finally. "He always sends me a photo."

She let her breath out in a rush as she sank down onto the top step. "Oh, Jennifer."

I sat down next to her and picked up her hand, giving it a tight squeeze. "I'm sorry about Laura," I whispered. "Are you okay?"

Her eyes glazed over as she turned to stare blindly into the misty rain. "Laura was a good person. She didn't deserve all that pain. She didn't deserve to die that way."

"In what way?"

She swallowed hard before turning to face me. "He gave her an icepick lobotomy."

《 》

BY THE TIME THE FIRST responders arrived, Joey had wrapped our shaken mother in a blanket and tucked her into his cruiser with the heat on full blast. We leaned side by side against the car, lights flashing around us, and watched the CSI officials swarm in and out of Laura's apartment like an army of ants. At some point, my mother emerged from the cruiser and joined us without speaking.

Eventually, Baratti descended the stairs, expression stony, and strode unhesitatingly toward us. My mother glanced at me, mouth slightly ajar, but didn't have a chance to say anything before he caught up with us.

"Good to see you, Kathryn." He gave her a rueful smile. "Wish it were under better circumstances."

She cleared her throat. "Likewise."

He gave her shoulder a reassuring squeeze before redirecting his attention to me. "Can I talk to you?" Without waiting for a response, he strode away.

Joey snorted. "He seems awfully confident you're going to follow him." Nonplussed, he watched me push away from the car. "Apparently with good reason."

I shot my brother a shut-up glare and followed Baratti to an SUV with state plates parked at the curb. He opened the passenger door and reached inside to retrieve an envelope.

"Sorry I didn't get this to you sooner," he said, handing it to me before slamming the door shut.

Nodding in thanks, I hugged it to my chest and stared up at him. "It wouldn't have made a difference, if that's what you're thinking."

He leaned against the car and crossed his arms over his jacket. "How did you get here before the rest of us?"

"He sent me her photo at about nine o'clock this morning. She wasn't dead in it, so I thought maybe..." I lifted a shoulder in a half shrug as my voice trailed off.

"You recognized her?"

"She works for my mom." I blew out a breath. "Worked. And she didn't have an ice pick through her skull yet."

Baratti nodded. "Have you given a statement yet?"

Dropping my eyes to the ground, I toed a pebble with my shoe. "Yes."

"You can probably go, then."

I let out a humorless laugh. "Not yet."

"I think the CPD knows where to find you."

"True, but—" Out of the corner of my eye, I caught sight of Mike striding toward us at a determined pace, his partner, Natasha Sardelis, close behind. "Uh oh."

Baratti followed my eyes and pushed away from the SUV, straightening to his full height. "Detectives," he said amiably.

Mike spared him a brief glance before directing his glare at me. "What are you doing here?" he demanded, hands on his hips.

I gave him a tight smile. "Getting in trouble, as usual." I nodded at Sardelis. "Natasha."

The hint of a smug smile twitched across her lips. "Jennifer."

Mike cleared his throat. "A word?" He spun me around, wrapped a firm hand around my forearm, and pulled me away, keeping his mouth tightly clamped until we were out of earshot. "What did we just talk about less than five hours ago?"

"Something about Orlando and North Korea nuking Napa Valley, and how you're a stalker." His eyes narrowed, and a surge of irritation filled my chest. "I didn't ask Orlando for anything. I came by this honestly. Jury's still out on the stalker thing."

He held out a hand. "Let me see the photo."

I hooked a thumb over my shoulder. "It's in my car."

"What's in there?" he asked, nodding at the envelope clutched in my arms.

"Christmas list for Santa. I knew the post office was on the way."

"Let me guess." He crossed his arms over his chest. "You sweet talked Baratti into getting you crime scene photos."

"I didn't do that, either."

He pinched the bridge of his nose. "Did he tell you the vic's name?"

"Who, Baratti?"

"No. The killer."

"I recognized her," I repeated, feeling like a scratched CD. "She worked with my mom."

"So he's getting closer." Expression squeezed tight, Mike lifted a hand and waved at Joey in a come-here motion.

He exchanged a few words with our mother, then jogged over to us. "Detective?"

"I trust that after the incident at Quinn's apartment, you didn't let her into the crime scene?"

A muscle in Joey's jaw tensed. "No, but—"

I cut him off before he hanged himself. "Mom and I got the key from the neighbor before Joey arrived. He couldn't have stopped us."

Mike scrutinized my face for signs I was lying, but found none—because technically I wasn't. It was just selective truth, which, as a journalist, I was pretty good at. But then again, so was he.

Seemingly satisfied, he turned back to Joey. "How's your mom doing?"

"Shaken up."

"She need a ride back to work?"

"Might be a good idea."

He nodded once. "Take her, then go back to the precinct to write up your report."

"Yes, sir."

Mike directed his piercing eyes back to me. "And you—back to the newsroom. I'll check in with you later."

"Yes, sir," I said, my tone much less polite than Joey's.

Mike gave me one last warning look before marching away in the direction of my mother. As Sardelis strutted by in pursuit, with Baratti close behind, she gave me a snarky salute. I made a rude gesture at her retreating back.

"I hate her," I muttered.

Baratti stopped about twelve inches from my right shoulder and slid his hands into his pockets. "I don't think anyone actually likes her."

"Demarco seems to like her enough to spend twelve hours a day with her," Joey said dryly. I pivoted slowly to stare at him, deadpan, earning myself a mischievous grin. "Though I'm sure he's suffering silently inside."

"The fact that he's getting paid probably helps," Baratti said.

"Speaking of getting paid," I said, "it's been nice chit-chatting, but I've got to get back to work." I held up the envelope. "Thanks for the photos."

"Anytime." His face was blank as he took a step back in the direction of his SUV. "Let me know if you need anything else."

Joey waited until he was out of earshot before speaking. "You're being awfully nice to Baratti."

"So are you." Eyes narrowed into slits, I folded my arms over my jacket. "You're supposed to hate him on my behalf."

"We work together," he reminded me. "But I give him a lot of dirty looks when his back is turned." He matched my defensive stance. "So what are you doing with him?"

"Nothing. I gave him back his ring and warned him about a potential stalker, and he got me the crime scene photos." I shrugged. "That's it. We're done."

"For your sake, I hope so," he said. "I doubt Mike would be thrilled to find out you're spending all this quality time with your ex-fiancé."

"Good thing I'm not."

"Yeah," Joey said, voice infused with skepticism. "Good thing."

《》

THAT AFTERNOON, I SPENT SEVERAL hours tracking down Laura Garrett's eConnections profile, followed by a fruitless search for the overlapping user names from Orlando's lists. When it hit me that the killer had probably created multiple accounts for this very reason, I called off the search.

I needed a new tactic.

So, I hauled all my files into an unoccupied conference room, spread everything out across the table, and drew a chart on a large dry erase board. I spent the rest of the day filling in the cells with what I knew—victims' names, ages, stats, and clues—and scouring the Record's people search database for what I couldn't.

When most of the table was filled in, I stepped back to survey my progress, irked to discover Mike was right: They had next to nothing in common. The only similarity was their relationship statuses, which had so far proven to be a dead end. Annoyed, I sank down into a chair and stared at the board in silence.

When Christine wandered in around five forty-five, my eyes felt like they'd dried into raisins, and I was contemplating putting my head through a wall.

"Yo," she said, tossing a small padded envelope on the table before plopping down adjacent to me. "That was sitting on your desk."

Yawning, I sat up straight and stretched my arms overhead. "Thanks." I scrutinized the envelope, finding nothing but my name and the newspaper's address written in thick black marker on one side. "Last time I got one of these, it had my—" I cut myself off and cleared my throat. "Baratti's ring in it." Taking a deep breath, I slid my finger under the flap and tore it open.

Christine's eyes widened. "You think it's from today's murder?"

"Let's find out." I tipped the envelope upside down, and several playing cards emblazoned with the Caesar's Palace logo fell out, one corner of each card snipped off at an angle. I arranged them on the table so they were all face up.

Two kings and three Jacks.

"Full house," Christine leaned in to inspect them. "What does that mean?"

I slid my forefinger lightly across the coated card stock, figuring the likelihood of lifting prints was nil. "In the photo he sent me this morning, Garrett was dressed up like a card dealer."

Christine grabbed the marker and filled in the box in Garrett's clue column. She stepped back and examined the board for a few long seconds.

"I've been staring at this for so long, I don't think my brain's actually registering anything anymore." I slid the cards back into the envelope and stood, sending her a questioning look. "Do you see any connections?"

She thought it over. "Quinn, Donnelly, and Garrett were all dark haired, and they all went to school in Ohio," she said, drawing small asterisks in the correlated boxes.

I nodded. "Goodwin's the redheaded oddball from Chicago who graduated from Northwestern." I stared at the board some more. "She and Garrett were both in healthcare."

"And then there's the blonde bartender who dropped out of community college." Christine shrugged. "Seems random."

"It can't be random," I insisted. "He planned this carefully. There's got to be a connection."

She handed the marker to me. "Sleep on it," she suggested on her way to the door. "I'll see you tomorrow."

I waved to her distractedly. "G'night."

Next thing I knew, Mike strode into the conference room at a determined pace. Before saying anything, he grasped my shoulders and pulled me close.

I blinked up at him. "What was that for?"

"You weren't answering my calls." He kissed my forehead and released me. "I got worried." He removed his coat and draped it across one of the chairs before turning to study the board, arms akimbo. "Now I see why."

I winced. "Sorry, I guess I left my phone at my desk."

He wiggled the marker out from my clenched fist. "Autopsy hasn't been done yet," he said as he filled in one of the blanks in Garrett's row, "but Baratti strongly suspects C.O.D. was a brain hemorrhage from the botched lobotomy."

"That's what my mom thought, too," I murmured.

Mike threw me a narrowed-eye glare over his shoulder. "Yeah, we're going to talk about that later." I managed not to roll my eyes until he had turned back to the board. "Any ideas on this one?" he asked, tapping Chelsea Quinn's clue column.

"The puncture wounds on her chest looked like they were arranged deliberately—"

"Agreed."

"But I haven't figured out yet what it means."

"We didn't find the murder weapon at the scene, but in the photo you gave me—"

"You mean the photo you stole," I muttered.

"Yes, that one." He turned and gave me a mischievous smirk. "She had so many wounds, we couldn't even guess what he might've used to kill her. Now I'm wondering if the murder weapon might have been an ice pick."

I frowned. "Like the ice pick he used for Garrett's lobotomy?"

"Bingo." Mike shifted back to the board, tapping the marker against his chin in thought. "Send me the digital photo, and I'll have it enhanced. We can give it to Baratti to compare."

"We?"

"Sure, why not?" His voice was falsely cheerful. "Seems like you two are already working together."

"He got me some photos. End of story."

"I'm not mad."

"I can tell."

"Seriously, Jen," he said. "Baratti's pretty level headed and by the book. He's a helluva lot safer than Orlando."

That was debatable. I kept my mouth shut and shifted my attention back to the board, feeling his eyes on the side of my face. "Have you identified any prints yet?"

"No. Might take a day or two to get results." He sent me a sideways glance. "Speaking of which, did you or your mom touch anything?"

"Of course not," I said, scowling. "We stood in the front hall for about thirteen seconds before we went back outside and Joey called it in."

"Good." He crossed his arms over his chest, and we stood side by side studying the chart. A few beats later, he tapped a finger on Allison Donnelly's clue column. "What kind of a clue is a napkin?"

I pivoted away and sifted through the photos from the second murder. "She had a cocktail napkin in her hand." I handed him Miguel's enlargement. "It had the Bartholomew's logo on it."

The restaurant was local entrepreneur Aaron Bartholomew's flagship eatery, featuring five-star food at five-star prices. I'd only been twice: Three years ago when my parents had treated all of us and our significant others to dinner for Joey's twenty-first birthday, and six months ago when Mike took me there for our one-year anniversary.

Mike studied the photo. "And?"

I shrugged. "And that's all I know."

"Hmm." He passed the photo back to me and stepped toward the board. "I can't offer any insight on that, but I might be able to help with this one." He tapped Gina Hadley's clue cell, in which I'd written BOTTLE??

"I'm listening."

"As you know, Hadley's neck was slashed with a broken beer bottle," he said. "I was comparing your photo to the West Madison P.D.'s crime scene photos, and I noticed the bottles were different. The bottle in your photo was Loch Ness Monster Scottish Ale. But the bottle extracted from her neck was a Thirsty Dog Labrador Lager, presumably from the club where she worked—or a gazillion bars, restaurants, and stores in a ten-mile radius alone."

My eyebrows furrowed. "Weren't Jason's prints found on the bottle?" I asked, and he nodded. "Labrador Lager is his favorite beer. That's...suspicious."

"I thought so, too." He swiveled to face me. "And even more mysterious is the fact that Loch Ness Monster is from a microbrewery in Chicagoland and isn't even sold in Ohio."

"Ah, the plot thickens."

Mike erased my notation and scribbled LOCH NESS MONSTER SCOTTISH ALE in barely decipherable caps in Hadley's clue box. "According to Jeff Simmons, the McKinley County coroner," he continued, "the Thirsty Dog bottle was inserted after she died."

"So he took that murder weapon, too."

"Not a big surprise. He's taken them all—at least, until now." He dropped the marker into the tray beneath the board and rounded the table, picking up the printout of Laura Garrett. "She's still alive here." He looked up at me. "That's new. Why didn't you mention that this morning?"

"Well, you didn't exactly stick around to chitchat."

He dropped his eyes back to the photo. "Maybe next time."

"He was mocking me," I said. "He knew I'd know who she was and—"

Mike's head snapped up. "And try to save her," he finished. "Which means he could have been waiting for you at Garrett's apartment."

"Damn. I hadn't thought of that." I blew out a heavy breath. "You guys still videotape murder scene investigations?"

He gave a curt nod. "I'll pull the footage tomorrow, but chances are, he was gone by the time CSI got there." Brow furrowed, he shifted his gaze back to the board. "Where'd you get her clue?"

I picked up the padded envelope Christine had delivered and passed it across the table to him. "This arrived a little bit ago."

He extracted the cards and studied them. "Do these mean anything to you?"

"Nope."

Frowning, Mike slid the cards back in the envelope and placed it on top of Garrett's photo, which he then separated into another pile. "Is this the only evidence he's sent you?"

"Um—" Taken off guard, I tried to think of a reasonable explanation that neither invited questions nor was a lie, but came up with nothing. "What?"

Mike opened his mouth to respond but was cut off by the shrill ring of his cellphone. Pulling it from the holster on his belt, he pointed a stern finger at me. "We're not done yet."

I released the air I was holding as he answered the phone and turned his back to me, grateful his attention was momentarily redirected. My thoughts darted around my brain haphazardly as I gathered up my files and wrote a note threatening a plague upon anyone who touched the dry erase board.

Mike shrugged into his jacket. "Nat found something," he announced, sliding Garrett's photo and the playing cards into an inner pocket. "I've got to go back to the precinct."

I gave him my best pouty face. "But Kellyn is making spaghetti for dinner," I said, hefting the pile of files into the crook of my elbow.

"She recently discovered there are other sauces and is going to try a new one."

He grinned, reaching out to tuck a strand of hair behind my ear. "Sorry, honey, but look at it this way: The more I can get done over the next few days, the more time we can spend together over Thanksgiving weekend."

"Do you think serial killers observe national holidays?" I flicked off the conference room light, and we trudged back to my desk. "Doesn't seem like something a psychopath would care much about."

"No, it doesn't," he said, smiling ruefully. "But let's hope we're wrong."

FOUR YEARS AGO
COLSBORO, OHIO

THE NEWSROOM AT THE COLSBORO *Record* was a tenth of the size of the *Sun-Times*' bullpen, and the tallest building I could see from the sixth floor window was less than forty stories. I swallowed the persistent feeling that I had taken a giant step in the wrong direction and reminded myself I had done the right thing. I would never have forgiven myself if something had happened to my mother and I hadn't been here for her.

She would be okay, though. My mother was religious about healthcare and self-exams, so she had found the invasive lobular carcinoma early. Her doctor began treatment right away, which gave her almost a one hundred percent survival rate. But the coming months would be rough for her, and she deserved all the support I could give her.

"Hey, Jen," Christine said, startling me out of my self-pity. I glanced up at her as she sat down on top of my desk and dropped her purse next to her. "It's Friday, it's five o'clock, and you survived your first week at the *Record*. Shut down your computer, and let's go celebrate."

"Celebrate what, exactly?" I saved the document I'd been distract-edly working on and closed all my open programs. "Everything sucks."

"Um, all the stuff I just said."

"All of which I could've done blindfolded, hog-tied, and dangling from a spit over an open flame." I shook my head and logged out of the computer. "Thanks, but I'd rather go home and mope."

"Okay, so maybe you don't live in the coolest city in the world any-more, and maybe you write for a paper with a circulation of slightly less than a zillion." She winced. "And maybe tomorrow you're taking your mom to chemo for the first time."

"And I gave up my boyfriend of two years and my future career for all this," I grumbled, gesturing dramatically to my surroundings, "because apparently long-distance relationships are too hard, and I need to focus on my family right now."

"Right, that too," Christine tucked a strand of blonde hair behind her ear. "And it also happens to be Friday the thirteenth."

I narrowed my eyes at her. "Is this supposed to be making me feel better?"

"I'm getting there." She sent me an admonishing look. "As I was about to say, there is at least one shining ray of hope you've completely overlooked. Under the circumstances, however, I'm willing to forgive the oversight."

"All right, sunshine, tell me: What's that shining ray of hope?"

"Me, of course." She flashed me a dazzling grin. "Which you obvi-ously already knew."

The corners of my lips lifted into a reluctant smile. "How could I have forgotten that?"

"Don't let it happen again." She winked and hopped down off my desk, hooking her bag over her arm. "So, there's this new bar a few blocks away from your apartment. We can park at your place and walk there. Some fresh, less-polluted air will do you good."

《》

"SO," CHRISTINE SAID, LEANING HER forearms against the table after the server at Boulevard Bar dropped off our drinks—hers, a very girly cosmo; mine, a very dirty vodka martini. "Gotten any morbid photos of dead people lately?"

I scowled. "No. I think the last Colsboro murder was in 1999."

Her eyes slid skyward. "Well, it's a good thing you're here, then. Surely your mere presence will inspire a few unbalanced lunatics on the cusp of committing murder to just go for it."

"We can only hope." I lifted the glass to my lips and took a tentative sip. "Hard to be a crime reporter when there's no crime."

"There's plenty of crime," she said. "Last week, I saw the greeter at my grocery store run out into the parking lot to stop some kid who'd pilfered a pack of condoms."

"Ooh, exciting."

"Maybe not as exciting as serial killers, but at least a shoplifter is less likely to cause you bodily harm."

I ignored her. "Once he finds out I'm gone, my homicidal stalker will find some other reporter to freak out." I glared into my martini, pouting. "Lucky bitch."

"You sure you're talking about your stalker and not Gavin?"

"Yes."

She eyed me skeptically but didn't call me out. "You lived here before; you'll get used to the slower pace. Just focus on your mom, and you'll forget all about it."

"Way to make me feel like a total asshat."

She waved a hand, as if shooing away my comment. "You're allowed. You just broke up with a pretty awesome guy." Frowning, she reached for her drink. "Or a pretty awesome guy broke up with you. I'm not one hundred percent sure what exactly happened."

I gave her a stony glare. "He broke up with me, and thanks for the reminder."

"I'm sure it was reluctantly."

"Either way, same result."

"Drink faster," she ordered, and demonstrated by knocking back about a quarter of her cosmo. "Much faster." Her eyes flitted down to her phone for a nanosecond before she flashed me a smile. "As your bestie, it's my responsibility to get you drunk as part of the post-breakup healing process."

"You're about two weeks late," I muttered. She narrowed her eyes at me, so I picked up my martini and swallowed three large gulps. "There. That better?"

"You tell me."

I considered it, and gave her a half-assed smile. "Getting there."

Grinning smugly, she glanced at her phone to check the time. "I'm going to order us another round before happy hour ends." She slid out of the booth. "Keep going."

Typically I didn't like to do what other people told me to, but this seemed reasonable, and I was probably going to do it anyway. So I took another sip, and then another, and then another, until Christine returned with two more drinks and I was starting to feel warm and moderately happier.

I shrugged out of my jacket. "So now that we've covered my pathetic love life, tell me about your latest beau."

She laughed. "Bo is long gone," she said with a flick of her wrist. "I thought you knew that."

"That's not what I meant."

Christine leaned back against the booth. "Seeing what you're going through doesn't really inspire me to seek a replacement."

I popped an olive in my mouth and chewed thoughtfully. "You're twenty-three," I pointed out. "Isn't it time to be a grown up?"

"I'm pacing myself. I've got a grown-up job and a grown-up car and a grown-up apartment. I don't want to go overboard; that's how you relapse."

I snorted. "Right."

She rolled her eyes. "We're twenty-three, Jen. We don't need to worry about this for another six years, minimum."

"Think about it." I polished off my martini and plucked the tooth-pick with the remaining olive from the glass. "You've got to be with someone for two or three years before you consider getting married, and then if everything goes well and you actually do get engaged, it takes another eighteen to twenty-four months to plan the wedding. Then you need three or four years to adjust to married life before you start having kids, and everyone knows that once you hit thirty-five, the chances of giving birth to a genetic nightmare increase exponentially."

Christine blinked at me. "Of course. Everyone."

"If you want to have more than one kid," I went on, "you really should start no later than thirty, and that's only if you want to have no more than three kids who are no more than two years apart each, or two kids that are no more than three years apart. Which means..." I slid the olive into my mouth and attempted the mental calculations while I chewed. "I would have to be with the person I'm going to marry by the time I'm—" I gave her a significant look. "Twenty-three."

"Hey, you're already twenty-three. Halfway there."

"Because that's the hard part."

"That theory is ridiculous." She waved a dismissive hand. "Despite your need to control every aspect of your life, love doesn't happen on a pre-determined timeline."

I dropped the toothpick into the empty martini glass and slid it to the edge of the table. "How would you know? You have commitment phobia."

"Because nothing ever works like that," she said, so undeniably reasonable that my annoyance grew. "Besides, I don't know yet if I want to get married. It's not like I've had a plethora of shining examples of long-term relationships in my life to model mine after."

I let out a poof of air. "I suppose that's fair."

Grinning, she slid my second martini closer, until it was right in front of me. "Keep drinking. I like when you agree with me."

I let out a short laugh. "If there's one thing I can always count on," I said, holding up the glass in a toasting gesture, "it's your aversion to commitment."

Christine lifted her glass and clinked it against mine before taking a quick sip. "Now, to answer your original question, I do have a new beau. Todd is a personal trainer, the proud owner of a four-year-old chihuahua named Señorita Rosita, and has muscles on top of muscles." She wagged her eyebrows up and down. "That's my favorite part."

I let out a bark of laughter. "I can see why you enjoy relationship debauchery so much." I paused for a mouthful of martini. "Maybe I should give it a try. Does Todd have a personal trainer friend, or any kind of friend with muscles on top of muscles?"

Christine froze with her drink halfway to her lips. "No. Sadly, he has anthrophobia."

I raised an eyebrow. "He's afraid of people, but he's a personal trainer?"

Clearing her throat, she put the glass down and folded her hands on the table in front of her. "You know, Jen, I don't think you should make any rash decisions right now. Just be alone for awhile. Think things over, grieve for your loss—"

"Gosh, that sounds like fun," I said dryly.

"And then when you've had some time," she continued, "perhaps you can think about possibly trying relationship debauchery. Maybe."

I stared at her, deadpan. "I'm getting the impression you don't think I should."

"I've known you a long time." She tapped a forefinger against the base of her glass. "You probably wouldn't be good at it, but if you want to give it a try, I can't stop you."

"Thanks for the wishy-washy support, bestie."

"Anytime." She peeked over at her phone again, then back to me. "Now, what else do you want to do tonight as part of the stage one healing process? Keep in mind that, per the rules, it must involve alcohol."

"This was your idea," I reminded her. "You must have something in mind."

She thought it over. "Black light bowling?"

"Shoes that have been worn by the entire population of central Ohio and balls that have a thousand million bacteria on them?" I snorted. "Where do I sign up?"

"Dancing?"

"Not in the mood."

"Well, maybe if you drank more," she said pointedly.

I took a few more sips of my martini and mimed deep contemplation. "Still no."

"Karaoke?"

"Veto."

Christine sighed. "I've got nothing."

"That's okay." I slid an olive off the toothpick, dropped it into my mouth, and sent her a fake smile while I chewed. "I'm more of a drink-wine-on-the-couch-in-my-sweats-and-mope kind of person."

"Not tonight you aren't." Her eyes darted to her phone and back again. "I'm not going to let you—"

"You got somewhere to be?" I cut her off. She tilted her head and frowned. "You keep looking at your phone."

"People in our age range check their phones an average of seventy-five times a day." Her eyes were wide to convey innocence. "I can't help it. It's ingrained in my DNA."

"I think I cap out at a mere fifty."

"Well, that's because you're the victim of a recent dumping, so looking at your phone would just disappoint you."

I let out a dry laugh. "This is supposed to make me not want to go home and mope?"

Christine opened her mouth to respond, but before she could, her phone chirped out a text notification. She snatched it up and ran her finger across the screen. "You're right. I'm not doing a very good job cheering you up."

I sighed, my shoulders sinking. "I'm sorry. I'm being a total bitch, and you're really trying to—"

"Oh!" she exclaimed. "Turns out Todd is free tonight, so—"

"Don't you dare finish that sentence," I warned, pointing an accusatory finger at her.

Dropping her phone into her purse, she gave me a sheepish smile. "Want to meet him? You can tag along, or he can meet us here." I gave her my best drop-dead glare, and she blinked at me. "Or maybe next time."

"There won't be a next time," I said irritably, "because I hate you, and we're not friends anymore."

She laughed and waved for the server. "In that case, the drinks are on me. Think of it as a parting gift."

"If I'd known that, I would've given tonight's activities more thought."

"Like dinner and wine at Bartholomew's?" she asked, pulling her credit card out of her wallet as the server approached.

"Why didn't you suggest that earlier?"

"Hindsight's twenty-twenty." She passed her card over to the server. "I'd say next time, but since we're not friends anymore—"

"And I hate you."

She grinned. "Exactly."

We finished what was left of our martinis, cashed out, and made the trek back to my townhouse, where her Acura was parked on the curb a few yards away from my front door. Somewhere around block four or five, while she was chattering on about a disagreement she'd had with one of the writers over his lame headline, I decided to forgive her.

Until we came to a stop in front of her car and she sent me a panicked look, hand deep inside her person.

"Shoot," she said, digging around. "I can't find my keys." She crouched down on the sidewalk and dumped out the contents of her bag. Trying to hide my annoyance, I leaned back against her car and watched as she sorted through. "Dammit."

I sighed. "And I had just decided to forgive you for insisting we go out for drinks and then immediately blowing me off."

She glanced up at me with narrowed eyes. "Not helping."

Biting my tongue, I knelt down and sorted through the pile. "Sorry," I said a few beats later. "I tried."

"For, like, seven seconds."

"It was my best effort." Rising to my feet, I crossed my arms over my chest and watched her shove everything haphazardly into her purse. "Did you check your pockets?"

Shooting to her feet, she slid her hands into her jeans and then her jacket, cringing. "Shit," she said, drawing them back out. "Shit, shit, shit."

"Before you freak out and run back to the bar, let's check inside." I rubbed my temple tiredly. My tenuous buzz was wearing off and irritability returning full force. "Maybe you left them on the kitchen counter or accidentally dropped them in my personal black hole."

She followed me up the porch steps. "Right, because dropping my keys into a black hole would make them easier to find."

I slid my key into the deadbolt and turned. "A black hole is a good thing to have on hand, you know."

"In case you need to hide incriminating evidence?"

"Sure." I extracted the key and shoved it into the lock in the handle. "Or when you need to get rid of the corpse of a former friend who bailed on you for a guy."

"Hey, you should have expected something like this," she said as I turned the knob and pushed the door open. "It is Friday the thirteenth, after all."

"Good poi..." My voice trailed off as I stepped inside and looked around at my living room. It glowed in the light of dozens of candles—on the coffee table, the entertainment center, the kitchen counter and dining room table—and soft blues music played on the stereo. And standing in the middle of it, cast in a warm yellow glow and holding a single red rose, was Gavin.

He took a few steps closer, sliding his free hand into his pocket and producing Christine's keys. Holding them out to her, he winked. "Thanks for the assist."

Beaming proudly, she grabbed her keys from his outstretched hand. "Call me tomorrow," she stage whispered to me on her way out.

Once she was gone, Gavin closed the distance between us, his eyes locked on me. My breath caught in my throat as he gently took my purse out of my limp hand and unzipped my jacket, tugging on the sleeves to take it off. "I'm sorry," he said, dropping both to the floor and handing me the rose.

Dumbfounded, I glanced down at the rose briefly and back up to him. I opened my mouth to speak but nothing came out, and the corners of his lips tilted upward, clearly amused by my flabbergasted state. Finally, I was able to summon a few words.

"What are you doing here?"

He shook his head slowly. "The real question is, why wasn't I here with you two weeks ago?"

I blinked at him. "Why weren't you here with me two weeks ago?"

"Because I'm a stupid, stupid man." His dark eyes sparkled in the candlelight. "And I'm going to make up for that."

My mouth twitched. "By burning down my apartment?"

"I located the fire extinguisher first," he assured me. "At most, I'll burn down your living room."

"If you do that, I probably won't get my security deposit back."

He mock cringed and glanced behind him. "You're right. Maybe I should put these out now. We're going to need that security deposit in a few months." As he turned back to me, I held my breath and waited, afraid to move. "Actually, I should amend that. What I should say is that I hope we're going to need it in a few months."

Butterfly wings brushed against the inside of my chest. "Why?"

"Because the last two weeks have been miserable for both of us, and it's completely my fault," he said, all humor gone from his face. "I handled the situation horribly and made a knee-jerk decision—the wrong decision." He lifted a hand and ran his fingertips lightly along my jaw. "I'm sorry."

I swallowed. "So—you want to try long distance?"

Gavin shook his head. "That's a hard no." He dropped his hand, and my heart sank with it. "And I can't ask you to come back; I know you need to be here right now. So this is where I need to be, too. With you."

I raised a brow at him. "Are you simultaneously un-breaking up with me and inviting yourself to move in?"

He grinned. "I'm giving up Chicago and moving across two states. The least you could do is take me back and give me a place to live."

"Assuming you don't burn it down."

Shaking his head in what looked like amusement, he let out a short laugh. "Shut up, Jennifer, and just let me propose already."

My stomach took a nosedive, making my heart pound harder. "Okay."

Smile fading, Gavin drew in a deep breath and let it out slowly. "When you left, I got a reminder of what my life is like without you, and I don't like it. It's bleak and cold and lonely. You're the light and warmth in my life, Jen; you're my sun." He gently slid the rose out of my hand, dropping it to the carpet as he sank down on one knee. My skin vibrated as he took both of my hands in his, sending a thrill up my arms and into my chest. "I want to do the same for you, if you'll let me." He gazed up at me with wide, vulnerable eyes. "Will you marry me?"

I sank down next to him, my mouth tipping up to form a smile, and folded my shaky legs underneath me. "Yes, Gavin. I will marry you."

His breath came out in a rush, as if he'd been holding it, and he ran his hands up my arms until they framed my face. "Good," he said, his voice husky, and leaned in to press his lips against mine. Too quickly he pulled back, releasing me to dig into his pocket. "That means you can have this."

He held out a small, ornate ring box and flipped the lid open to reveal a sparkling white diamond encircled by small sapphires and set in a silver band lined in tiny diamonds. My breath caught in my throat as he removed it from the blue velvet, dropped the box to the floor, and reached for my left hand.

"This was my grandmother's." Gavin slid it onto my ring finger. "My grandfather had it custom made." He raised his eyes to mine. "One of a kind—like you."

I stared down at it, suddenly overwhelmed. "It's beautiful."

He smiled. "Also like you."

Wrapping my arms around his neck, I pulled him close and kissed him softly. "I love you, Gavin."

"I love you too, Jennifer," he said solemnly, his warm breath skimming across my lips. "Dead or alive."

CHAPTER 6
PRESENT
COLSBORO, OHIO

AFTER MY STORY HIT THE RECORD'S home page, Laura Garrett's murder took over the news cycle, even earning a brief segment on the national news on Tuesday morning. Two homicides in one week was big news in a city the size of Colsboro.

I called my mother on my way to work to see how she was handling it now that the shell shock had worn off.

"We closed the practice today," she told me, avoiding my question. "We were going to be closed the rest of the week for Thanksgiving, so I suppose I should thank him for the convenient timing."

I winced. My mother's sarcasm only made an appearance during times of high stress or exhaustion. My guess was this time it was both.

"Is there anything I can do?" I slowed to a stop at a red light. "Do you want some help tomorrow with Thanksgiving preparations?"

"Actually, I want to help you."

"Oh, thanks," I said, brightly, then added: "With what?"

"Identifying this killer," she said. "How many victims are there now?"

"Five."

She let out a heavy sigh. "Pete and Holly Lockwood invited us over for dinner last night. He agrees with your serial killer theory."

"I knew it," I said. "CPD had a press conference last week, and he dodged all my questions—even when I talked to him in private afterward."

"He doesn't want to cause panic, and the fact that eighty percent of the cases are outside CPD jurisdiction complicates things further."

The light flicked to green, and I tapped my thumb on the steering wheel as I waited for traffic to respond. "Did you tell him you wanted to help?"

"Of course not. He would've slapped an ankle monitor on me and put me under house arrest."

"True." Throwing a glance over my shoulder, I changed lanes and passed the slowpokes in front of me. "Not that I don't appreciate your offer, but this guy is dangerous."

"I'm aware of that, Jennifer." Her usually soothing voice had a sharp edge. "I'm not suggesting we play *Murder, She Wrote.*"

"What do you want to do, then?"

"I want to construct a psychological profile," she said. "It's time to give this son of a bitch a face."

《》

O'MALLEY'S WAS ON THE CUSP of the happy hour rush when my mother and I seated ourselves in a booth at the back of the restaurant that evening. Before the server had a chance to introduce himself, I put in an order for a bottle of cabernet without consulting my mother, to which she had no objections.

"This is worse than I thought," she said, once our nameless server disappeared.

I braced myself. "How do you mean?"

"This has nothing to do with Laura—or any of the other victims, for that matter." She pulled out a thick accordion file, which I presumed contained the pages I'd scanned and emailed her this morning, and placed it on the table in front of her. "It has to do with our family. More specifically, you."

Uncomfortable, I looked away and dug out my notebook. "Why do you think that?"

"The fingerprints, the personalized emails, the photos, the fact that he's sending you tokens…" Her voice trailed off until I lifted my eyes back to hers. "But you know that." Reluctantly, I nodded. "The million-dollar question is, why?"

"I can think of several reasons, and none of them are good."

"So can I." She clasped her hands together on top of the folder. "You first."

I drew in a deep breath and blew it out quickly. "He's using me for fame, and he's planting fingerprints of people close to me to make sure I'll pay attention."

She nodded. "That's probably the best-case scenario."

We paused as the server returned with our bottle of wine and took his sweet-ass time opening and pouring it. Once he was finally gone, we each took a long sip before continuing.

"If fame were his goal," my mother continued, "he'd be sending photos to other journalists, far and wide. As many as he feasibly could." She put down her wine glass and stared at it. "However, I don't believe that's the case."

I nodded. "Someone else would have reported on it by now."

She lifted her head. "Not only that, but he couldn't personalize the fingerprints and the clues—like Gavin's ring—for each reporter."

"Well, I guess the best-case scenario is out." I swirled my wine absently. "So you don't think fame is his goal."

"Most serial killers enjoy the attention, but no, I don't think notoriety is his primary goal."

"All right. Your turn for a theory."

"He could be obsessed with you for some reason," she suggested. "Your accomplishments, your looks, your job, your proximity to the police…" Her voice trailed off, and she fell silent. When she spoke again, her voice was cool and detached. "He may have started watching you from afar and constructed a fantasy centered on you. He thinks he knows you. The murders are his way of simultaneously expressing his frustration and getting your attention."

"He wants me to know who he is." I lowered my eyes and traced the outline of the base of my glass. "I think I do know him—at least well enough to be able to piece together his identity."

She appraised me for a few beats. "You've figured out that he's leaving you clues," she said, and I nodded. "There's no other logical reason he would stage such an elaborate scene, only to mess it up for the police. He wants someone to see it."

"He wants me to see it."

"Yes." She drew in a shaky breath and gave me a tight smile. "We need to figure out who this guy is."

I flipped to a fresh page in my notebook. "Let's do it."

"He's organized, patient, and intelligent," she began. "I'd peg him at somewhere between thirty and forty years of age—fifty at most."

"White?" I glanced up from my scribbling. "All the victims are white."

"The majority of serials stay within their own race, so he's most likely Caucasian." Her eyes glazed over as she drummed her fingers on the table. "He's too deliberate to be schizophrenic, but I wouldn't be surprised if he was on the higher end of the psychopathy scale."

"So he's charismatic. Uses his charm to seem nonthreatening and coax his way into the vics' homes."

"Yes, but—" She paused and shifted in her seat. "Once he has his chosen victim where he wants her, I don't think he would continue to be charming."

"Why not?"

She lifted her gaze to mine. "He wants his victims to fight back," she said. "It's more thrilling. It makes him feel powerful."

I swallowed, trying to dislodge the lump that had formed in my throat. "What would he do if they didn't fight back?"

"That's difficult to predict," she said carefully. "He would certainly be angry."

"Seems to me he's angry either way."

"True." She sighed deeply. "The fact of the matter is, he would have killed them no matter how they reacted. It just wouldn't have been as satisfying."

"So he would have been frustrated."

"Most likely, he already is—but for now he has to be careful not to go overboard."

I laughed humorlessly. "Rape and murder isn't overboard?"

"To you and me it is. To him, it's a game. A challenge."

"How far he can go without getting caught."

"Exactly."

"What does he think I'm going to do when I figure out his identity?" I demanded. "Keep it a secret?"

She shook her head, eyes wide as golf balls. "I can't say."

I looked away and took a long sip of wine. "And what about the rapes?"

"Sexual assault is common with serials." Her voice was neutral again, as if she were giving a college lecture. "It's more about dominance than sex."

"He likes to be in control."

My mother nodded. "A position of power would be an ideal career choice for him, especially if it allowed him opportunities to practice manipulating people into doing what he wants without garnering suspicion."

"Like a politician?"

"I think that would attract too much attention," she said, frowning. "He needs to stay under the radar."

"It might also be good cover," I pointed out. "No one expects the city council president to be a serial killer."

"Maybe." She picked up the wine bottle and poured us each some more cabernet, even though neither of our glasses was empty. "But the added public scrutiny would be difficult to control. He'd be safer as someone average with a behind-the-scenes job."

I scribbled a few notes on my legal pad. "What about the ways he's killed these women?" I asked. "We've got five different victims and five different methods. Do you think that's significant?"

My mother opened her folder and extracted a stack of papers from one of the sections. "Absolutely. Look at Laura." She slid her eyes up to mine and gave me a significant look. "A psychiatrist given a lobotomy? That definitely means something."

"Maybe he just has a morbid sense of humor."

"The M.O.s might all be different, but they have a common thread." She ran a finger down her notes. "One victim was stabbed in the chest. Another had her femoral arteries slashed. Impaled with a broken bottle. Slit wrists. Lobotomy." She lifted her eyes to mine. "What do they all have in common?"

"They're all exceptionally bloody?"

"And they involve knowledge of anatomy—likely more advanced, given the lobotomy."

I frowned, debating my next question. "Could he be a doctor?"

My mother studied me for a moment. "Do you think Gavin did this?"

"Of course not." I scowled and reached for my wine.

"Of all the people whose fingerprints were found at these murder scenes, he's the odd one out. He's not part of your family."

"I'd be hard pressed to call Kenny my family," I said dryly. "Besides, why would he leave his own prints at the scene of a murder he committed?"

She leaned forward and calmly folded her hands together on the table. "The same reason we discussed earlier—to get your attention."

"How'd he get the other fingerprints?"

Her gaze drifted skyward as she deliberated. "He works with Joey. He could've bought medical supplies from Kenny. But Jason—" She shook her head. "I can't figure out how he would've gotten to Jason without being noticed."

"You've put a lot of thought into this." I swallowed hard, my throat suddenly dry. "Mom, you don't really think he did this, do you?"

"He fits the profile."

I gaped at her. "Except he's not a psychopath!"

She gave me a smile that didn't reach her eyes. "That's precisely what a psychopath wants you to think." She paused, as if gauging how I might react to her next statement. "And they have no problems with betraying people, even those who love them."

"And now he's back." I said, my voice accusing. "Why? If he was done with me, why reappear three years later?"

"It could be anything." She shrugged helplessly. "He could have a specific goal, or he could just be bored."

I sat back in the booth and crossed my arms over my chest, glaring at nothing in particular.

"I'm sorry, honey," She tilted her head slightly, her jade eyes sympathetic. "I hope I'm wrong, but you should be aware of the possibility. I don't want you to be blindsided."

"Again?" I muttered.

"You gave him his ring back, and he gave you the crime scene photos. For all intents and purposes, his obligation to you and yours to him has been met."

I blew out a long sigh. "What you're saying is, if he shows up again, that means his plan isn't working, and he's trying a new tactic."

"He has no reason to contact you again, but if he does…" Her voice trailing off, my mother gave me a tight smile. "Just be careful around him, okay?"

AFTER I GOT BACK FROM my three-mile run early Wednesday morning, I had a vague but foreboding voicemail from Mike, asking me to stop by the precinct on my way to work. Asking for more information would be a fruitless venture, so I didn't respond until I was on my way out the door at seven-thirty.

"Gibbs." The desk sergeant nodded to me when I signed in. "They're waiting for you in the eighth floor conference room."

I thanked him, not bothering to ask who he meant. I already knew Mike would be there, and the eighth floor meant the chief would be, too.

When I burst into the conference room adjacent to the chief's office, I was surprised to find Joey and Baratti as well. All wore grim but unreadable expressions.

"Well, this can't be good," I muttered.

At the head of the table, Lockwood stood. "Shut the door, and have a seat."

I obeyed without hesitation, dropping down into the chair next to Joey as I wriggled out of my jacket.

The chief wasted no time getting to the point. "We lifted about half a dozen prints from Laura Garrett's apartment." He slid his hands into his pockets and gave me a significant look. "We were able to identify two sets."

I frowned. "Mom and I didn't touch anything." I slid my gaze to Mike, finding his face taut. "I told you, we were barely even in the apartment."

Chief shook his head. "Not yours. Garrett's and..." His voice trailed off for a few seconds, as if he were purposely drawing out the tension. "Your mother's."

My brows drew together as I replayed the scene in my mind. "She might have touched the doorknob when we unlocked the door. Plus, Laura worked for her. It's feasible that Mom had been there before, or she touched something at the office that Laura brought home."

"True," Mike said carefully. "But her prints were on the ice pick."

My heart skipped a beat as I swung my eyes back and forth between Mike and Lockwood, waiting for the punchline. None came.

"Per the detective's suggestion," Baratti said, folding his hands in front of him, "I compared the murder weapon to the photos you received from Chelsea Quinn's murder." The vein in his forehead twitched as he scrutinized me, gauging my state of mind. "I'm ninety percent certain it's the same tool."

Joey sat up straighter in his chair and leaned his elbows on the table. "So what you're saying is that Chelsea Quinn and Laura Garrett were both killed with an icepick that has our mother's fingerprints on it."

Baratti gave a curt nod. "Given her educational background, she could feasibly perform a lobotomy."

"A botched lobotomy?" Joey interrupted.

Lockwood rested his palms on the back of his chair. "If the goal was to kill Garrett, it wasn't botched."

Joey let out a heavy sigh. "Go on."

Baratti exchanged a wary glance with Lockwood before proceeding. "As far as Chelsea Quinn, the killer would almost certainly have used a mallet or hammer to ensure the precise pattern of wounds on her chest, rather than stabbing her freely, which means—"

"A woman could have done it," Joey finished.

"Yes."

A short hysterical laugh bubbled past my lips. "So now you think my mother's a murderer." I swiveled to glare at Lockwood. "That's ridiculous."

The chief's bushy eyebrows rose. "We didn't say that."

Joey's eyes shrank into slits. "No, but it kind of sounds like that's what you're inferring."

I let out a fake cough and covered my mouth. "Implying," I said from behind my hand. Joey redirected the evil eye toward me but otherwise let it go.

Mike lifted a hand in a stop gesture. "We don't think she killed either Quinn or Garrett. We're more concerned about why the killer drew her into his game by choosing someone close to her."

"If you don't think she's the perp," Joey interjected, "how do you explain her prints on the murder weapon?"

"With a little know-how, it's relatively easy to transfer fingerprints from one surface to another," Baratti said. "You can do it with cocoa powder, a paintbrush, and packing tape. The hardest part would be getting the fingerprint itself, especially without attracting suspicion."

"Which means," Lockwood cut in, pivoting his steely stare to me, "this guy knows you and your mother personally. And not just you two." He glanced at Joey and Baratti. "Both of you as well."

Mike frowned. "I understand Joe, Jason, Kenny, and Kathryn, but what's Baratti got to do with this?"

Damn. It. All. To. Hell.

Lockwood's forehead wrinkled as he shot me a puzzled look. "It's possible the perp's trying to discredit him, just as he tried to discredit Joe." He slid his eyes to me and smiled tightly. "I'm sure we'll find out soon enough."

Joey quickly redirected the conversation. "Is Mom in any danger?"

Mike shook his head. "Unlikely. If he can get close enough to get her fingerprints, he can get close enough to kill her."

I stared at him, deadpan. "Gosh, that's comforting."

"But he hasn't. If he wanted to, he could—but he hasn't."

Joey rubbed the back of his neck. "Better, but I'm still not going to rest easy tonight."

"I'm sorry, but obviously we can't make guarantees."

I angled myself toward Lockwood. "Did you tell Mom when you had her and Brian over for dinner?"

He shook his head. "We didn't find out until this morning, but I will."

"When?"

"Given the fact that we're going to have to interview her, pretty damn soon."

I snorted. "Not to mention a serial killer is stalking her, and she has no idea."

"I don't think he's stalking her." Lockwood placed a slight emphasis on 'her,' and I clamped my mouth shut and looked away. "That's all we've got, so unless you have any further questions, you're dismissed." He strode to the door, calling over his shoulder, "Demarco, a word?"

Rising to his feet, Mike gave me a significant look. "Don't go anywhere," he said, pointing a stern finger at me before turning to Baratti. "You too. I want to talk to you both."

Joey sent me another nervous glance as he stood. "See you tomorrow, sis." He followed Mike and the chief out of the room and closed the door behind him. Agitated, I pushed back my chair and jumped to my feet.

"So," Baratti said as I turned my back to him. "Any particular reason you didn't answer Demarco's question?"

"Any particular reason you're here?" I shot back, staring out the window at the dismal gray morning.

"We got the results from AFIS early this morning, and I brought the report straight here." Something rustled behind me, and I sensed him moving closer. "I figured you'd want to know."

I whirled around, finding him only a few feet away. "I would have found out from Joey or the chief. You didn't have to deliver the news yourself."

"Same goes for you the other night." He shrugged. "And maybe I just wanted to see you again."

I crossed my arms over my chest. "Maybe you shouldn't have."

"Most definitely," he agreed, his expression giving nothing away. "But I figured it might be my last chance, so—"

"Why aren't you in Chicago?" I cut him off.

"My flight doesn't leave until ten." He raised a brow suggestively. "Want to come?"

I pushed past him, putting some space between us. "I hope you fly through turbulence."

"It's a fifty-minute flight."

I let out an annoyed groan and began pacing. "Why are you still here?"

Baratti frowned. "Because Demarco said he wants to talk to us."

I shook my head. "I don't mean right here and now. I mean Colsboro. Why are you still in Colsboro?"

"I signed a five-year lease."

"You did not."

"Okay. I like it here."

"You do *not*," I said, drawing out the syllable to indicate my annoyance.

He sighed. "I didn't have a compelling enough reason to move back. I have a good job here, and I pay a lot less in property taxes."

"Those are stupid reasons."

Baratti laughed humorlessly. "Well, I don't know what else to tell you."

Before I could summon an appropriate retort, the door opened behind me. I hurled one more dirty look at him and swiveled around to face Mike.

"So, here's the deal," he said, hands on his hips as he assessed us: Me with my arms stubbornly crossed and a death glare tacked on my face, Baratti with his hands casually stuck in his pockets and a placid expression on his. Mike directed his attention to me. "I know I said it was okay the other day, but I've changed my mind. I don't think it's a good idea for you two to work together anymore."

"No problem. As I told you the other day, we're not working together."

Baratti cleared his throat. "May I ask why, Detective?" I rolled my eyes in his general direction, and he shrugged again.

"Because it's too dangerous, and you're civilians." Mike's eyes swung toward me. "And that goes double for you."

I scowled. "That's so sexist."

He shook his head, annoyed. "Someone is going to extreme lengths to get your attention—and that someone is a serial killer who happens to be in your social circle."

"We aren't certain of that," I argued. "He might just be an avid fan with a vivid imagination."

Mike snorted and crossed his arms over his chest, matching my standoffish stance. "Has anyone new popped up recently? Anyone you haven't seen in awhile?"

I could feel Baratti watching me again, but I ignored him. "Nope."

"And you'll let us know if that changes."

"Of course. Now, if that's all, I need to be going." I gave him a sarcastic smile. "Lots of things not to do and people not to see."

"Not so fast." He stepped in between me and my jacket. "I need a guarantee."

"But Detective," I said innocently, "I obviously can't make any guarantees."

He let out a harsh breath. "I wish for one day, you were not a human tape recorder."

"Sorry. It's built in."

"Fine." Mike shrugged, unconcerned. "I only need agreement from one of you." He turned away, and I followed his gaze to Baratti. "How about you, Baratti? Can I count on you?"

Baratti shifted his eyes to me. "Of course," he said. "You can trust me—dead or alive."

I froze, and a few beats of silence passed before I realized I was capable of moving. Jaw clenched, I grabbed my coat and purse and strode to the door, yanking it open and storming away without another word.

«»

MIKE LET HIMSELF INTO MY condo at nine-thirty that night, after not speaking to each other since I'd stomped out of the precinct fourteen hours earlier. Murphy barged in, sending the door into the wall, and pranced over to the couch. He hopped up between me and Kellyn, sniffed my mug of hot tea and Kellyn's fuzzy socks, and finally settled down to watch the Charlie Brown Thanksgiving special with us.

"So, funny story," Mike said as he locked the door and hung up his coat. "I figured out how Baratti fits into this puzzle." He took a few steps into the room and parked his fists on his hips. "You used to be engaged to him."

Kellyn choked on her hot cocoa and shot to her feet. "Dammit. I hate to be rude, but I just realized it's way past my bedtime." She patted Murphy's head. "C'mon, boy."

She scurried out of the room and disappeared down the hall, Murphy alert as he watched her go. Yawning, he slid off the couch and lumbered out of the room in her wake. Neither Mike nor I moved or spoke until Kellyn slammed the guest room door shut, likely for our benefit.

"It's nice to be in the loop now," Mike continued. "Serial killer apparently knew the connection, but I didn't."

I mentally steeled myself. "Who told you?"

He strode over to the coffee table and snagged the remote. "Hmm, let me see if I can remember." He flicked the TV off and tossed the remote down with a clatter. "Oh, yeah. It was Baratti."

"Huh." I sipped my tea while I contemplated how to respond. "That's unexpected."

Arms akimbo, he stared at me with a flat expression. "Among other things."

I closed my eyes and pinched the bridge of my nose. "Okay, I know I should have told you, but I didn't think I'd see him after Monday." I opened my eyes to find Mike staring at me incredulously. "And I didn't want to upset you."

"That the only reason?"

"I might also be a little bit scared of you."

"Try again."

Blowing out a sigh, I put my cup down on the coffee table and stood. "All right. I didn't want to upset me, either." I took a few tentative steps closer to him, until we were only inches apart. "And I thought that saying it out loud would make it important, and it's not. He's not."

"How would you feel if you heard from one of my exes that we'd been working together, and I'd purposely neglected to tell you?"

I held up a finger. "First of all, we were not and are not working together." I held up a second finger. "Second of all, who is she? I swear I'll cut a bitch."

The joke had the intended effect; he cracked an infinitesimal smile. "Still," he said, threading his fingers through mine and gently pulling me closer, "I wish you would have told me."

"I don't have an excuse, and I'm sorry."

"You should have told me from the beginning."

"Define 'beginning.'"

"I knew you'd been engaged. I just didn't know it was to a Colsboro M.E."

"I figured the chances were pretty good that you had or would at some point work together. I didn't want to make it weird."

"For me," he asked, "or you?"

I nodded definitively. "Yes."

His deep blue eyes probed mine. "Do I have anything to worry about?"

"Well, serial killers—"

"Jen."

"No. Of course not. I love you."

"Okay," he said after a long pause. "As long as he knows that we're..." His voice trailed off as he read my pinched expression. "He doesn't know about us, does he?"

"Did you tell him?"

"No."

I cleared my throat. "Then no. There's a high probability he doesn't."

Dropping my hands, he took a few steps back and ran a palm over his short hair. "Because saying it loud would make it important, and it's not?"

"Well, look who's the human tape recorder now."

Mike let a few beats of silence pass. "Do you still have feelings for him?"

I swiped a hand down my face, shoulders drooping. "No. I wasn't planning on seeing him again. It was just simpler keep it professional."

"Based on the evidence, how do I know that—"

"That what?" I interrupted. "That I don't intend to see him again? That I don't still have feelings for him? That I didn't keep it from you because I secretly want to get back together with him?"

Mike crossed his arms over his chest. "Yeah. All of that."

"Um, because I said so, and you trust me?"

"If 'because I said so' were the basis of truth, my job would be a helluva lot easier."

"Because I broke up with him," I snapped, throwing my arms wide. "Because he did something selfish and unforgivable. Because he reminds me of my father and Kenny and all the other jerks who betray the people who love them. And, most importantly, because I love you."

"Your father got Baratti out of questioning last week." A thick silence passed as he scrutinized me with sharp eyes. "Did you call your father for Baratti?" I clamped my mouth firmly shut and matched his defensive stance, saying nothing. "You did, didn't you?"

I swallowed. "Yes."

Shaking his head, Mike turned away and began pacing. "You called Pierce to save Baratti." He said the words as if he were trying on a pair of shoes to see if they fit. "You asked the father you hate to help the ex-fiancé you hate." He spun around, planting his hands on his hips. "Why?"

"He was being set up," I insisted. "Just like my brothers, just like Kenny, just like my mom. They're all being set up."

"How do you know?" Mike demanded. "Prior to this, you hadn't seen or spoken to him in..." He raised his eyebrows and waited.

"Three years."

"And all of a sudden, he shows up. Don't you find that a little suspicious?"

I pushed away the conversation I'd had with my mother the night before, and the warning that had been banging around in my head ever since.

"I hate to admit this when I know I'm on thin ice, but I'm the one who initiated contact."

"Which you were prompted to do based on his fingerprints showing up at a murder scene," Mike said. "Right?"

Uncomfortable, I shifted to my other foot. "Partially."

His eyes narrowed. "Explain."

"Stephanie Goodwin was wearing an engagement ring in the photo the killer sent me." I drew in a deep breath and exhaled slowly. "It was mine."

His Adam's apple bobbed as he swallowed. "How can you be sure?"

"It's one of a kind."

"Maybe he got a copy made," he suggested, and I gave a minuscule head shake. "He sent it to you, didn't he? And you gave it back to Baratti." I didn't respond, and he scraped a hand across the back of his neck. "You should have turned that in."

"Honestly, Mike, what could you have done with it?" I asked. "You know the killer wiped it clean. There was no trace evidence."

"Probably not," he admitted. "You still should have told me."

I let out a puff of air. "Well, that would have meant I'd have to tell you about Baratti—and you know I'd rather avoid uncomfortable conversations."

Dropping his gaze, he stared at the carpet for a few long seconds. "From here on out, no more secrets." He lifted his chin. "About Baratti, about serial killers, about everything."

"You really want to know everything?"

"Every last detail."

I nodded soberly. "You should know, then, that I've been ignoring the brake light in my car for about two weeks, and I accidentally broke your favorite mug."

The corners of his mouth twitched. "I'll take care of your brakes this weekend," he said, "and I already knew about the mug."

"See, I can't keep secrets from you." My eyes widened to convey my innocence. "Not for long, anyway."

He gave me a lopsided smile. "Side effect of dating a detective."

I stepped closer and circled my arms around his neck. "I suppose that's a better side effect than dating a calamity magnet."

"Actually, it sounds like a fantastic combination to me."

I let out an unexpected laugh. "Doesn't it?" I looked up at him, my smile flattening. "I'm sorry I didn't tell you up front. Are we okay?"

"Do you have any more ex-fiancés lurking around the city?"

"Most definitely not."

He lowered his head and gave me a soft kiss. "Yeah. We're okay."

CHAPTER 7

WHILE MIKE VISITED HIS PARENTS on Thanksgiving morning, Kellyn and I drove up to my parents' house early to help with whatever my mother ordered us to do. But when we arrived, the turkey was in the oven, the potatoes were peeled and sliced, the table was elaborately decorated and set, and the only thing left to do was drink wine.

"Not that I'm complaining," I said to my mother as she handed us each a glass of cabernet from an already half-empty bottle, "but how did you finish all this by—" I glanced at my watch. "Eleven o'clock?"

My step-dad, Brian, gave me a significant look. "She's been up and at 'em for six hours." He paused to fold me into a bear hug. "Plus, she's had half a pot of coffee."

"And half a bottle of wine," Kellyn added before she disappeared into her own bear hug.

"It's a holiday, and it's been a rough week." My mother dumped the rest of the wine into her glass. "I've been trying to keep busy so I don't start brooding."

Brian released Kellyn and strode around the island to drape an arm across my mother's shoulders. "Where's Mike?"

My mother winced. "He found out about Gavin, didn't he?"

Brian's forehead creased. "Gavin's back?"

"No!" I exclaimed. "I just happened to run into him on Monday." I shifted to my other foot. "And a couple of other times."

"How?"

I cleared my throat and glanced down at my shoes. "I might have called Pierce to bail him out of an interrogation."

"With Mike and his partner?"

"Maybe."

"Judging by Kellyn's expression, I'm guessing he's not too happy about that." He raised his eyebrows quizzically. "Is he still coming to dinner?"

I sent Kellyn a narrowed-eye stare before answering. "He stopped by his parents' for a bit. He'll be here in a couple of hours."

"So he says." Kellyn appraised me over the rim of her wine glass. "He didn't seem mad this morning, but something tells me he's not thrilled about the situation."

"Go ahead. Get all the gossip out now." I made circle motions with my hand. "Because if you bring it up after Mike arrives, you're going to be homeless."

She stood up straighter and gave me a snide salute. "Sir, yes, sir."

Brian let out a low whistle. "You keep that up, kid, and you might end up homeless anyway."

«»

BY THREE O'CLOCK, MY BROTHERS, Mike, and Murphy had arrived, and the house was in a state of controlled chaos as all the Thanksgiving preparations and football excitement reached a simultaneous crescendo.

"Imagine if we had a couple of grandkids running around," Brian shouted to my mother over the cacophony of the carving knife and hand mixer. Murphy danced around his feet, hoping for a morsel of meat to fall magically into his mouth.

"Keep imagining." Kellyn transferred the stuffing to the dining room table. "Unless someone forgets to take their birth control, you're going to be waiting awhile."

Jason wandered into the kitchen and snagged a piece of turkey off the serving plate. "You can thank my darling ex-wife for that." He popped the sample into his mouth. "Among other things."

The potatoes having achieved the perfect consistency, my mother turned off the hand mixer and glanced at me. "You're my only hope."

"That is not true." I flicked off the stove burner and retrieved the gravy boat from the cupboard. "Jason and Kellyn might be lost causes, but you still have Joey."

"You're right." She spooned the mashed potatoes into a serving bowl. "Now that I think about it, Joey might be my only hope."

"Hang on." I poured the gravy into the boat. "I'm the only one of us who's not single, newly divorced, or about to be divorced."

"You can't have kids. You'd lose them or smash them or blow them up."

"Mother!" I said, indignant. "I never lose things."

Grinning, she handed the potatoes to Jason and waved him away. "Of course not."

"Thanks for your conditional faith in me, Mom." I grabbed the basket of rolls and took it and the gravy to the table. "Means a lot."

"Hello!" a voice called from the front hall seconds before Kenny appeared in the kitchen with a bottle of wine. "Sorry I'm late."

The house fell silent as everyone stopped what they were doing and turned to stare at him in disbelief.

"Kenton," Brian said finally, his voice neutral. "We weren't expecting you."

"Probably because we didn't invite him." Kellyn crossed her arms over her chest as she glared at her estranged husband. "What are you doing here?"

Kenny handed the bottle of wine to my mother, who accepted it with an robotic thank you. "Sorry if I'm intruding. I just didn't want to be alone today. I hope you don't mind."

"Nope." Kellyn smiled coldly. "We don't mind at all if you're alone today."

My mother handed Kellyn the bottle of wine, along with an unspoken warning with her eyes. "Open that, please." She looked back at Kenny. "So long as you don't cause any arguments, you can stay for dinner."

"Yes, ma'am." He gave her a little bow. "Thank you."

Mike slid an arm around my shoulders and leaned in. "I've been telling your parents for a year and a half that they need to keep the doors locked even when they're home," he whispered. "Think it's too soon for an 'I told you so'?"

"Yes." I snorted. "But don't worry. Now they have incentive."

My mother laid out an extra place setting for Kenny in between Joey and Brian and across from Jason and Mike. It was her subtle way of telling him to behave himself, lest he wanted to end up at the bottom of a four-man pileup.

Dinner began, unusually quiet for the first five minutes. Meals at my parents' house typically involved four different conversations occurring simultaneously, contributing to a noise level I would call a low roar.

"So, Jason," Kenny finally said, "where's Megan? She sick?"

Jason's eyes flashed. "I hope so."

When no one else volunteered an answer, Joey spoke up. "Megan and Jason split up."

Surprised, Kenny dropped his fork to his plate with a clatter. "I'm sorry, man." He fumbled to pick it up. "When?"

"September," Joey said, when Jason refused to answer. "Divorce was final about six weeks ago."

"Hey, Jase, look on the bright side—now you can do whatever you want and don't have to answer to anyone." Kenny gave him a bright smile. "Trust me, it's worth it."

"If that's all you wanted out of life," Jason said, his voice controlled, "you shouldn't have gotten married in the first place."

"Eloped," he corrected. "It was a spur-of-the-moment thing."

I eyed him dubiously. "Like buying a pack of gum at the cash register?"

"Exactly," he said, pleased that I had gotten it. "Everybody who gets married in Vegas knows that."

"I guess I misplaced my copy of the official Vegas wedding handbook," Kellyn muttered.

"I haven't heard about this either." Mike sent Kenny a sarcastic smirk. "What are the other rules?"

"It's a short list. First, both parties must be intoxicated, and second, an Elvis or Cher impersonator must be present." A mischievous grin spread across Kenny's face. "Why so interested? Are you planning something?"

I inhaled a sharp breath and coughed as my mashed potatoes were sucked into the back of my throat. Staunchly avoiding looking at Mike, I reached for my water and gulped some down.

Kenny's grin widened. "I wish you two could see your faces right now."

"I was only making conversation." Mike's voice was neutral. "I have no interest in getting married in Vegas."

"That's good." Kenny forced his lips into a flat line. "Because I don't think your girlfriend wants to get married."

Mike glanced at me, brows furrowed. "Is that true?"

I cleared my throat. "I never said that."

Kenny laughed. "Sure, you did. Remember that time when—"

"I called off my wedding?" I snapped. "Yes, but thank you for reminding me."

"Well, yes. But more specifically, the time after that when you said you were never going to get married."

My eyes slid skyward. Kellyn and Kenny had just gotten back from Vegas, and we had not been thrilled with their news. The official party line claimed it was because they'd only been dating six months, and we hadn't been invited to the wedding. At the time, it had only been three months since Baratti and I had split up, so for me, it was more because I thought love was a giant pile of horse poo, and I wanted nothing to do with it or anyone who'd fallen in it.

"I also said I was going to find out where Baratti lived and burn his house down," I said, annoyed that he'd remembered. "I wasn't being logical."

Kellyn snorted. "Sounds reasonable to me."

Jason lifted his glass and reached across the table to clink it against Kellyn's before both polished off their drinks.

"There's more wine, right?" I stage whispered to my mother. She nodded and scooted her chair back.

"I got it." Kellyn jumped to her feet and bolted toward the kitchen.

"Don't get drunk yet," Joey warned me. "We still have to go to Dad's for dessert." I froze with my fork halfway to my mouth, and he narrowed his eyes. "You forgot, didn't you?"

I scoffed. "Of course not."

"We're going to your father's for dessert?" Mike asked in a flat voice.

"You don't have to go." I put my fork down so I didn't use it to stab myself in the temple. "But I do."

"Why?"

I tried not to squirm. "I owe him for doing a favor for me."

"Let me see if I can figure out what it was." Mike rubbed his chin in mock thought. "Could it be for getting Baratti out of interrogation?"

Jason's head snapped up, and he gaped at me. "You, Gavin, and Pierce all in the same confined place?" he asked. "I don't know which part of that statement to tackle first."

"Then don't," I said irritably.

He laughed humorlessly. "Oh, Panda," he said, using my childhood nickname, short for 'pandemonium.' "And I thought my life was complicated."

I made a snarky face at him before turning back to my plate.

Brian coughed loudly. "So, what's everyone doing for the big game on Saturday?" He delicately cut his turkey and dipped it in the pool of gravy atop his mashed potatoes. "I heard Colsboro U is favored to win by only one field goal."

Things had to be pretty bad for Brian to talk about football. And I knew they were only going to get worse.

AFTER DINNER, JASON VOLUNTEERED TO take Murphy for a walk with Kellyn, who happily agreed until my mother snatched her wine glass before she made it out the door. Meanwhile, Brian took Joey downstairs to the man cave to show off his new Glock, Kenny helped my mother clear the table and put away the food, and Mike and I washed the dishes.

Once they were out of earshot, Mike slid me a sideways glance. "Is what Kenny said true?"

"About getting married?" I asked, and he nodded. "I did say that, but it was three years ago, when I was cold and dead inside." Smiling up at him, I nudged him playfully with my shoulder. "Things are different now."

He finished drying a platter and added it to a stack of clean dishes on the opposite counter. "How so?"

"I'm not cold and dead inside anymore." I rinsed off another plate and handed it to him. "Feel free to take credit for that."

"I think I will." His lips curved upward. "So you do, then? Want to get married, I mean."

I focused intently on scrubbing a glob of congealed gravy in the gravy boat. "I'm open to it." A few beats of silence passed, and I sneaked a glance at him to gauge his reaction, but his face was unreadable. "But it's not like I have to," I amended quickly. "There's no pressure—"

He slid a hand along my jaw and turned my face toward him before leaning down to kiss me softly. "You don't need to backtrack," he said when he pulled back. "You're going to need more than a wishy-washy desire to maybe get married possibly sometime in the future to scare me off."

"I guess I'm not trying hard enough, then." I rinsed off the gravy boat. "Spending an evening with Pierce might do the trick."

My mother appeared at my side with a few empty wine glasses. "Your father is very charming when he wants to be—which is usually only when he's getting paid for it or wants something."

Mike turned his laugh into a cough as he took the dripping dish from me.

"Gee, Mom, how do you really feel about it?" Smirking, I snatched one of the glasses and dunked it in the soapy water. "Is this all of the dishes?"

"I think so." She glanced over her shoulder at the table, then back to the wine glasses. "Did you already wash one of these? There are only seven here."

"Maybe Kellyn found a way to sneak out with hers," I suggested.

"No, I watched her leave without it."

Mike added the gravy boat to the collection of clean dishes. "Where's Kenny?"

"He's gone. I told him it would be best if he left before Kellyn got back."

I rinsed the wine glass and handed it to Mike. "Let's blame it on him, then. He crashed Thanksgiving, riled everyone up, broke a glass, and then ran away."

My mother shrugged. "Works for me."

《》

AT SEVEN FIFTY, JOEY, MIKE, and I trudged up the front steps of Pierce's Colonial-style house in Marble Hill, a swanky suburb a few miles northwest of downtown Colsboro, with Murphy in tow. Mike had been concerned about bringing him without prior permission, but we hadn't had time to take him home, and also, I didn't give a hoot.

"You brought a dog," Pierce said flatly when he opened the door and Murphy darted inside. He lifted his sharp hazel eyes to us and frowned. "And Detective Demarco."

Mike nodded at him. "Nice to see you, too, counselor."

I stifled a nervous giggle and gave my father a huge fake smile. "Pierce, this is my boyfriend, Mike." I used my matching fake cheerful voice. "Mike, this is my father Pierce."

Pierce pressed his mouth into a flat line but otherwise kept his disappointment to himself. "Pleasure." He spared Mike a brief glance before stepping aside. "Please come in."

Mike squeezed my hand in reassurance as we stepped over the threshold. After stowing our jackets in the coat closet, we followed Pierce single file into the formal dining room, where my stepmother Elle and her two children quietly awaited our arrival. They stood to greet us, perfectly in sync, as if they'd choreographed it. Murphy plopped down in a corner with a groan and watched us in a half-awake tryptophan haze.

Elle gave us a warm smile and floated around the table with her arms open. "Jennifer, darling, so lovely to have you here." She leaned in for the lightest of hugs and air-kissing my cheeks. "It's been too long."

I made a noncommittal noise before backing away and introducing her to Mike, who also got a pseudo-hug. After she gave Joey his hug, she turned to the children, who were neatly dressed in their Sunday best, their blond hair perfectly arranged.

"Felicity, Phillip, come say hello to your sister and brother."

They obediently strode around the table and gave Joey and me each a stiff hug and Mike a formal handshake before returning to their places.

Elle turned back to us, her pink lipsticked mouth frozen in a wide smile that showed off her unnaturally white teeth. "Please have a seat, and I'll get the pies. Coffee?" We nodded in unison, and she turned to Pierce. "Darling, will you help me, please?"

Joey sat down next to the kids and struck up a conversation, while Mike and I sank resignedly into the two remaining chairs without speaking. Once she and Pierce had returned and distributed dessert and coffee, Elle turned her pale blue eyes to me.

"So," she said, tucking her platinum blond hair behind her ear, "how long have you two been dating?"

I stirred some sugar into my coffee and chased it with a splash of cream. "About a year and a half."

"How did you meet?"

I placed my spoon on the china saucer. "We went to the same high school."

She beamed at us. "You were high school sweethearts?"

A short laugh bubbled out. "How old do you think I am?" When Pierce cleared his throat loudly, I stifled a sigh and revised. "No."

After her initial disappointment passed, Elle made a motion with her hand, encouraging me to continue. I pointed at my mouth, into which I'd just shoved a bite of pie, and shrugged self-deprecatingly as I chewed. Her smile faded into a pout.

Mike broke the silence before my father could chastise me. "I graduated a couple years before Jen. We met again when Joe graduated from the Academy last spring."

Pierce glanced up from his pie. "You were in Jason's class," he said to Mike, who nodded. "Were you friends?"

"We were friendly. Played on the hockey team and had a few classes together."

"Hmm. Strange we haven't met before." Pierce's lips twitched ever so slightly, his version of a smirk. "Except when you're railroading my clients in interrogation."

Mike's smile didn't reach his eyes. "Strange we never saw you at any hockey games."

"Speaking of Jason," Pierce continued, redirecting his attention to me, "how is he doing?"

"Fantastic. I'll let him know you asked."

"Jason's been staying with me," Joey cut in. "He's having a hard time with the divorce."

Pierce nodded, expressionless. "He should have known better than to marry a dentist." He pushed away his empty plate with his fingertips, as if it were covered in maggots. "Physicians have one of the highest divorce rates."

"So do lawyers," I countered.

He slid his eyes to mine. "So do police officers."

Before I could retort, Joey quickly shifted the topic of conversation. "I doubt Megan's profession had anything to do with it."

"Of course it didn't," Elle piped up from the other end of the table. "They loved each other; that was all that mattered."

Pierce raised a brow. "I think he was talking about why they split up."

She blinked. "Oh. What happened?"

Joey shrugged. "It's complicated, but suffice to say that Megan is a manipulative bitch—"

"Joseph," Pierce said sharply, cutting Joey off mid-sentence. He hated being called by his full name, but he clamped his mouth shut without argument.

Elle jumped to her feet. "Come on, kids," she said, practically shouting in an attempt to drown out words already spoken. "Let's give Daddy and your big brother and sister some alone time to visit." She reached out and grabbed both their hands before dragging them out of the room, even though they had dutifully stood to follow her instructions.

Once they were gone, Pierce swiveled his glare between Joey and me. "You both seem to have forgotten how to behave in front of children."

I opened my mouth to respond, but Joey beat me to it. "Sorry, Dad. I've been spending too much time at the precinct."

"And what about you?" Pierce asked, directing his judgmental scowl toward me.

I gave a half shrug. "I don't spend that much time at the precinct."

His eyes drifted downward, and he pinched the bridge of his nose. "I wish we could get along." His face was blank when he lifted his gaze back to mine. "Just for one night."

"And I wish I were a best-selling novelist with a villa overlooking a Tuscan vineyard, but it would take more than one hour of half-assed effort every two years to make that happen."

His jaw tightened briefly. "Half-assed effort is better than no effort at all—which is more than I can say for you."

"Would I be here if I hadn't called you first?"

Sighing, Pierce rubbed his temples with his forefingers. "Why did you even come tonight?"

"Because we made a deal, and I fulfill my commitments."

"How honorable of you." He picked up his mug and took a leisurely sip of coffee. It was one of his favorite courtroom tactics to draw out the tension before the drama reached its climax. "Your mother and I divorced more than seventeen years ago, yet you appear to be harboring a great deal of anger about it."

"Not at all. It was a good thing you got divorced."

"So you're angry about something else."

"Don't worry." I gave him a tight smile. "It's nothing to do with you, of course."

"We're all stressed out," Joey cut in. "This serial killer has everyone on edge."

"Ah, yes." Pierce topped off his coffee and set the carafe back down without offering anyone else a refill. "I take it your fiancé is no longer a suspect?"

"Ex-fiancé," I muttered from behind gritted teeth.

Mike shifted in his chair, sitting up straighter. "We don't consider Dr. Baratti a suspect at this time."

"Any other persons of interest?"

"No."

His piercing gaze locked on Mike. "Three of my children are tangentially linked to this case and could very well be in danger, and you're telling me you have no suspects?"

"Dad, we're not in any—"

Without breaking eye contact, Pierce held up a hand to silence him, and Joey slumped back in his chair. Under the table, I rested my hand on Mike's thigh and gave it a tight squeeze, both in reassurance and warning.

Pierce's brow arched, betraying his impatience. "Detective?"

"Yes, counselor." Mike's voice was taut with restrained annoyance. "That is what I'm telling you."

Pierce pressed his lips together. "I see."

"We are exploring several possibilities," he added, "none of which I'm at liberty to discuss at this juncture."

Pierce smiled at him—a menacing smile that didn't reach his eyes. "I'm sure Pete Lockwood would be more than willing to share those possibilities, given the circumstances."

Mike met his gaze head on, expression equally devoid of emotion. "You'll have to ask the chief yourself."

He nodded, bringing his coffee cup to his lips again. "And so I shall."

NINE YEARS AGO
COLSBORO, OHIO

"WOULD YOU LIKE A GLASS of wine?" my father asked me unexpectedly. "We haven't gotten to celebrate your birthday yet."

I glanced surreptitiously at the server, who waited patiently next to our table, hands clasped behind his back. "Dad, I turned eighteen, not twenty-one." A month ago, but who was counting?

"Per the Ohio Revised Code, individuals under age twenty-one are permitted to drink alcoholic beverages when supervised by a parent or guardian." He eyed me over his menu. "Which I am." He redirected his attention to the waiter without moving. "She will have a glass of the riesling, and I will have a double Johnnie Walker Blue with exactly one ice cube."

"Very good, sir." He turned on his heel and glided away.

"I apologize for missing your birthday," Pierce said once the server was gone. "I'm sure your mother told you about the trial."

I placed the cloth napkin on my lap and twisted it around my fingers. "It's fine. I understand."

At least one of those things was true. I may not have understood, but I was fine with it. I'd grown accustomed to being low on my father's list of priorities, and truth be told, my birthday without him had been a lot more fun than this.

"Here." He slid a narrow, perfectly wrapped box across the table. "A belated birthday gift."

I tentatively picked up the box. "You didn't need to get me anything."

"Of course I did. You're my daughter, and you deserve much more than what you've gotten." He cleared his throat. "I want to do whatever I can to make up for that."

Swallowing hard, I looked up at him. "Really?"

His brows furrowed. "Of course. How could you think otherwise?"

"I don't know," I mumbled, frozen with shock. It was a lie, but to answer honestly would make the next two hours about as comfortable as wearing a cactus sweater.

He sighed and leaned forward, clasping his hands in front of him. "I realize our relationship has been strained, especially since your mother and I split up. I admit I hold some responsibility in that."

That was an understatement. Ever since I'd walked in to his home office nine years ago to find Melanie Davenport's mother on her knees at his feet, our relationship had wavered between strained to downright hostile.

"Jennifer, I was hurt by what happened, too," he continued. "And I had hoped you would see that." He tilted his head, softened his eyes. "But you were so young, and I should have been more sympathetic to the position I put you in."

"The position you put me in?" I stared at him incredulously as hot lava clogged my veins. "You mean bribing me into lying to Mom?"

His brows furrowed slightly, but his face remained otherwise impassive. "I only wanted some time to talk to her myself. I'm sorry my request made you uncomfortable."

My father was a master at twisting the English language. I'd been blind to it until my first journalism class freshman year. Once I'd learned about context, about how to manipulate verbs by using whichever tense achieved your goal, about which statistics and direct quotes were most powerful, everything he'd ever said had become suspect.

"Thanks," I said carefully. "I'm sure that was a difficult situation for you." *What with all the lying to your family so you didn't get caught.*

His lips formed an unconvincing smile. "And thank you for understanding."

"Of course. I completely understand." *That you're a selfish ass.*

Obviously relieved, he gestured toward the gift. "Well, go on. Open it."

Not wanting to get sidetracked into any other uncomfortable memories, I ripped through the paper, crushed it into a ball, and tossed it on the table. I jiggled the lid off the box and stared down at the slips of paper atop a layer of white cotton.

"Airline vouchers," he explained, as if I were illiterate. "To fly to Europe first class with Melanie." I jerked my head up to stare at him. Melanie and I hadn't been friends for nine years, since I'd politely informed her that her mother was a home-wrecking whore, and she'd tried to rip my hair out to prove I was wrong. "Or whoever you want. Whenever you want." He smiled again, reaching across the table to awkwardly pat my hand. "Happy birthday—and congratulations."

I frowned. "Congratulations?"

"On your graduation." He leaned back in his seat as the waiter returned with our drinks, nodding at him once to simultaneously thank and dismiss him. "It's a shame you aren't the valedictorian, but fourth in your class is respectable."

"Thanks. Are you coming to the ceremony?"

He paused to sip his drink, and for some stupid reason, my heart sank. "Unfortunately," he began slowly, "I will be out of town next weekend. Didn't your mother tell you?"

I shook my head. "Where are you going?"

"Las Vegas," he said. "For a conference." He nodded at my glass. "How do you like the wine?"

"Good," I murmured obediently.

But not quite as good as the lie he'd just told.

CHAPTER 8
PRESENT
COLSBORO, OHIO

AFTER WE LEFT PIERCE'S HOUSE and said good night to Joey, Mike didn't run away, shouting some excuse over his shoulder about not being ready for a committed relationship, as I'd half-jokingly predicted. Instead, he wrapped me in a tight embrace before we climbed into his truck, while Murphy tugged impatiently on his leash.

"How did your parents ever get married," he asked, "let alone fall in love?"

"I think they met in the Bermuda Triangle on Friday the thirteenth," I said, my voice muffled against his sweater. "And it was a full moon."

He leaned back and smiled down at me. "Whatever the reason, I'm glad they did." Then he kissed the tip of my nose, tucked me into the passenger seat, and drove me home, where we went to bed early and stayed awake late talking. After surviving a traumatic experience together, I found it easier to discuss adult things, like childhood scars (his, literal; mine, metaphorical), getting married, and making tiny humans.

When I opened my eyes the next morning, though, my brain had reset, and the sweetness of the previous night had gone sour. I blinked, allowing my eyes to adjust to the dull gray light of reality peeking in from beyond my curtains. I realized Mike's side of the bed was empty seconds before the bedroom door opened and he tiptoed in.

He sat down on the bed next to me and brushed my hair away from my face. "Good morning."

I frowned up at him. "You're wearing a tie."

"Sadly, yes. I'm going to work."

"But today is the day we're supposed to do festive things—like decorate the tree and drink spiked cider and not talk about serial killers."

"We can still do all those things," he assured me. "It's only seven, and I plan on being home by one."

"But spiked cider..."

"This afternoon, I promise. Besides, that needs to sit in the crockpot for a couple hours."

"Not the way I do it," I muttered.

He bent and gave me a kiss before rising to his feet. "Do me a favor and stay out of trouble, okay?"

"Can't guarantee anything if you're not here to supervise." I smiled up at him. "When the cat is away..."

"You mice have fun today," he called over his shoulder. "And try not to drink all the spiced rum before I get home."

I couldn't fall back to sleep after Mike left, so I dragged myself out of bed and got dressed. After breakfast, I prepped the spiked cider, dragged my Christmas decorations out of storage, and rearranged the living room furniture to make space for the tree, all under Murphy's unblinking supervision. When that was finished, Kellyn still wasn't out of bed, so I half-heartedly sifted through emails and re-examined crime scene photos until my cellphone rang an hour later.

"Gibbs!" Gus shouted from the other end of the line. "You talked to Phelps today?"

"No." I closed my laptop and set it aside. "Why, did she find out the reason you sometimes close your blinds and lock your door during lunch?"

"She's a no call, no show," he barked. "Didn't file her copy last night, either—and on the biggest sports weekend of the year."

"That's not like Tori." I frowned. "Maybe she was so depressed because the Browns crashed and burned yesterday that she couldn't get out of bed."

Gus snorted. "Like that came as a surprise to anyone."

"Well, did you call her—"

"Of course I called her," he interrupted. "Several times. Why d'you think I'm calling you?"

I cleared my throat. "What I was going to say is, did you call her dad? Maybe one of her brothers fell through the floor of a burning building during a three-alarm fire."

Gus mumbled something under his breath and hung up.

While I waited, I dialed Tori's number to check on her myself. My first three calls went to voicemail, so I sent her a text message, in case she was in a place where she couldn't talk on the phone. By the time Gus called back, she hadn't responded to that, either.

"Her dad hasn't talked to her since she left his house early yesterday evening," he said. "Nor have her brothers, none of whom have fought any fires in the last twenty-four hours, so there goes your theory."

"I have a bad feeling about this." I blew out a breath and reached for a notepad. "Give me her address."

《》

ON THE WAY TO TORI'S place, I called Mike to apprise him of the situation.

"I'll meet you there." Some papers shuffled in the background as he exchanged a few hushed words with someone. "Where's she live?"

"It's probably nothing," I said dismissively. "I'm probably just being paranoid."

"Under the circumstances, I'd rather play it safe." He blew out a puff of air. "And anyway, it's never nothing with you."

I couldn't argue with either point, so I rattled off the address. He promised to meet me there in fifteen minutes or less.

Tori lived about six miles north of downtown on a quiet, tree-lined street in Beechwold. I parked in her driveway behind her black Kia and cut the engine, the cinderblock in my stomach growing heavier. There was only one way to get rid of it, so I climbed out of my car, shoved my keys and cellphone into my jeans pockets, and trudged up the brick sidewalk.

I rang the doorbell and stepped back to wait impatiently as the seconds dripped by like thick syrup. Impatient, I pressed the doorbell several more times in rapid succession.

"Dammit, Tori," I murmured, peering inside the narrow side window. The front hall was dim and silent, and nothing changed when I shouted her name against the glass. As a last resort, I jiggled her doorknob and was surprised when it turned without resistance.

I pushed the knob away, and the door creaked open as I stood on the threshold, debating. The smart thing to do would be to wait for Mike—but if Tori was in danger, waiting could be the deciding factor in whether she lived or died.

Decision made, I stepped into the quiet foyer, gently closed the door with my elbow, and glanced around the narrow townhouse. Small living room with fireplace on the right, dining nook and kitchen on the left, staircase in front of me. Still no sounds or movement. A little voice in the back of my head told me to go upstairs, and I listened, shoving my hands into my jacket pockets so I didn't touch anything.

I tiptoed up the stairs as if walking barefoot over thumbtacks. Once I made it to the top, I paused and looked around. One bedroom on either side of the stairs and, straight ahead, two closed doors next to each other.

Before I could overanalyze the situation, I turned right and peeked into a small, spartan office: Utilitarian desk and bookshelf, short filing cabinet, various sports paraphernalia on the walls, several boxes in the closet. Across the hall, the master bedroom was similarly appointed—and similarly devoid of life. Not even a monster under the bed.

With the bedrooms clear, that left the two closed doors. I pulled the sleeve of my sweater over one hand and opened the door on the left. Linen closet. I closed it and, stomach tightening, turned to the final door.

I knew three things at this point: One, it had to be the bathroom. Two, no one ever closed the bathroom door unless they were inside said bathroom. And three, if she were inside this bathroom, by now she would have heard me, and I would have heard her.

Unless...

Holding my breath in apprehension, I rotated the knob and slowly nudged open the door. I half-expected someone to clobber me with a plunger and push me down the stairs, but after a few long seconds, nothing happened. Relieved, I released my breath and fumbled for the light switch with my left elbow. The overhead light flicked on, and as I drew in a deep breath, the odor of dead fish filled my nostrils.

I could deny it before, but now it was undeniable: Something was very wrong.

Covering my nose and mouth with my palm, I inched closer to the frosty glass-doored shower. My fingers brushed against it and, of their own accord, yanked the door open, releasing the stench full force. The miasma assaulted my nose and throat, making me gag, and I forced myself to look down despite every instinct telling me to get the hell out of there.

I gasped, blinking a few times as my brain tried to make sense of what my eyes were seeing. Tori slumped awkwardly in the stall with her head hanging uncomfortably to one side. She stared sightlessly from beneath drooping lids, her mouth ajar in a soundless scream. Her knees rested crookedly against the wall, and her arms laid boneless next to her bruised and naked body atop a greenish-blue sludge.

My head spun and nausea rose in my throat as I stumbled backward out of the small bathroom and toward the staircase. I staggered down the first stair, then the second, and fumbled for my cellphone. Halfway down, I managed to free it from my pocket, but it promptly slipped out of my numb fingers and tumbled the rest of the way down the stairs. As I bent to reach for it, my chest twisted painfully, and I groaned, teetering precariously on the second to last stair.

Then my vision swirled, my body grew heavy, and I fell into pitch black nothingness.

CHAPTER 9

I OPENED MY EYES TO find two homicide investigators staring down at me from above. One was Mike; the other was Chad Davis, Baratti's friend and fellow medical examiner.

"Omigod," I croaked from behind the oxygen mask he held to my face. "So this is what it feels like to be a murder victim."

Mike blew out a breath. "Are you okay?"

I nudged the mask away from my nose. "If Chad is here, I'm guessing not."

"So far, so good," Chad said. "You definitely haven't been murdered."

"Where am I?" I blinked a few times and glanced around, trying to figure out why I was lying on a gurney in someone's driveway, surrounded by flashing lights. "What happened?"

Mike exchanged a glance with Chad. "I found you crumpled at the bottom of the stairs." When I stared blankly at him, he added, "At Tori's house."

"Oh." I squeezed my eyes shut and rubbed my temples as the memory of Tori's body permeated my mind. "Right."

After exchanging a few hushed words with Chad, Mike put a hand on my shoulder, and I opened my eyes. "The medic's going to check you out now." His face was deliberately blank. "We'll talk afterward."

Chad and I watched him walk away and join Sardelis on the other side of the caution tape, neither of us speaking until they disappeared amongst the other investigators.

He turned back to me. "How are you feeling?"

I drew in a shaky breath. "That's a broad question."

"Let's start with physically, then."

"I've been worse. Did you go inside?" I asked, and he nodded. "What was that smell?"

"Toxic phosphine gas," he answered. "My preliminary theory is he dumped her and a shit-ton of rodenticide in the shower, turned on the water, and closed the door. The chemicals in the rat poison reacted with the liquid to form a toxic gas, which was then trapped in the bathroom with her."

I swallowed the lump in my throat. "How did she die?"

"Likely multi-system organ failure." He gave me a rueful smile. "I'm sorry, Jen."

I blinked rapidly to keep the tears at bay. "Thanks," I managed to say. "Now what?"

"We focus on you." He signaled to someone behind me, and a medic appeared on my other side with a medical kit, which he immediately seized from her. "Any dizziness or double vision?"

I took a deep breath to steady myself before answering. "Not at the moment."

He rooted around in the kit, pulled out a stethoscope, and inserted the tips into his ears. "Abdominal pain or headache?"

"A bit of a headache," I said. "But I think I fell partway down the stairs."

He nodded and pressed the diaphragm to my chest. "Take a few deep breaths." We fell silent for a minute while he listened to my heart and lungs, checked my pupils, and took my blood pressure.

"Did you get demoted at the coroner's office?" I asked as he unwrapped the blood pressure cuff.

His lips tilted upward as he handed the equipment back to the medic and thanked her. "No, I just know certain people will prefer a doctor's assessment over a paramedic's."

"Certain people being Baratti?"

Chad's eyebrow lifted, but he didn't comment on my use of his surname. "And Demarco," he said. "You're lucky he got you out of there so fast, or I'd be sending you to the hospital for seventy-two hours of observation, IV fluids, and EKGs."

I let out a humorless laugh. "I'm also going to be lucky later when he lectures me for breaking and entering and tampering with a crime scene."

"The crime scene was fine. No signs of forced entry, either."

"Thanks, but I don't think that'll be enough to escape a lecture."

Chad studied me for a few long beats. "How long have you guys been together?"

I didn't answer right away. "Year and a half."

He nodded. "So you're happy?"

"Today notwithstanding?" I gave him a weak smile. "Yeah, I'm happy."

"Good." He surprised me by reaching out and picking up my hand and giving my fingers a light squeeze. "He just wants you to be happy. That's all he's ever wanted."

Without asking, I knew he meant Baratti. I slid my eyes away and stared blindly at the melee of crime scene investigators. "He had a funny way of showing it."

"Maybe, maybe not." Chad's voice was barely audible. "Things aren't always what they seem."

I jerked toward him too fast, making my head throb. "What do you mean?"

He glanced away, shoving his hands into his jeans pockets. "From what I've seen and heard, your intuition is spot on—today, for example."

"This one was pretty easy to spot."

"Yet no one else was here checking on her." His eyes slid up to mine. "Just you."

I blew out a sigh. "What's your point?"

Chad shook his head, opening and closing his mouth a couple times before the words materialized. "Don't ignore your instincts, no matter what anyone else tells you. Ninety-five percent of the time, they're right."

"Are we speaking generally, or do you mean Baratti?"

"What does your gut say?"

"My gut says you're being frustratingly vague."

"Your gut also makes you a very good judge of character. You know that, right?"

"I used to." I shook my head and looked down at my fingers, twisted together on my lap. "I was wrong about him, in a big way. Now I second-guess myself."

"Why do you think you were wrong about him?"

I lifted my head from the pillow and stared at him incredulously. "Because he told me so," I said, my voice rising. "It came straight from the ass's mouth."

One corner of his lips twitched upward. "I believe the actual phrase mentions a horse, not an ass."

"Whatever," I muttered. "They're both equines."

He grinned. "I've missed you."

I couldn't help but smile back. "And I you."

"You know, we don't need Gavin to hang out. I can be Switzerland."

I flipped my hand over and held out my palm. "No, you can't," I said as he laid his hand lightly on mine. "And you're not supposed to. You're his friend first. You're supposed to be on his side."

"I am, but I'm also on yours. This isn't Axis and Allies."

I smiled weakly. "You are such a nerd."

Chad smiled. "See what a good judge of character you are?"

"I had prior knowledge."

"You don't give yourself enough credit." He released my hand and patted it gently. "Just think about it, okay?"

As he relinquished custody of me to the paramedic and rejoined the other crime scene investigators, I found myself wondering what he was really trying to tell me.

My gut said it had nothing to do with a serial killer.

《》

THE EPIPHANY CAME AT THREE o'clock on Saturday morning, as epiphanies generally did, and I wasn't able to fall back asleep. Four hours later, Mike checked to make sure I was still breathing—per Chad's doctorly advice—and left for work. Less than an hour after that, I plunked down at Tori's desk in the newsroom.

What was the one commonality among the victims? They were all registered on the same dating website.

And I had access to one of the vics' computers.

I switched on her computer before my butt was even in the chair and removed my coat while I waited for it to boot. When presented with the login screen, I drummed my fingertips on the keyboard for a few beats while I wracked the depths of my memory for her password.

She'd given it to me several months ago, after she'd gotten a quick manicure over her lunch and didn't want to risk smudging her nails, but wanted to appear as though she were working. I tried a few options, the panic intensifying with each failed attempt, until I stumbled across the right one.

"Dear technology gods," I muttered to myself as I clicked on the browser icon, "please let Tori be the kind of person who saved all her passwords in her browser."

Not wasting any time, I pulled up the eConnections website, where, to my relief, Tori's user name and password automatically appeared on the login screen. I clicked the button to sign in and navigated to her inbox. Starting at the top with the most recent, I scrolled through and read every message in her inbox, sent folder, and trash.

When I had read all the messages back to early August, an instant message popped up in the lower right corner of the page. I recognized the screen name as someone she'd exchanged a few emails with during the past month.

Who is this?

I stared at the chat box, my fingers hovering over the keyboard as my mind raced. The CPD hadn't given the media the official go-ahead to release Tori's name, so none of the news reports had named her; they had so far all referred to her as "an unidentified Beechwold woman."

Which meant whoever had just sent the IM could be her killer.

Holding my breath, I thought quickly and typed out a response.

What do you mean?

A few long seconds passed while I watched the chat window without blinking, afraid I would miss something if I closed my eyes for even a fraction of a moment. An ellipsis inside of a speech bubble appeared, indicating the user was typing a response.

You're not Tori.

I gaped at the screen for a few surreal seconds before my heart started beating again. My hands shook as I typed out a response, deleted it, and started over. On the third try, I tapped enter to send the message.

How do you know?

So much time passed that I began to think he wasn't going to respond. But then the speech bubble popped up for a few brief seconds, followed by four words that stopped my heart.

Because I killed her.

I blinked and rubbed my eyes, convinced I was hallucinating—but when I opened my eyes again, the words were still there, just as I remembered them.

It was incredibly risky for him to admit that, especially knowing that a tech guru could follow breadcrumbs though the virtual forest and find exactly where his gingerbread house was hidden—which meant only one thing.

He was playing with me.

"You want to play?" I typed out my response. "Let's play."

Then I guess it's my turn to ask: Who are you?

The next message came only a few seconds later.

Nice try, Jennifer. You're going to have to do better than that.

My heart jumped into my throat at his use of my name, but I swallowed it back down and forced myself to focus. He was obviously challenging me. He wanted me to challenge him back. But how? If my response fell short of his expectations, he'd get bored and end the conversation. And if I pushed too hard, he'd get pissed and end the conversation—or worse.

But in my gut, I knew he would kill again, no matter what I said. I had to take the risk. So I cast out my fishline before I could talk myself out of it, half hoping he'd pass on the bait.

Bartholomew's. 7pm tonight. I'll be at the bar.

Jaw clenched, shoulders tensed, back ramrod straight in the chair, I waited. For a long time, nothing happened. No speech bubble. No message. Finally, I took a deep breath, blew it out slowly, and played my last card.

Alone.

Again, I waited with bated breath for his response. Seconds oozed by like tar. I aged about ten years. I almost gave up on life.

"Come on, come on, come on," I whispered.

After a full two minutes had passed, a message appeared.

Don't be late.

Immediately, the green dot next to his profile picture turned red, indicating he was no longer online, and the conversation was over.

I sank back against the chair, mentally exhausted and on the verge of hyperventilating. As the first wave of panic rippled across my belly, I dug into my purse and pulled out my cellphone. Following a brief inner debate, I tapped on the name and pressed the phone to my ear.

"Hey, Steve," I said when he answered. "Feel like making detective tonight?"

《》

WE MET AT BARTHOLOMEW'S AT six o'clock to scope out the place and claim two stools next to each other, staggering our arrivals so it didn't look like we'd planned it. I went in first and slid onto a barstool, casually dropping my purse on the seat next to me. Shortly thereafter, I had a glass of cabernet—which I was going to attempt to nurse over the next hour—and the bar was rapidly filling up. I texted Steve, sipped my wine, and sat back to wait.

I had met Steve Ford a few years ago during my first investigative exposé with the *Record*. Now a third-year beat cop trying to work his way into homicide, he was always ready to push the boundaries—a valuable quality to find in an informant.

Five minutes later, Steve appeared to my left. "Excuse me. Is this seat taken?"

"Oh, sorry," I said, snatching my purse. "No, go ahead."

He flashed me a dimpled grin. "Thanks."

"No problem."

Sliding onto the stool, Steve grabbed the menu and held it up to cover his face while he spoke. "Is Demarco aware of what we're up to tonight?"

"No," I said from behind my wine glass. "But don't worry. I made sure you're covered."

Out of an abundance of caution, I'd called Mike several times that afternoon, even though I knew he wasn't likely to answer. I also knew he was not going to be pleased when he found out what we'd done. But the killer was so well-informed about my life that he'd been able to track down my ex-engagement ring. It was a sure bet that he was also familiar with Mike. Partnering with Steve had been a gamble, but he was the least likely person to be a known associate of mine.

The bar was full by the time seven o'clock rolled around. Wondering if he was already here, I re-scrutinized every man I'd already ruled out. Twenty-something Asian geek with thick plastic glasses: No. Paunchy middle-aged white guy sipping white wine with paunchy middle-aged white woman: No. Two African-American miming football moves and laughing hysterically: No and no. Balding Latino man trying to discreetly pick his large nose from behind a cocktail napkin: Definitely no.

Brown-haired Caucasian man in his mid-thirties whose eyes darted away when I glanced at him: Maybe.

I lifted my wine glass to shield my lips. "Eleven o'clock," I murmured to Steve. "Blue shirt."

Following my line of sight, he covered his mouth for a mock yawn. "He's been here longer than anyone else and hasn't spoken to anyone except the bartender."

I picked up my phone to check the time, surprised to see twenty minutes had gone by, and I had racked up a few missed calls from an unknown number over the last hour—but no voicemails. I wondered if it was the killer calling to cancel: "Sorry, but something came up. Can we reschedule?"

Smiling in morbid amusement, I polished off my wine and figured I might as well have another, since I'd probably been stood up. I slid the glass to the edge of the bar and waited.

Within seconds, the lanky blonde bartender arrived and gave me a bright smile. "Another cabernet?"

I shrugged. "If you insist."

To my left, Steve turned a laugh into a throaty cough, which I ignored. While the bartender retrieved my wine, I redirected my attention to the man in the blue shirt.

But he was gone.

I made a show of scratching my nose to hide my lips. "Where'd he go?"

Steve pressed his phone to his ear and shouted, "Hello?" A second later, he added, "Some lady came to pick up the dry cleaning. Took the blue shirt with her."

"Any other possibilities?"

"How about that green shirt you like?"

Placing my elbows on the bar, I tapped my phone randomly with both thumbs as if I were texting. Meanwhile, I scanned the bar until I found someone in a green shirt: A Middle Eastern man in his late forties who sipped from a pint glass, eyes roaming the room as if cataloging its contents.

"Shifty, but doesn't fit the profile. Anyone else?"

Steve cleared his throat. "The other shirt I was considering has mysteriously disappeared." He went silent for a few seconds. "Damn. Seems like we're out of shirts."

My shoulders slumped in defeat as the bartender returned with my wine, and I nodded in thanks before checking the time. Seven thirty. Most likely, we'd blown it.

"So," I said, my voice hollow as I spoke into my wine glass, "should we stick around to see if perhaps we didn't scare him off?"

Steve shrugged. "Doesn't hurt to try, but my gut says he's gone."

"Mine too."

"Okay, talk to you later." He disconnected his fake call and resumed scanning the bar with sharp cop eyes, while I swallowed a few large gulps of wine because who cared anyway.

It was a few minutes past eight o'clock by the time we both finished our second round and I requested the tab.

"I'll leave first in case he's waiting for you in the parking lot." Steve shrugged into his jacket. "Wait a few minutes before you go outside and then another few minutes before you leave, okay? Then I'll follow you home."

"Ooh, a police escort?" I said. "Fancy."

He slid off the barstool and stood, sending me a sideways grin. "More like a babysitter than an escort, but whatever makes you feel better."

《》

I MADE IT TO MY car without incident, which was both a relief and a disappointment. Once inside, I locked the doors immediately, started the engine, blasted the heat, and waited with an eye on my rearview mirror. After about three minutes had passed, no one had attempted to murder me, so I shifted the car into gear and swung out of the parking lot. Less than sixty seconds later, a pair of headlights turned onto the street behind me.

Reassured by the close proximity of my babysitter, I let my mind wander. Tonight may have been a bust, but the day wasn't totally wasted. I still had Tori's computer, which—with a little magic and a forensic digital analyst—could be the rainbow that led to the proverbial pot of gold.

The problem was, neither data recovery nor hacking were among my list of professional skills. Even if they were, the CPD would probably take possession of the computer before I had a chance to ask Orlando for another favor. And if Mike got his hands on it, I'd likely never find out what secrets it held—unless Steve made the homicide squad in the next twelve hours.

I slowed to a stop at a red light and glanced up at my rearview mirror to check in with my tail. Rather than the blocky headlights of Steve's older model Ford Explorer, the car behind me had the halo headlights signature to BMWs.

"Look at that," I said to myself. "Steve's been holding out on me."

Or maybe it wasn't Steve at all.

"One way to find out," I muttered as the light turned green.

Once the traffic in front of me cleared, I checked my mirrors and quickly shifted into the left lane without signaling. A few seconds later, the BMW followed. Inching the speedometer a few ticks past the speed limit, I flew past the trio of vehicles in front of me. The BMW followed again. When I'd cleared the sedan at the front by several car lengths, I cut back over to the right lane.

The BMW stayed in the left.

"So you're not Steve," I said to him as he inched closer.

Either Steve had gotten caught behind a slow driver and was farther behind me than I'd realized, or he wasn't behind me at all.

A shiver ran down my spine.

We sailed through the next intersection, the BMW picking up speed before disappearing into my blind spot. Keeping my eyes on the road, I reached across the center console to grab my purse from the passenger seat and dropped it on my lap.

As I fished around for my cellphone, the blind spot warning on my side mirror blinked off, and in my peripheral vision, I saw the BMW inch closer. I chanced a look to my left, but the tinted windows blocked my view into the driver's seat.

My fingers finally brushed against my cellphone, and I yanked it out with a triumphant "aha!" No sooner had it been freed from my purse than it slipped out of my hand and fell to the floor. I shot a quick look in the direction it had fallen, but it had disappeared into the darkness.

Son. Of. A. Bitch.

When I looked back up, the BMW's nose had edged slightly ahead of me. I gripped the wheel tighter.

"Let's be reasonable here," I told myself. "This could just be the typical, asshole BMW driver. Or maybe he's trying to get to his pregnant wife to the hospital." I paused to consider other scenarios as the car's taillights inched into my peripheral vision. "Or he's exactly who you think."

To test the theory, I took my foot off the gas and fell back. A few beats later, so did the BMW. He kept his front bumper just barely ahead of mine.

Clenching my jaw, I nudged my car to go a few MPH faster. When I had almost caught up with him, he sped up again.

This wasn't a regular asshole BMW driver. This wasn't a guy trying to get to the hospital. This was a serial killer.

I was on to him—and he knew it.

"Game time," I whispered.

The street ahead of me was clear for at least a mile. No brake lights. No stoplights.

This was my chance to catch a killer.

Adrenaline flooded my veins, and my senses crystallized. My surroundings sharpened—colors, lights, sounds. My mind blocked out everything but the dangers right in front of me.

I stomped on the accelerator and shot ahead of him for a brief second. He caught up, and I glanced over quickly to see we were head to head.

So far, we hadn't run into much traffic. Although the road ahead of us was clear for the next few blocks, red lights shone not too far off in the distance. The game, whatever it was, would quickly be over.

He seemed to realize it at the same time. As the BMW shot forward and swerved into my lane, I jerked the wheel to the right and slammed on the brakes. A grinding sound and the crunch of metal on metal under my feet sent vibrations of panic directly to my heart.

I braced myself as my front headlight screeched across his passenger-side door. The sound of crumpling steel and breaking glass filled my ears as my car's front end smashed into a vehicle parked at the curb.

The instant explosion of the airbag knocked me backward and took my breath away. A second later, my rear bumper rammed into something behind me with a crunch. My ears rang in the sudden silence. Head spinning, it took me a few beats to realize my car had done a one-eighty before coming to an abrupt halt.

Bright light illuminated the dust swirling around me, and I blinked in confusion. By the time I realized I was trapped in front of an oncoming vehicle, it was too late.

Blinding headlights.

The screech of tires and shattering glass.

A flash of sharp pain.

And then there was just silence.

CHAPTER 10

WHEN STEVE ARRIVED AT THE emergency room, I was lying boneless on a gurney having a gash in my left temple stitched closed.

"Well," he said, surveying me with hands on his hips, "that did not go as planned."

I let out a hysterical giggle, which I immediately regretted. "That should not surprise you." My voice came out hoarse.

The doctor pursed her lips. "Please hold still—unless you want to add getting stabbed in the eye with a needle to your injuries."

I stifled another laugh. "Sorry."

Steve grinned. "They must have given you the good drugs."

I held up my right arm to show him the IV. "Morphine."

The smile faded. "So you're hurt pretty badly."

"Nothing broken," the doctor said without looking up. "Whiplash and bruised ribs are the worst of it."

I had no idea how much time had passed since my arrival, but I'd been there long enough to have my blood drawn and vitals checked twice. I'd also visited radiology for a CT scan and, as a bonus, made a quick stop in the cardiac department for an EKG.

It seemed excessive to me, but when they found out I'd been exposed to phosphine gas yesterday, they ordered some extra tests.

I was too tired to argue, and after they gave me IV painkillers, I didn't care much.

The doctor snipped the thread, tossed the scissors and needle onto the metal tray, and affixed a small square of gauze over the wound. "You're all done. I'll get your discharge papers." Standing, she removed her gloves and dropped them in a can by the curtain. "Sit tight."

Once she was gone, Steve sat down on the doctor's stool and appraised me. "You look terrible, so I'm betting you feel pretty shitty."

"Thanks for the compliment." I shifted so I could face him directly, wincing at the dull pain that would be ten times worse tomorrow. "What happened?"

"Guy in a Beemer pulled out behind you and followed you like a magnet, and I couldn't get around him," he said. "He's either a really skilled offensive driver, or he can control traffic lights and other cars with his mind."

"He didn't escape unscathed, at least." I paused to cough; the powder released by the airbags had irritated my throat, but the doc said it would improve by morning. "BMW's not the car I would choose to drive when I'm running someone off the road, but I'm not a sociopath."

"Agreed."

"Did you get his plate number?"

"Yeah—and I finally got ahold of Demarco."

"After how many attempts?"

He cleared his throat. "Let's just say it was more than one, and I needed reinforcements."

I grimaced. "How mad is he?"

"About as mad as I've ever heard him." Steve raked a hand through his hair. "Though I don't think it's directed at us."

The long breath I drew in tickled my throat, and I coughed again. "Where is he?"

"On his way." His phone started ringing, and he stood. "I've got to take this. Be right back."

Closing my eyes, I let my head drop back against the pillow. "I'll be here," I murmured, my voice drowned out by the sound of the curtain swishing closed.

I must have drifted off after Steve ducked out of the cubicle, because the next thing I knew, a tingle ran up my left forearm as something brushed lightly against it. I jolted awake to find Mike hovering over me.

"Shit," I squeaked through my sore throat. "You scared the crap out of me."

"And you scared the crap out of me." Giving me a tight smile, he slid his fingers down my arm and grasped my hand. "I hate finding you in a hospital bed."

"I'm not too fond of it, either."

Without releasing my hand, he rolled the doctor's stool closer and dropped down onto it. "How are you feeling?"

I relaxed back against the pillow. "Peachy. Thinking about running a half marathon." I cleared my throat again. "Where've you been?"

He let out a humorless laugh. "Work. It's been a helluva day."

"I'll say," I retorted.

"I'm sorry." He let out a deep sigh that tickled across my face, still partially numb from the novocaine. "If I had been there—"

"You probably would have scared him off."

"Maybe so, but you wouldn't be here now." He shook his head in contempt. "We could have caught him and ended this whole thing."

"Possible, but unlikely. I don't think he's going to get caught until he wants to." If he wanted to, which was a ridiculous thing to want.

"This was the best chance we've had," Mike insisted. "He didn't have time to plot out fifteen contingency plans. I just wish I'd known, so we could've plotted out fifteen contingency plans of our own."

I narrowed my eyes at him. "It wasn't for lack of trying."

"I know, honey. This one's on me."

Though the morphine was doing a damn good job of dulling my senses, it couldn't tamp down the rising wisp of guilt. I was ninety-five percent sure that if I'd really wanted Mike to be there, I could've made it happen. I figured, though, that we were both paying the price for the choices we'd made, so I kept my mouth shut.

Somewhat reassured, I let my eyes drift shut again. A few minutes later, the cubicle curtain rustled, and Mike whispered he'd be right back. I tried to respond, but it came out an indecipherable mumble.

My body felt heavy and weightless at the same time, and with no one to help me stay awake, I stopped struggling and let the darkness take me again.

«»

WHEN I WOKE LATE THE next morning, I found myself sprawled across the middle of my bed, disoriented and confused—until I rolled onto my side, and my aching body reminded me of the previous night. Seeing as I was alone, I allowed myself a few minutes to wallow in self-pity before slowly rolling out of bed.

Once standing, I paused to let my spinning head right itself and took a deep breath, wincing at the pain in my ribs as my chest expanded. Excellent. Tracking down a serial killer would be so much easier now that it hurt to breathe.

After a pit stop in the bathroom for one of the pain meds the E.R. doctor had given me last night, I threw a sweatshirt on over my jammies and stumbled out to the living room. Kellyn sat cross-legged on the couch, newspaper in one hand and a mug in the other.

"Wow, you must've had too much fun last night." She tossed the section she'd been reading onto the coffee table. "Last time you slept this late was—" Kellyn cut herself off as she took in the sight of me and jumped to her feet, sloshing coffee on herself in the process. "Omigod, Jen, what happened?"

"A non-accidental car accident." I grimaced as she embraced me in a tight hug. "Guess I look pretty awful, huh?"

She leaned back. "Wait, someone purposely caused an accident?"

I nodded once. "Ran me off the road."

Her mouth dropped in shock. "Who?"

"We don't know. Some asshole in a BMW."

"Omigod," she said again, her voice going up an octave. "He got away?"

"Unfortunately—but Steve got his plate number, so we should find out soon enough." I frowned and glanced around. "Where's Mike?"

Something flitted across Kellyn's face as she took a step back. "Um, I haven't seen him." She stepped around me in the direction of the kitchen. "Sit down. I'll make you some tea."

I obeyed and, after pulling my favorite fleece blanket around me, sank back against the leather cushions with a groan. A few minutes later, Kellyn returned with a mug of hot tea and set it down on the end table to cool.

She plopped down on the love seat and faced me. "Okay, now tell me what happened." I filled her in on the highlights of my misadventure with Steve. By the time I reached the end, her expression had hardened. "So, let me get this straight: After being MIA all day, Mike finally shows up at the hospital, brings you home, and then promptly disappears again."

I blinked at her. "Yeah, I guess so."

"Boyfriend of the year," she said, rolling her eyes.

"I didn't expect him to answer." I shifted uncomfortably. "He was at work all day."

She lifted a brow. "And all night?" My shoulder twitched in a barely discernible shrug. "Plus, why isn't he here now?"

I sighed. "Are you going somewhere with this?"

Kellyn hesitated for a few beats before leaning forward to grab a section of the Sunday *Record* she'd haphazardly folded and left separate from the rest of the newspaper. Without a word, she held it out to me.

"What's this?"

She shook her head. "Just read it."

I grabbed the paper and leaned back against the couch. It was a page of several news briefs from the metro section. I scanned the page. "Which 'it' are you referring..." My voice trailed off when I saw the headline. "Oh."

ARSON SUSPECTED IN FIRE THAT LEFT CPD DETECTIVE HOMELESS

At approximately 7:15 p.m. Saturday, the Colsboro Fire Department (CFD) responded to a residential fire on the city's northeast side. Although they eventually gained control of and were able to extinguish the blaze, the house was deemed a total loss.

"We found evidence of an accelerant, which leads us to believe this fire was purposely set," said CFD Lieutenant Timothy Jenkins. "However, we can't definitively state this was arson until fire investigators take a closer look."

Colsboro Police Department (CPD) Homicide Detective Natasha Sardelis, who was renting the property, was not home at the time of the fire. A next-door neighbor noticed smoke and reported the fire at 7:02 p.m.

"Thank God she wasn't home," said Glen Ritter, 43, who called 911. "I guess there's one good thing about all these murders happening."

The murders in question, which Sardelis is rumored to be investigating, have occurred at various locations across Colsboro and its contiguous counties over the past several months.

Record crime journalist Jennifer Gibbs has been following this string of homicides since late May and was first to suggest they had all been committed by one individual—although CPD officials have neither confirmed nor denied the theory. Most recently, Gibbs reported on the suspicious death of Record sports reporter Tori Phelps on Friday, dubbing it the serial killer's sixth victim this year. (For more coverage, please visit www.cboro-record.com/crime.)

Attempts to reach Sardelis for comment were unsuccessful, though a source at the CPD said she was "understandably upset, but would be staying with a colleague." The source would not comment on whether the fire could be linked to the murder investigations.

I read the article three times, my jaw clenching tighter with each read-through. Finally, I took a deep breath and let it out slowly, noticing vaguely that the ache in my ribs had subsided somewhat. Dropping the paper on the end table, I calmly picked up my mug and took a sip of my tea, aware that Kellyn was watching me.

She leaned closer to inspect me. "Are you all right?"

I smiled coolly at her. "Of course."

Her brows sank, wrinkling her forehead. "That's the voice you use when you're trying to keep your head from exploding because you're so mad."

"My head almost never explodes." My face twitched from maintaining the fake smile.

"But you are mad."

"Hey, it's Captain Obvious," I said, the sarcasm seeping through despite my best efforts to contain it. "The superhero of the conspicuous."

"I knew it." Kellyn nodded definitively. "You're mad."

"Of course I'm mad!" I snapped, slamming my mug down on the table so hard that tea sloshed over the edge. "But when I'm mad, I want to flail and yell and punch things, and I know that's going to hurt—" Cutting myself off, I closed my eyes and took a few more deep breaths. When I opened my eyes, my voice was serene again. "So I'm trying to stay calm."

"Did they give you any good painkillers at the hospital?" Kellyn asked. "It might make you feel better enough to flail and yell and punch things, or at least not care as much."

I let out a pathetic whine and dropped my head back against the couch cushion.

"Look on the bright side. You hate Natasha, and her house burned down. Maybe it's karma."

"Except karma forgot to take into consideration the possible repercussions. Like—oh, I don't know—where she would live after burning her house to the ground."

"Well, it could be bad karma."

"I've had quite enough of that, thank you very much."

Kellyn grinned mischievously. "Maybe you were a murderous dictator or a Republican in a previous life."

"Yeah, I'm sure that's it." I lifted my head and blew out a sigh. "I'm not being logical. Of course he wouldn't have told me about it last night. I'd just been in a car accident. I was shaken up and hurt and exhausted."

"Fair," she conceded. "But where is he now?"

"I don't know," I said irritably. "Maybe he's picking up breakfast or decided to attend mass for the first time in five years."

"On the off chance he's not picking up breakfast, I can make you something to eat." She sent me a questioning glance. "Are you hungry?"

I considered. "Yes," I said, realizing I hadn't eaten in about twenty-four hours. "Famished."

As Kellyn hopped off to the kitchen, glad to be doing something useful, I sank farther into the couch and let my thoughts drift into the deep end.

Although Mike inviting Natasha Sardelis to stay with him was troubling, especially if he neglected to inform me, it wasn't the worst part of the situation. The implications went far beyond housing arrangements.

Fact one: Her house burned down, and arson seemed likely.

Fact two: The fire had been reported at seven o'clock—the precise time of my meeting with the killer.

It wouldn't surprise me one bit if someone hated Sardelis enough to burn her house down, but at the exact time I was meeting a serial killer? No. Someone had wanted to keep Mike occupied last night to ensure I was alone. That someone was the killer—that much was obvious. There was only one question left.

Was Sardelis in on it?

《 》

MIKE RETURNED AROUND FIVE O'CLOCK with Murphy and a take-out bag of Kentucky-fried comfort food. Kellyn and I had spent the afternoon watching movies and avoiding topics that required higher thinking. At first, I had difficulty reining in my thoughts about Mike and Sardelis, but another pain pill made everything much easier to forget about.

Until he arrived, sans duffel bag, and reconfirmed what I already knew.

I frowned up at him as he bent to give me a kiss on the fore-head. "You're not staying tonight?"

His brows sank as he straightened. "Unfortunately, I have an early day tomorrow," he called over his shoulder as he took the food into the kitchen, Murphy trailing hopefully behind. "I don't want to wake you when I have to leave at the ass crack of dawn."

Kellyn exchanged a skeptical glance with me. "I wouldn't worry about that. Thanks to some killer prescription narcotics, Jen's been conked out most of the day."

"Good, she needs some extra rest." He rejoined us in the living room and sat down next to me. "I don't want to risk it. You've been through a lot the last few days."

It was hard to argue with that, but I stuck out my lower lip in a pout anyway.

His shoulders drooped. "Don't give me that face."

I tilted my head to one side and sniffed. "But what if I need help?"

"That's what Kellyn's for."

"Yeah," she muttered. "I sell medical supplies for my husband. I'm practically a doctor."

"But what if I need help in the shower?"

He was quiet for a few beats, then shook his head. "Nope, not gonna give in. I'm standing firm."

I settled back into the cushions and sighed deeply. "I actually would like some help."

Mike appraised me for a few beats, the crevasse in between his eyes deepening. Finally, he gave a nod. "After dinner."

The three of us ate in the living room, replacing conversation with the second half of It's A Wonderful Life. Murphy situated himself on the floor between me and Kellyn, knowing full well that we were the weakest links. I sneaked him several nibbles of chicken, half my biscuit, and a few green beans to round out his meal.

Once we were finished and the movie was over, Mike gathered up the dirty dishes, took them to the kitchen, and began rinsing them.

"Mike, don't worry about those," Kellyn called to him. "I'll clean up." She leaned closer to me and lowered her voice. "He's got some explaining to do, after all." She jumped to her feet and bolted for the kitchen before I could even open my mouth to respond.

"Thanks." He turned off the faucet and dried his hands on a towel before returning to the living room. "Well, Calamity Jane," he said, holding his hands out, "would you prefer a bath or a shower?"

I placed my hands in his and allowed him to haul me upright. "Bath. It requires less energy."

"As you wish." He pulled me gently into my room, closed the door behind us, and flipped on my nightstand lamp. "I shall go draw your bath. You, m'lady, get naked."

After he disappeared into the bathroom, I shuffled to my bed and sank down on the edge. I'd only moved from the couch once since I collapsed into it late this morning, and I was annoyed to find myself a bit winded after the long journey from the living room. I managed to wriggle one arm out of my sweatshirt by the time Mike returned.

"I'm stuck," I said pathetically.

He stifled a smile and closed the distance between us in two strides. "I guess this wasn't a ploy to coerce me into staying." He eased the sweatshirt off. "I'm a little disappointed."

"Sorry." The hoodie muffled my voice, making me sound even more pitiful. "I don't have the energy to devote to lost causes that I typically do."

Mike picked up my arm and pulled the cuff over my hand, followed by the rest of the sweatshirt. "Don't be sorry." He tossed the garment to my bed and smoothed my hair. "None of this is your fault."

To his—and my—utter surprise, I burst into tears. "Yes, it is," I wailed. "The whole thing was my idea. None of this would have happened if I hadn't suggested meeting him last night."

He dropped to the bed next to me and squeezed me to him. "I know, honey. We picked up Tori's computer today, and we read the messages."

I sniffled. "You did?"

"It wasn't your fault," he repeated. "You saw an opportunity, and you took it. If anyone's to blame, it's me. I should have been there."

"But—"

"No buts. This one's on me, and I'm sorry." He leaned back and wiped away the tears on my cheeks with his thumb, smiling down at me. "And now I have to stay, don't I?"

I let out an unexpected laugh. "That would be nice."

"Okay." He gently straightened me so I was sitting upright and rose to his feet. "Ready for that bath?"

Nodding, I took a deep, calming breath and blew it out slowly. Mike helped me to my feet again, led me into the bathroom, and closed the door to keep the heat in.

"Arms up," he said, and I complied so he could ease my t-shirt over my head. When I emerged, he was staring at me with an unreadable expression. "Jesus."

"What?" I asked hoarsely.

He lifted a hand and touched my left collarbone. "You're really hurt."

Uncomfortable, I glanced down at myself as he traced the purple line that ran diagonally across my torso. "It's just a flesh wound," I said lightly, summoning a British accent. "I'll be fine."

His Adam's apple bobbed as he swallowed. "I'm going to get this guy, Jennifer. I promise you that."

I rose up on my tiptoes and gave him a kiss. "I know."

Neither one of us spoke much while he helped me bathe, but I could tell by the way his jaw had tensed that he was struggling to keep his anger in check. I felt too vulnerable, too exposed, to say anything that might unleash it, even if it weren't directed at me.

After I was out of the tub, he helped me dry off and dress in a fresh set of pajamas. While he retreated to the kitchen to make some chamomile tea—and maybe punch a hole in a wall—I wove my wet hair into a sloppy braid, took a pain pill, and crawled into bed. He returned ten minutes later with two steaming mugs and Murphy, who hopped up on the bed and plopped down at the foot with a contented sigh.

"Before you fall asleep," Mike said once he was situated next to me, "there's something I should tell you."

A mix of emotions swirled in my chest, and I braced myself for the news about his new roommate. "Okay, shoot."

"Steve recorded the plate number of the driver who ran you off the road. We got a hit."

I blinked at him, nonplussed. "And?"

"And I need you to promise not to interfere. You have to let me handle it."

"Well, of course," I said, as if it were obvious. "Handle the hell out of it."

"One more thing." He paused to extract the mug from my hands and placed it on the nightstand next to his. "You should know, the only reason we've got this guy is because of what you did yesterday—"

"Omigod, Mike, who was it?"

He took a breath, blew it out, and met my eyes dead on. "Gavin Baratti."

THREE YEARS AGO
COLSBORO, OHIO

"I'M NOT GOING HOME," I told Gus, crossing my arms over my chest. "I'm fine."

He rolled his eyes at me from behind his desk. "You almost cried when Peterson bumped into you at the staff meeting."

"I did not," I said, indignant.

Gus sighed. "Gibbs, you were in a car accident. It's normal to not be fine. You're just a regular human like the rest of us."

Accident was a definite understatement. A few days ago, a cowardly driver had run a stop sign, T-boned me in the middle of an intersection, and took off into the sunset. Missing the stop sign could have feasibly been an accident, but the whole fleeing-the-scene-of-the-crime thing sure wasn't.

I shot Gus a dirty look as I eased into a chair, stifling a wince. "You don't know that."

He smirked but didn't comment on my obvious discomfort. "Go home, Gibbs. Superhuman or not, if you haven't found the guy in the last ten months, you're not going to find him today."

The guy he was referring to was the latest homicidal maniac who thought sending me photos of his victims would be his ticket to fame. After the murders I'd followed in Chicago, I was a bit concerned about what this said about me, but I figured it said more about him—namely, that he was a psychopath.

"Your faith in me is inspiring."

He snorted. "To be fair, there's only six hours left."

I heaved a dramatic sigh. "Fine, I'll go, but you've gotta help me up."

He grabbed a pen and turned back to the stack of copy for Saturday's paper. "Get out, Gibbs."

I hauled myself out of the chair, returned to my desk to collect my things, and shuffled out of the newsroom. Truth be told, I was pretty sore—which was a secret between me and God—but it wasn't anything I couldn't handle. Jane the Jetta, on the other hand, had left this world for car heaven.

I arrived home to find Gavin pacing from one end of the kitchen to the other. At the sound of the front door, he whirled around, eyes wide. "You're home early."

I raised a brow. "So are you."

"Are you feeling alright?"

"Spectacular." I dropped my purse and keys on the table by the door. "Gus sent me home. What's your excuse?"

Gavin rubbed the back of his neck, glancing away. "Oh, uh, I had to..." His sentence trailed off when I joined him in the kitchen, standing up on my tiptoes to give him a kiss, but he jerked away before I could. "Can I get you anything? Tea? Pain pill?"

Dropping my heels back to the floor, I frowned up at him. "What's going on?"

He reached for the kettle and yanked the lid off. "Nothing," he said, filling it up with water. "I mean, uh, something, but—" He replaced the lid and dropped the kettle heavily onto a burner, but didn't flick the knob to light the gas. "Maybe you should sit down."

"Gavin, I'm fine." I took a few steps closer and reaching out to touch his shoulder. He jolted, a cartoon character who's been taken by surprise, and pushed past me, putting the dining room table between us. "Are you?"

He'd been acting strangely for the past couple of weeks, and the behavior had intensified since my accident on Tuesday. I'd wondered if the reality of getting married was finally setting in, but Gavin wasn't the freak-out type. Gavin was the type who carefully weighed decisions before acting. Not very romantic when the decision in question was proposing marriage, but at least I'd never doubted it was what he wanted.

"Yeah, I'm okay." He tugged on his earlobe. "I mean—no. I'm not." He gripped the back of a chair until his knuckles turned white. "We need to talk."

"What's wrong?"

Too agitated to stand still, he released the chair and strode into the living room pace. I leaned a hip against the kitchen counter, allowing him several feet of space. I crossed my arms over my chest and waited, trying to look casual despite the wisps of panic rising in my gut.

"Something happened. I don't know how—" He stopped abruptly at the opposite side of the living room and scrubbed his face with his hands, back to me. "I don't know how it happened."

"Gavin," I whispered, my heart rate kicking up a notch. "Whatever it is, we'll figure it out. We can—"

"No, we can't," he blurted, turning around to finally meet my eyes. "I slept with someone else."

Frozen, I stared at him for a few long beats, the air thick between us. His chocolate eyes were wide and solemn, body rigid as we both waited for my response.

I let out a short hysterical laugh. "You can't be serious."

A flash of pain crossed his face. "I am."

"I know you." I kept my voice low so it wouldn't crack. "You're not a cheater, Gavin, so what's this really about?"

"Jennifer—" He dropped his head to his chest and clasped his hands behind his neck. "This is real. I'm sorry."

"Why are you lying? What happened to 'dead or alive'?"

When he didn't respond, I bolted forward and pulled his arms down to his sides so I could grasp his hands. He tried to squirm free, and I held tighter.

"Look at me, dammit." I released one hand so I could tip his chin upward and see his eyes. "I know you, Gavin, and I know this isn't you. This. Is not. You." He tried to back away, but I squeezed his hand tighter, curled my fingers around the back of his neck until my nails dug into his skin. "Tell me what happened."

His throat pulsed as he swallowed. "You don't really want to know, do you?"

"Yes, I want to know," I said firmly. "Whatever happened was so bad that you've invented a fake affair, and you can't keep something like that to yourself when we're about to start a life together."

Gavin's face darkened, and he broke free of my grasp. "We are not going to start a life together," he said, in a tone of voice I'd never heard before. He pushed past me, putting several yards between us. "I'm sorry, but this is over."

I pivoted to stare at his retreating back. "Turn around and tell it to my face. Look me in the eyes and tell me what you're saying is true."

A few long beats passed before he complied, and when he did, his face was blank, empty. "It's true, Jennifer. I slept with someone else, and we are over."

I stared at him, every muscle in my body squeezing painfully tighter. "When?"

He blinked. "What?"

"We just set a wedding date three weeks ago," I said, my voice dangerous. "When did this happen?"

He shrugged, the casual gesture infuriating me further. "Does it matter? The end result is the same."

I threw my hands wide. "Yes, it matters, and 'end result' is repetitive!" I sputtered nonsensically. "When—why—dammit, what the hell happened?"

"I told you—I don't know how it happened. I don't know, okay?"

"No, it is not okay. You left Chicago—your job, your friends, your family, your home—to move here, because you wanted us to be together." I crossed my arms over my chest so I didn't take a swing at him. "That's not something you would do if you weren't sure about us."

"Yes, but—"

"And if something were wrong between us, you would have talked to me about it before it got to the point where you—" I clamped my mouth shut, gnashing my teeth together until my jaw hurt.

"Yeah, I should have done that." Gavin's eyes flashed. "But I didn't, and shit happened, and there's nothing you or I can do to change it now."

"So let me get this straight." I held up a hand, as if trying to stop an attack. "It took you a month to work up the nerve to ask me out for coffee. Three weeks to invite me to move in with you after dating two years. Two weeks to decide to propose and move across two states. Nine months to choose a wedding date. And then, after all that, you spontaneously decide to sleep with someone else."

He looked away. "Yes."

I shook my head at him, eyes wide in dismay. "That makes no sense!"

Blowing out a deep breath, he resumed pacing. "Not everything has a logical explanation. How often is there simply no reason for someone's behavior?"

"We're not talking about someone. I don't know someone." Bewildered, I watched him pace; usually he was the calm to my nervous energy. "We're talking about you. I know you. I know there's something else going on. So the question is, are you going to come clean, or do we need to get you a CT scan?"

"I have come clean!" he shouted, whirling around to face me, and I sucked in my breath. "That's what I'm doing right now, but you're not listening." He stepped closer, so close that I had to tilt my head back to meet his eyes, and gripped my arms tightly. "I do not have a head injury. I do not have a brain tumor. I have no explanation or excuse for this, so stop trying to give me one."

He pushed me away from him, released me, and stepped back. We stared at each other in silence for a few long beats as my mind tumbled down a dark path dotted with long-buried memories that were clawing their way back to the surface like zombies. Soon I would pick up this memory—carefully, barely touching it, so I didn't stain my fingers—and dig a hole next to the others to bury it in, the deepest of them all. Imagining it as if it were dead, as if it were rotting in the cold, dark earth, helped me put distance between it and myself.

"Okay." Somehow my voice was calm, normal. "I'm going to give you one more chance to be honest and let me help you. And whatever you say, I swear I will believe you, because I trust you." He stood completely still, not even blinking; I had finally gotten him to listen. The rest would be up to him. "I want you to think about this very carefully, because there is no going back."

This time, he didn't look away. He stepped closer to me, gently took my hands in his, and looked down at me with wide, vulnerable eyes. Relief surged through me as I threaded my fingers through his.

"I love you, Jennifer," he said softly. "And that's why I can't give you another story. I know this is a non-negotiable for you—because of your father, yes, but mostly because you have too much self-respect to accept it. Because you are confident and you know what you want, and you should have it. Because you are an amazing person, and you deserve someone equally amazing." He shook his head, eyes glistening. "I can't take that from you. I've already taken enough, and that's something I have to live with for the rest of my life. So I have to let you go."

A heavy silence fell, and the wave of relief I'd felt seconds ago froze into a barren tundra. Biting the inside of my cheek to keep from showing any emotion, I dropped my eyes and pulled my hands out of his, brushing past him as I strode toward the stairs. I made it to the bedroom without falling or screaming or exploding into a thousand sharp pieces.

At least, not on the outside.

CHAPTER 11
PRESENT
COLSBORO, OHIO

ON MONDAY MORNING I SLEPT late again—apparently Mike had turned off my alarm clock and called in sick on my behalf—and spent most of my waking hours on the couch, avoiding reality with trash TV and more pain meds.

But before the drugs further fogged my brain, I devoted a few minutes to calling Orlando for another favor, which I knew would probably require more time and caution than usual. When Kellyn got home from work, she presented me with a carton of chocolate chip frozen yogurt and an annoyingly sympathetic expression.

"I'm sorry about Mike." She switched on the end table light, temporarily blinding me, and sat down on the coffee table. "Want me to let the air out of his tires? Or Natasha's?" She wiggled her eyebrows. "Or both?"

I grunted and forced myself into a sitting position. "He didn't tell me."

Her lips formed a surprised O. "So, he just gave you a sponge bath and left?"

"He stayed, at least until I passed out."

"And left her alone in his apartment?"

"Presumably." I raked a hand through my hair, which was a mess of disorderly curls. "I guess my pathetic state outweighed hers."

"Is he coming back tonight?"

I picked my phone up off the end table and glanced at it. No new messages. "I haven't heard from him today." I slid my eyes back to hers. "I'm guessing he and *Nat* are interrogating their new suspect."

"Omigod." She grabbed my free hand, eyes wide. "They caught the killer?"

"They caught the guy who ran me off the road."

Kellyn frowned. "Isn't it the same guy?"

I blew out a breath and shrugged. "Theoretically."

"Why aren't you more excited?"

"The narcotics dull my senses," I said.

"But—"

"It was Baratti," I interrupted, and she gasped. "The car that ran me off the road was Baratti's."

Her mouth opened and closed a few times before she responded. "I should have gotten the full-fat ice cream."

《》

"IT WASN'T HIM," MIKE INFORMED me when he called later that night. "Baratti was in Chicago."

I was quiet for a few beats. "Are you sure?"

"Reasonably," he said. "He flew out late Wednesday morning and came back last night. Had a friend drop him off and pick him up at the airport."

"What about in between?"

"We couldn't account for every minute of every hour," he said, "but he stayed with family, who vouched for his whereabouts Saturday night."

"As they would."

"It's a pretty solid alibi, even without them. With them, it's even stronger. Apparently the Barattis are a well-respected family in Chicago—" He paused to clear his throat. "Which I suppose you already know."

I let the remark slide by without comment. "He didn't rent a car and drive back to Colsboro?"

"A number of people not biologically related to him confirmed seeing him that evening," he said. "Trust me, Jennifer, I've covered every possible angle. Unless he has a twin or can fly faster than a 747, I just can't see how it could've been him."

I rubbed my temple, not yet sure how to react. "So his car was stolen."

"And then put back into his garage with a nice big dent in the front passenger-side door."

"Any prints?"

"Clean."

"So where does that leave us?"

Mike blew out a breath. "Back at square one."

《》

TUESDAY MORNING AFTER KELLYN DROPPED me off at work, I found a cellophane-wrapped gift basket and a padded yellow envelope on my desk. Eyeing the deliveries suspiciously, I dropped my purse into my bottom drawer and slid off my coat. I had a pretty good idea what was in the envelope—not specifically, but I assumed it was Tori's clue.

Not ready to face it yet, I shifted my attention to the basket and untied the scarlet ribbon that held it closed. Inside was a bottle of red wine, a box of chocolates, a bag of mixed nuts and dried fruit, and a small white envelope. Curiosity piqued, I extracted the envelope and sank down into my chair to read the hand-written note.

They say wine and pain meds don't mix, but I think that's a conspiracy. Hope you feel better. Kenny.

"What the hell?" I muttered. Unable to come up with a logical answer, I slid the card back into the envelope and buried it at the bottom of my purse. I now faced a moral dilemma: To drink the wine and eat the chocolate would represent a betrayal to Kellyn, but not to would represent a betrayal to wine and chocolate. After a few beats of contemplation, I shoved the basket under my desk and out of my mind.

While I waited for my computer to boot, I stared at Tori's empty desk. Unexpected tears pricked my eyes, and I blinked rapidly as my vision blurred. The past few days had been such a whirlwind that it hadn't had a chance to sink in.

Tori was dead, and it was my fault.

I grabbed my mouse with numb fingers and sifted through my emails until I found a message entitled "Number Six," buried under three days of other unread emails. I mechanically opened the message and gaped at the photo of Tori, my mind unable to process the information. I sent the image to my printer and closed out of the message.

Taking a deep breath, I hauled myself to my feet and trudged into the conference room to update the clues chart—but it was gone. Wavering between screaming and sobbing, I marched to Gus's office and burst in, sending the door flying into the wall with a crash.

"Where is my murder board?" I demanded, annoyed to hear a quiver in my voice.

Gus glanced up at me briefly. "I knew there were going to be meetings in there for most of the day, so I had it moved."

"Where?"

"Gibbs, I'm in the middle of something here. Can you give me five minutes?"

"No."

He eyed me for a few beats, then yanked open his desk drawer and fished out a set of keys. "Come on," he said, rising to his feet. "I'll show you."

I retrieved my case files from my desk before following him up the stairs to the mezzanine, pretending not to notice how he slowed his breakneck pace so I could keep up. Once we made it to the top, he led me down the balcony that overlooked the newsroom and stopped in front of a door a few offices down.

"I figured you might need to get away from those nosy reporters," he said, inserting a key into the doorknob and turning. "So I moved your board up here." He pushed the door open, stepping out of the way so I could enter.

Shuffling over the threshold, I glanced around the office—large desk, cushy chair, widescreen iMac, an entire wall of windows overlooking downtown Colsboro. It was the epitome of professional accomplishment in a small Ohio city, and it was undeserved.

"What's this?" I asked, my voice scratchy.

Gus jiggled the key off the ring and held it out to me. "Your new office," he said. "Once you catch Tori's killer, that is." He smiled ruefully. "Thought you might need a pick-me-up today—not to mention some damn peace and quiet."

When I made no move to take the key, he dropped it on the desk and gave my shoulder a light squeeze on his way out, closing the door behind him. I stood still as an ice sculpture for a long time. When my arms started to ache, I dumped the files onto the desk and deflated into the chair. I couldn't call them mine yet. Because I didn't know if I wanted this anymore.

《》

ALTHOUGH I WASN'T IN THE mood, Christine forced me to go out for lunch with her. Worse still, she made me walk the three blocks to Brenen's, insisting the fresh air and exercise would be good for me. After we ate and closed out our checks, the gray sky split open and released a cold downpour.

"As long as it took us to get here, we'll be well on our way to pneumonia if we walk back through this," she said, pulling out her phone. "I'm ordering an Uber."

I had no protests, though it took longer for the car to arrive than the trip itself. The driver dropped us off as close to the door as possible, and Christine dashed inside without a second thought, leaving me to trail behind. When I eventually pushed my way through the revolving door, she stepped in front of me, blocking me from going any farther.

"I made it this far," I said as she grasped my arms. "I think I can manage to get to the elevator."

"Don't look, but Gavin's here." She slid her eyes from me to the security desk and back again. "Do you want me to cover for you while you make a run for it?"

I snorted. "You remember the walk to lunch, don't you?"

"Yes, it was very slow. But avoiding him might be stronger motivation than food."

The truth was, I'd been expecting him to show up at some point today. Avoiding him would only compel him to get creative and ultimately result in undesirable long-term effects—like him finding out my phone number or address—and my motivation to dodge that bullet was stronger than my urge to delay an inevitable conversation.

"I'm a big girl." I extracted myself from her grasp. "I can handle it."

Nodding, she took a step back. "Want me to stay?"

"Thanks, but I don't think he'll do anything inappropriate in the middle of the *Record* lobby."

"Fair." She glanced toward the security desk, where Baratti was arguing with the guard, his back to us. "In that case, you'd better go break that up, before he lands himself back in an interrogation room."

I sighed, thanked her for lunch, and dragged myself across the lobby to intervene. The guard caught sight of me as I approached and waved me over. "Okay, Hunter, what's the problem?"

He gestured to Baratti, who immediately calmed down at the sound of my voice. "This gentleman has been blacklisted, but he refuses to leave the premises."

"Blacklisted?" I asked, frowning. "We have a blacklist?"

"Yes, ma'am—"

"Who put him on the blacklist?"

Hunter glanced down at his clipboard. "A Detective Mike Demarco. Called yesterday morning when you were out." He swiveled to glare at Baratti. "Said he was wanted for questioning in connection with a hit and run."

Baratti opened his mouth to defend himself, but I spoke up before he could. "He's been questioned and, as you can see, released. Can you please un-blacklist him?"

"Afraid I don't feel comfortable doing that without confirming he's been cleared." He reached for the phone on the desk and eyed Baratti suspiciously. "Don't do anything stupid."

I grabbed Baratti by the arm and hauled him into a relatively quiet corner of the lobby. "What are you doing here?"

"You had a busy weekend, and I wanted to check on you." He looked me up and down, as if reconfirming I was in one piece. "How are you feeling?"

"Kind of like I found my colleague's dead body, fell down the stairs, and then got hit by a car."

He winced. "That wasn't me, Jen, I swear—"

"I heard."

"But do you believe it?"

Unbidden, my mother's words whispered across my memory—*He has no reason to see you again, but if he does...Be careful.*—and I hesitated. Only for a few seconds, but he noticed. He opened his mouth to argue, but I spoke first.

"You were in Chicago," I said wearily. "You couldn't have also been here, running me off the road."

He shoved his hands into his jacket pockets and swallowed nervously. "Is that the only reason you believe it?"

"Does it matter?"

"It does to me."

"Why?"

"Because I—" He paused and looked down at the tiled floor, and I knew he was sifting through his vocabulary for a convincing explanation. "I need you to believe me." He lifted his eyes back to mine. "To trust that I would never purposely hurt you."

I let out a humorless laugh. "Historically speaking, you and I both know that isn't true."

He ran a hand across his cleanly shaven jaw. "Technically, you're right, but—"

"Technically?" I interrupted. "What other way could there be?"

"Look, the thing is—" He cut himself off and shook his head, frustrated. "If you really believe I could have done this to you, you're going to focus on proving that I did, and you'll be caught off guard again when..." His voice trailed off.

"When what?" I asked, deadpan. "When he comes back to murder me?"

Baratti took a deep breath and let it out slowly. "Yes."

"Thanks for the advice, but I won't be caught off guard again."

"Listen to me, Jennifer." He stepped closer and gripped my shoulders, and I was annoyed he had caught me off guard despite my assertion he wouldn't. "Him running you off the road wasn't an attempted murder. That was a warning."

"What makes you think that?"

"Trust me or don't, but you have to trust yourself," he said, ignoring my question. "And trust your instincts, because they're always right. They will keep you alive."

I frowned. Chad had said the same thing to me last week. Did Baratti have an underlying message, too? Were they both trying to tell me the same thing? I opened my mouth to ask, but Hunter was crossing the lobby, ready for a fight.

"Sir—" he called, his voice echoing against the high ceiling.

Baratti swung his gaze toward him and held up a hand in a stop gesture. "I know, I know. I'm going."

Hunter halted about three feet from us but didn't retreat.

He turned back to me, dropping his hand heavily on my shoulder. "I understand why you can't trust me." Baratti lowered his voice. "I'm sorry, Jennifer, for everything." He stepped backward, releasing me, and watched me with wide, dark eyes. "And I won't bother you again."

Without waiting for a response, he pivoted on his heel and strode away, pushed through the revolving doors and out of my life, without looking back.

Again.

《》

I SPENT THE REST OF the afternoon reanalyzing the updated murder board, alternating between pacing and staring out the window as my mind warred over which problem to focus on: Mike and his new roommate, Baratti's thinly veiled warning, Tori's brutal death, or the serial murderer lurking nearby.

Eventually I gave up and let my thoughts run rampant. By the time Christine appeared in the doorway with Mike in tow, the rain clouds had forced night to descend earlier than usual, and the street lamps seven stories down had flicked on to compensate.

"I brought you a gift." Christine gestured toward Mike and plopped down in one of the chairs facing the desk. "Sorry it's not wine."

"Congrats on the new office." Mike smiled at me as he removed his coat and draped it on the back of the empty chair. "Does this mean you got the promotion?"

I shook my head. "Gus was trying to isolate me so I didn't make anyone cry."

He chuckled and leaned in to give me a kiss, which ended up on my cheek when I turned away. "You okay?" he asked uncertainly.

"Peachy. It's been a wonderful day."

"You did get an office on the mezzanine," Christine pointed out in an attempt to lighten the mood.

Mike grabbed my hand before I could pace back to the window. "What happened?"

A few beats of silence passed before Christine answered for me. "She's upset about Tori—and her Vicodin has probably worn off."

"True," I said. Although after the incident in the lobby and Baratti's ominous warning, I'd decided not to take any more pain meds, worried they might do more harm than good. "And I'm having a hard time being objective about this one."

"I understand." He slipped a hand around the back of my neck and massaged with his fingertips. "Let's go home, open a bottle of wine, and relax for a bit. Then we can figure it out together."

"Before you sneak off in the middle of the night again?"

His eyes sharpened as he studied me. "Chris," he said, keeping his gaze glued to my face. "Can we have a few minutes?"

"Sure." She eyed me warily as she rose to her feet. "Holler if you need a mediator."

Once the door clicked shut, Mike let a few beats of silence pass before speaking. "You're not going to like this."

I sank down into the desk chair and swiveled to face him. Resting my elbows on the armrests and clasping my hands over my belly, I sent him an expectant look. "Hit me."

"I wasn't entirely honest with you about where I was Saturday when you called," he said carefully. "I was with Nat, but we weren't at work."

Despite the fact that I already knew this, my heart plunged sickeningly into my toes. I covered my nerves by sending him a sarcastic smile. "God, I love stories that start like this."

"It's not like that." He held his hands up as if surrendering. "Her house burned down."

I pressed my lips together and nodded slowly. "That's unfortunate." Which wasn't a complete lie; I couldn't have cared less about her house, but the repercussions sucked.

"She's still sort of new to the area, so..." His voice trailed off, and he shoved his hands into his pockets.

"So?" I asked, raising my eyebrows. No way was I going to make it easier for him.

"So, I invited her to stay with me." He shifted his weight to his other foot. "Just for a little while, until she can find an apartment. A week at most."

I watched him, forcing myself not to blink or look away. "How odd that her insurance doesn't cover lodging in the event of a fire, flood, or other miscellaneous act of God, and that every hotel room in the metro Colsboro area is booked for the next week." I smiled humorlessly. "At most."

Mike sighed and ran a hand over his hair. "Jennifer, I'm just trying to do the right thing. What would you do if Baratti's house burned down?"

I laughed. "The right thing is asking another woman to move in with you and lying to your girlfriend about it?"

"I didn't lie. I just omitted—"

"Lie by omission," I cut in. "And if Baratti's house burned down, he'd be on his own. Because, among other reasons, he's a grown-up and can find his own damn place to live."

Mike's eyes flashed, the first sign of exasperation. "Are you sure about that?"

"Well, if he's not a grown-up, he's a very convincing fraud, particularly with that fake medical license."

"That's not what I meant."

Annoyed, I pushed out of the chair and resumed pacing. "I know that's not what you meant," I snapped, "but it was an asinine question. There's no way in hell I'd invite my adulterous ex-fiancé to move in with me, especially when I'm in a relationship with someone else." I whirled around to glare at him. "And if I did, how would that make you feel, three days later when I finally told you?"

"Maybe you wouldn't invite him to move in with you," he said, ignoring my question, "but you're still seeing him. I know he stopped by today. Hunter called me."

"*He* stopped by. I didn't invite him."

"My neglecting to mention this to you is no different from your neglecting to mention him to me." He laughed sardonically. "Except, of course, that you've slept with Baratti."

"Three years ago!" I exclaimed, throwing my arms wide. "And it's not like I'm seeking him out; he just keeps showing up."

"Because you let him." Mike folded his arms across his button-down shirt. "Are you sure you don't still have feelings for him?"

"Omigod," I said, threading my fingers into my hair. "We are not having this conversation again."

"I don't hear you denying it."

"Again, you mean? We talked about this last week."

Glancing away, he ran his palm along his jaw. "I believe what you said was I didn't have anything to worry about," he muttered. "Not that you didn't have feelings for him."

I rolled my eyes dramatically, making my head ache. "I'm pretty sure those things are mutually exclusive. If I had feelings for Baratti, you definitely would have something to worry about."

"Or maybe you don't plan on acting on your feelings."

"You're absolutely right," I said from behind clenched teeth. "I don't. It's been a struggle, but I've managed to ignore my feelings of wanting to kick you in the shin."

"What do you think is going to happen, Jennifer?" he demanded. "Do you think that because she's staying with me for a few days, we're going to sleep together? Is that really how little you trust me, after a year and a half?"

"No." I squeezed my eyes shut and rubbed my temples, trying to ease the throbbing. "It's not that."

"Then what is it?" he asked, his voice softer.

I dropped my arms and opened my eyes. "I trust you, but because of what I've gone through, I'm paranoid. And the fact that you didn't tell me right away makes it worse."

Mike let out a long sigh. "I'm sorry I let you down." He grasped my arms and gently pulled me closer. "How can I make it up to you?"

"Throw her out."

"It's forty degrees outside."

"She'll be fine," I said with a stiff shrug. "She's cold blooded, anyway."

He studied me for a few beats. "You don't like her."

I gave him a wide-eyed look of mock awe. "Gosh, Mike, you should be a detective."

"Why didn't you tell me?" His brows drew together in confusion.

"Because you would've started tiptoeing around the subject and omitting things—kind of like you are now—and I would've gotten paranoid and started to wonder, and when I start to wonder about things, I have a tendency to go off in the deep end." Annoyed, I shook my head. "You know this. I'm like a dog who's lost a bone; I get obsessive and start sniffing around."

"Yeah, I've noticed." Mike released my arms and ran a hand over his hair. "So what do you want me to do?"

"Um, throw her out," I said irritably. "You already asked me that."

He parked his hands on his hips. "Seriously, Jen. Do you want me to get a new partner?"

I shook my head. "That would make you resentful of me."

Not to mention it would become a helluva lot more difficult to watch her. Keep your friends close; keep your enemies within spitting distance.

"Okay, then what?" He stared down at me, raising his eyebrows as he waited for an answer. "What can I do to fix it?"

I blew out a poof of air. "I don't know, Mike."

"Well, then, I don't know what else to do," he said, holding his arms out.

Swallowing hard, I strode to the window and stared blindly out at the rain-drenched city. "Just go."

He blinked, taken aback. "Are you serious?"

"With everything that's happened over the past few days, I can't think logically right now, and I don't want to say something I'll regret."

"Like what?" His voice was edged in barely controlled anger. "Like we're done?"

I whirled around to face him. "No! Of course not." The back of my eyes began to sting, and I blinked rapidly. "I just need to clear my head."

He snatched his coat from the chair and spun toward the door. "Fine. Let me know when you figure it out."

Before I could say anything else, he strode out and slammed the door behind him. Wincing at the sound, I squeezed my eyes shut and focused on the pounding pain in my head instead of the dull ache in my heart.

CHAPTER 12

BETWEEN THE SELF-INDUCED VICODIN EMBARGO and my dog-with-a-bone tendencies, I didn't sleep much Tuesday night. When I dragged myself out of the wrong side of the bed the next morning, I couldn't summon enough motivation to care if I arrived late to work. I told Kellyn to go ahead without me and putzed around until nine-thirty, when the Hyundai Elantra or similar mid-sized rental car I'd ordered yesterday was dropped off.

When I arrived at the newsroom with a heavily doctored mug of strong coffee in hand, I opted for my desk in the bullpen rather than the mezzanine office, which was entirely too quiet. Today I needed some background noise to keep my mind from wading back into the deep end of the pool.

While my computer booted up, I drew out Tori's photo and forced myself to study it. Compared to the other vics' photos, this one was a completely ordinary headshot, set slightly off-center against a nondescript blue background. Tori looked straight at the camera, unsmiling and eyes wide, her skin pale in the light of a camera flash. There was nothing else to go on—no props, no hidden message, no stolen jewelry. It could have been a BMV photo.

With a sigh, I pulled out the padded envelope, slit it open, and tipped it upside down. When nothing fell out, I peered inside to make sure I wasn't about to be stabbed with a Swiss Army knife or stung by an angry hornet. At first glance, I thought the envelope was empty, but when I turned it over, I saw a white rectangle stuck to the other side.

I fished out a narrow piece of slippery white paper printed with faded block text. It wasn't completely illegible—I was able to decipher the words TAXI, FARE, and CHICAGO—but getting any detailed information off it would be tricky, if not impossible.

Until then, back to the haystack of case files I went, to search again for the elusive needle.

When I got to Gina Hadley's file, I paused. The murder weapon had been a broken bottle of Loch Ness Monster Scottish Ale, which Mike had said was from a microbrewery in the Chicago area. And now I had what appeared to be a receipt from a cab ride in Chicago.

The obvious conclusion was that the killer was from Chicago as well. As far as clues went, this was minimally more helpful than the killer's gender; after all, I'd been operating under the assumption this was the same killer I'd followed during my stint at *The Chicago Sun-Times*.

So how was this receipt a clue?

"Yo," Christine said, plopping down on top of my desk and jolting me out of my analytical trance. "What are you doing here?"

I leaned back in my chair and appraised her. "I work here. Same as you."

She crossed one leg over the other. "I mean, why aren't you upstairs in your shiny, new office?"

"It's too quiet." I snagged a pen off my desk so I had something to fiddle with. "Besides, it's not really my office."

"Is it currently occupied by anyone else?"

"No, but—"

"Do you have a key?"

"Yes, but—"

"Well, then, it's yours." Glancing down at my desk, she spotted the edge of Tori's photo underneath the stack of files and wiggled it out to inspect it. "This is nothing like the other photos." Her voice had lost its usual levity. "Do you think it's not gruesome because he knows you knew her?"

I frowned and thought it over. Laura Garrett's photo had been fairly tame as well, and I knew her—not well, but there was an obvious connection through my mother. "Interesting theory," I mused, "but I doubt he'd sacrifice his own satisfaction just to spare my feelings."

"You're probably right." Blowing out a breath, she returned Tori's photo to the bottom of the stack. "What's the clue?"

I fished out the receipt and handed it to her. "Useless is what it is, until I can sweet-talk Miguel into working his magic."

Christine squinted down at it. "Chicago Cab Company," she read. "Maybe you shared a cab with him."

"That would certainly narrow down the suspect pool if I'd asked for identification from everyone I shared a taxi with."

"Ooh, better yet, what if he was a cab driver?"

I pursed my lips as I thought it over. "That would be a helluva way to vet your victims."

"He'd be able to isolate them easily."

"And if not, he'd have their addresses to track them down later."

She let out a low whistle. "Contact the cab company and find out if they have a record of the ride." Her face scrunched up in a grimace. "Assuming Miguel can enhance this enough to make it reasonably legible."

"And if not?"

She shrugged, placing the receipt back on my desk. "Ask for a new clue."

I laughed. "Good idea. Why didn't I think of that?"

"Hey, that's what I'm here for." She smirked. "Harebrained ideas you're too logical to concoct on your own."

"I will take any ideas, harebrained or otherwise." Leaning forward, I pulled out Chelsea Quinn's file and sifted through until I found the photo the killer had sent me. "What's your hare brain say about that?"

Christine swallowed as she studied the photo of Quinn's bare chest, carefully dotted with red puncture wounds that oozed blood down her ribs. "Do four-letter words count?"

"I'd prefer more descriptive words, if you have them." I twirled the pen in between my fingers. "I've been able to at least figure out what the other clues were, if not necessarily their meaning—like the cocktail napkin, the playing cards, and the beer bottle. But this one has me stumped."

"Probably because the mind fixates on the dead body," she said under her breath.

"Accurate."

"So, you need to remove the dead body so you can see the clue."

I fought an amused grin and failed. "Another brilliant idea."

Sliding off my desk, she snatched a sheet of paper from my printer, layered the paper on top of the photo, and then lifted them up to the light.

"Hold these," she ordered.

I stuck my pen behind my ear and rose to my feet to comply. "Yes'm."

Once she'd handed them over to me, she whirled around and plucked a Sharpie from my pencil cup. I watched in amazement as she drew a black dot on the paper over each puncture wound in the photo. When she was finished, she capped the marker and tossed it back on my desk.

"Voila," she said, smiling smugly. "How d'you like me now?"

I beamed at her. "You, my friend, are a harebrained genius."

She gave a little bow, then snagged the pages from my fingers. "Now, let's see what we have to work with."

Smiles fading, we fell silent as we inspected the diagram, comprised of five large dots connected by half a dozen smaller dots. Together they formed what resembled a lopsided, upside-down Y. Christine rotated the image a few times so we could study it from different angles, but nothing clicked.

"Got any more harebrained ideas?" I asked, shoulders slumping.

She blew out a sigh. "I'm working on it."

We scrutinized it for a few more beats. "Could it be Braille?" I suggested.

"Doubt it. No way this guy is blind."

"Fair." I straightened as an idea crossed my mind. "Hey, hold it up to the light again, except without the photo behind it."

She tossed the photo onto my desk and lifted the paper toward the ceiling. "Now what?"

I took the pen from behind my ear, removed the cap, and poked a hole through each of the five bigger dots. The fluorescent lights shone through the holes like stars against a night sky.

"I'll be damned," she breathed. "It's a constellation."

I dropped back into my chair and jiggled the mouse to wake my computer. Christine peered over my shoulder while I searched the internet for constellations, and we sifted through the image results until we found one that matched.

"Cancer," she said as I clicked on the corresponding website. "The crab."

"The dimmest of all the constellations of the zodiac," I read aloud, "it is sometimes referred to as the dark sign." I snorted. "Seems appropriate."

Christine leaned closer and read over my shoulder. "Cancer birth-dates fall between June twenty-first and July twenty-second, and they're most compatible with Capricorn and..." She glanced down at me. "Taurus."

"That doesn't mean anything," I said, waving a hand dismissively. "There's no way this guy believes in astrology, and even if he does, there are a thousand million other Taurus women in the metro Cols-boro area aside from me." I frowned. "Including Kellyn."

"But he's not sending a thousand million other women pictures of his murder victims." Straightening, she folded her arms over her chest. "Just you."

«»

A POKER-PLAYING CABBIE FROM CHICAGO who drank Scottish ale, ate at expensive restaurants, and had a summer birthday wasn't something I could search for in the white pages. Until I had more information or an epiphany, I needed a new tactic.

That new tactic was exposing Natasha Sardelis.

I left work early and drove to Drake Security to hunt down Orlando, who had agreed to go on a scavenger hunt after I'd exaggerated my damsel in distress status. Forty-eight hours had passed since my request, and my patience was running on fumes. If he didn't have anything by now, I was going to put his head through a wall.

When I strode into the lobby, the poker-faced receptionist—who looked like he'd be more at home working as a strip club bouncer—greeted me with a cordial grunt.

"Mr. Drake is expecting you." He hooked a thumb over his shoulder in the direction of glass door labeled AUTHORIZED STAFF ONLY. "Take the staff elevator down to the basement."

"He's waiting for me in the basement?" I asked dubiously. "That's not at all suspicious."

"The shooting range is in the basement."

"That doesn't help."

He attempted to smother an amused grin. "The whole building is under twenty-four-seven video surveillance." He swiveled his widescreen computer monitor toward me, then clicked on the top left square of the grid to enlarge it. "See? No chainsaw murderers or boogeymen."

"How fast can you get down there if one shows up?"

He winked. "Faster than a speeding bullet."

Minimally reassured but not wanting to look like a sissy, I thanked him and rode the elevator down to the basement. I stepped out into a small anteroom stocked with various equipment and lined in concrete but for the wide window overlooking the range beyond. A couple of burly black-shirted men milled about on the other side, oblivious to the pop-pop-pop of gunfire. Taking a deep breath, I donned a pair of goggles and earmuffs, pulled open the heavy door, and strode in.

One of the burly men directed me to lane two, where Orlando stood still as a sculpture, his back to me as he fired one round after another. Once the clip was empty, he ejected the magazine and put it and the gun down on the table before turning to me.

"You say you're not psychic," I yelled, "but do you have eyes in the back of your head?"

He laughed. "I have no hair. You'd know if I had eyes in the back of my head."

"Omniscient, then?"

"Observant," he corrected. "I make it a point to be aware of what's going on around me at all times."

"Smart. So, why are we meeting in a gun range?"

"Thought you might like a change of scenery from the bar." I stuck my tongue out at him, and he grinned. "Besides, we're less likely to be overheard here."

"By each other?" I shouted.

Orlando picked up his gun, quickly reassembled it, and shoved it into the holster on his hip. "Come with me," he said, tapping my arm before sliding past me and out of the booth. I followed him out of the range and back into the anteroom, where we removed our gear and waited briefly for a couple of guys to disappear into the elevator.

I eyed him with a barely suppressed smile. "All this mystery makes me think you found something interesting."

"Don't get too excited." Orlando leaned a hip against the window and crossed his arms over his chest. "We're dealing with a cop here. I thought it prudent to take extra precautions."

My brows sank. "I'm getting mixed messages. What did you find?"

"She's clean—"

"You made me come down to this sensory overload chamber to tell me she's clean?" I exclaimed.

He held up a hand. "Hang on a minute. Her record is clean, but I did find something you might be interested in."

Appeased, I nodded once. "Go on."

"She's from the Chicago area—"

"Wait, what?"

"You know, that big city where you used to live and this little fairytale began?" Orlando said dryly.

"Yeah, I'm familiar." I shook my head. "It's just a helluva coincidence."

"Mind if I continue now?" he asked, and I waved a conciliatory hand at him. "As I said, she's from Chicago. Grew up with four siblings in an unstable household."

"Demon worshippers?"

The corners of his lips twitched. "More than a few reports of domestic violence against her father. Nothing stuck, though.

"Anyway, she got into some trouble at school in her teen years," he continued. "Bullying and fighting, mostly, and a few instances of stealing. She cleaned up her act when her father died. Eighteen months later, she applied to the police academy."

I mimed falling asleep. "Wake me up when it gets interesting."

"Patience, grasshopper," he said mildly. "Couple of years after graduating from the academy, she met a filthy rich guy and conveniently managed to get herself knocked up."

I gaped at him. "She's got a kid?"

He nodded. "His family was concerned about appearances, so they had themselves a lovely shotgun wedding. They'd been married for a few years when—"

"Ooh, let me guess what happened to him," I interrupted, clapping my hands. "When he realized he was married to Medusa, he threw himself off his rich parents' penthouse balcony onto Michigan Avenue."

"Close. They got divorced."

"So, where's the kid now?"

"Her ex has full custody. She gave up parental rights."

"Why?" A round of gunfire erupted, and I waited for it to cease. "Call me cynical, but I would think she'd want to keep that paycheck coming."

Orlando glanced out the window. "Your guess is as good as mine. However—" He turned back to me and straightened to his full height. "It happened shortly after she transferred to homicide."

"Maybe they didn't want to risk putting the kid in harm's way," I mused. "All it takes is one psycho to follow you home from work."

Orlando's obsidian eyes sparkled. "You would know."

I gave him a drop-dead glare. "Bite me."

"Anytime." He winked and moved on before I could protest. "Now, this is where it gets really interesting. After that, Sardelis was instrumental in apprehending a serial who tortured and raped his victims before killing them in creative and grotesque ways. You may have heard of them, since you covered them for the *Sun-Times*."

My eyes bulged. "She collared that guy?"

"In collaboration with her partner."

"Austin Fletcher, right?"

"They got a lot of credit for that bust," Orlando said. "I'm surprised you worked with him and never encountered her."

I clicked my tongue against the roof of my mouth as I contemplated. "Chicago P.D. is huge," I pointed out. "Plus, if I were her C.O., I sure as hell wouldn't want her anywhere near the media with her inability to play nice with other humans. Wouldn't do any favors for their public image."

"Rumor has it she was one mistake away from getting fired when she miraculously caught the killer."

"How convenient." I crossed my arms over my chest and leaned my back against the wall. "Is it also a coincidence that now she's here, following the same killer I am—again?"

"Might be intentional. Colsboro P.D. could've brought her in specifically for this purpose, given her experience."

I stared at him, deadpan. "I'm sure Chicago and every other city in a five-hundred-mile radius has thousands of more experienced detectives Lockwood could have brought in."

He was quiet for a few beats. "I know you're friends with half the CPD, but you have to be careful with this one. You can't ask a cop to investigate another cop unless you don't want to keep it a secret."

"Why do you think I'm here?" I asked, eyes narrowed. "I mean, you can't even express uneasiness when a cop invites his female partner to move in without starting a cold war."

"I presume you're referring to Demarco?"

I let out a sigh. "Sardelis' house burned down on Saturday night."

Orlando's brows arched slightly. "And now she's living with him."

"Yep."

"Babe." He gave me a pained look, lifting one large hand to rub the top of his head. "Please tell me that's not why you asked for a background check on a cop."

"Orlando, the fire occurred at exactly the same time I was supposed to meet the killer," I said, and gave him the full run-down of the night's events. "I got suspicious. The fact that she's now living with my boyfriend is just the cherry on top of the whipped cream on top of the hot fudge on top of—"

"Okay, I'm familiar with what's in a sundae." Orlando held up both hands in surrender. "So this isn't just a jealousy thing?"

"I'm not jealous," I said, sounding defensive even to myself, and he lifted an eyebrow. "Pissed off and paranoid, maybe. Hurt, yes." I pushed away from the wall and dropped my hands to my hips. "Not jealous."

"Right. So now that we've established this is definitely personal, what was the other reason?"

"A gut instinct brought on by years of training and experience in investigative journalism."

Orlando studied me for a few beats. "D'you think she's working with the killer?"

"At the very least, he's using her," I said. "But now that I know she's from Chicago P.D. and worked the same cases..." Voice trailing off, I shrugged. "There are striking similarities between these murders and the ones in Chicago."

"Except for one minor problem. What was it, again?" he said, scratching his chin in mock thought. "Oh, yeah. They caught the guy."

"They caught a guy. Doesn't mean it's the guy."

He let out a short laugh. "Not only do you think Sardelis arrested the wrong person, but you also think the same perp committed both series of murders—with five hundred miles and three years between them?"

"Okay, I know it sounds about as realistic as a herd of unicorns, but hear me out." Snorting, he gestured a hand as if inviting me to continue, and in between bursts of gunfire, I filled him in on the crime scene photos. "There are only a few people who knew about them, then and now," I concluded. "I didn't mention them in any of my articles, and I didn't report them to the police."

Orlando shook his head in disbelief. "You didn't report them," he repeated. "Are you trying to get yourself killed?"

"Um, I don't think so."

"If the journalism thing doesn't work out, you can have a job at Drake. Reckless abandon and an aptitude for risk taking are job requirements."

I narrowed my eyes at him. "Not the point."

He nodded. "The point is your ridiculous theory."

"A serial killer in my ex-fiancé's car ran me off the road a few days ago." I waved a hand. "Ridiculous is the new norm."

He ran a palm along his jaw, eyes drifting downward. "Other than the photos and the fact that women are being creatively murdered, are there any other similarities you've seen?"

"No," I admitted. "I can't connect them."

"When did Sardelis transfer here?"

My eyes slid skyward as I thought it over. "April, I think."

"And when did you start receiving photos again?"

"Late May."

He reached past me and tapped the button to call the elevator. "If Sardelis arrived before the murders began, that blows the consultant theory out of the water," he said in a low voice. "So that leaves either one hell of a coincidence, or..." Pausing, he glanced down at me. "Maybe you're actually on to something."

I wiggled my eyebrows up and down. "Not such a ridiculous theory after all, is it?"

"There is a slight chance it is not." The elevator doors slid open, and Orlando motioned at me to go first. He remained silent until we were inside and on our way to the top floor. "We need to do more research to confirm."

"We?"

"Your resources are limited," he said. "You're right—you can't ask around about this."

"I know," I agreed. "Now would be a good time to reveal you are psychic after all."

When the doors slid open, he launched himself into the foyer, and I trailed behind him. "So that means you're going to have to surveil her yourself." He dug a set of keys out of his pocket and rifled through them as we approached a door at the end of the hall. "You're dating her partner, so you won't come off as suspicious when you invite her to a slumber party."

"That's going to be tricky since Mike and I aren't speaking."

He jammed a key into the door handle and sent me a sideways glance. "I'd lend you a white flag, but I'm not in the business of surrendering."

I sighed. "Point taken."

"Until we find out what we're dealing with, you need to be very careful with her—even if Demarco's around." The lock clicked, and he pushed the door open, flipped on an overhead light, and led me into a small storage room lined from floor to ceiling with shelving. He scanned the neatly organized shelves until he found one labeled "GPS - WEARABLES" and pulled out a plastic tote.

"I'm beginning to see how you came to be omniscient," I said dryly as he placed the tote on the floor and peeled off the lid. "Technologically advanced stalking."

Grinning, he sorted through the box. "Not stalking," he corrected. "Security management."

"My bad."

Orlando handed me a small box before replacing the tote's cover and lifting it back to its assigned shelf. "This," he said, wiggling the lid off the box to reveal a square-faced watch with a thick silver band, "is more than an ordinary watch."

I let out a faux gasp. "I did not see that coming."

"Not only can you use it to make calls, presuming your phone is within range," he explained, smirking, "but it also has a built-in GPS tracking device."

"Naturally." I eyed the gadget suspiciously. "What's 'within range' equate to?"

"Three hundred feet, give or take." He gave me a quick rundown of the watch's features and instructions for syncing it with my smartphone. "Do you want me to set it up for you?"

I scoffed. "I'm a Millennial. I think I can handle it."

"Set it up tonight and start wearing it at all times." He replaced the lid and peeled a sticker off the back, which he slid into his pocket. "And remember, I'll be watching."

I dropped the box into my purse. "I'm not sure if I should feel nervous, creeped out, or reassured."

"Reassured, definitely." His smile faded. "I hope we don't need it, but as the old adage goes, it's better to be safe than get brutally murdered. Especially when we're dealing with a serial killer who's taken a liking to you."

I couldn't come up with a cheeky remark or clever argument, so I merely nodded. Whether my theory was on base or totally off, we both knew the likelihood that I'd come face to face with a killer wasn't just good.

It was likely.

«»

ORLANDO SENT ME HOME WITH a file of Sardelis' background information, and I spent the remainder of the evening sifting through it, accompanied by a gargantuan glass of wine. The next morning, I continued my research from the newsroom, but I swapped out my adult beverage for a similarly sized coffee.

So far, I'd found nothing to back up my theory. Like Orlando had said, there was no real evidence that Sardelis had done anything illegal, let alone frame an innocent man for murder. Just a big pile of coincidences.

And a deep-seated gut feeling that something was off about her.

Despite what Orlando thought, this wasn't based on jealousy; I'd had this feeling since the moment I met her, months before she'd weaseled her way into my boyfriend's apartment. And if what every-one had been saying about my instincts was true, it would be a mistake of epic proportions to ignore it, especially when the stakes were this high.

With the thought, I took a deep breath and forced myself to call Mike. Time to wave the white flag, probably via voicemail.

"Hey," I said, surprised when he picked up on the second ring. "You answered."

"After last weekend, I figured it would be prudent." His voice was neutral. "Everything okay?"

"Of course." My tone went up on the second syllable, an obvious clue I was trying too hard to be cheerful. I cleared my throat and started over. "Well, no. I mean, I'm okay, but..."

Mike blew out a breath. "Yeah. Me too."

"This whole silent treatment thing really sucks." Agitated, I picked up a paperclip to fiddle with. "How would you feel about not doing it anymore?"

"I could get on board with that. Have you been able to clear your head?"

I let out a short laugh. "Not remotely—though refraining from prescription narcotics has helped."

"You're feeling better, then?"

"Yes. Not one hundred percent, but better." I pried apart the paperclip so it resembled an exaggerated S. "I'm clear headed enough to know that I'm sorry. I hate the way we left things."

"I'm sorry, too. I should have told you about Natasha immediately."

"Maybe, but I understand why you didn't."

"And I understand why you were upset."

"It was all just—" I sighed. "Terrible timing."

He laughed. "To say the least."

"And before I talk myself out of it, I think I might've made a snap judgment about her. I should at least give her a chance to prove me right—or, you know. Wrong."

A few beats of silence ticked by. "Really?"

"Well, I know it doesn't happen often," I said lightly, "but I've been known to eat my words on occasion."

"No offense, but I hope this is one of those rare times."

"Me too." I was only half lying.

"Thanks, Jen, this means a lot." His voice was lighter, as if a weight had evaporated, and my guilt deepened. "Do you have plans tonight?"

"Hmm," I mused. "Do I?"

"As a matter of fact, you do. Dinner, my place?"

"You're not working late?"

"Assuming no one's murdered in the next few hours, I can make it happen." He paused, and a muffled voice filtered over the line. "Listen,

I need to get back to work, but I'll call you this afternoon after I talk to Nat, and we can figure out the details, okay?"

I swallowed a bunch of feelings, not the least of which was annoyance. "Sure. Love you."

"Yep. We'll talk later." Then he hung up.

I went back to my research with renewed enthusiasm.

《》

A BRIEF TEXT MESSAGE FROM Mike later that afternoon confirmed they'd be home—I rolled my eyes at the phrase—around six-thirty. By then, I'd had plenty of time to contemplate and discard several different plans, finally settling on one involving a combination of grand gesture and good, old-fashioned distraction.

At a quarter to seven, I hauled myself up to his second-floor apartment—laden with groceries, a duffle bag, and determination—and kicked the door with the toe of my boot until he opened it. Murphy shoved his way out and sniffed me, tail wagging happily.

"Surprise," I said, a cheerful grin tacked on my face as he stared at me dumbfounded. "I come bearing gifts."

"Wow." Mike looked me up and down. "I was just going to suggest ordering takeout."

"But takeout isn't made with love." I smiled beatifically at him.

His lips twitched. "That's probably a good thing."

"Um, can I come inside? The gifts are kind of heavy."

"Oh, right." Knocked out of his stupor, he bolted forward and relieved me of a few of the grocery bags looped over my arm. "Sorry, long day."

I pushed past him, directing the beatific smile at Sardelis, who was slumped in the recliner. "Hey, Natasha. Hope you're hungry."

She eyed me dubiously as I hobbled through the living room. "I might be thirsty."

I shot her a dazzling smile. "I've got you covered." I strode around the corner into the kitchen and dumped the bags on the counter, with Mike right behind me.

He flipped on the overhead light and placed his bags next to mine. "Have you been drinking?" he asked under his breath, leaning in close.

I rooted around in one of the bags and produced a bottle of red wine, which I handed over to him. "Not yet, but just as soon as you open that, we will be." I gave him a quick kiss before turning away to unload the bags.

He watched me twirl around his kitchen, pulling out plates and wine glasses and preheating the oven. "What's all this?"

"Oh, nothing fancy. Just some tapas—bread, cheese, hummus, some cured meats, and other assorted crudités. Things like that." I sent him a sideways glance. "And wine, if you would be so kind as to open it."

Because wine was integral to my plan. Wine would grease wheels that I didn't have enough finesse or patience to grease myself—at least when it came to Sardelis.

"I see that." He dug a corkscrew out of his silverware drawer. "I meant, what's going on?"

"What? I'm making a gesture." In my peripheral vision, I saw Sardelis slink over and rest her arms on the bar so she could watch us, and I turned to face her. "I don't think it would surprise anyone if I said we didn't get off on the right foot. So, I wanted to remedy that."

Her brows sank. "Why?"

I smiled sweetly at her. "Because you and my beloved are partners." She snorted, but otherwise remained silent. "We're going to be around each other for a very long time, so wouldn't it be nice if we got along?"

"You brought all this—" She gestured toward the containers I'd laid out on the counter. "To make me like you?"

"Nah, this is just phase one." I held out a wine glass for Mike to fill, and then slid it across the counter to her. "Ultimately, I plan to make you like me with my sparkling wit and undeniable charm. And alcohol."

She sniffed the wine suspiciously. "How many phases are there?"

I pretended to count on my fingers. "Seventeen. You're in for a long night, so you'd better drink up."

"If it means that much to you..." With a shrug, she knocked back half her wine.

Mike's eyes widened. "You're not a wine drinker, are you?"

Sardelis held her glass out to him expectantly, a hint of a smile on her lips. "I am now."

CHAPTER 13

TWO HOURS LATER, WE WERE deep into our second bottle of wine, all our wheels were well greased, and Sardelis was beginning to resemble a human. I'd insisted on bringing the food into the living room and gathering around the coffee table—which I thought would be more relaxed than staring at each other from opposite sides of Mike's dining table under a bright light, interrogation style.

"So, Natasha, you're one of only a few women in the homicide unit, right?" I spooned some hummus onto a wedge of pita bread as she nodded from behind her wine glass. "Was it like that in Chicago, too?"

Sardelis lifted a shoulder in a half shrug. "Chicago P.D.'s a bit more balanced than Colsboro, but still, only about a quarter of the entire force was women." She speared a garlic-stuffed olive and popped it in her mouth. "What about you? Can't imagine the media's much better."

I swallowed before answering. "Average newsroom is around forty percent female. Here it's more like thirty."

Mike leaned his forearms against his thighs, wine glass dangling from his fingers. "Explains why you're so damn pushy."

Sardelis pointed an accusatory finger at him. "That is such a typical man thing to say," she declared. "Women have to work twice as hard to even be recognized in the workplace, let alone advance, and as a result, we're seen as pushy." Her mocking tone reminded me of how I used to taunt Jason when we were kids, and I giggled.

"And you know why?" I asked. "It's because we can't pee standing up."

She snorted. "Plus, we get too emotional."

"In our line of work," Mike cut in, stabbing a slice of salami with his fork, "we have to be unemotional to deal with all the shit we see every day."

"It's easier for men, though," I said. "Take the case you're working on now."

"We're," Sardelis corrected, reaching out a fist.

Grinning, I bumped my knuckles against hers. "Take this case we're working on now," I continued. "All the vics are women, and they were all raped before they were killed."

Mike's eyes bulged in incredulity. "You think that doesn't bother me?"

I held up a finger. "I didn't say that."

"Yeah, she didn't say that." Sardelis shot him a scathing look. "Geez, Demarco, just let the woman talk."

He held up his hands in surrender, and I laughed again. "Not used to this, are you?"

"This is a new experience on many levels."

I patted his knee reassuringly before continuing. "Women have a different perspective on rape than men do. For you, it's about—" I waved a hand to indicate he could answer.

"Power and dominance," Mike filled in. "Complete control over another human being."

"Right, but to a woman, it's much worse. It's a fusion of shame and guilt and humiliation." I paused to sip my wine. "It's the highest level of violation imaginable."

Sardelis nodded, her eyes vacant. "For it to be the last thing a woman experiences before she dies..." She shook her head, bringing her wine glass to her lips. "Unforgivable."

Mike exchanged a glance with me. "Nat," he said slowly, "were you—"

Her head jerked up. "No! But that's exactly the point. It's something that every woman can understand simply by virtue of being a woman, but the majority of men never will."

I bobbed my head in an exaggerated nod. "Not only that, but an alarming number of women actually do experience it firsthand."

"One in five," Sardelis said. "One in five women, versus one in thirty-eight men." She turned toward Mike. "You know what that means, Demarco?"

"Sure." He frowned. "Twenty percent."

She let out a humorless laugh. "Twenty percent, he says. What a genius!" She polished off her wine, then reached for the bottle. "That means, of the two of us—" She pointed at herself and then at me. "And, say, all three of our mothers..." She tipped the bottle over her glass to refill it. "Of the five of us, at least one of us will come face to face with a rapist, if we haven't already." She passed the bottle across the table to me and turned back to Mike, whose expression was indecipherable. "That's what one in five means."

"And too often, it's not random," I added. "It's someone we know—maybe even trust."

"A colleague or friend." Her voice was low as she locked eyes with me. "If we're especially unlucky, maybe even a family member or spouse."

Mike seized the wine bottle from my hand. "I'm aware of the statistics." He divvied up the remaining wine between us. "Where are you going with this?"

She shrugged. "Maybe we should take a closer look at the vics' families and social circles," she said, in that arrogant indifference that typically infuriated me. "See if there's any overlap."

"We've looked." Blowing out a sigh, he reached across the table to put the empty bottle back down. "Other than having active online dating profiles, they have nothing in common."

"Well, that's not entirely true." I cleared the lump out of my throat. "They have something else in common. The same killer."

Mike threw a hand up in the air. "We can't even prove that, seeing as though the guy has no consistent M.O., struck in multiple jurisdictions, and doesn't leave any trace evidence."

"Except other people's fingerprints." Sardelis appraised me with sharp eyes. "People linked to you."

My jaw clenched involuntarily, and I took a slow sip of wine. "I'm the common denominator."

"Seems so."

I tapped a finger against the side of my glass, debating. "By that logic, though, so are you."

Mike's brow wrinkled. "How do you figure?"

"You didn't tell him?" I swiped a slice of prosciutto from the platter and bit into it, aiming for nonchalance. "Natasha investigated the same murders I did when I was at the *Sun-Times*."

"I worked a lot of murders in Chicago," she said. "Why would I mention those specifically?"

"No doubt," Mike eyed us both suspiciously. "Awfully coincidental if it's true, though."

Her face remained impassive. "But coincidental all the same."

"Right," I agreed. "That would be tricky to pull off on purpose, wouldn't it?" I smiled as I finished off the prosciutto. "You'd almost definitely need inside help, or a respectable amount of money."

She snorted. "Yeah, I left Chicago so I could buy my way into the Colsboro police force."

"Sounds ridiculous when you put it like that." I tilted my head to one side, as if curious. "So, why did you leave Chicago?"

Sardelis focused her attention on scooping the perfect amount of hummus onto a cracker. "Needed to put some distance between me and my ex-husband. You?"

"My mom was diagnosed with cancer."

"She okay now?" She rolled her eyes before I could answer. "Well, she must be, if her fingerprints were found at the scene of a murder last week."

"Planted, but yes." I selected a wedge of pita bread from the basket. "And your ex?"

"What about him?"

"He okay now?"

"I expect so." She rubbed her temple wearily. "Last I heard, he was living it up in Forest Glen, spending weekends on his parents' yacht on the lake."

I let out a low whistle. "Not too shabby."

"Yeah, well, bully for him." She jammed another cracker into the Brie, which had long ago cooled, and it snapped in half. "Fat lot of good it does me now."

Mike avoided looking at Sardelis as he reached for another slice of salami. "I didn't know you were married."

"I'm not," she said flatly. "I'm divorced."

"Hence the past tense." He folded the meat and stuffed it into his mouth, then rose to his feet. "This conversation calls for another bottle of wine."

After Mike carefully stepped over me and grabbed the empty bottle on his way to the kitchen, I eased myself up off the carpet and took his place on the couch. "Another side effect of being a female police officer?"

"What, divorce?" she asked, and I nodded. "Fairly common for cops in general." She retrieved the rest of her broken cracker from the congealed Brie, sending me a sideways look. "Which I'm sure you know."

I patted Murphy's head absently. "I'm aware of the trend."

Sardelis glanced over her shoulder to make sure Mike wasn't within earshot. "Doesn't that make you nervous?"

I rubbed the back of my neck, uncomfortable with the shift in conversation. "I guess I hadn't really thought about it."

"You're lying. You're all butt hurt because I'm living with Demarco, and you're not."

I jerked my eyes up to hers. "That has nothing to do with whether we get married."

"No?" Her lips twitched in the beginnings of a smirk. "You're afraid it will. You don't want me here, do you?"

Mike breezed back in with the third bottle of wine and stood over us. "Okay, bottoms up."

Sardelis and I obediently drained our glasses and held them out toward him. He refilled them, put the bottle down on the only vacant spot on the table, and nudged Murphy off the couch so he could sit down next to me. Just before his butt hit the cushion, Sardelis snatched her water glass off the end table and held it out to him.

"Demarco, be a pal, and get me some more water." She batted her eyelashes and beamed. "Please."

Letting out a soft sigh, he stood again and wordlessly disappeared into the kitchen with her glass.

Sardelis leaned in closer, lowering her voice. "Tell me I'm wrong."

"About you living with my boyfriend? It's not exactly a dream come true, but I get it. Someone burned your house down, and you have no friends." I swirled my wine and summoned a smug smile of my own. "Any leads on that, by the way?"

Her eyes narrowed slightly. "No." She raked a hand through her obsidian hair. "I don't know. I've been distracted."

"Mm." I plucked another olive from the platter and popped it into my mouth. "Had anything like this ever happened to you before?"

"Nah, I'd never lived in a house before now." She sank back into her chair and sipped her wine. "If you don't have a house, no one can burn it down."

"Other things can be burned down or otherwise destroyed." I swallowed the remainder of my olive. "Motor vehicles. Relationships. People."

"Speaking from experience?"

I snorted. "Yeah, I guess I am." I snagged another olive. "Well?"

"Are you asking if I've been targeted before?" She considered it for a few beats, then let out a short laugh. "Yeah, I guess so."

"Because you're a cop?"

She nodded in thanks as Mike reappeared with her water. "Kind of comes with the territory," she said, sliding the glass back onto the end table without drinking from it. "But you know how that goes, right? I mean, you've got yourself a psychotic secret admirer."

The look Mike shot her could have melted tungsten. "Not necessary."

"Let's be honest here, Demarco." She flipped her hair over her shoulder. "Your girlfriend is a psycho magnet."

Gritting his teeth, he reached for the wine bottle and gave himself a healthy pour. "Why do you have to do this? We were having a nice evening, finally getting to know each other—"

"I know why," I interrupted, keeping my eyes glued to Sardelis.

Something flicked across her face before disappearing just as quickly. "Oh, yeah?"

"You don't want to talk about your divorce." I lifted a brow. "Right?"

Her shoulders dropped, and she let out the air she was holding. "Yeah. You're right."

"All you had to do was say so." Emboldened, I patted her knee lightly, quickly retracting my hand when her eyes narrowed slightly. "No need to project."

"Hell, Nat." Mike ran a hand over his hair. "I'm sorry, I shouldn't have pried."

Her eyes darted back and forth between us. "You're forgiven."

"But if you do ever need someone to confide in, I'm a good listener." I locked eyes with her. "And I protect my sources."

"Sources?"

I waved a hand. "Just an expression among journalists. We take confidentiality very seriously."

Mike threw an arm around my shoulders. "Especially this one," he said proudly. "Never has anything I told her in confidence ended up in the *Record*."

"Wow," Sardelis said with her usual disdain. "What a resounding endorsement."

"Hey." He pointed a stiff finger at her in warning. "I'm sorry it came up, and we're not going to say anything else about it—but just know nothing you tell her will ever come back to me." He slugged some wine. "I know you don't have a lot of friends here—"

"Okay!" She let out a dramatic sigh and slid her gaze skyward in a remarkable depiction of a sullen teenager. "I get it, Demarco. Enough already."

He held up a hand in surrender. "Fine. On that note—" He gave me a kiss on my cheek before rising to his feet. "I'm going to take Murphy on a quick walk."

We fell silent as Mike shrugged into his coat, clipped on Murphy's leash, and sauntered out the door. Finally, Sardelis put her wine glass on the table with a clang and grabbed a couple of dishes.

"I'll clean up," she said sullenly, rising to her feet.

"Hey, Natasha?"

She halted halfway to the kitchen and turned around slowly to face me. Her entire demeanor had changed; her usual arrogance had dissolved into something that looked a lot like defeat. "What?"

"I mean it. If you want to talk, I won't tell anyone."

She held my gaze for a few beats and eventually turned away without another word, leaving me to wonder if my grand gesture would end up being a grand failure.

AFTER A FRUSTRATING EIGHT HOURS of research gridlock, I waved another imaginary white flag and admitted defeat around five-thirty on Friday. The world wide web had proven to be frustratingly narrow when it came to my specific research needs, and everyone I'd sent an S.O.S. to had been out of the office. To top it off, there was nothing but radio silence from Mike, who had evidently been wholly reassured by my satisfactory mental state that morning.

"Want to grab a drink at Press Club?" Christine asked as she waited for me to ease my stiff body into my coat.

"God, yes. More than you know."

Giving me a rueful smile, she turned toward the elevator. "Rough week, huh?"

I zipped my jacket and slung my purse over my shoulder. "You could say that."

Outside, I was surprised to find a light snow falling against the darkening sky, and even more surprised to find Baratti leaning against the side of the building, engrossed in something he was reading on his cellphone.

I halted a few feet away from the door, appraising him with a frown. Snowflakes dusted the shoulders of his wool coat, and there were no footprints across the sidewalk where he stood, indicating he'd been here for a while.

"This is like deja vu," Christine said when she joined me on the other side of the revolving door. At the sound of her voice, Baratti looked up from his phone and pushed away from the wall. "Except this time it's snowing, and he's standing between us and alcohol."

"Yes," I agreed as he strode toward us. "The stakes are indeed much higher."

Baratti nodded hello to Christine and turned to me, face blank. "Sorry to cold call twice in one week. Can I have a word? It's important."

"More important than happy hour?" Christine asked.

His expression didn't change. "Yes."

She let out a sigh and sent me a sideways glance. "I'll save you a seat at the bar."

I nodded. "I'll be there in a few." We watched her stride away in the direction of the crosswalk. "So much for not bothering me ever again."

Baratti shot me a brief glare as he reached into his coat. "Sorry to disappoint you," he said, extracting a letter-sized envelope and handing it to me, "but I thought you should know about this."

Not bothering to voice the questions that flooded my mind, I slid my thumb under the flap of the envelope, pulled out the single page inside, and inspected it. It was an analysis of a fingerprint found at the scene of Tori Phelps' death. Specifically, on a box of rodenticide. More specifically, the murder weapon.

And it belonged to Christine Morgenstern.

"Shit." I raised my eyes back to Baratti's. "Do they know?"

He nodded. "Likely. The lab would've sent the report by now."

"Yet it's a quarter to six, and they haven't shown up."

"Does anyone else know where you two are headed?"

I shook my head. "It was a spur-of-the-moment decision."

Baratti slid his hands into his coat pockets. "If you keep her busy, that'll buy her some time."

"To what end? They'll be able to find her through me."

"Of course." His words were faint against the swish of passing cars. "Because Demarco knows Christine's your best friend, right?"

Nonplussed, I lowered my eyes to the report still clenched in my hand, wondering why Baratti would think Mike, rather than Joey, would be the one to track her down using me. To buy time, I folded the paper, deliberately and slowly, and slid it into the envelope before lifting my gaze to Baratti's. I studied his face for a few long seconds, trying to decide how to respond.

"Chad told me," he said finally.

"I see."

His throat pulsed as he swallowed. "You could have told me you were dating someone."

Giving a slight head shake, I held the envelope out to him. "It doesn't matter when they track her down. She didn't kill Tori."

He plucked the envelope from my fingers and returned it to his inner pocket. "I know that. So do they."

"They're still going to interrogate her." My face hardened as anger crept into my voice. "Just like my brothers, just like my mom, just like you."

"Yes. They have to."

"Meanwhile, the actual killer is still out there." Shoving my clenched fists into my pockets, I turned away again and looked around, as if expecting him to be standing on the other side of the street. "Finding more women to rape and torture and kill. Right now. And they're going to waste time with Christine." I shook my head and let out a dry laugh. "I mean, she probably doesn't even know where to buy rodenticide, let alone how to turn it into a weapon."

Baratti was silent for a few beats. "So maybe you should tell him where she is. Get it over with, so he can go back to protecting you."

I jerked toward him. "That's not what this is about."

"Of course it is," he said, eyes flashing. "I've never seen anyone else work so hard to protect another person—" He cut himself off abruptly and diverted his glare to his shoes.

"Anyone else? What does that mean?"

I waited for him to finish his sentence, but for a few beats, the only sounds were the click of heels as a woman dashed past us, a light honk from a car at the intersection, the buzz of streetlights overhead. But I'd known he wasn't going to finish it.

"Nothing." He swiped a hand across his jaw. "It doesn't matter." When he lifted his head again, his expression was carefully blank. "I'll walk you to Press Club. I think you've left Christine waiting long enough." He waved a hand and turned in the opposite direction.

Frowning, I followed him. "How did you know that's where we were going?"

Baratti glanced down at me briefly. "Oh, come on," he said, as if scolding me. "Just because we broke up, doesn't mean my memory was erased." He let out a short laugh. "Though sometimes I wish it had been."

"Yeah." I blew out a breath, increasing my pace slightly to keep up with him. "Me too."

Automatically, he slowed, and we magically fell into step with each other. It was startlingly easy, and we both pretended we hadn't noticed.

"Are you—" Baratti cut himself off and drew in a deep breath. "Are you happy?"

I looked up at him; his face was momentarily obscured by the white cloud of his exhale. "I suppose Chad didn't tell you about that part?"

"No, he did." We came to a stop at the crosswalk, and he pressed the call button to trigger the signal before turning toward me. "I wanted to verify it for myself."

I leveled my gaze with his. "When are you going to realize you can't repeatedly commit emotional suicide?"

"What's that supposed to mean?"

"It means stop sacrificing yourself for other people, and think about your own needs for once," I spat. "Do you honestly think it's going to make you feel better to know if I'm happy?"

"Yes."

"Why?" He opened and closed his mouth a few times without vocalizing anything, and I nodded. "My point exactly."

His expression hardened, and he stepped closer to me. "Maybe it's what I deserve. Maybe watching you be happy with someone else is my punishment."

"Jesus, Baratti." Agitated, I raked a hand through my hair. "It's been three years. Don't you think it's time to forgive yourself?"

"Have you forgiven me?"

I shook my head and looked away. "I don't know."

"How am I supposed to forgive myself, Jennifer, if you haven't?"

The traffic light changed, and the crosswalk sign lit up. Without waiting for an answer, Baratti stepped out into the crosswalk, and I grudgingly followed.

"I'm not exactly the foremost authority on forgiveness," I told him, hurrying to keep up. "I mean, look at me and my father—"

"He neglected you and your brothers from the minute you were born, cheated on your mother literally right in front of you, guilted you into keeping it a secret, and added writing monthly child support checks to his secretary's job description so he wouldn't be bothered with it." Baratti snorted derisively. "The guy doesn't deserve your forgiveness."

"And what about you?" I pressed a hand to my ribs, a vain attempt to contain the growing ache as we walked faster. "Do you deserve forgiveness?"

"You tell me."

"I just told you I'm lousy at forgiveness."

He stepped up on the sidewalk and took a hard right. "I'll take that as a no."

"Baratti, I've spent the last two and a half years forcing myself not to think about you, and—"

"Two and a half years?"

"Well, I thought about nothing but you for the first six months," I said breathlessly, annoyed at myself for being winded. "I needed a break."

A few yards from the club's entrance, he grabbed my arm and halted abruptly. "You're in pain." He looked me up and down, as if that would confirm his diagnosis. "Why didn't you say anything?"

"Nah, I'm—" I dropped my hands to my hips and took a few seconds to catch my breath. "I'm fine. Just haven't run at all this week, so I'm a little out of shape."

"They didn't give you any pain meds at the E.R.?"

"They did, but I stopped taking them." At his quizzical head tilt, I elaborated. "You freaked me out the other day with your dire warning to stay alert."

"Good." He crossed his arms over his chest. "Have you made any progress?"

"Oh, yes. When it hurts to breathe, that really keeps me on my toes."

Baratti opened his mouth to respond, but before he could, the Press Club door swung open and Christine stomped out.

"So, Detective Demarco just called," she barked, directing her glare at Baratti. "Could that have anything to do with your urgent message?"

He cleared his throat. "Might."

"And you didn't think it was relevant to me?"

"Well, I—" She punched his bicep before he could formulate an answer, and he jumped back in surprise. "Ow," he said pointedly, rubbing his arm. "What was that for?"

"Oh, so many things." She narrowed her eyes. "Unfortunately, I can't go over them with you right now. My immediate presence is requested in homicide interview room four." With that, she marched away, back in the direction we'd come from. A few steps later, she whirled around and held her arms out wide. "Aren't you coming?" she demanded.

"Of course." I sent Baratti an apologetic look. "Um..."

He smiled tightly. "I know."

«»

MIKE WAS WAITING FOR US in the lobby when we arrived at the precinct twenty minutes later. As we approached, I wrapped a hand around Christine's arm and pulled her closer.

"I hope I don't need to tell you this, but don't punch him."

Her jaw tensed. "I can't make any promises."

"At least wait until we're not surrounded by cops and surveillance cameras, okay?"

"I'll do my best."

After signing in and obtaining our visitors' passes, we joined Mike at the elevators.

"Hey," he greeted us, leaning in to give me a quick kiss on the cheek. "I'm sorry about this. I know it's not what we had planned for tonight, but—"

"Hello," Christine exclaimed, throwing her arms wide. "I'm the one who's about to be interrogated."

He raised a brow. "You want a kiss, too?"

"Not from you," she muttered, crossing her arms over her chest.

"Relax, it's not an interrogation." He jabbed the up button a couple times. "She's just going to ask you a few questions."

"She?"

"Well, I can't do it. We're friends. It's a conflict of interest."

Her eyes shrank into slits. "Not anymore we're not."

Mike's lips formed an O. "Harsh."

"Just be glad she's not punching you," I told him in a stage whisper.

The elevator doors slid open and, after the car emptied, we filed in one by one. Mike pushed the button for the fifth floor, stepped back to stand next to me, and slid his fingers through mine. None of us spoke, not until we'd stepped out of the elevator and Mike had led us back to the interview room.

He opened the door and gestured for Christine to go in. "It won't be long," he said. "You want anything to drink? Water, coffee, soda?"

She sank into one of the chairs. "I'll take a skinny double shot sugar-free caramel macchiato, extra hot, no whip." Folding her hands on the table, she gave him a pleasant smile. "Please."

Rather than volley back a snarky comment of his own, he returned the smile and closed the door. "It really is a wonder you two are friends, what with being so different." He tapped my arm. "Come on."

I followed him down the hall to the kitchen. "I wouldn't have gone quite that far. The normal serving temperature would have been satisfactory."

"How considerate." He wiggled a Styrofoam cup off the stack by the coffeemaker and filled it, leaving an inch of space at the top. His hand hovered over a jar containing individual-sized creamers. "One or two?"

"Two. And one of those generic Splenda packets."

He scoffed but followed my directions anyway, and a few seconds later, we were on our way into the observation room, where Sardelis watched Christine through the one-way mirror. She appraised us as Mike closed the door.

"Seriously?" Brow raised, she tilted her head slightly toward me.

Ignoring the comment, he handed her the coffee. "That's for Christine."

Sardelis took the cup, scowling. "What, no caramel macchiato?"

220 « KRYSTEN BENNETT

"Unfortunately, our imaginary barista is on vacation," he said. "You may want to step back when you break the news to her, unless you want to wear that coffee."

"Thanks for the advice," she said dryly. "Anything else?"

Mike planted his hands on his hips. "Remember she's not a suspect. We're just covering our bases."

Sardelis rolled her eyes and pushed the door open before disappearing into the interview room.

Exhaling heavily, Mike dropped his hands and pivoted to face me. "I guess I can kind of see why you don't care for her, but she's not that bad once you get to know her."

I smirked. "What a convincing review."

He let out a laugh and hooked an arm around my shoulder, pulling me closer. "She's hard to get to know. I'm still working on it."

I tilted my head back so I could see his face. "Do you trust her?"

"If we're going to be partners," he said, smile fading, "trust is crucial."

"Mm." I stepped out from under his arm and faced him. "Sounds like we might be talking about more than you and Natasha."

He kept his eyes on the window. On the other side, Sardelis asked Christine how well she knew Tori. "It bothers me, Jennifer. That you don't trust me."

"Of course I trust you. What happened the other day—" I sighed. "I wasn't being rational."

"Are you sure?"

"Why wouldn't I trust you?" I asked. "You've never given me any reason not to. It's everyone else I don't trust—and that includes Natasha." I slid my hand into his. "And if we're being honest, I'm not convinced you do, either."

"I don't think one person can fully trust another person without a certain level of intimacy." He looked down at me. "Which she and I don't have yet."

I swallowed. "Yet?"

"Not that kind of intimacy." He squeezed my hand. "With cops, there's a baseline of trust you share by virtue of being a cop. But when you're put to the test in a life-or-death situation, that's when you find out how deep it goes. And you either become closer, or you can't be partners anymore."

"And you haven't had any life-or-death situations with her yet."

"Nope." He smiled down at me. "But I've had so many with you, I'm surprised we're not literally joined at the hip."

I grinned up at him. "How awkward would that be?"

"Awkward?" He made a *psh* sound. "Close-range people watching you would become so much easier."

"You may get your wish yet," I whispered, and both our smiles faded.

"No." Mike leaned in and rested his forehead against mine. "We'll just have to find another way, because I'm not going to let another life-or-death situation happen, okay?" He pulled back a few inches. "I promise."

But that's the thing about promises. They inevitably get broken.

CHAPTER 14

AT SEVEN THE NEXT MORNING, I buckled myself into a window seat on a plane bound for Chicago, with Christine sitting next to me. I'd had to make promises just short of offering him a piece of my liver, but I'd been able to persuade Lockwood to grant my favor. When Mike had unsurprisingly asked for a raincheck on our original plans, I'd gone home and spent the remainder of the night booking an expensive last-minute flight and hotel room and prepping for what could be the most important interviews of my career to date.

"So what did you tell the chief?" Christine asked, flipping through the SkyMall catalog.

"The truth." She sent me a skeptical sideways glance. "Well, some of it."

"Did you mention your suspicions about his hiring a dirty cop?"

"I trust Lockwood, but I'm not sure that would stay secret for long." I shifted uncomfortably in my seat. "Until I know more, I'm not making any accusations."

"So what rationale did you give him?"

"I told him my new working theory is the Chicago killer had a partner who wasn't caught."

"And he bought it?"

I snorted. "It's much more believable than my actual theory."

Once we landed at Midway, we took the L orange line downtown, dropped our bags off with the hotel concierge, and walked four blocks to the Sunshine Cafe. First on the agenda was a breakfast meeting with Detective Austin Fletcher, my source for the original Chicago murders more than six years ago.

"Good to see you, Gibbs." He stood as we approached the table and thrust a hand toward me. "How's exciting Ohio treating you?"

I smiled, accepting his firm handshake. "We'll get to that." I gestured to my sidekick. "This is my colleague, Christine Morgenstern."

"I'm the bodyguard," she informed him. "I'm way stronger than I look."

Fletcher let out a bark of laughter. "I guess that answers my next question." We made small talk while we waited for the server to bring coffee and take our orders. Once she was gone, Fletcher's expression sobered. "So, you've got yourself a serial."

I pulled a thick accordion file out of my tote bag and placed it in front of me. "Yes, and there are a number of similarities to a string of murders you and Sardelis investigated about six years ago."

He raised a brow. "Solved or unsolved?"

"A guy by the name of—" I consulted my notepad. "Gary Rogers was convicted for the murders of Hannah Percy, Bethany Collins, and Yvonne Gardner."

His pale blue eyes lit with recognition. "I remember those. Some of the most gruesome murders I've ever seen." Pausing, he lifted his mug to his lips and gulped some coffee. "Glad we got the bastard."

I dumped a French vanilla creamer into my coffee and stirred, mentally steeling myself. "How sure were you that he was the right guy?"

"Sure enough to testify in a court of law—which I did," he said evenly. "Where are you going with this?"

Christine put down her mug. "Obviously we're not as familiar with the cases as you are, but we have reason to think he's still out there."

Fletcher's eyes slid back and forth between us. "Chances are, it's a coincidence—or, at most, a copycat."

"I figured you'd probably say that." I thumbed through the file, extracted the trio of photos from the original murders, and slid them across the table. "Do you recognize these?"

The crevasse between his eyebrows deepened as he stared down at the three images. "Percy, Collins, and Gardner. How'd you get these?"

"He sent them to me."

Fletcher's jaw dropped open briefly. "And you never reported them?"

"I was fresh out of J-school back then, green as the grass on the other side of the fence." I shrugged. "Harvey advised me to keep it under my hat, and I trusted him."

He shook his head in disbelief. "Forgetting for a moment that you withheld evidence in a murder investigation," he said, his voice tainted with disapproval, "what does any of this have to do with your killer?"

I extracted two more photos and passed them over to him. "I got these after I moved back to Ohio four years ago. Look familiar?"

He nodded. "When and where did these occur?"

I flipped through the pages of my notebook. "First one was in December of the same year; second was in the following August. Both in Colsboro, both unsolved."

Fletcher spread out the photos in chronological order in front of him, falling silent for a minute as he studied them. "We arrested Rogers early the next year, so the one in December—" He tapped a knuckle on the first photo. "Could've been him. But by August, his trial had started."

"Was he released on bail?" Christine asked.

He lifted his gaze to Christine. "Judge denied bail due to the heinousness of the crimes. He was in jail the whole time."

"Tell us about Rogers." I pulled a pen out of my bag and clicked it open. "What convinced you he was your guy?"

Fletcher blew out an exhale. "To be honest, I wasn't sold on Rogers as the killer at first. He was guilty of something, that much was obvious, but I wasn't sure it was serial murder."

Christine rested her forearms on the table. "What do you mean?"

"Rogers had originally been brought in as a suspect in a burglary case—several cases, in fact—but they couldn't definitively pin anything on him. Everything was circumstantial." He locked eyes with me. "Sardelis was in burglary before she transferred to homicide."

I frowned. "How'd Rogers become involved in the murder investigation?"

"He was caught on video a couple of blocks from Gardner's apartment within the time frame of the M.E.'s estimated T.O.D.," he said. "Knowing his background, Sardelis insisted on bringing him in for questioning. After the interrogation, we pulled fingerprints and DNA off a water glass he used. Forensics didn't get a hit on the DNA, but his prints were in AFIS from a prior arrest—and they matched some that CSI lifted from the vic's apartment."

I ran a hand along my jaw, frowning. "Why wouldn't he wear gloves?"

"Especially if he was a career criminal who'd already killed two other women," Christine added.

"Both good points," Fletcher admitted. "But what are the odds that he was in that building for a legitimate reason in the middle of the night?"

"Remind me," I said, "where did Gardner live?"

"A high-rise in Gold Coast." I let out a low whistle, and he nodded. "Even if he didn't murder her, he sure as hell wasn't there for an innocent midnight visit. They didn't exactly run with the same crowd."

Christine put her mug down on her placemat. "When did you start drinking Sardelis's Kool-Aid?" I elbowed her in the ribs, and she let out a grunt. "Uh, I mean, what persuaded you he was guilty?"

Fletcher snorted. "Other than the fingerprint? His alibis were so full of holes, they might as well have been fishnet stockings."

When the waitress appeared at his side, laden with plates and accoutrements, he paused and leaned back. After we all had our meals, he thanked her and continued.

"During the first murder, he was at home alone, so no one could vouch for him." Fletcher reached for the salt and sprinkled a generous portion over his eggs. "Then he claimed to be out of town during the second, but he had no documentation to back it up, and his cellphone records showed he was in the city during part of the estimated T.O.D. window. And he flat out couldn't give us an alibi for the third."

I unrolled my silverware and placed the napkin on my lap. "Still plenty of room for reasonable doubt."

He held up an index finger. "Wait, it gets better. In between the first and second murders, he took an eighteen-month contract job in Memphis."

I eyed the photos upside down as I thought it over. "After Collins' murder, I didn't get any photos for almost two years."

"That's because Rogers wasn't here." He tore open the silverware and cut into his omelette ferociously. "He moved back to Chicago less than two months before the third murder."

"Well, that's a little less doubtful," I muttered.

We fell silent for a few beats as we worked on our meals. After finishing his omelette, Fletcher picked up the conversation again.

"A couple of months after Gardner's murder, we renewed our media efforts. Guess that must've been after you left." He paused to gulp some coffee. "A witness came forward, and not only did she positively ID him from a lineup, but all the details she provided matched our evidence—even those that weren't released to the media."

"Maybe she was the murderer," Christine said, her voice as dry as the English muffin she was spreading a thick layer of jam across.

Grinning, Fletcher winked at her before continuing. "Her testimony was instrumental in his conviction. I don't think we'd've been able to nail him without it."

"Don't you find that awfully convenient?" Before he had a chance to respond, I barreled on. "Plus, I'm having a hard time believing he would be careless enough to leave his prints in the third vic's apartment, especially when he didn't leave anything behind at the first two."

Christine gave me a significant look. "Or perhaps someone left them there intentionally."

Fletcher eyed her skeptically. "That's about as plausible as finding a pot of gold at the end of a rainbow."

"You would think so, but—" I popped a strawberry into my mouth and put down my fork. "Not only is he still sending me photos of his handiwork," I said, extracting the last set of photos and dropping them on top of the others, "but he's somehow planting fingerprints of people I know at each crime scene."

He dropped his fork to his plate with a clatter. "Hell, Gibbs. You should've led with that."

I smiled humorlessly. "Just building anticipation, Detective."

"These are the latest ones?" He sifted through the photos.

"Yes. First one was in late May; the most recent one was a few days ago. All in different jurisdictions. All with different M.O.s."

He ran a hand over his hair, letting out a gust of air. "I presume none of these people were anywhere near the scene where their fingerprints were found?"

"Not exactly." I filled him in on the particulars while he resumed working on his breakfast. "Even if they were all physically at the crime scene when police arrived, it wouldn't make any sense. These murders were committed by the same person, despite the obvious differences."

"You didn't report the photos, but did anyone else know about them?"

"A few people I trusted."

"That blows the copycat theory out of the water, but there is another explanation."

Christine smiled sweetly at him. "Like the wrong guy went to prison?"

"Another reasonable explanation." He took a few sips of coffee before continuing. "Rogers could've had a protégé or an accomplice who carried on in his absence."

"Yes." I carefully unwrapped a butter packet and scraped its contents out with a knife. "I agree."

Fletcher reached for the ketchup bottle and gave it a shake. "Sounds like you have a theory."

"I have something resembling a theory." I spread the butter onto my cinnamon bagel. "But you have to keep an open mind."

"Oh, boy." He waved an impatient hand at me. "Let's hear it."

"There is one more similarity." I locked eyes with him. "Natasha Sardelis is investigating these murders, too."

As he stared at me incredulously, a dollop of ketchup slid from the bottle and plopped down on his placemat. Just before another one oozed out, Christine extracted the container from his frozen fingers and put it down.

Fletcher cleared his throat. "I might be hallucinating, but it sounds like you're accusing Sardelis of being a dirty cop."

Christine forced out a laugh. "To her former partner? No way," She waved a dismissive hand. "Wondering is a better word for what we're doing."

He snorted. "And are you wondering if I'm in on it, too?"

"The thought never crossed my mind," I said, frowning. "I've been more focused on how many more people have to die before this serial killer is caught."

Eyes flinty, Fletcher braced his arms against the table and leaned in. "Do you have any idea the damage you could do if you pursue this line of inquiry?" he hissed. "You could ruin her career and mine, not to mention the ripple effect it would have. We're talking about every case we've ever touched being reopened and reexamined under a microscope. Every criminal we have or ever will put away will use this to cast doubt on their guilt. And every hour we put into these closed cases will be an hour taken away from open ones." He straightened and rubbed his fingers along his jaw, as if trying to erase the tension. "And killers like Gary Rogers will get away with murder, so they can do it again."

We stared at each other in silence for a few tense seconds, neither one of us blinking or moving. Finally, I folded my hands in front of me and leaned forward. "Only if I'm right. So, prove me wrong."

He shook his head definitively. "I don't need to. You're the one who needs to prove it." He threw his napkin down and stood. "Thanks for breakfast."

Christine swiveled to watch him stride away. "Well," she said as he pushed his way out the door, "that did not go as planned."

NEXT ON THE AGENDA WAS a trip to the MCC Chicago, a federal prison masquerading as an ordinary building a few blocks from Buckingham Fountain and Millennium Park. Lockwood had hacked through some of the red tape surrounding media visits and waiting periods, but beyond that, I was on my own. After a laborious sign-in process, a guard escorted me to a noisy visitation room.

"That's him there." He pointed to a table in the corner, where a khaki-clad, middle-aged man leaned back in his chair, hands clasped behind his head as he surveyed his surroundings with a casual vigilance. When his gaze brushed against mine, he locked eyes with me and smiled slowly.

Steeling myself, I thanked the guard and wove my way through the tables. "Mr. Rogers?"

He stared at me in mild amusement for a few beats. Finally, he dropped the chair to the floor with a clang and rested his hands on the table. "Mr. Rogers, that's me," he said in a gravelly voice. "And you are?"

I perched on the edge of the chair across from him and met his eyes, a cold gray that matched the cinderblock walls of the visitation room. "You don't know who I am?" I asked, even though I already suspected the answer.

This time, the laugh broke free. "Sorry, but no." His grin widened, revealing a set of slightly crooked teeth. "Should I?"

"I just figured you would, after all the photos you sent me."

"Nope." Clasping his tattooed fingers together in front of him, he raised a brow at me. "All I know is you're a reporter from Ohio."

"Jennifer Gibbs. *Colsboro Record.*"

Rogers grunted as he appraised me, the smile settling into an unnerving smirk. "Tell me about these photos I supposedly sent you. Were they sexy?"

"No. They were rather memorable photos of your handiwork a few years ago."

"Those girls who were murdered?"

"Those girls you murdered."

His lips flatlined, and he sat back in his chair, expression stony. "That's why I'm here." He crossed his arms over his chest, another tattoo peeking out from beneath his left sleeve. "Doesn't explain why you are."

"I have some questions about them."

"That's old news, princess. Already been covered to death." He let out a humorless snort at his pun. "So unless you've got a new angle, there's nothing I can tell you."

I clasped my hands on the table and stared at him, unblinking. "Why'd you do it?"

"Christ." He dropped his arms heavily on the table. "What the hell difference does it make? The girls are dead either way. The reason doesn't mean shit."

I shook my head. "That's not what I meant."

"That's what everyone always wants to know." He leaned in close enough that I could see flecks of blue in his eyes. "And what no one will ever understand."

Heart pounding hard in my chest, I fought the urge to back away from the convicted killer. Instead, I inched a little bit closer. "You're right. I don't understand why you'd go down for three murders you didn't commit."

Rogers blinked as surprise flitted across his face, but it quickly disappeared. His forehead creased while he considered the best response, ultimately deciding on silence. He sat back and crossed his arms over his chest again, clamping his mouth shut.

"I suppose I could understand if the alternative was worse," I said, "but what's worse than going to prison for the rest of your life, and two more on top of that?"

"You have to ask that, princess," he spat, "you'll never understand."

"You've been labeled a serial killer." I watched him carefully as I fished for his secret. "You have no chance of getting out of here. No chance of living a normal life. No chance of being with the person you love or watching your kid grow up." His eyes flickered, and my gut said I was getting close. "Meanwhile, the real killer is out there, living the life you should be living. Seems like an awful waste, doesn't it?"

"You have no idea what you're talking about." The din of conversation surrounding us nearly drowned out his voice. "You shouldn't go snooping around in other people's dirty laundry."

"Snooping around is kind of my bread and butter." I flashed him a tight smile. "But while you're in here pretending to be Jesus for all of mankind, he's still out there, raping and torturing and murdering young, innocent women. Eleven, in fact, that we know of."

He shook his head, shifting his gaze away. "Not my problem, princess."

"Those victims were people." I squeezed my fingers into a fist and pounded the table. "They had friends, families. People who cared about them. They were somebody's little girl." The muscles in his jaw tightened, as if he were gritting his teeth together to keep from screaming at me. "How many more have to die for it to be your problem?"

Without blinking, he leaned forward, until his face was only a few inches from mine. "There's nothing I can do, and if you know what's good for you, princess, you'll stay out of it."

"Is that a threat?"

He gave a curt shake of his head. "A warning."

"I don't need a warning. I'm aware of what's at stake. What I need is a name."

Rogers sneered. "Do you know what happens to snitches in prison?"

"If you cared about yourself, you wouldn't be in here right now," I said evenly. "It's someone out there you're worried about. Isn't it?"

His dull eyes narrowed into slits. "Back off," he said from behind clenched teeth, "or I'll—"

"Or you'll what?"

"I might be stuck in here, princess, but I know people," he seethed. "People who would be your worst nightmare. Make you afraid of the dark. Make you disappear."

"I have a serial killer stalking me." My voice was flat as I met his blazing eyes. "He followed me five hundred miles across two states. He knows who my friends and family are and plants their fingerprints at crime scenes to make sure I pay attention. He sends me souvenirs from his victims and morbid photos of his handiwork, just to remind me he could kill me any time he wanted." I smiled humorlessly at him. "You want to send someone after me to save me from that fate? Make me some concrete boots and dump me in the lake, quick and painless? Go ahead, but remember: I'm the only one who's willing to help you and whoever you're protecting."

A few beats went by, and something in his face changed. "What do you want?"

"Your alibi for the third murder."

He shook his head. "Can't."

Sitting back in my chair, I crossed one leg over the other. "That's the only one where you left a fingerprint behind." I fell silent, giving him the opportunity to explain, but he didn't. "The way I see it, there are three explanations."

His eyes slid skyward. "Can't wait to hear them."

"First," I said, listing on my fingers, "you really did murder those women, and by the time you got to Yvonne Gardner, you'd just gotten lazy or cocky or more stupid."

Rogers' eyes narrowed. "Thanks."

"Second, someone planted your prints at the crime scene," I continued. "Or third, there was one hell of a coincidence, and you really were in Gardner's apartment that night, but for a different—yet no less illegal—reason."

He grunted noncommittally. "You have quite the imagination."

I tapped my forefinger on the table. "My money's on the third scenario, or a combination of the second and third. I find it a little farfetched that you would be careless enough to leave your fingerprints at the crime scene."

"Can someone do that?" Rogers asked, sounding interested. "Transfer a fingerprint from one surface to another?"

"Someone is doing that, Mr. Rogers, in Colsboro. With a little practice, it's surprisingly easy."

"Would you need special police equipment for that?"

"Why would you ask that?"

The crease between his brows deepened as he considered his response. "Just seemed like a logical question."

"I understand why you're reluctant," I said in a low voice. "You're in a difficult position. On the one hand, you could give up your alibi—and along with it, the people you were working for—and potentially get out of here, only to face a different kind of punishment later. On the other hand, the people who could prove it wasn't you and get you out of here—even without your alibi—are the ones who put you here, so you obviously can't trust them." I leaned forward and smiled conspiratorially. "And to answer your question, no, you don't need special police equipment, but forensic knowledge would come in handy."

"What do you want?"

"It's very simple. I really don't want to be raped, tortured, and murdered—which means I need to find this guy yesterday. But so far, I haven't been able to find him on my own, nor have the police." I stared at him with wide, earnest eyes, afraid if I blinked it would ruin my credibility. "But I think you can help me. And in return, I'll help you."

He shook his head slowly. "I'm sorry some sicko's got his sights set on you," he said, sounding genuine. "But I don't know who he is."

"Maybe not. But if I can prove you didn't kill those three women—or at least cast doubt on it—then that casts doubt on the entire investigation."

"Why would that help you find him?"

It was my turn to hesitate. "Because I think he's got inside help. I think he had it then, and I think he has it now."

Glancing away, Rogers ran a hand over his head. "You're talking about that detective, aren't you?"

"What detective?"

Snorting, he swiveled his eyes back to mine. "That bitch who tried to nail me for burglary, then when she couldn't, transferred to homicide and tried to nail me there, too."

I gave him a slight nod. "She's in Colsboro now. Transferred a month before the first murder."

Rogers let out a harsh laugh. "You think she knows who the killer is, and she's helping him?"

"It would explain why they've made no progress in the last six months."

"Why would a cop do that?"

"Glory. Money. Blackmail. Possessed by a demon." I shrugged. "Take your pick."

He scrubbed his hands across his face. "This doesn't change the fact that I can't help you," he said, voice muffled. Finally, he dropped his arms to the table and met my eyes. "I can't give you my alibi. So that means she needs to admit to framing me, or we're both shit out of luck."

CHAPTER 15

THE FOLLOWING NIGHT, I WAS lingering on the edge of sleep when a shrill ring tore into the silence, bringing me back to consciousness with a gasp. It took me a few beats to realize it was my phone. Dragging myself into a sitting position, I grabbed it and frowned down at the screen.

"Who is it?" Mike demanded.

"I don't recognize the number." Groggy, I tapped the answer button and pressed the phone to my ear. "Hello?"

"Sorry to wake you," he said, "but this is important."

I rubbed my eyes with my free hand. "Baratti?"

"Oh." He cleared his throat awkwardly. "Yeah. Sorry."

To my left, Mike sat up straight and flicked on the lamp. I blinked in the sudden brightness, smacking his hand as he tried to snatch the phone away from me.

"How'd you get my number?"

"Uh—I know a guy."

I sighed. "Joey?" He muttered something unintelligible under his breath, which I took as a yes. "What happened?"

"Got a D.B. in Middlebury, and—"

"In Dover County?" I interrupted. "What are you doing there?"

"Nina Woods called me. I asked the M.E.'s offices in the surrounding counties to contact me if they caught any unusual homicides."

"And?"

"And it's definitely unusual." He paused to clear his throat, and I imagined him raking a hand through his brown hair, slightly disheveled from sleep. "I was hoping you could check your email and see if you have a new photo."

I blew out a breath. "Yeah. I'll call you back."

"Well?" Mike asked expectantly as I disconnected. "What's going on?"

I rubbed my eyes tiredly, letting out a long groan before I answered. "Homicide in Middlebury." I opened my phone's mail app. "They're not sure if it's our guy."

He peered over my shoulder. "So Baratti wants to know if you got a photo."

I didn't have to scroll far before I found a message titled "NUMBER SEVEN," timestamped one o'clock—only ninety minutes ago. Neither of us spoke as I tapped on the attachment.

It was a full-length portrait, taken in profile from her left side. She lay supine on a long table underneath a bright overhead light, nude but for a dark cloth draped across her midsection that hung over the edges of the table. Her neck was arched over a tall block that forced her head to dangle downward at an awkward angle. She was blonde and Caucasian, but beyond that, I couldn't make out any distinguishing features.

Mike's exhale tickled across my neck, and I shivered. "Who is she?"

"He didn't say." I closed the email and returned to my call history.

"Forward that to me," Mike ordered as he rolled out of bed.

Baratti answered halfway through the first ring. "Is it him?"

"Yes," I said. "Caucasian, short blonde hair—"

"That's her." He swore under his breath in Italian. "Was she alive in the photo?"

"Looks like it." On the other end of the line, he let out what sounded like a relieved sigh. "Who is she?"

"Rebecca Ramsey. She's a realtor. Lives in Northville. A colleague found her late yesterday in an unoccupied house she was showing in Middlebury on Saturday afternoon."

"Give me the address."

"No. This one is bad."

"They're all bad," I said irritably, "and if you don't tell me, I have plenty of other people I can call."

Not only did Baratti know I was right, but he'd never been able to tell me no. As I ended the call, I wondered what it meant that he still couldn't.

《》

IT WAS ALMOST FOUR A.M. when Mike parked his truck a block away from the flashing lights and yellow tape and cut the engine. As soon as my feet hit the pavement, he grabbed my hand in his, as if afraid I might otherwise wander off.

Once Sardelis had parked and joined us at the scene's perimeter, Mike flashed his badge at the uni, who gave him a salute and held up the tape so we could duck under. About a hundred yards away, we found Baratti outside Ramsey's house with a woman in a medical examiner's jacket, whom I presumed was Nina Woods.

"Detectives," she said in a dry, gritty voice. "Glad you could join us." Without relaxing his grip on me, Mike shook hands with her and thanked her for waiting. She nodded curtly, her gaze darting between the three of us. "Shall we?"

He looked down at me, obviously torn between protecting me from whatever was inside the house and leaving me alone with Baratti and a serial killer lurking nearby. I figured it was probably a toss-up which was worse in his mind.

"Go." I gave him a tight smile. "I'll stay right here."

He gave my hand a squeeze before pulling away, following Woods into the house with Sardelis tagging along behind. Neither of us spoke until they'd disappeared.

Baratti scrutinized me warily. "So, have you and Demarco adopted Sardelis, or have Demarco and Sardelis adopted you?"

I swiveled slowly to face him, eyes narrowed. "Bite me."

He ducked his head to hide his reaction. "Sorry. Just wanted to know if the rumors were true."

"Most rumors contain a modicum of truth," I said flatly.

When he lifted his chin again, his face was carefully blank. "Run into some rush hour traffic on your way?"

"We made an unexpected discovery that slowed us down," I explained, shoving my hands into my pockets. "Apparently Rebecca Ramsey was dating a CPD cop."

His eyes darted away. "Shit."

Neither Mike nor I had voiced the implications of this break from pattern, both of us tacitly hoping it was a mistake: Either Ramsey wasn't a cop's girlfriend, or the killer hadn't known. Deep down, though, we knew it wasn't.

"What did he do to her?" In response, Baratti clamped his mouth shut and refused to look at me. "You know I'm going to find out anyway."

His Adam's apple bobbed as he swallowed. "She was raped and tortured, like the others." A few beats passed before he met my gaze again. "And then decapitated."

I sucked in a gasp and looked away, mind reeling. In the last few months, I'd managed to maintain enough distance between myself and the victims to hang on to my sanity. Although that distance had shrunken considerably in recent days, I hadn't yet panicked. But now I was damn close.

I took a deep breath, held it, and let it out slowly before facing Baratti. He was trying to hide it, but I could see it in his eyes: Fear.

"You're right," I said finally, my voice thin. "This is bad."

《》

I WASN'T SURPRISED THAT AFTERNOON when Baratti let himself in to the conference room, where Christine and I had been holed up for most of the day. He appraised the mess of photos, coffee mugs, laptops, and partially empty carry-out containers strewn across the table as he hung his coat up by the door.

"Is this what mad genius looks like?" he asked, closing the door behind him.

I tossed down the dry erase marker I'd been twirling in my fingers. "This is what the early stages of panic look like."

Christine whirled around in her chair to stare up at him. "What are you doing here? Thought you were blacklisted."

"Apparently not anymore." He pulled out the chair next to me and sat down. "As it happens, I too am in the early stages of panic."

She nodded once. "Fair enough."

"So, what have you found out?"

I handed him a printout of the photo the killer had sent this morning and pushed back my chair. "Miguel's working on enhancements, but the only clue I see is that plaid blanket she's covered with." I rose to my feet so I could pace. "The internet has proved useless in yielding helpful information."

"I did find a nice fleece-lined flannel shirt to order my dad for Christmas," Christine said dryly. "So it hasn't been a complete loss."

Baratti studied the photo for a few beats. "Maybe it's a family tartan."

Christine drummed her fingertips on the table. "Or maybe he lives in a wigwam and dances with wolves."

I shot her an annoyed look, earning myself an unconcerned shrug, before pivoting to face Baratti. "I thought of that. Do you know how many family tartans are green and blue?"

"I'm guessing based on your expression it's a lot."

"A literal shit ton." I flashed him a fake smile. "So it'd be nice if you had something solid to contribute."

Baratti snatched up the dry erase marker and stood. "Woods believes the vic was alive when she was decapitated," he said in the soporific voice he used to distance himself from unpleasant things like death and infidelity. "Good news is, he used a very sharp instrument, so it was quick. Bad news is, he gutted her like a fish first." He popped the lid off the marker and wrote DECAPITATION under Ramsey's cause of death column. "Either would have killed her, but he didn't make her wait long for the decapitation."

A wisp of nausea rose in my throat like smoke. "Murder weapon?"

"He left behind a Lochaber axe." At my confused frown, he added: "An antiquated battle axe. You'd know it if you saw it."

Behind us, Christine tapped the keys of her laptop. "Here we go. A Lochaber axe is a two-handed pole weapon used in Scotland beginning in the sixteenth century." She spun it around so we could see the screen.

Leaning over the table, I scanned the accompanying photos. "And he just happened to have one handy?"

Christine laughed. "Handy."

Baratti sent her an admonishing glare. "In addition to the blade, this particular weapon was also equipped with a spear and a hook." The muscle in his jaw twitched. "I'm not going to explain how he used those, but whatever you're thinking, double it."

I straightened, swallowing hard. "Was it authentic?"

He shrugged. "The lab is analyzing it, but my guess is no."

"It'd probably be difficult to get his hands on a real one," Christine pointed out, "not to mention expensive."

"Both the axe and the tartan have strong connections to Scotland." Baratti turned back to the board to scribble in Ramsey's clue column. "So my guess is this is a hint to his heritage."

Christine stood and appraised me, arms akimbo. "Know anyone who's Scottish?"

"Maybe. Probably." I raked a nervous hand through my hair. "I don't go around asking people I meet what their genetic composition is."

"Right, but I just figured that since he knows you so well—"

"That I know him well, too?" I snapped. "If that were true, we wouldn't be here right now."

Christine held up her hands, as if I had a bomb strapped to my chest. "Don't go off in the deep end yet," she said, her voice unnaturally soothing. "We'll figure it out."

The question wasn't whether we'd figure it out. I had no doubt that we would. At some point, one of us would flip a puzzle piece around and everything would suddenly fit.

The real question was, how many more clues would it take—how many more people would he kill—for us to see the complete picture?

«»

AFTER BARATTI LEFT THE NEWSROOM and Christine went back to her actual job, I spent the remainder of the day mentally arguing with myself over telling Mike my suspicions about Sardelis, until my anxiety was so high I couldn't sit still any longer. By the time he let himself into my condo that night, I was well on my way to wearing a permanent footpath in my living room carpet.

Mike eyed me warily as he removed his coat and hung it up. "Something bothering you?" he asked, flipping the deadbolt on the front door. "You seem nervous."

"Maybe a little."

He stepped over the threshold but left me enough room to continue pacing. "Want to talk about it?"

"Yes." I reached the other side of the room, turned around, and trudged toward him. "And also no."

"Where's Kellyn?"

I gestured toward the hallway. "Upstairs watching TV."

"Go on, then. Rip the Band-Aid off."

I came to a halt a few feet from him and dropped my hands to my hips. "I have reason to believe," I said, slowly lifting my gaze to his, "that Natasha may know more about the killer than she's letting on."

"Like how much more?"

"Um." I raked a hand through my hair. "Like who he is."

He was quiet for a few beats. "You're not serious, are you?"

"Yes, and—"

"Oh, you're not done yet." Laughing humorlessly, Mike shook his head and gestured a hand toward me. "Don't let me—or logic—stop you. Go on."

I narrowed my eyes at him. "Trust me, I don't want to want to be the lunatic girlfriend any more than you want to have one, but here we are."

"We're running that risk either way." He scrubbed his face with his hands. "Might as well keep going." He dropped his arms to his sides. "Let's hear it."

"So, you know last weekend, when I got run off the road, and her house burned down—"

His brows sank low. "Please tell me this isn't because you don't like her staying with me."

"At the same time," I finished, sending him an admonishing glare. "I thought that was a little too coincidental to be a coincidence, so—"

"Maybe it is," he agreed. "But it doesn't mean she knows anything about it."

I crossed my arms over my chest. "Can I get through my whole theory before you start poking holes in it?"

Letting out a sigh, he shuffled over to the couch and sank down. "Fine."

"So, while I was off on Monday, I did some research—"

"Hang on," he interrupted. "You knew about the fire before I told you?"

I gave a dramatic, full-body eye roll. "Mike, it was in the newspaper. Three quarters of a million people could've known about it before you told me. Also, shut up."

Eyes narrowing slightly, he clamped his mouth into a thin line and mimed locking it shut. I waited ten seconds to make sure he wasn't going to protest before continuing.

"Additionally," I continued calmly, "you know she investigated the same murders in Chicago as I did—the ones where the murderer also sent me photos of his vics. The guy she liked for it and eventually helped put away was someone she'd been after since before she'd even transferred to homicide. He was convicted on some shaky evidence, including a fingerprint at the third crime scene." I held up my index finger. "One single fingerprint.

"Her partner wasn't sold on him as the killer," I barreled on before he could interject. "That is, until a witness came forward in the eleventh hour and hammered the final nail into his coffin—a witness who, after the trial, mysteriously disappeared from planet Earth. And then Natasha transfers here, right before Chelsea Quinn's murder, and is somehow assigned to the case."

"This is all very interesting," Mike said evenly, "but what's her motive?"

"Well, this is where my theory gets a little shaky—"

"Gets?"

I ignored his sarcasm, opting instead to resume my pacing. "She and her ex-husband have a kid together. She didn't fight him when he sued for full custody, and she hasn't seen the kid in over three years."

"How do you know all this?"

"I heard a rumor."

"From a credible source?"

"I talked to her ex-husband." I waved a hand. "Not important. But what if she's not totally evil, and she's protecting her ex and their kid? Maybe she figured out who the killer was, and he threatened her, so she had to pin it on someone else. She chose someone she knew was a criminal and planted his fingerprint to make sure he got caught." I pivoted on my heel at the edge of the room and began pacing back toward the window. "Or, hell, maybe she is totally evil. Maybe she's always known who he is and has been sabotaging the case ever since."

"That's a lot of maybes."

I whirled to face him and threw my hands out wide. "I know that," I said, my voice edged in desperation. "I know this makes me sound like a total schizo, and I know there's no evidence beyond a gut feeling and a lot of coincidences, and I know she's a cop as well as your partner." I drew in a long breath, letting my arms fall to my sides. "But I also know if I keep my mouth shut, and she is involved, and more people die..." I shrugged helplessly. "I would rather be wrong than have that on my conscience for the rest of my life."

Mike shot to his feet and rounded the coffee table. "You're right." He pulled me into a embrace. "So would I. Especially since—" He cut himself off and squeezed me tighter.

"Especially since what?" My voice was muffled against his chest, and I tilted my head back to look at him. "Especially since I'm the one he's really after?"

His eyes darkened. "No. You're not."

I gave him a tight smile. "Come on, Mike. Let's be honest here."

Something that looked a lot like fear flashed across his face. "What happened to the theory that he's infatuated with you and is using you for fame?"

I pulled out of his arms, shaking my head. "He probably is, but that's just gravy. It's not his primary driver."

"Have you considered the possibility that you're misinterpreting the evidence and jumping to conclusions?" he asked, his voice controlled.

"Have you considered the possibility that you're ignoring the evidence because you don't like it?"

He sighed. "Yes, I've considered it. But until there's solid proof, I'm choosing to be optimistic for my own sanity."

I watched him silently for a few beats before padding away to fish my notebook and a pen out of my tote bag. As I flipped through it, I felt him come up behind me to watch over my shoulder. When I found the page with the victims chart, I clicked the pen open and went through the details I'd collected, methodically circling the one thing each victim had in common with me.

Chelsea Quinn: Brown hair, green eyes.

Allison Donnelly: Divorced parents, both remarried.

Gina Hadley: Two brothers—one older, one younger.

Stephanie Goodwin: Northwestern graduate.

Laura Garrett: Studied psychology.

Tori Phelps: Reporter for *The Colsboro Record*.

And Rebecca Ramsey: Dating a CPD cop.

When I finished, I closed the pen and turned to face him, handing him the notepad. "Sorry to sabotage your sanity, but is that enough to convince you?"

He stared down at it in silence for a few beats, the muscle in his jaw tightening. "Fuck."

"So you see why I'm willing to follow any viable lead, even if it is a cop who's your partner."

Mike nodded, swiping a hand across his cheek. "Give me everything you have on her. I need to see it for myself."

«»

"YOU'RE LATE," LOCKWOOD INFORMED ME as I dropped into the booth across from him at Brenen's the next morning. He'd chosen a table in the back corner with a direct line of sight to both the main entrance and the back door. Once a cop, always a cop.

I took in his stony expression and opted not to trifle over a few minutes. "Sorry, Chief," I said, sliding out of my coat. "What's with all the espionage?"

I'd woken this morning to an ominous text message he'd sent in the middle of the night asking me to meet him for coffee before work—and instructing me not to mention it to anyone, not even God. I'd known it couldn't be good, but at least it wouldn't be another decapitated body. Probably.

"How was Chicago?" he asked, and I shrugged noncommittally. "Didn't find what you were looking for?"

When the server returned to refill Lockwood's coffee, I put in an order for a peppermint mocha and chocolate chip scone. "Circumstantial evidence," I said when she disappeared. "Nothing concrete."

"You going to tell me what that was all about?"

I gave him a skeptical look. "You going to tell me what your mysterious message was all about?"

He lifted his coffee mug. "You first."

"You're not going to like it."

"Neither are you, and I expected as much."

I spent ten minutes filling him in on the highlights. When I finished, he fell silent for a while, finally speaking up when I was about halfway through my scone.

"When did you get back?" he asked, eyes cast downward at the table.

"Late Sunday afternoon."

"Did you take Demarco with you?"

"No."

Lockwood rubbed the back of his neck. "I think we're past the point where we can pretend we're dealing with multiple perps," he began slowly. "To that end, I think it's also safe to say Ramsey was murdered by the same person who murdered the six others, including your friend and your mother's colleague."

"Agreed."

"The Northville P.D. crime lab shared the autopsy report with us. The M.E. put Ramsey's time of death between nine p.m. Saturday and one a.m. Sunday."

Nonplussed, I tilted my head slightly to one side. "Where are you going with this?"

He blew out a breath, finally lifting his gaze to mine. "Demarco's prints were identified at the scene."

I stared at him, body frozen as my mind raced through the implications. Mike's fingerprints had been found at the scene of a murder—just like my brothers, just like Baratti, just like my mom and Christine and Kenny. However, something—possibly Lockwood's pinched expression and this whole clandestine meeting—implied this time wasn't like the others.

"Well, that's not a total surprise, right?" I said tentatively. "You've ID'ed prints at every scene."

"This is different."

"How?"

"It wasn't a single print. They found a couple dozen."

I shrugged. "So he copied it over and over, and—"

The chief folded his hands on the table. "No, Jennifer. They found a full set of prints."

I blinked in surprise. "Like an index finger and thumb and pinky and—"

"Yes," he cut in. "And lip prints."

"Lip prints," I repeated. "On what?"

"They were all on a wine glass." He gulped some more coffee and let the information sink in. "The bottle had Ramsey's prints on it, as well as a few other unidentified sets—probably from wherever the wine was purchased."

"Have they found his prints on anything else?"

"Not to my knowledge."

I drew in a shaky breath. "Are you suggesting Mike is the killer?"

"That would be a very large leap."

"Exactly." My voice was laced with the beginnings of anger. "Why would he leave his prints on a glass and wipe everything else down? Or, better yet, why wouldn't he wear gloves if his intention was to kill her?"

Lockwood gave a minute shake of his head. "You're right—which means, if he was there, his intention was not to kill her."

My mouth opened and closed twice before any words materialized. "Chief, what are you trying to tell me?"

"One of two things," he said, pinching the bridge of his nose. "Either Demarco's being set up like everyone else—only much more elaborately, for reasons I can only speculate at. Or, he really was with Ramsey in an empty but fully furnished house on a night you were five hundred miles away."

My heart leapt into my throat, and I swallowed hard. "Let's focus on the first option: He's being elaborately set up."

"Unlike the other pieces of evidence we've found prints on, it appears that the wine glass was legitimately touched by Demarco." The chief shrugged helplessly. "If that's the case, that brings us back to option one: He left it there himself—"

"No," I interrupted, shaking my head definitively. "He wasn't there."

"Or someone close to him stole a wine glass that he had used and planted it." Lockwood drained his coffee mug and slid it to the edge of the table before continuing. "In light of the information you've just given me, the second option has gained some ground—especially knowing Sardelis has been staying with him and has had access to everything he owns." He leveled his eyes with mine. "But Jennifer, both are possible—and if I'm being honest, the first option seems more likely. Transferring the glass from one location to another without destroying the prints or picking up any outside evidence, while not impossible, would be much more difficult."

"Sure, but this guy had already gotten six people's fingerprints and planted them at six different crime scenes—all without attracting suspicion." I cleared my throat, which had gone desert dry, and paused for a sip of coffee. "I'd say that's pretty damn difficult, too."

"True, and you're probably right. In all likelihood, the glass was planted, like everything else." Lockwood paused, nodding up at the waitress as she refilled his coffee mug. "But there's plenty of room for doubt. You should be prepared for the alternatives."

I let out a short humorless laugh. "There's no way to prepare for finding out your boyfriend's either a closet killer or a cheater."

Lockwood gave me a tight smile. "I know. Maybe you don't have to." He reached across the table and gave my hand a brief squeeze. "Question is, do you believe he could do either?"

"No, but I've been wrong about this kind of thing in the past." Swallowing hard, I dropped my gaze to my almost-empty coffee mug, annoyed at the unexpected sting in the back of my eyes. "And apparently a murderer is lurking somewhere in my social circle, and I have no idea who he is despite the plethora of well-planned clues he's left for me—so I wouldn't trust my judgment if I were you."

"Hey." He gripped my hand and waited until I looked up at him. "Don't be so hard on yourself. None of this is your fault."

A savage psychopath was killing women to get my attention—and had been for years. How was that not my fault? I shook my head and changed the subject.

"So what happens now?"

Releasing me, he wrapped his oversized hands around his mug, making it all but disappear. "Well, I suspect you're going to spend the next eight hours trying to prove me wrong." He blew out a heavy sigh. "And I have to talk to Demarco."

"Are you going to do anything about Sardelis?"

"I'll look into it."

"What about Northville P.D.?"

"They've agreed to give me twenty-four hours as a professional courtesy, but they're like a pack of hungry hyenas. They want to move on this before a third murder happens in their jurisdiction and the governor demands their heads on a pike."

Thinking of Ramsey, I wrinkled my nose. "Chief."

Lockwood let out a dry laugh. "Sorry. Bad joke." He glanced around the coffee shop and signaled for the check. "The point is, we're running out of time. If Demarco's innocent of murder, as I suspect he is, we need to prove it fast. The longer we focus our attention on him, and the longer we're distracted from the real evidence..." He gave me a taut smile. "The closer the real killer gets to his next victim."

I could tell by the chief's expression—face tight, eyes drawn, jaw set—that he was thinking the same thing I was.

That the next victim could be me.

EIGHTEEN MONTHS AGO
COLSBORO, OHIO

"SO THEY DID, IN FACT, remove the tumor, but they also left a seven-inch scalpel in the guy's abdomen," Kenny told me with a cheesy grin, bringing his story to its painful conclusion. "And that's why you check medical instruments four times during a surgery."

It was the day after Joey's graduation from the police academy, and we were on my parents' backyard patio under the warm mid-May sun. I'd been stocking the cooler with soda and bottled water when Kenny had cornered me, wielding two giant bags of ice and claiming my mother had sent him out to help. That had been at least fifteen years ago.

I frowned, wishing again that I'd grabbed my drink before I came outside. "What hospital was this?"

Kenny waved a hand. "It wasn't around here, and I'm really not supposed to tell that story." He laughed. "But it's the best icebreaker at parties."

"You should tell Megan," I suggested. "As a doctor, she'd think it was hilarious."

He blinked, obviously confused. "She's a dentist, not a surgeon."

"And I'm not any kind of doctor." I shifted the empty plastic bags and flattened cardboard boxes I'd been holding for a quarter of an hour and pretended to check my watch. "Shoot, I promised my mom I would make meatballs. You want anything while I'm inside?" I turned on my heel and strode toward the door without waiting for an answer, relieved when Kellyn stepped outside.

"Mom's freaking out." She held the door open for me. "Something about meatballs."

Even though Kellyn was technically Brian's niece, she'd been so young when she came to live with us that she'd eventually transitioned from "Aunt Katie" and "Uncle Brian" to "Mom" and "Dad." They'd both been thrilled, particularly Brian, who didn't have any children from his first marriage.

"Thanks." I tilted my head in Kenny's direction and lowered my voice. "Go ask your husband to tell you a riveting tale about a scalpel."

"Again, you mean?" she muttered.

Inside, I found my parents, both my brothers, and my sister-in-law gathered around the kitchen island. I gaped at them as Brian pushed away from the bar to take the trash clutched in my hands.

I planted my hands on my hips. "You've all been in here having fun while I've been stuck out there listening to stories about scalpels?"

"Chill, sis," Joey said. "We sent Kellyn to rescue you."

"Took you long enough." I marched to the island to retrieve my cocktail, which was now severely watered down.

"That was a test to see if you could bluff your way out." Jason's green eyes sparkled as he looked down at me. "What do I keep telling you, Panda? You need to get better at bluffing before I let you play poker with us."

"I'm good at bluffing. It's being rude I'm not good at."

Jason snorted. "You sure about that?"

I elbowed him in the ribs, and he let out a grunt. "I feel much better." I smiled up at him sweetly. "Now make me another drink."

《》

SOON THEREAFTER, THE KITCHEN CLEARED out, save for me, my mother, and the occasional new arrival who passed through on the way to the patio. The oven was preheating, I was on my second pan of mozzarella-stuffed meatballs, and Joey and Jason had just returned for drink refills.

Joey stopped next to me and eyed the meatball I'd just dropped on the pan. "You're making some of those without cheese, right?"

My mom sent him a sideways glance from the other side of the island, where she was artfully arranging crudités on a platter. "Honey, I already tried."

He sighed. "I'll take that as a no."

"Actually, it's a hell, no," I corrected.

"But Dad's lactose intolerant."

"I know." I smiled gleefully. "Tell you what: I'll make one without cheese, and if he finds it, he wins a prize."

He sighed. "You're mean."

"Karma's a bitch, bro." Before Joey could respond, the doorbell rang. "Can you get that? Mom would not be happy if I got E. coli all over the place."

"That's true, hon," my mother confirmed.

He rolled his eyes, dropping his empty beer bottle on the counter next to me, and stalked away.

Jason grabbed the bottle as he breezed by. "The better approach would've been to bluff," he called over his shoulder en route to the pantry. "You need the practice."

"He could see what I was doing," I pointed out. "It would've been the worst bluff ever."

"And unnecessary." My mother's eyes slid skyward. "Your father won't show up anyway."

"Ooh, Mom!" I grinned. "How do you really feel?"

"This is probably why you can't bluff," she said. "You got my resting bitch face."

I let out a bark of laughter as Joey returned to the kitchen with the newcomer. Judging by his delighted expression, my transgression had been forgotten.

Joey gestured grandly toward us. "Detective, I'd like you to meet my family. Mom, Jen, this is Detective Demarco."

I appraised the newcomer as my mother stepped forward to give him an enthusiastic handshake. He was tall—not as tall as either of my brothers, but at least six foot—with short dark hair, a Mediterranean complexion, uncharacteristically blue eyes, and an uncanny familiarity.

When he turned to me, hand outstretched, I held up the ground beef I'd been rolling around in my palms. "I'll catch you later."

He winked. "Promise?"

I smiled coyly. "I don't suppose you're Mike Demarco, are you?"

"Wow. You're really good at this game."

"That, or you might've graduated high school with my brother." Raising a brow, he shifted his eyes from me to Joey and back again. "Not that one. My older brother, Jason." I glanced around. "He was here a minute ago."

A few seconds passed before I saw recognition dawn. "Good memory." He nodded in approval, lips curving upward in the beginnings of a smirk. "I suppose that makes you little Jenny Gibbs."

"I suppose it does."

His eyes slid down and back up. "Good job growing up."

I laughed again. "Thanks. You too."

"The party's out on the patio, Detective," my mother interjected, pointing at the back door. "Can I get you something to drink first?" She rattled off the extensive selection of beverages she'd purchased for the occasion.

"The IPA sounds good," he said. My mother beamed happily at him before ducking into the fridge, and he slid onto a barstool across from me. "I don't remember you being the apron-wearing domestic type."

I glanced down at myself. "Much to my mother's disappointment, I still am not." I dropped another meatball onto the baking sheet. "The apron is hers. She's afraid I might accidentally smear raw beef all over myself and ruin my chances of finding my future husband at my little brother's graduation party."

My mother reappeared at my left side and passed a bottle of beer across the counter to Demarco. "Don't listen to her." She gave a nonchalant wave. "She's just being modest. Jennifer is very domestic."

As she turned away, I sent Demarco a wide-eyed look. "See?" I whispered, and he grinned.

"And a smart ass," she added, returning to her vegetable tray.

"Well, that goes without saying."

Joey gave me a pained look. "Sis."

I shook my head in disappointment, mushing the last of the ground beef around a mozzarella ball. "Nearly twenty-three years, and you still don't know what big sisters are for."

"The same thing big brothers are for," Jason said, reappearing in the kitchen with a bottle of bourbon. "Embarrassing you." He clapped Joey on the shoulder and handed him the bottle. "And buying you alcohol."

As Jason caught up with his former classmate, I popped the meatballs into the oven and began warming the marinara. My mother flitted between the kitchen and the dining room table with trays of food; Joey meandered back and forth between the front door and patio; and Megan wandered back inside to tuck herself under Jason's arm and join him in conversation with Demarco. All the while, I pretended not to notice his eyes following me around the kitchen.

"So, what are you up to these days?" he asked when there was a brief lull. "Still chasing people around with dozens of questions and a notebook?"

"Someone else has a good memory." My lips twitched as I attempted to suppress a smile. "But no. I'm a yoga instructor now."

Jason didn't bother hiding his smirk. "Nice try, Panda, but you're just not ready."

"For yoga?" Demarco lifted a brow. "She looks ready to me."

"No." Jason narrowed his eyes. "She's a crime reporter."

"Quit sabotaging me!" I punched his bicep in frustration before turning back to Demarco, who was fighting a smug smile. "He's been teaching me how to play poker."

"Trying to," he corrected.

I ignored him. "His curriculum places particular emphasis on effective bluffing, which he seems to think I'm not good at."

"You couldn't be. You're my itty bitty baby sister."

I turned back to the stove to give the marinara another stir, then flipped off the burner. "Oh, but I think I learned a thing or two from you in high school."

My mother eyed him suspiciously. "And here I thought you were the perfect firstborn son."

Jason grinned down at me. "See, that's how you bluff."

"Some of us couldn't ride the perfect firstborn child train." I yanked the apron over my head and tossed it onto the counter, now that the danger of spilling on myself had mostly passed. "I had to develop my own techniques."

Demarco gave an exaggerated nod. "I'm willing to bet they're just as—if not more—effective," he said, earning himself a drop-dead glare from Jason.

"What's that face for?" Megan barked at him, arms akimbo. "You didn't have to listen to that damn scalpel story."

"Well, not the entire thing." Jason shrugged. "But I caught some of it, and that was more than enough."

She picked up her empty glass and marched to the refrigerator. "If you'd heard the whole thing, you'd have shoved a saliva suction up his nose, too." She wrenched the freezer door open and tossed him a glare before dropping a few ice cubes into her glass. "At least I would have, if I'd had one on me."

"Do you usually?" Demarco asked dubiously.

"Be careful what you tell this guy," Jason told her in a stage whisper. "He investigates murders."

A mischievous smirk played on her lips as she splashed vodka into her glass. "In that case, no, I do not."

"Too bad." I fought against a persistent grin. "I think it would have a kind of poetic justice if Kenny's cause of death was impalement by saliva sucker."

Megan let out a delighted laugh as she slid onto a barstool. "Especially if I bought it from him."

Demarco shot her an incredulous look before turning back to me. "Who's Kenny?"

"We can't give you any more information than that, Detective." I leaned a hip against the counter. "Don't want you to do something silly like try to save him."

"You don't have to call me Detective." His blue eyes sparkled. "You can call me Mike."

I stifled a pleased smile. "Only if you never call me little Jenny Gibbs ever again."

"I think you're getting the better end of the bargain, but you have yourself a deal." He forced his mouth into a flat line. "As long as I don't hear about a vic who's been killed with a dental device."

I winked. "We'll be discreet."

"What did I tell you?" my mother said, pouring the marinara into a crockpot. "You should have gone outside."

He shrugged. "But then I might have lost twenty minutes of my life to the infamous scalpel story."

I let out a laugh. "That's the thing about Kenny," I said, just before the back door opened again. "He's better in small doses."

"Who's better in small doses?" Kenny asked, striding past me to the fridge.

"George W. Bush," I said smoothly. "He's always making up words and generally butchering the English language." I shot him a look of mock dismay. "C'mon, Kenny, you know I hate that."

Laughing, he ducked into the fridge and reemerged with a Scotch ale. "I may have picked up on that." He closed the refrigerator and retraced his steps to the door. "Carry on with your political gossip."

We fell silent until Kenny was gone and had shut the door behind him. Mike eyed me before shifting his smirk to Jason. "You thought she needed help with bluffing?"

He leaned a hip against the island. "My little sister? Of course. She never lies."

Shaking my head, I reached for my drink. "Or he doesn't want his little sister at guys' night, because he knows I'd distract all his friends and win every round."

Jason snorted. "Quite the modest one, aren't you?"

I crossed my arms over my chest. "Don't believe me?"

His mouth lifted in a lopsided smile. "Sounds like you're about to prove me wrong."

I wagged my eyebrows up and down, then forced my face into a neutral expression and turned back to Mike. "You know," I said hesitantly, "this is so embarrassing, but I used to have a huge crush on you in high school."

A slow smile spread across his face. "Really?"

I bobbed my head up and down. "In fact, there was this one time you came over to study with Jase, and—"

"Hold it right there." Jason pointed a stern finger at me. "We swore we'd never speak of that again. If I hadn't run into you in the hallway—"

"Come on, Jase," I said, rolling my eyes. "It's been, like, thirteen years."

"Nope." He shook his head definitively, then finished off his drink. "Never again."

I turned back to Mike, wincing. "Sorry, I guess I can't tell that story. But yeah. Big crush." I held my arms wide to indicate its relative size.

"Wow. I had no idea—" He cut himself off as his mouth flattened. "Wait." His eyes darted back and forth between me and Jason. "Is that true, or are you bluffing?"

My lips lifted in a leisurely smile, and I shrugged again. After a few beats of silence, Jason let out a laugh.

"Okay, Panda. You win." He held up a hand.

Without taking my eyes off Mike, I gave Jason a high five. "Thanks for the backup." Grin spreading wider, I turned away to remove the meatballs from the oven, and Jason strode over to the freezer.

"Hang on a second," Mike said, holding up a finger. "You're not finished with that story yet."

"You heard me, Demarco." Jason dropped an ice cube into his glass. "Never again."

"Sorry, Detective," I said innocently. "I guess you're just going to have to find out for yourself."

He gave me a smug smile, blue eyes smoldering. "Challenge accepted."

CHAPTER 16
PRESENT
COLSBORO, OHIO

SOMETHING THE CHIEF SAID AT Brenen's nagged at the back of my mind, so instead of pointing myself in the direction of the news-room, I took a detour to Mike's apartment. To my relief, neither his truck nor Sardelis' Mustang were present in the sparsely populated parking lot when I arrived a few minutes after nine o'clock.

I did a quick perimeter check to be sure, then backed into a space at the rear of the lot. After silencing my cellphone, stowing it and my keys in my jacket pockets, and shoving my purse under the front seat, I locked up the car and made my way across the asphalt.

The apartment was dim and quiet when I let myself in and threw the deadbolt behind me. As I glanced around, trying to ignore the irrational feeling that I was breaking and entering, there was a thump from the direction of the bedrooms that sent my heart up into my throat. Seconds later, Murphy padded around the corner and sauntered up to me, the tags on his collar jingling softly against each other. My shoulders sank in relief.

"Hey, buddy," I whispered, scratching his ear. "You scared me."
He stared up at me with dopey brown eyes, eyebrows twitching as if
mildly surprised. "You be the lookout, okay?"

First things first: The kitchen. Mike's fingerprints had been found
on a wine glass, which Sardelis could have easily pilfered at any point
over the last week. I glanced in his cupboards and in the dishwasher,
finding all four wine glasses present and accounted for.

"Damn." I closed the cupboard and spun around, nearly bowling over Murphy in the process. He looked up at me expectantly, tail wagging lazily. "What are you doing?" I hissed at him,
hands on my hips. "Didn't I tell you to be the lookout?" His tail slowed
to a stop, and I sighed in defeat. "Okay, I forgive you. But don't
screw up this time."

I stepped around him and strode down the hallway to the bedrooms.
Mike's door was wide open to allow Murphy unrestricted access to
his human's bed. The door to the guest room was shut; when I turned
the knob, I was half relieved to find it unlocked. The other half of me
thought rooting through a cop's personal effects was a terrible idea,
even if that cop was potentially corrupt.

I took a deep breath and blew it out. "Desperate times," I murmured, propelling myself into the tiny bedroom. I glanced under the
pillows and inside the pillowcases, pried the mattress up and ran my
hands underneath, and filtered through layers of blankets. Nothing.

Inside the nightstand drawer, I found a small flashlight, a tube of
lip balm, a couple of old magazines, a travel bottle of aspirin, and a
few stray bullets. I grabbed the flashlight and crouched down on the
floor to shine it under the bed, where all I discovered was that Mike
really needed to vacuum in here when Sardelis moved out. I drew in
a dust-laden sigh and sneezed, bumping my head on the bed frame
in the process.

After letting out a string of hushed curses, I returned the flashlight
to the drawer and hauled myself to my feet. Next up, the closet. I slid
the door open and flipped on the overhead light. Cardboard boxes

labeled in Mike's all-caps handwriting lined the shelf above the clothes rod. A handful of collared shirts and dark trousers hung crookedly from white plastic hangers, and a pair of practical leather shoes rested on the carpet next to an overstuffed duffel bag.

I bent down to grab the strap and dragged the bag out of the closet, finding it heavier than expected. Before the angel on my shoulder had a chance to interject, I lugged it up onto the bed and unzipped it.

Inside were a couple pairs of jeans, an array of shirts and sweaters, undergarments, and socks, which I placed on the bed in the order I withdrew them. A pair of sneakers was tucked against one end and a cosmetics bag against the other. With all the contents laid out on the bed, I ran my hands along the inside of the bag, disappointed when I could find nothing else—no inner pockets, nothing sewn into the lining, not even a stray bobby pin.

"Well, that's anticlimactic," I muttered, picking up the bag, which was still strangely heavy, and shaking it to see if anything fell out. Nothing did, so I carefully returned the neatly folded clothing to the bag and zipped it back up.

And that's when I noticed: The bag was taller on the outside than the inside was deep. I ran my fingers along the outer seams until I found a well-concealed zipper a few inches from the bottom, hurriedly yanked it open, and sifted through the contents.

The hidden compartment was about a third of the size of the main section, but its contents were much more valuable: A couple dozen prepaid Visa gift cards rubber banded together. A cheap pay-as-you-go cellphone and charger. A driver's license and passport issued to a blonde version of Sardelis named Nancy Smith. A compact handgun and box of ammo. And the coup de grâce, a zippered bag stuffed with bundles of cash.

A cold sweat broke out at the base of my spine, and for a few long seconds, all I could do was stare at the items as my mind raced through the implications. This was a go bag, and it hadn't been thrown together overnight. Which meant...

Out in the hallway, Murphy jumped to his feet and let out a low growl, ripping me from my thoughts. Half a second later, there was a click, followed by the creak of a door swinging open. As Murphy tore down the hallway, barking fiercely, I propelled myself into action, shoving everything back into the bag as fast as I could.

The sound of a surprised yelp and a few choice words spoken in an undeniably female voice filtered down the hallway. Yanking the zipper back in place, I wondered what the hell Sardelis was doing here at nine-thirty in the morning, and I froze.

What if she was here for the bag?

Outside the room, Murphy's angry barks had morphed into excited yips. Tick tock, Jennifer. Gritting my teeth, I pulled the top zipper open a few inches, slid off my watch, and tucked it into one of the shoes. As the yips died down, I lifted the bag and gently dropped it back to the closet floor, zipping the top compartment shut en route.

I didn't want to risk drawing attention to myself by sliding the door shut, so I left it ajar. The jingle of Murphy's collar grew louder, and I knew it was only a matter of seconds before he led her right to me. No time to hide.

Thinking fast, I tiptoed out of the room and eased the door closed behind me. Then, tacking a startled expression on my face, I bolted around the corner and burst into the living room, nearly colliding with Sardelis.

"Omigod, Natasha," I said, pressing a hand to my chest and jumping backward. Her hand froze at her hip, and she stared at me, eyes bulging. "I'm so relieved it's you. I was afraid it was—"

"Jesus, Jennifer," she spat, taking a few steps backward. "You scared the shit out of me. I could have shot you."

I held up my hands in surrender. "Sorry, you startled me too. Wasn't expecting anyone." I tilted my head to one side, mimicking confusion. "What are you doing here?"

She blew out a hiss. "What am I doing here?" she demanded. "What are you doing here?"

"Oh, I was just, um—" I gestured in the direction of Mike's bedroom. "Something for Mike. For our anniversary. A surprise."

Sardelis scraped a hand through her dark hair. "Well, it worked. You surprised the hell out of me." She eyed me suspiciously as she dropped her hands to her hips. "I thought your anniversary was in the spring."

I frowned, taken aback. "It's weird you know that."

She shrugged. "Well?"

"Um, it's..." I rubbed the back of my neck, glancing away. "A different kind of anniversary."

"Oh." Her nose scrunched up, and she waved a hand. "Don't need the details."

I laughed awkwardly. "Wasn't going to offer them."

"Okay, great." She shifted to her other foot. "So..."

"Oh, right!" I lurched forward, gesturing toward the door, and she stepped out of the way. "I'll just come back later and finish up."

She bobbed her head in an exaggerated nod. "Cool," she said. "And I'll make myself scarce tonight so you guys can—" She scratched her nose. "Celebrate."

"Hell, I didn't think this through." I let out a self-deprecating laugh. "You know what, don't worry about it." I shuffled into the foyer, waving at her over my shoulder. "I'll just do it—the surprise—at my house."

"But isn't your cousin staying with you?"

Stifling a wince, I whirled back around to face her. "Well, yes," I said slowly, shoving my hands into my pockets. "But you know what—I think she's traveling tonight. For work."

Sardelis' lips formed an O. "Well, there you go."

"I don't know why I didn't think of that before now." I rolled my eyes at myself, fumbling behind me for the doorknob. "Anyway, I'll get out of your hair now. See you later."

She mumbled a bewildered goodbye as I launched myself out of the apartment, pulling the door closed behind me. I forced myself to descend the stairs one at a time, walk across the parking lot at a normal pace, and then get into my car, start the engine, and drive away without hesitation.

I was halfway back to the office before my heart slowed to its normal pace and my hands stopped shaking enough to unlock my cellphone. At the next red light, I opened my phone book and tapped Orlando's name. To my great frustration, he didn't answer.

"Call me as soon as you get this," I ordered his voicemail. "I need to know how to track the watch."

《》

I HAD BARELY MADE IT to my desk in the bullpen when the door to Gus's office opened, he stuck his head out, and looked straight at me.

"Gibbs!" he shouted unnecessarily, since I was only about twenty feet away. "Get in here." Leaving the door open, he strutted back inside. With a sigh, I dropped my purse on my desk and trudged into his office.

I closed the door and sent him a skeptical glance. "Omigod, are you firing me?"

"Not yet." He leaned a hip against the edge of his desk. "I'm upping the ante. Apparently the promotion wasn't enough incentive."

I dropped into a chair facing his desk and crossed one leg over the other. "Throwing in a company car as well?"

"Not even close," he said. "A little competition."

I sighed dramatically. "Is that necessary?"

"While you were M.I.A. this morning—"

"I wasn't M.I.A. I was following a lead."

Gus held up a hand. "Not the point. Your pet serial killer is apparently getting impatient, because he's chosen a new mouthpiece."

My face sank into a glare. "What?"

"One of your television colleagues received an email this morning from the Colsboro Killer, as he dubbed himself." His eyes slid skyward as he shook his head. "Not very creative, if you ask me, but we can work on that."

"Gus."

"Right, not important." He crossed his arms over his chest. "The email also contained a tip that someone is being questioned in connection with the murders."

"Who?"

He hesitated. "Mike Demarco—your Mike," he added, in case it wasn't clear. "You didn't know?"

"No, I knew. I meant, who got the email?"

Gus eyed me warily for a few beats. "Davenport."

I shot to my feet. "Melanie Davenport? That's my competition?"

"Gibbs, it wasn't my choice," he said, holding his hands up. "But if she's what lights a fire under your ass—"

"The fire under my ass is not getting raped and murdered." I crossed my arms tightly over my chest and began pacing across his office. "You don't need to throw Melanie fucking Davenport into the flames, too."

He snorted. "I didn't. That was him—"

"Oh, did he also offer her the crime desk?" I shot Gus another dirty look, and he pressed his lips together. "I didn't think so."

"I didn't offer her anything." He scraped a hand through his curly hair, leaving a few tufts standing up at awkward angles. "Between you and me, she couldn't handle a single day of the obits section, let alone the crime beat, but this is where we are."

"No shit," I muttered. "How many people has she slandered this year?"

"None, or she wouldn't have a job."

"None that you know of."

"You're looking at this all wrong." He straightened to his full height. "This guy doesn't think Davenport can crack the case. Hell, even she knows that." He rolled his eyes. "Not that she'd ever admit it."

"So, how should I look at it?"

"He chose her for one reason." He held up an index finger. "To piss you off."

I blew out a breath. "And light a fire under my ass."

"Which means he knows of your professional rivalry."

"It's not a professional rivalry." I stopped pacing and pivoted to face him. "I mean, it is, simply by virtue of working at competing news organizations, but—"

Gus's forehead wrinkled. "But it's more than that?"

"About fifteen years more." I let out a humorless laugh. "And there aren't that many people who know about it."

"Good," he said. "It's another clue."

"How did you find out about the email?"

"He blind copied me."

A shiver zipped down my entire body. "Hell."

"You're not about to freak out, are you?" he asked, and I shook my head automatically, though I wasn't certain. "Good. You have all the information you need, or he wouldn't be poking you with this stick."

"He can poke me with as many sticks as he wants. It's not going to make me figure it out any faster."

"Gibbs, you know what to do and how to do it. Detach yourself and look it this logically."

"How am I supposed to be unbiased about this?" I demanded, throwing my arms wide. "The guy's been following me for years. He knows my history, the people I associate with, what kind of car I drive, my elementary school arch-enemy. He's planting fingerprints of my family while he kills people that somehow remind him of me. How is that not personal?"

"I didn't say it wasn't personal. It's very personal," he said. "That's exactly why the bastard's doing it: To unnerve you. To keep you off balance. To make you doubt yourself and the people closest to you." He raised his brows at me. "Don't let him. Find a way to detach yourself."

I dropped my eyes to the floor, feeling slightly out of breath, as though the wind had been knocked out of me. It wasn't like I hadn't been faced with a challenge before. Murder investigations were always difficult, on multiple levels. But this was different. I couldn't see the entire picture—only strangely shaped pieces that didn't fit together. Something was missing.

"Do you need help?" he asked in a neutral voice.

My gut instinct was to say no—I hated needing or, worse, asking for help—but that would've been a lie. I was in over my head.

"Yes." Letting out the air I was holding, I lifted my gaze to him. "But that's the thing. He's made sure I'm the only one who can I.D. him."

He lifted his shoulders in a shrug. "Doesn't mean you can't benefit from a fresh perspective."

Uncomfortable, I glanced away. "Maybe."

Gus gave me time to elaborate, but I didn't. Finally, he rounded his desk and sank into his chair, the leather creaking loudly under his weight. "If you change your mind," he said, reaching for a pen, "I'll be here."

WHEN I EMERGED FROM GUS'S office, I was shocked and more than a little annoyed to see Kenny sitting in my desk chair. Nonchalant and completely comfortable, casually glancing around the newsroom like he belonged there.

Annoyed, I slammed Gus's door harder than necessary and marched over to him. Once I was a few yards away and closing in, he caught sight of me and sat up straighter—as if the reason I were charging toward him with a grim expression was because of his poor posture.

"What are you doing here?" I barked, arms akimbo.

He held his hands up in mock surrender. "Before you get mad—"

"Little late for that."

"I just wanted to apologize for being an ass the last time we saw each other."

I blinked down at him, nonplussed. "What?"

He raised a brow. "Which part of that was confusing?"

"Definitely not the ass part," I muttered.

The corners of his mouth twitched. "I'm guessing it's the apology part, then?" he asked. "I'm choosing to believe you have so much on your mind that you merely forgot when we ran into each other at Bartholomew's."

"Don't you mean Viva Vino?"

He tapped his temple, as if remembering. "That's right," he said. "Anyway, I'm sorry for being an ass—which is part of the reason I sent you the gift basket last week."

I removed my jacket and threw it on top of my purse. "And what was the other part—a bribe?"

"I plead the fifth."

I narrowed my eyes. "Get out of my chair."

Kenny jumped to his feet and shuffled awkwardly around me so I could sit down. He wheeled Tori's chair to my side of our desks and sat down.

I swiveled to face him. "What do you really want?"

"I know you're skeptical—and you have every right to be—but I truly did want to apologize."

"Great. Is that all?"

One side of his lips lifted in a half smile. "You must be having a rough week."

I blew out a breath. "Yeah, but that's not your fault." I closed my eyes and rubbed my temples for a few beats. When I opened them again, his smile had flattened. "Sorry, I shouldn't take it out on you."

His expression sobered. "I understand. I guess I'm so used to cold calling people that I think it's normal."

"I do it, too. Occupational hazard." I waved a hand. "What's on your mind?"

"I think I made a mistake." At my inquisitive expression, he added: "With Kellyn."

"Undoubtedly," I agreed. "How far back are we going?"

"Ouch."

"Well, you guys did elope in Vegas, so..." I shrugged, voice trailing off.

He nodded, glancing down at his hands. "And tomorrow is our anniversary. I didn't think it would bother me this much, but it does."

"Bother you?"

"It's more difficult than I thought it would be."

"Is the paperwork confusing?" I asked. "You could hire a lawyer to help with that."

Kenny slid his narrowed eyes back to mine. "Not what I mean."

"Then what do you mean?"

"I—" He shifted uncomfortably in his chair. "I want her back."

I stared at him for a few beats, the muscles of my face tightening into a frown. "I can't do anything about that."

"If it were you, what would it take?"

"It has been me, Kenny," I said edgily.

"I know. That's why I'm asking you."

"Nothing short of a time machine, or—" I cut myself off with a shake of my head.

"Or?" he prodded.

"I don't know." I opened and closed my mouth a few times, trying to find the right word. "A hoax."

His eyes sparkled as he attempted to smother a smile. "A hoax."

"That's less plausible than a time machine?"

"Well, not in daytime TV."

"Those are the only things I can think of to make up for infidelity."

"In other words, making it so it never happened." Kenny shook his head ruefully. "So I'm screwed."

"If it were me, yes. As for what it would take for Kellyn..." I shrugged. "You'll have to ask her yourself."

"Do you think she'll talk to me?"

"There's a simple solution to that." When he didn't respond, I raised an eyebrow at him. "Ask her. And if she doesn't talk to you—well, that probably means she won't talk to you."

"Simple in theory." Kenny ran a hand across his clean-shaven jaw. "Not so much in practice."

"Most things are that way."

He let out a humorless laugh and lifted his chin. "Will you put in a good word for me?"

"On what grounds?"

"On the grounds that she wants to talk to me, and I've already bribed you."

"You're awfully confident for a guy who won't call the wife he cheated on because he's afraid she won't answer."

"You said she's reluctant to admit our relationship is over."

"And you said no one cheats because they're in a happy relationship."

"Actually," he said slowly, "what I said was that our relationship was ruined before I strayed." His lips lifted in a smile that didn't reach his eyes. "Some people can be in a perfectly happy relationship and cheat anyway." He stood and zipped up his jacket. "Just think about it."

As I watched him walk away, I wondered what part of the conversation he wanted me to think about.

ORLANDO CALLED JUST BEFORE LUNCH with an IP address to track the watch from my web browser. I spent the rest of the day alternating between staring at the blinking red dot hovering over the map of downtown Colsboro (specifically, the CPD) and scrutinizing the clues chart.

At five o'clock, I let myself back in to Gus's office, where he'd already switched his wall-mounted TV to the local FOX affiliate. The anchors wasted no time volleying the feed to Melanie fucking Davenport, who was stationed outside Colsboro police headquarters with a breaking-news story only on channel eight.

"A homicide investigator is on the other side of the interrogation table today after being questioned in connection with the brutal murder of real estate agent Rebecca Ramsey, whose body was found early Monday morning," she said, somehow managing not to look like a ghost in the garish white lights of the camera. "Detective Mike Demarco's fingerprints were identified at the scene of the crime, an unoccupied house Ramsey's agency was selling."

"I hope she chokes on her microphone," I muttered, crossing my arms over my chest.

Gus snorted. "That would save me from having to replace you when you're arrested for strangling her."

"I'd still be able to do it," I said darkly. "I know people in the M.E.'s office."

"Really, Gibbs?" He sent me a skeptical glance. "That's what you want to go to jail for—desecration of a human corpse?"

I shrugged. "Might be worth it for Melanie Davenport."

"Don't expect me to bail you out for anything other than protecting a source."

"Although a CPD spokesperson assured me Demarco is innocent of murder, they are being tight-lipped about the details," Davenport concluded. "In the mean time, the detective has been placed on administrative leave pending further investigation." She signed off and sent the feed back to the studio.

Gus muted the TV and stood, tossing the remote down onto his desk. "You know, they are right about one thing. They did break the story."

"Good. They can be the ones to get sued when the truth comes out."

"Nothing she said was untrue," he pointed out. "Sensationalized, yes. But not untrue."

I groaned dramatically. "What do you want me to do about it, Gus? I can't exactly write a rebuttal."

"No, I'll get Peterson to follow up for tomorrow's paper." When I opened my mouth to argue, he held up a hand in a stop gesture. "Like you said, it can't be you. It's a conflict of interest."

"This whole story is a conflict of interest," I said, waving my arms. "We may not have known it at the beginning, but we sure as hell know it now, so why don't you just give Peterson the assignment? Hell, give him the crime desk while you're at it."

"I'm not going to reassign you," he said edgily. "But if Peterson breaks the story, then yes, I'll give him the crime desk. That was the deal."

"Meanwhile, I'm still next in line to get murdered." I clapped my hands in mock glee. "Thanks for believing in me, boss."

"Go home, Gibbs." He flicked a hand toward the door. "Drink some wine, break some stuff, yell at your elderly neighbors—whatever you need to do to reset. Then get your ass back in here tomorrow morning and act like the goddamn professional you are."

I clamped my mouth shut and stalked out before I said anything stupid enough to force Gus to fire me—or worse, give Peterson my story.

«»

"HEY," MIKE SAID AS I SLID ONTO the barstool next to him about an hour after I'd stomped out of the newsroom. "I was afraid you were ignoring me."

"Sorry." I glanced around for the bartender as he leaned in to kiss me. "I didn't notice your messages until I got home."

"Oh." Straightening, he appraised me solemnly. "You saw the news, didn't you?"

I let out a short laugh. "Honey, I write the news. Sometimes I even am the news. Of course I saw the news."

Mike winced. "How bad is this?"

"You tell me."

"I didn't kill Ramsey, nor does Lockwood think I did."

"I know."

"Jen, I didn't sleep with her, either," he said, exasperated. "You know that, too, right?"

"Of course."

He studied me for a few beats. "Do you?"

"Yes, Mike." I rubbed my forehead tiredly. "But that doesn't mean I didn't think about the possibility."

"We've talked about this. I would never—"

"Yes. That's what I told the chief." I blew out a breath. "He was just trying to prepare me a variety of worst-case scenarios."

He blinked. "Wait—Lockwood told you?"

"This morning. He wanted to know if I could alibi you for Saturday night." I held up an index finger. "And before you ask, he didn't tell me that's what he was doing until after I couldn't."

Turning away, he ran a hand down his face. "That's okay. I'm sure Nat told him we were together all night."

"Great," I said from behind gritted teeth. "Problem solved."

He jerked to face me again. "Jen, I didn't mean it like that."

"Like what?" Avoiding his eyes, I lifted a hand to signal the bartender. "Logically speaking, any of the scenarios are plausible."

"The scenarios being what?" he demanded. "That I either slept with Ramsey or killed her?"

"Yeah, those are two of them," I said. "There's also the one where the killer planted that wine glass while you and Nat were together all night."

"In the majority of cases, the most obvious answer is the right one."

I swiveled to face him. "Which one is that?"

"He planted the glass with my prints on it—just like all the others."

"While you were with Nat all night."

He closed his eyes briefly and sighed. "Yes."

"But this one isn't just like all the others." I gave him a tight smile. "Is it?"

Before he could respond, the bartender finally arrived. "What can I get ya?"

"Vodka martini. Really, really dirty."

He nodded once. "ID?"

"Seriously?" I whined. "No way could I pass as younger than twenty-one. I'm wearing a blazer, for crying out loud."

"Agreed." At my deadpan expression, he added: "Not that you look a day over twenty-one. It's just my manager is a hard-ass. I have to card anyone who looks under forty unless I want to get fired."

"It's also the law," Mike muttered, but we ignored him.

I stifled the urge to pound my fists on the bar top in frustration and instead pulled my wallet out of my purse. When I didn't see my license in its usual spot, I rifled through the rest of my handbag with no success. "Okay, so, I seem to have lost it," I said a minute later, "but I can tell you the exact date, time, and location of my birth."

The bartender opened his mouth to respond, but Mike beat him to it. "You can't find your driver's license?"

I flashed him a brilliant fake smile. "That is what 'lost' means."

His brow furrowed, deepening the crease between his eyes, but he said nothing. So I turned back to my purse and dug around for something to prove my age.

"Oh, look! I'm old enough to rent a car." I pulled out the crumpled invoice and passed it to the bartender. "That should count, right?"

He scanned it and shrugged. "Works for me. Got a preference on your vodka?"

"Grey Goose."

"Coming right up." He winked and strode away.

Once he was out of earshot, I turned back to Mike. "I know I rarely lose stuff, but you seem overly concerned about this." I zipped up my wallet and dropped it back in my purse. "If you're worried about me driving without a license, I promise I won't roll through stop signs or do anything else life threatening."

"It's not that."

"Then what?"

Mike hesitated for a few beats. "We went back through the crime scene photos and reports with a fine-tooth comb, and we identified another commonality among the vics."

I blinked at him. "What is it?"

He took a deep breath and blew it out. "All of their driver's licenses were missing."

CHAPTER 17

"I DON'T WANT YOU GOING home by yourself," Mike said as we walked out of O'Malley's.

"So come with me."

"I also need to keep an eye on Nat." He shoved his hands into his coat pockets. "You should stay with me until we have something solid on her involvement."

I dug my keys out of my purse and pressed the remote to unlock my car. "I don't think that's necessary."

"I need to keep you safe, and I need to keep an eye on her." He followed me from the sidewalk to the driver's side door. "I can't do that simultaneously unless you're both within sight."

I exhaled heavily and turned to face him. "Fine. But I still need to go home to get an overnight bag."

He nodded. "I'll go with you."

《》

"THANK GOD YOU'RE HERE." KELLYN jumped up from the couch as soon as we walked in the front door and embraced me in a tight hug. "I really don't want to be alone tonight."

I sent Mike a glare over her shoulder, and he glanced away sheepishly. "What's wrong, cuz?"

She stepped back. "You don't remember?"

"I remember," I said, wincing. "I was hoping you wouldn't."

"Yeah, right."

Mike flipped the deadbolt and removed his coat. "Remember what?"

"Tomorrow is Kenny's and my anniversary." She stared at us, deadpan. "We'll be celebrating three wonderful years of wedded bliss."

I dropped my purse on the foyer table, then took off my jacket and handed it to Mike to hang up next to his. "How are you planning to commemorate it?"

"I'm taking the day off to spend some quality time with Jack Daniels. He's an old friend of mine." She pivoted and padded into the kitchen, picking up her wine glass from the coffee table en route.

"Kell, there's something you should know." Joining her in the kitchen, I leaned a hip against the counter and crossed my arms over my chest. "About Kenny."

"If you're going to say I should never have married him, I am already aware." She dumped wine into her glass. "You guys want some?" Without waiting for a response, she pulled two more glasses out of the cupboard, filled them up, handed one to me, and slid another across the bar toward Mike.

"Thanks," he said carefully.

She lifted her glass in an air toast. "Cheers." She took a few long gulps, then faced me. "Now, what's this you need to tell me about my darling husband?"

I hesitated for a few beats, until she waved a hand at me impatiently. "He wants to talk to you about getting back together."

Kellyn snorted, spraying wine across the floor. "What?"

"He says he misses you. Thinks he made a mistake."

She let out an unexpected laugh. "He thinks he made a mistake?" she repeated. "Just one?"

I shifted to my other foot. "He didn't provide a comprehensive list."

"When did he tell you all this?" she demanded.

"Today. He came to the newsroom."

"Why?"

"He wanted me to put in a good word with you."

Her eyes narrowed. "Is that what you're doing?"

"No. I'm just relaying the message." Uncomfortable, I took a sip of wine before continuing. "And he wanted to ask me, as an expert in being cheated on, what it would take to get you back."

"What did you tell him?"

"That it was essentially impossible."

She let out another dry laugh. "I don't even know what to say."

"You don't have to say anything. I just didn't want to keep it from you." Putting my glass down on the counter, I gave her shoulder a squeeze. "Be right back." I glanced over at Mike and tilted my head in the direction of my bedroom, and he followed me inside, shutting the door behind us.

"I know what you're going to say," he told me as I switched on the light.

"I can't leave her like this." I gestured emphatically in the direction of the kitchen. "Her marriage is falling apart, and—"

"So is she." He rubbed his temples as he considered the dilemma. "All right. Don't answer the door, and keep your cellphone nearby at all times—preferably in your pocket. I'll pick you up for work at seven-thirty tomorrow. If anything feels off between now and then, call me immediately."

"Don't worry." I gave him a weak smile. "I know the drill."

And I did. We'd done this enough times that I knew the list of do's and don'ts by heart. But this time, something felt different.

This time, I was terrified.

《》

AFTER KELLYN PASSED OUT ON the couch—having finishing the rest of the bottle of wine, along with Mike's untouched glass and half of mine—I took my files to my bedroom, flipped on all the lights, and spread the photos out on the carpet in chronological order. Maybe a different perspective would help me spot something I had missed before.

Midway through the eleven o'clock news, I realized something was missing from my clues chart, and had been the whole time: The first series of victims.

I dug the original photos from my accordion file and lay them at the front of the array. First, I stood above and studied them as a group, looking for any macro details that linked them together. After that, I used a magnifying glass to scrutinize each photo and wrote down everything I could make out.

When I had finished, the only conclusion I could draw was that the first five murders—which occurred between four and seven years ago in both Chicago and Colsboro—were random and spontaneous, whereas the current series of seven were purposeful and carefully planned.

"Really impressive work, Gibbs," I muttered, flopping down onto my bed. "You've got it all figured out now."

If they had been impulsive kills, the first five victims wouldn't help me figure out who the perp was; with no advance planning, he wouldn't have intentionally left any clues behind. If it had occurred to him in the heat of the moment, he could have improvised. Etched his birthdate onto one of the victims' foreheads or something equally morbid. But he hadn't. Why?

And then it hit me: Those clues wouldn't have meant anything to me. Because I didn't know him then.

That realization left me with a new question. What had compelled him to kill all those years ago? Given that he had sent photos only to me and had followed me here from Chicago, the logical conclusion was obvious.

I had.

«»

BY THE TIME MIKE STROLLED into the conference room the next morning, accompanied by Gus, I'd nearly filled another whiteboard with scribbles. While Gus hovered in the doorway, Mike gave me a brief but firm hug, then stepped back to stare at me with his stern cop face.

"I told you I'd pick you up," he said, arms akimbo. "Why didn't you wait for me?"

"I sent you a text so you'd know I probably wasn't kidnapped."

"What time did you get here?" Gus called from his vantage point.

I spared him a brief glance. "Around six-thirty. Couldn't sleep last night."

He eyed the whiteboard. "Looks like you've been busy."

"Any progress?" Mike asked, evidently deciding to forgive me.

"Depends."

He raised a brow. "On what?"

"On whether my mental train is heading in the right direction."

Gus ventured farther into the room. "Which direction is that?"

"I determined last night that, whoever this guy is, he stumbled into my world within the last seven years." I stepped closer to the board and pointed at the first chart, which listed the dates of all the murders for which I'd gotten photos. "The first victim was Hannah Percy, who was killed six and a half years ago while I was an intern at the *Sun-Times*."

"You've got to've been the luckiest intern ever to walk into a news-room," Gus muttered.

I shot him a glare over my shoulder. "Yes, just look at me now."

"Point taken. Go on."

I summarized the theory I'd formulated last night, and they thought it over for a few beats. Just as I was about to urge them to think faster, Mike spoke up.

"So, you think the dates of the first five murders are significant."

"Maybe. With the exception of the first, they all occur within a few days of some major—specifically, romantic—life event." I tapped a knuckle against the third victim's name. "Yvonne Gardner, for instance. She was killed right after Baratti and I moved in together."

The crevasse between his brows deepened. "What about the newer ones?"

"Chelsea Quinn was the first in three years. She was found the day after our one-year anniversary in May." I ran my thumb along the base of my right ring finger, touching the delicate band of the emerald ring Mike had given me to commemorate it. "After that, there doesn't seem to be any correlation."

"Sounds like he really doesn't like it when you're dating someone." Gus sat down on the edge of the conference table. "But how does that help you identify him?"

"Right now, it doesn't. But it'll help narrow down the suspect pool." I turned back to the board and tapped the next chart—a large Venn diagram consisting of three overlapping circles. "I'm compiling lists of people I've met in the last seven years, people who know I hate Melanie fucking Davenport with the fire of a thousand suns, and people who could feasibly get close enough to members of my family to get their fingerprints without attracting suspicion."

Gus stepped forward to scan the diagram. "This is a lot of people."

"A lot" was stating it lightly. Among a few dozen others, I'd included Mike (who was on all three), Baratti (also three), Kenny (at least two), Gus (two), Orlando (at least one but potentially three), Steve (one, maybe two), and Chad (one)—not to mention the entire *Record* staff and every source I'd ever spoken to.

I nodded. "Seven years for a journalist is a lot of ground to cover."

"Well, you aren't exactly discreet about your dislike of Melanie Davenport." He nodded at the foreboding stick figure next to the circles. "Self-portrait?"

"No, this is the killer. It helps if I can visualize him."

He squinted at its evil toothy grin. "Do you suspect he's a werewolf?"

"Not at this time." I pointed to the list below the stick figure. "That's not among the clues he's left me."

"Yet," he said, smirking. "So once you identify the overlapping names in your list, you'll cross-reference them against the clues he's given you."

"Bingo."

"Looks like your mental train has almost made it to the end of the line." He clapped my shoulder and turned for the door. "Nice work, Gibbs. I knew you had it in you."

Mike watched Gus stride out of the room, then shifted back to me. "So, Baratti and I are your top suspects," he said neutrally. "How long has that been on your mind?"

"You're the only ones so far who for sure fit in all three circles. Doesn't mean I consider you suspects."

"I think you're missing a fourth circle." He tilted his head toward the first clue listed under the stick figure. "Cancer."

"Good point." I grabbed a dry erase marker from the tray and added another circle to the diagram. "Looks like you're both off the hook."

"Never thought I'd be saved by astrology," he said dryly.

I sent him a sideways glance. "You didn't need to be saved by anything. I never thought it was you."

"How can you be so sure?"

Shrugging, I flashed him a smile. "That stick figure doesn't resemble you at all."

WHILE MIKE WENT TO GRAB lunch, I took a mental break. When I returned to my desk, a fresh cup of coffee in hand, there was a neon yellow sticky note on the middle of my computer monitor with three words printed in thick block letters: PHOTO LAB, ASAP.

"*Hola, compañera,*" Miguel said when I burst through the door. "I found something interesting on that receipt you got."

I narrowed my eyes. "You mean the one I asked you to enhance a week ago?"

"That's the one," he said cheerfully, and waved a hand in a come-here gesture. "Take a look at this." I hovered behind him as he pulled up the digital scan, which barely resembled the original. "It was pretty faded, so I had to fiddle with the curves and levels—"

"Lives at stake, Miguel," I interrupted. "Give me the bottom line."

His reflection in the computer screen rolled its eyes. "I was able to pull out some details." He clicked on a panel to change the view, and zoomed in to the top of the receipt. "Check it out—it's part of the cab driver's license number."

"Looks like five, oh, seven..." I leaned in closer and squinted. "And a smudge."

Miguel swiveled to face me. "Call the city and sweet talk them into giving you a list of all drivers whose license numbers start with five, oh, seven."

Straightening, I crossed my arms over my chest. "Do you know how many chauffeur licenses have been issued in Chicago?"

He shrugged. "No sé. A few thousand?"

"More like fifteen to twenty—maybe more. We're talking about pending, current, *and* expired."

"Well, it's a good thing I found something else, yes?" He turned back to his computer and reached for the mouse, clicking a few times to adjust the view. "Look, it's the date."

I gaped at it in disbelief. "That's *today's* date."

He leaned back in his chair and cracked his knuckles smugly. "Seven years ago today."

A chill crawled down my backbone. "Anything else?"

Miguel zoomed out so the entire receipt was in the frame. "That's all I can make out."

I turned on my heel and bolted for the door. "Email me that photo," I called over my shoulder.

"You're welcome," he shouted after me.

Back at my desk, I pulled up the website for Chicago's city government and searched for the division of transportation. Commercial driver licensing was buried under several layers of pages, but I finally found a database of public chauffeurs, which, as predicted, dated back to the dawn of time.

For being one of the largest cities in the U.S., Chicago should've had a more robust search feature. However, most of the search parameters were either far too general or much too specific—including the license number filter, which required the full seven-digit code.

"Sonovabitch," I swore loudly. A few reporters in my immediate vicinity glanced up but, upon seeing my expression, quickly turned back to their work.

I shot to my feet, sending my chair backward a few feet, and began pacing around the newsroom. I was missing something.

Today was important for some reason, but what? Hell, I didn't even know where I'd been on this day *last* year, let alone seven years ago. Lost in thought, I reached the end of the row of desks and pivoted to pace back toward mine.

It would have been my junior year at Northwestern, so most likely, I'd have been in one of three places: Evanston, Chicago, or Colsboro. Being that it was mid-December, Northwestern was probably on its holiday break, so I felt comfortable ruling out option one. As for option two or three, it could've gone either way, but seeing as though this guy followed me to Colsboro, I ruled that out, too.

Everything came back to Chicago.

Winter break, junior year. Five months before I began my internship at the *Sun-Times*. I'd wrapped up my interviews prior to going home for winter break. In fact, if I recalled correctly, I'd had my final one right before I was supposed to catch a flight to Colsboro.

Supposed to—but didn't. Because the cab I'd taken had been in an accident.

With a gasp, I came to a halt in the middle of the aisle. "Omigod."

"Are you okay?" someone said to my left, derailing my train of thought.

I whirled to face the reporter whose desk I was standing next to and stared at him wide eyed. Unsure of the answer, I opened and closed my mouth a few times before giving up and darting back to my cubicle without another word.

Back at my computer, I scoured the City of Chicago's user-unfriendly website for accident reports and discovered online records only went back five years. I let out another curse, quieter this time, before picking up the phone. Three transfers later, I was connected to a human being in the division of transportation.

"I need a crash report from seven years ago," I said before the operator could get through her greeting. "And I need it now."

«»

AFTER I HUNG UP, I called Mike and filled him in on what I'd learned, hoping he could cut through the red tape and speed things along. He promised to make a few calls.

While I waited, I returned to the whiteboard. Now that I knew Chicago was the link, I needed to reevaluate the list of suspects. I was able to eliminate quite a few, but most of those people I'd only listed in the interest of being thorough—which meant this newly deciphered clue hadn't had much of an impact.

A short time later, I caught movement out of the corner of my eye, and turned to find Christine leaning against the doorway.

"Judging by your expression, you've solved the mystery and are just waiting for the opportune moment to strike."

I snorted. "Actually, I'm about ready to put my head through a wall."

"Well, I've got something to cheer you up."

"Unless it's the answer to this mess, I don't care." I waved a hand at her, inviting her to join me. "Maybe your hare brain can help me again."

"It can try." She came to stand beside me and studied the board. "You need another circle."

I blew out a sigh. "For what?"

"People who are Scottish." She threw me a glance over her shoulder. "Remember?"

"Chris, adding another circle isn't going to help if I don't know who to put in it."

"Then I guess it's time to consult Google and find out which of these surnames is Scottish."

"Oh, goodie. Let's waste more time researching things that could be completely useless and definitely can't be used in a court of law."

"I'll do it," she offered. "You look like you need a break." She spun on her heel and headed to the door.

"Wait a sec," I called after her. "You didn't cheer me up."

Christine paused and whirled back around. "You should check out your desk for something else."

"My desk is low on the list of things that would cheer me up."

"Ordinarily, yes. But you just received an embarrassingly large bouquet of roses." She wagged her eyebrows up and down. "Either somebody's making up for a very big mistake, or something momentous has happened."

"Neither," I said, frowning. "At least not recently."

"Why else would you get flowers on a day that's not your birthday or anniversary?"

"Good question. If anyone should be getting flowers today, it's—" I cut myself off as a dangerous idea electrified my brain like lightning.

"Well, don't leave me in suspense," Christine said, startling me out of my trance. "Who should be getting flowers today?"

"Omigod," I said, my voice breathy.

"Omigod what?"

Without answering, I launched myself back in the direction of my desk, where a vase of red-and-white roses in a black vase waited for me. I plucked the envelope out of the plastic holder, ripped it open, and extracted the handwritten card.

Seven years ago today. Do you remember yet?

Before the message had made it from my eyes to my brain, Christine seized it from my fingers and read it. Meanwhile, I bent to open my bottom desk drawer, yanking it out so far that it hit her in the shin, and she let out a grunt as I pulled out my purse.

"Dammit, Jen." She bent to rub her leg. "That's going to leave a bruise."

I overturned my purse and dumped its contents onto my desk, sorting through with trembling hands until I found the other tiny envelope—the one I had buried so I didn't have to think about it—and slid out the card.

They say wine and pain meds don't mix, but I think that's a conspiracy. Hope you feel better.

I snatched the second card back from Christine and compared the handwriting.

They matched.

Letting out a strangled yelp, I dropped the cards and sank into my chair. "Fuck."

Injury forgotten, Christine picked them up from the floor and straightened. Her eyes shifted back and forth between the two cards several times before meeting mine.

"Omigod," she whispered.

"So you're thinking the same thing I am—that my cousin's married to a serial killer." My voice wavered slightly. "I'm not crazy, right?"

She shook her head. "You're not crazy."

"Okay." Uncertain whether that was a good thing, I took a deep breath and let it out slowly. "None of this is definitive evidence."

"Maybe not alone, but together—"

"No judge is going to issue an arrest warrant based on what may or may not be a constellation stabbed into a murder victim's chest or a bouquet of poinsettias or any of the other vague clues that could mean literally anything or nothing."

"True." Her forehead wrinkled as she thought it over. "So you need DNA or some kind of trace evidence from the crime scene."

I gasped. "Or a fingerprint."

Her eyes widened. "Exactly."

CHAPTER 18

BY THE TIME BARATTI FOUND me pacing in the lobby of the coroner's office, I'd called Kellyn a couple times with no success and renewed a long-broken habit of biting my fingernails.

"Something's wrong," he said, arms akimbo as he appraised me. I was too anxious to muster a snarky response, so I simply nodded. "Come on. Let's talk in my office."

I stuffed my hands into my pockets and followed him down the sterile white hallway into a tiny windowless room. He closed the door and gestured to a plastic chair in the corner. Instead of sitting, I dropped my bag onto the chair and sifted through my folder.

"Allison Donnelly was found on August thirteenth around nine P.M. in a bathtub of bloody water." I spun around and handed him the file from the second murder. "The Corine M.E. estimated her time of death between six and ten A.M. that same day." I hugged my arms across my chest. "Tell me how he could have made it look like it occurred earlier or later than it actually did."

Brow furrowed, he silently sank into the desk chair and opened the file. As he thumbed through the pages in silence, I paced the tiny office, checking my cellphone for messages and shooting off a couple of vague texts to Kellyn. When Baratti cleared his throat, I forced my feet to still and turned to face him.

"She bled out, so there was no lividity to go on, and by the time they found her, rigor was complete." His voice was calm and detached. "The only thing the M.E. had to base T.O.D. on was body temp and decomp—both of which could have been thrown off by extreme heat or extreme cold. She was in a bathtub." He held up Donnelly's photo as proof. "It's conceivable he covered her in ice to slow down decomp. The ice would've melted and drained from the tub by the time the authorities arrived, so they wouldn't have known."

"Is there any way to prove that?"

"It's possible," he said dubiously. "What's your theory?"

"My theory is that he planted his own fingerprints at the scene, because he knew he'd have a solid alibi for the estimated T.O.D."

Baratti flipped through the pages until he found the fingerprint analysis. "Shit," he said under his breath. He looked back up at me. "I presume you have other evidence to support this theory?"

"Nothing solid from a legal standpoint, but I'm working on it."

He closed the folder and, rising to his feet, handed it back to me. "Take this to Demarco."

I nodded, absently shoving the file back into my purse. "I'll call him."

Baratti's eyes narrowed. "You're not going to do anything stupid, are you?"

"Of course not."

"For some reason, I don't believe you."

"Really. I'm going back to the newsroom."

"Sure." He waved a hand in circles, palm up, indicating he knew there was more. "After what?"

Sighing, I slung my purse over my shoulder. "After I go home to check on Kellyn. She took the day off work, but she's not answering her phone."

"All right." Baratti removed his white lab coat and reached around me to pluck his jacket from a hook on the wall. "Let's go."

DURING THE SHORT DRIVE TO my condo, heavy clouds opened up and released a steady rain that darkened the sky to an early twilight. Baratti thumbed through my files and quizzed me on the clues and their meanings, playing devil's advocate wherever possible. If he intended to help me gain perspective or to prove me wrong, he failed. By the time we reached my condo complex, we'd fallen into a tense silence.

My knuckles whitened as I gripped the wheel, steering us through the maze of quiet residential streets. I parked in front of my garage and cut the engine but made no move to get out. Anxiety oozed out of my pores like sweat, making it hard to think clearly. Though I wouldn't admit it, I was glad Baratti had insisted on accompanying me. He was level-headed and calm, two vital qualities to have in life-or-death situations, and I had neither.

"We don't have to go in, you know," he said in a low voice—the voice of reason. "We could call the police."

"You don't have to go in." I let out a heavy sigh. "But I do."

His face contorted into a scowl. "No, you don't, but if you do, of course I'm going in. If there's any chance he's in there—"

"Then your coming in would only make him suspicious," I interrupted. "At least give me a head start."

The muscles in his jaw tightened. "I'll give you three minutes to check on Kellyn. Then I'll break down the damn door if I have to."

I unbuckled my seat belt and reached for the door handle, leaving the car key dangling from the ignition. "Fair enough."

"Hey," Baratti said as I pushed the door open. "Be careful."

Unable to find my voice, I nodded and climbed out of the car. On the way to the front door, I took a few deep breaths to slow my racing heart. By the time I pulled my house key out of my coat pocket and slid it into the deadbolt, the extra oxygen coupled with the cold rain had cleared my head and steadied my nerves.

The living room was dim when I pushed open the door, lit only by a few flickering candles and the blazing fire in the fireplace. Kellyn was snuggled up to Kenny on my couch, feet tucked under her and a glass of red wine in her hand. Stunned, I stood frozen in the foyer as she jumped to her feet, equally surprised.

"Hey, cuz." Her demeanor was somewhere between cheerful and embarrassed. "You're home early."

"I was worried about you. You weren't answering your phone."

"Shit, I'm sorry." Kellyn blew out a breath, running a hand through her hair. "Kenny called, and we talked for a long time, and—" She gestured behind her. "Things went well."

"I see." I slid my eyes from her to Kenny, who sprawled against the cushions, one arm thrown casually across the back of the couch, a glass of wine in his other hand.

His lips curved up in a smile as I appraised him. "What a pleasant surprise," he said, eyes sparkling in the light from the fire. I made a noncommittal noise, and the smile grew wider. "Why don't you come in? You can close the door and take off your coat, if you want."

My irritation flared, but I thrust it back down. "Only if I'm not interrupting."

"Well..." Kellyn's voice trailed off as she gave me a significant look.

Kenny waved a hand. "Relax, Kell. She can hang out with us if she wants." He winked. "We have time enough at last."

"Don't you also have your own house?" I said pointedly, dropping my purse to the table and tearing off my jacket. "Unless I really am in *The Twilight Zone*."

He smiled again, pleased I'd gotten the reference. "You're not. This is bona-fide reality."

"What a relief." I turned away to hang up my jacket. "I guess this is better than being the only survivor of an apocalypse."

Kenny let out a laugh. "Please, temper your enthusiasm."

"You're having another rough day," Kellyn declared. "I've got just the thing for that. You're not going back to work, right?" Without waiting for a reply, she bolted for the kitchen, leaving me standing stiffly in the foyer, eyes locked on Kenny as my mind raced.

He looked like his usual cocky self; if he knew that I knew, he wasn't giving it away. There was a possibility, however slim, that he didn't know that I knew, in which case the best plan of action was to keep pretending I didn't until reinforcements arrived.

Unless I could strangle him with my bare hands. That might be an acceptable alternative.

Kellyn reappeared, jolting me out of my thoughts, and presented me with a glass of wine. "Here, this should help."

I glanced from her to the glass and back again. "What's this?"

"Wine." When I didn't move, she thrust it into my hand and wrapped my fingers around it. "You've heard of it, right?"

I forced a laugh. "Might have."

Satisfied, she bounded away and plopped back down on the couch next to Kenny. "I'm sorry if we startled you. I figured by the time you got home, we'd be gone."

"Gone?"

"Well, yeah. Like to dinner or something." She grinned and wiggled her eyebrows up and down. "Today is our anniversary, after all."

"So I heard." I traipsed into the kitchen, ignoring the ting of a text message, muffled from inside my purse. "Which one, again?"

"Third," she answered.

"Hmm." I dumped the contents of my glass into the sink and reached for the open bottle on the counter. "What's the gift for the third anniversary?" I tipped the bottle upside down and watched the liquid splash against the stainless steel sink.

"Leather," Kenny called from the couch.

"Isn't that the traditional gift?" I asked. "I think the modern gift is glass." I swiveled away from the sink to face them, wine bottle clutched in my fist. "Did you pick this out?"

He nodded. "Do you like it?"

I flicked my gaze down at the bottle to read the label. "Taxi Cab Sauvignon." I let out a sardonic laugh. "Cute."

He gave me a lopsided grin. "I thought so, too."

"Did you bring leather as well?" I asked, dropping my arm back down to my side.

"Unfortunately, no," he said carefully. "I was unprepared to exchange gifts."

I clicked my tongue against the roof of my mouth in a tsk sound. "Not cool, Kenny."

"Well, after our conversation the other day, my expectations were pretty low."

I took a few steps closer, hand still clenched around the bottle's neck, and leveled my gaze with Kenny's. "You should have at least stopped at a grocery store for a bouquet." I made a show of looking around. "But you didn't."

"I wanted to get here as fast as I could."

"How romantic," I said dryly.

Kellyn giggled, and the sound made me cringe. "You must've stopped for the wine, though, right?"

Kenny shook his head. "I happened to have it on hand for this special occasion."

My jaw clenched tighter as I realized he was baiting me, trying to determine if I'd figured it out. Though I wanted nothing more than to ram the wine bottle into his temple and watch him crumple to the floor in an unconscious heap, I had to be careful. No matter how angry I was, he had an advantage over me.

I had a weakness: Right now, Kellyn. As far as I could tell, he had none.

"Good thinking." I forced a smile that didn't reach my eyes. "I like to have wine on hand for many an impromptu occasion as well."

Something flashed in his eyes—disappointment?—but was gone just as quickly. "One of your many attractive qualities."

Kellyn's eyebrows sank in confusion, but before she could respond, the front door swung open. Both she and Kenny swiveled to look, while I stifled a wince.

"Gavin?" Taken aback, Kellyn glanced from him to me. "What is he doing here?"

"A very good question." Eyes locked on me, Kenny slid his wine glass onto the coffee table and slowly rose from the couch. "Especially given the fact that you're not at all surprised."

Baratti pushed the door closed and cleared his throat. "Well, I, uh—"

"Shh," Kenny hissed, shaking an impatient hand at him. "We weren't talking to you."

A few beats of tense silence passed while I debated my response. If I wanted to maintain my semblance of ignorance, there was only one answer. Finally, I held my hands out wide. "All right," I said reluctantly. "You caught us."

"You told me yesterday that forgiving him was impossible."

I exchanged a glance with Baratti, who quickly redirected his gaze to the floor. "Not exactly. What I said was that—"

"You'd need a time machine, or to find out it was a hoax." Kenny's pale blue eyes sharpened. "We all know at least one of those is impossible."

I opened my mouth to respond, but Baratti beat me to it. "That's right," he said, stepping forward until he stood at my right side. "We built a time machine."

Kenny let out a humorless laugh as he glared at Baratti. "Of course you did."

I wasn't sure where Baratti was going with this, but I played along. "Just like you guys: We've got time enough at last."

His hands turned to fists at his side. "That's bullshit."

"As much as your apology to Kellyn was bullshit," I said, my voice controlled. "Whatever you told her doesn't change the fact that you are—"

"An adulterous bastard," he filled in. "Right?"

"No!" Kellyn jumped to her feet and rounded the coffee table to stand in front of me. "He didn't cheat. The whole thing was a big misunderstanding."

I blinked in dismay. "A misunderstanding?"

She nodded emphatically. "The fingerprint they found didn't match after all," she explained. "Kenny had the lab run it again, and there was some kind of anomaly in the first test."

"Wow," Baratti muttered. "I didn't realize you had that kind of pull at the Corine M.E.'s office."

"Why did he say he had an affair with Allison Donnelly if he hadn't?" I asked Kellyn.

"To get the police off his back."

I snorted and redirected my glare to Kenny. "So, what you're saying is, it was a hoax."

He smiled. "The truth has been uncovered, thanks to you."

Kellyn's eyes widened hopefully. "You did this?"

"It was Jennifer's idea to figure out the hoax." Kenny held out his arms and took a step closer, as if inviting me to hug him. "This is all happening because of you."

"You son of a bitch," I retorted, raising the bottle I'd forgotten I was holding. "How dare you lie to her and make it look like this was my idea?"

Baratti grabbed my arm and pulled me back a few steps, keeping his hand firmly in place to prevent me from advancing again. With a sigh, Kenny dropped his outstretched arms.

"It was easier than building a time machine, wasn't it?"

"What's all this about a time machine?" Kellyn asked, nonplussed.

Kenny swiveled to face her. "According to Jennifer, those are the only ways to make up for infidelity—going back in time to prevent the infidelity from occurring, or proving it to be a hoax." He slid his eyes back to Baratti, a slow smile spreading across his face. "Or in other words, nullifying the affair so it's as if it never happened. Isn't that ironic?"

Behind me, Baratti went so still and silent I wasn't sure if he was breathing. I swiveled toward him, finding his expression stony and face pale.

"You never did explain why you were here," Kenny said, rubbing his chin in mock thought. "Rather suspicious, isn't it? But then again, there's a lot of things you haven't explained."

"What are you talking about?" I asked, my voice dangerous. Kenny merely smiled, so I turned back to Baratti. "What's he talking about?"

"I don't know," he said hoarsely, keeping his eyes locked on Kenny, who let out an unexpected laugh.

"Now who's the lying son of a bitch?"

Baratti managed to keep his tone cool and even. "I think we're all more interested in the things you haven't explained."

"Agreed." Kellyn crossed her arms over her chest. "Just give me a straight answer: Did you cheat or not?"

Kenny groaned, his eyes sliding skyward. "You are much too fixated on this infidelity thing. In the grand scheme of things, it really doesn't matter, just as our marriage doesn't matter, just as you don't matter." He stared at her, shrugging indifferently. "At least, not anymore."

Kellyn's breath shortened into quick puffs, and her hands clenched into fists at her sides. "Get out."

His lips peeled back into a humorless smile. "You should be more careful, Kellyn. Once you invite a vampire in, he can come and go as he pleases."

"Unless he's dead," she seethed.

Before I could react, she yanked the wine bottle out of my hand and bolted forward, arm raised and ready to attack. In one fluid movement, Kenny pulled a gun from the waistband of his jeans and pointed it at her, halting her mid-swing.

"Drop it," he said. "Or I'll show you just how little you matter."

CHAPTER 19

FREEZING IN PLACE, KELLYN LET the bottle fall from her fingers. It hit the carpet with a dull thud as she stared at him, wide eyed and slack jawed. She didn't resist when I reached out and grabbed her by the sleeve, pulling her closer to us.

"Who are you?" she breathed.

He gestured at me with the gun. "Ask your cousin."

"Up until about sixty seconds ago," I said carefully, "you were Kellyn's soon-to-be ex-husband. Now I'm not so sure."

Kenny sighed dramatically, dropping his arms to his sides. "Then why did you bring him?"

"We already covered this."

"And determined it to be a giant pile of bullshit." Kenny waved a hand. "Try again."

"Like I said when I got here, I was worried about Kellyn."

"So you brought your ex-fiancé instead of your boyfriend?"

"Don't overanalyze. It was a proximity thing."

"And why was he in such close proximity?"

I rolled my eyes. "Why does it matter?"

He lifted a shoulder in a half shrug. "You have your reasons. I have mine."

On the other side of the room, my phone began ringing from inside my purse, and we all turned toward the sound. I glanced back at Kenny. "You're not going to shoot me if I get that, are you?"

"Hard to say." He shrugged as it rang again. "Might be safer if you don't."

Baratti stepped around me and Kellyn, putting himself in between us and Kenny. "It's time for you to go." He inched toward him. My phone rang a third time. "You've said what you wanted to say, and Kellyn's not changing her mind. This is over."

"Over?" Kenny repeated. "It's definitely not over, and I definitely haven't said everything I want to say."

He shuffled a little closer. "We're not interested," he said firmly, and my phone rang a fourth and final time. "Now go, before things turn ugly."

"I'm calling your bluff." Kenny raised the gun and pointed it at Baratti, who froze and held his arms out. "I think Jennifer is very interested."

"We can all agree Jennifer is very curious by nature," he said carefully. "But surely you don't think we were stupid enough to come here without backup."

"Why would you need backup?" Kellyn asked, her eyes darting back and forth.

Kenny smiled. "Why, indeed?"

"We had no idea if Kellyn was safe or how you were going to react." My voice wobbled a little, and I hoped he hadn't noticed. "Over the past few months, your behavior has been erratic at best."

Someone else's phone started ringing, and Kenny dug into his pocket with his free hand. He glanced down at the caller ID, frowning.

"That will be the negotiator," Baratti said. "Answer it."

Anger flashed across his face. "You're bluffing."

"Look at me." Baratti stood straight and still as a sculpture, his voice equally steady. "Does it look like I'm bluffing?"

I knew from personal experience that he could lie convincingly, but over the last few days, I'd realized he also had a tell—and right now, it was nonexistent. A minuscule bit of tension drained from my muscles.

The phone rang again, and Kenny poked a finger at the screen. The ringing stopped, and he slid it back into his pocket before refocusing his attention on us.

Baratti sighed. "They're just going to keep calling."

As if proving his point, another phone began ringing. Nobody moved, and a few seconds of silence passed before it rang again.

"I'm not interested in negotiating anything," Kenny said, an edge to his voice. "I have everything I want right here."

"Are you sure about that?" Baratti asked. "You don't want anything else—like a way out of here?"

Kenny laughed dryly. "Maybe you are that stupid." Another shrill ring. "We both know it's not going to be that easy, after what I've done."

"You've showed us your gun," I pointed out. "That's all. There's no reason we can't—"

"Stop lying!" he shouted over the ringing phone, making me jerk in surprise. "I've waited seven years for this, and you're ruining it."

"Seven years?" Kellyn exclaimed. "What are you talking about? We didn't know you seven years ago."

"But that doesn't mean I didn't know you." He directed this comment to me.

I swallowed, trying to regain my composure. "No, you didn't. And you still don't." This time, when Kellyn's phone began vibrating against the coffee table, I didn't hesitate to step forward.

Kenny shifted, redirecting the barrel of his gun at me. "Jennifer, I'm warning you."

"I have a feeling," I said slowly, fingers closing around the phone, "that if you were going to kill me, you'd have done it by now." I turned to face him, phone vibrating against my palm. "Am I right?" Eyes locked on him, I tapped the answer button and lifted the phone to my ear, daring him to prove me wrong. "Hello?"

"Jesus Christ," Mike said on the other end of the line. "Is everyone okay in there? Are you?"

"Peachy keen. We're just having a friendly chat."

"Does he have any weapons?"

"Yes."

"Gun?"

"Yes."

Mike muttered an expletive under his breath. "What does he want?"

"He hasn't told us yet, except that he doesn't want to negotiate."

Kenny stepped forward, yanked the phone out of my hand, and pressed it to his ear. "Detective," he snarled. "To what do I owe the pleasure?" He fell silent for a few seconds, and we held our collective breath. "Nope, not gonna happen." Another beat of silence. "I would be more than happy to discuss it, but no one's leaving. So either you come in here, or this conversation's over." A menacing smile spread across his face. "I knew you'd come around."

Without another word, Kenny disconnected, tossed the phone back onto the coffee table, and redirected his smile toward us.

"Have a seat," he ordered. "The show's about to start."

THOUGH IT WAS PROBABLY ONLY A COUPLE of minutes, it felt like we sat on the couch for hours, waiting in silence for Mike to arrive. Even though I was expecting it, a heavy knock on the door made me jump and sent my heart racing.

Kenny waved the gun at Baratti. "Get the door."

Without a word, Baratti stood and strode into the foyer. While his back was turned, Kenny grabbed my wrist and yanked me to my feet. I let out a surprised yelp and Baratti whirled around, but before either of us could react, Kenny wrapped an arm across my chest to anchor me to him. Baratti took a step forward, but stopped when Kenny lifted the gun and pressed it to my temple. I sucked in a breath and held it.

"Don't try anything heroic," he warned, his voice dangerous.

Jaw tight, Baratti reached behind him to open the door, keeping his gaze on us, and stepped aside. Mike charged in, eyes darting around the room to assess the situation, and froze when he saw me locked in Kenny's grip with a gun to my head.

"Thanks for joining us, Detective." His voice slithered across my face, making me shiver.

"Wouldn't miss it." Mike lifted his hands slowly. "Now, why don't you let her go before you get yourself into more trouble?"

Kenny laughed dryly. "Because letting her go is going to save me, after everything I've done?" he asked. "No, I think keeping her is what's going to save me."

"If letting her go is the difference between life in prison and the death penalty," Mike said evenly, "I'd say it's worth it."

Kellyn gasped and shot to her feet. "The death penalty?" she demanded. "What the hell is going on?"

Kenny's grip tightened, and he dragged me backward a few feet, putting some space between us and the angry mob. "All in good time, Kellyn," he said. "Detective, if you'd be so kind as to disarm yourself, we can get started."

Mike gave a barely perceptible head shake. "I'm not armed."

"Bullshit."

"I'm on administrative leave, thanks to you," he said, voice simmering with anger, "and I didn't exactly have time to raid the armory."

"I can shoot her faster than you can pull out a hidden weapon."

Mike's eyes flashed. "I know."

Kenny thought it over for a few beats. "Fine. Take a seat."

The room fell silent, and nobody moved.

In one swift movement, Kenny removed the gun from my temple, aimed it at the ceiling, and squeezed the trigger. The gun exploded, and bits of drywall rained down on us. "Everybody *sit down*," he screamed. "Now!"

Kellyn collapsed onto the love seat as if her legs could no longer support her. Baratti gave her shoulder a reassuring squeeze before he sat down on the side of the couch closest to her. Mike stood statue still for another few seconds before complying, his hard glare glued to us as he settled on the opposite end.

Behind me, Kenny loosened his grip slightly. "Your turn," he whispered, and I barely heard him over the ringing in my ears. "Can you follow directions for once?" I nodded obediently. "You only get one chance. Misbehave, and I'll shoot one of your friends." I nodded again. Satisfied, he let me go.

Without him holding me up, I discovered my entire body was shaking. It took all my strength to remain upright as I stumbled toward Mike.

"Hold it," Kenny warned, and I stopped in my tracks. "You stay right where you are." I held my breath and waited for orders. "Now turn around and face me."

I exchanged a brief glance with Mike. His eyes softened, and he nodded. Feeling somewhat bolstered, I straightened and turned to face Kenny, keeping the others in my peripheral vision.

"Okay, Kenny, you've got us where you want us," I said, my voice impossibly calm. "As you said, you've been waiting seven years for this, so get on with it."

He leveled his gaze with mine and stared at me for a few long moments. "You know, if you'd figured it out sooner, a lot of innocent people would still be alive right now."

"And if you'd just killed me seven years ago and been done with it," I said from behind gritted teeth, "they'd all still be alive."

His laugh was genuine. "Sweetheart, you have no idea how relieved I am that moron rear-ended us and ruined my plans. It would have been a huge mistake to kill you."

"Why?"

"Because I would have killed my one true equal."

"Equal?" The word came out choked. "Don't you dare call me your equal. I'm nothing like you."

"Equal but opposite," he amended. "Where I am weak, you are strong. The light to my dark. Yin and yang." He made a circle with his hand. "And so on."

"There are millions of people you could've chosen," I said. "Why me?"

His icy blue eyes sparkled in the fire light. "I think everyone here can agree there's something special about you. Something memorable." He paused, his lips peeling back in a sinister smile. "Something worth killing for."

I swallowed hard against the bile that bubbled just below my throat, my head spinning slightly as my breathing grew increasingly shallow.

"I tried three more times after the day you got into my cab, and each time I failed." He stared at me, unblinking, and I struggled not to look away. "I'm not accustomed to failure, and eventually I concluded there must be a reason why I couldn't kill you. But I needed to find out for sure, so I devised a little experiment to test you."

"Hannah Percy?"

"I thought she and her successors would be more than enough to get your attention, especially with the photos. You know I only sent those to you, right?"

I nodded slowly. "I do now. I didn't then."

"If you had been paying closer attention instead of allowing yourself to get distracted..." His voice drifted off as he shifted his glare toward Baratti. "I blame you for that."

Baratti stared back at him impassively. "Sorry."

Kenny snorted. "Yeah, I bet you are," he said. "No matter. I took care of it."

My heart jumped into my throat. "What did you say?"

"I took care of it," he repeated, loud and defiant. "Or, rather, Gavin did it for me." He smiled, and I followed his gaze as he slid his eyes back to Baratti. "Why don't you tell us what you did?"

"She already knows what I did." Baratti's face was pale but unreadable. "There's no reason to dredge up the past."

"I disagree. There's every reason to dredge up the past." He smiled, gesturing casually with the gun to remind us he was in charge. "Humor me, won't you?"

Baratti sighed and shifted uncomfortably. "A little over three years ago," he began, scratching his earlobe, "I met a woman at work, and we—"

Kenny darted over to Kellyn, grabbed a fistful of her hair, and dragged her to her feet. She shrieked and tried to claw herself free, but Kenny held tight.

"Try again," he said, jamming the gun into her neck.

Letting out a deep sigh, Baratti nodded and raked a hand through his hair. "All right. Just take it easy." He glanced up at me briefly before dropping his eyes to the floor. "Out of the blue, I started getting calls and texts from someone I didn't know," he said, his voice steady, as if he were talking about rush hour traffic. "They seemed innocuous at first—creepy, but nothing to worry about. Things like 'How long have you lived on Harper Street?' and 'I like your blue shirt today.'" Pausing, he lifted his gaze to mine. "Then they became more serious. Menacing. Threatening—not toward me, but you."

Paralyzed but for my racing heart, I locked eyes with Baratti and held my breath.

"I was given a week to break off our engagement, or this anonymous person would kill you." His voice faltered, and he dropped his gaze back to the floor. "At first, I didn't believe it. I wavered back and forth over what to do—telling you what was going on, calling the police, packing up our things and driving us to the other side of the country. But he escalated." He paused, shoulders lifting and falling as he took in another deep breath and let it out. "You were in a car accident—a hit and run. In my gut, I knew leaving wouldn't change anything; he would follow us wherever we went. And I realized I couldn't put it off any longer." He drew in a shallow breath and blew it out, and when he spoke again, his voice was barely audible. "I did what he wanted me to do. I did what I had to do to protect you."

"So you—" My voice caught in my throat, and I cut myself off. I swallowed hard and tried again. "You didn't—"

He shook his head. "No."

No one spoke for a few long beats as Baratti and I stared at each other, unblinking and unmoving. I felt numb and blurry, disconnected and disoriented—as if my mind had detached from my body, and I was watching the scene from afar.

"That worked for awhile," Kenny said, cutting into the silence. I jerked back toward him, my muscles hardening as he came into focus. "You didn't have one iota of desire to be involved with anyone. But you're human. The pain faded, and you forgot."

My hands clenched into fists until my nails dug into my palms, and an intense desire to scream flooded through me. But my jaw was clamped so tightly, I couldn't force myself to move my lips.

"I knew I needed something to get your attention, to make you see me the way you didn't before. Something more than photos." Letting the gun drift away from Kellyn's neck, he released her hair and ran his hand around her shoulder and across her chest. Eyes drifting closed, he ducked his head and pressed his face to the base of her neck, breathing deeply. She tensed and turned away, and he lifted his eyes back to mine, smiling as if he were drunk. "Once again, I had to take control."

"So you married Kellyn," I said, my voice sounding hollow and far away. "Murdered some more women. Sent me clues hidden in their portraits and planted fingerprints at the crime scenes."

Kenny smiled, evidently pleased. "Yes, but it's so much more than that. I may not have been able to force Gavin into infidelity, but..." Voice trailing off, he slid his eyes toward the couch, and I followed his gaze.

Mike's eyes were cold and flinty as he glared at Kenny. "You don't really think she's going to believe that, do you?"

"Believe what?" Kenny asked innocently. "I'm not sure what you're implying."

He let out a humorless laugh. "We've already figured out the fire was a setup."

"Good work, Detective, but the fact remains—" Kenny leaned into Kellyn, his arm encircling her shoulders; though he looked relaxed, he had her in a death grip. "We still don't know what happened afterward." He turned back to Mike, smiling maniacally. "Did you or didn't you? Fill us in, Detective: What happened when you were alone with her?"

My breath came out as a strangled growl, and I whirled toward Kenny before Mike had a chance to answer. Without thinking, I lunged at him, fingers bent like claws, ready to rip out his throat. But before I could reach him, I was jerked backward into an unyielding body; an arm slammed across my chest and another across my waist as I struggled ineffectually to break free.

"Fuck you," I screamed, struggling to free myself. "Who the hell do you think—"

"Jen, stop!" Mike shouted, suddenly in my line of sight. I blinked to clear my vision; beyond him, Kellyn scratched ineffectually at Kenny's arm around her neck as she gasped for air.

I deflated against Baratti, whose embrace tightened to keep me from collapsing. He whispered something in my ear—some lie about how everything would be okay—and I knew down to my bone marrow it wasn't true, and it never would be.

Kenny's expression was intense as he locked eyes with me, and when he spoke, his voice was impossibly gentle. "You don't want to know, do you?"

I glared daggers at him, taking quick, shallow breaths. "Go. To. Hell."

"But I want to hear the end of the story." One corner of his lips jerked up in a cruel half-smile. "And you need to know how it ends, or you're always going to wonder."

Kellyn made a choking sound, and my rage morphed into fear.

"Please let her go. This has—" I paused again, out of breath, as if Kenny's arm was compressing my neck instead of Kellyn's. "This has nothing to do with her."

He eyed me suspiciously. "Are you going to be good?"

I couldn't force myself to verbalize agreement, so I merely nodded.

"Are you going to come with me voluntarily?" When I hesitated, he lifted his other arm and laid it on top of his other, tightening his grip on Kellyn's neck. Her eyes widened in panic.

"Yes," I blurted, sounding desperate even to myself. "Yes, I'll come with you, but please let her go."

Kenny loosened his grip on Kellyn, who sucked in a ragged gasp. Baratti tightened his on me. "No." His breath whispered into my ear. "You're not going anywhere with him."

Mike stepped in front of me, blocking my view of Kenny's triumphant smile. He was close enough that I could feel the heat radiating off his body, and the desire to curl up in that warmth overwhelmed me. My throat closed as a treacherous tear slid down my cheek.

"If you want to take her," Mike said, his voice dangerous, "you're going to have to kill me first."

Kenny laughed. "Although I would be delighted to honor your request, I've no plans to kill you or anyone else tonight. It would be counterproductive to my goal—but I will if I have to, so don't tempt me."

"Is that supposed to scare me?" Mike retorted. "Let's settle this, right here and now. Let Kellyn go."

"And if I don't?" Kenny asked, and something in his voice compelled me to lift my head and try to peek around Mike. Baratti held me firmly in place. "I could very easily just—" He paused, and Kellyn whimpered. "Shoot her."

"Go ahead," Mike said. "If you do, you'll have nothing left to protect you, and it'll be just you and me." He reached his left arm around, fumbled for my hand, and squeezed it tightly. "And I swear to God, you won't get out of here alive."

Kenny snorted. "You don't have it in you."

"Wanna bet?" Mike countered. "Let's find out."

With that, he gave me a hard shove backward and released me, and the last thing I saw before Baratti dragged me out the front door was Mike lunging for Kenny as Kellyn's scream fused with mine.

Momentarily stunned, I stumbled along behind Baratti until the cold rain jolted me out of my stupor, and I dug my heels into the sidewalk. "No," I said desperately, tearing away from Baratti and pivoting back toward the house. "We can't leave them—"

He caught my arm and whirled me around to face him. "There is no way I'm letting you go back in there. That was our deal before he got here: Mike agreed to take down Kenny if I got you out." He pulled me tight against his chest, so close I had to tilt my head back to meet his steely eyes. "And this is one promise I'm not breaking."

Baratti turned and resumed dragging me toward the car, and I let my body go slack, knocking him off balance so he fell to the ground with me. "I can't let him win again." Tears streamed down my face, mixing with the rain. "I won't."

Baratti levered himself off me and crouched on one knee. "He's not getting out of this, I swear. I called for backup. It should be here..." Frowning, he glanced around. "By now."

I followed his gaze, finding nothing but a quiet neighborhood, devoid of life on a cold, rainy day. "Call again."

He shook his head and stood. "Come on, we have to go," he said, pulling me to my feet. "I'll call once we're..."

Voice trailing off, Baratti's eyes rolled backward, and he crumpled to the ground in a heap. Natasha Sardelis stood behind him, face shadowed under the hood of a raincoat as she opened her fist to release an empty syringe. With her other hand, she leveled a gun at me.

"Backup's here." She grabbed my arm. "Let's go."

I gaped at her. "What did you do to him?"

She whirled me around and pushed me toward a car parked at the curb. "I'd be more worried about myself if I were you."

"One of the many ways you and I are different," I retorted.

Sardelis reached around me and pulled open the passenger-side door. "Lucky for you, I don't think Demarco and I will be partners much longer." She flicked her gun in the direction of the seat. "Get in."

I pivoted to face her, steeling myself. "No."

She let out a humorless laugh. "It's not optional. Get in the car."

"No," I said, raising my voice.

"You have no idea who you're dealing with, Jennifer," she spat. "I'm almost free, and I'm not going to let you screw it up. Now get in the car, or I will *make* you get in the car."

"No!" This time I shouted my defiance as I stepped closer to her, so we were almost nose to nose. "I think you got very specific instructions not to hurt me, so unless you want to risk your life further, we're not going any goddamn where."

"You still think this is all about you, don't you?" She shook her head in disgust. "News flash, Lois Lane: If you die, he'll just pick someone else. I sure as hell don't want that on my conscience, so if I have to sacrifice myself to stop that from happening, so be it."

With one quick movement, she lifted her arm and jammed a needle into my neck. I winced at the sharp pain, but it quickly faded as an icy numbness spread through my veins. My legs weakened and head grew heavy as I blinked at her.

"Why?" I whispered, head swirling.

"We aren't so different, you and I," she said, her voice inflectionless. "To protect the people you love, you'd sacrifice anything." She smiled tightly. "Including yourself."

Then my vision darkened, my body went limp, and I fell into darkness.

CHAPTER 20

I WOKE WITH A RAGGED gasp, blinking into darkness as I tried to orient myself. All I knew was the room was pitch black and silent, I was lying on something cushioned, and my thoughts were fuzzy. The light in my mind slowly brightened, revealing snippets of recent events: Kellyn's blue-tinged face as she gasped for air. Mike squeezing my arm before lunging away from me. Baratti dragging me through the rain. Sardelis's cold eyes and a sharp prick in my neck. The realization struck me a second time, leaving me breathless and afraid.

Kenny.

As soon as his name snaked through my mind, I heard a rustling somewhere in the room, and I jerked upright. I was able to sit, but something pulled against my wrists and legs, preventing me from going farther.

"It would have been much easier," Kenny said in a low voice, "if you'd've just cooperated." The cushion on my right side sank slightly before a low-wattage light flicked on. I blinked rapidly in the sudden brightness. "But you had to make it difficult."

Still groggy from whatever drug Sardelis had injected, my mind wasn't able to summon any words. Instead, I took a mental inventory of my physical state, relieved to find I was still fully clothed.

"But I suppose that's what we do, you and I." He made no move to grab me as I inched away from him. "Back and forth, push and pull—even if it would be simpler just to give in."

Daring to glance up at him, I found him stony faced as he watched me in silence, and I struggled not to look away. Kenny held my gaze for a few beats, then leaned into me, close enough that I could feel the heat from his body and smell the booze on his breath. I tensed and turned away. Sighing lightly, as if mildly disappointed, he began loosening the bindings on my wrists.

"What remains to be seen," he said in a low voice, "is whether you live up to my expectations now, when it counts."

"What do you mean?" My words dragged out, slurred and hoarse.

He pulled the ropes until they slid free of the iron bedposts and, dropping them to the floor, met my eyes. "Fight back. If you can get past me, I'll let you go."

I blinked. "That sounds like a lie."

"I'm not surprised you think that." He turned away and began working on the ties around my ankles. "After all, I have been deceiving you for as long as you've known me."

"And you tried to kill me," I mumbled, a trickle of sarcasm oozing out from the mush of my brain.

He let out an unexpected laugh. "Thrice—but now that everything's out in the open, I have no need to lie anymore."

"I still don't believe you."

"Understandable." With one final tug, he freed my ankles and rose to his feet. "But why else would I untie you?"

I shook my head. "I can't explain your motivations any more than I can explain time travel."

"I guess there's only one way to find out."

"Sodium pentathol and a game of twenty questions?"

His eyes sparkled in amusement. "It seems your signature sarcasm is making a comeback," he said. "Guess the ketamine is wearing off."

"Is that what Sardelis gave Baratti?"

"Ah, so, the game has begun." He smiled, pleased I was participating. "Bear in mind that this is reciprocal. You have to answer my questions, too."

I nodded once. "You're the boss."

His smile widened. "I like this game already," he said. "And yes, Gavin got a nice big hit of Special K. He's probably feeling pretty crappy right now."

"So he's alive." I phrased it as a statement, but we both knew I was asking for confirmation.

"Most likely."

This—keeping him talking—might be my best and only chance to delay my forthcoming rape and murder so Mike had more time to find me.

Mike. The syllable reverberated between my ears, bringing forth a fresh wave of panic. I swallowed hard and swung my legs over the side of the bed. The movement was too quick, making the room wobble nauseatingly, and I dropped my head heavily into my hands.

"What about Mike and Kellyn?" I asked, my voice muffled.

"Not so fast—it's my turn." He waited patiently until my head had stopped spinning and I sat up straight. "I want to go back to Gavin before we move on." I sighed but didn't argue. "Are you still in love with him?"

"No," I said without hesitation.

"Are you sure about that?" he prodded. "Even now that you know the truth?"

I stared at him, deadpan. "I've been unconscious for most of the time since I found out, and I believe it's my turn."

His eyes slid skyward. "Fine. Go."

"Are Mike and Kellyn still alive?" I asked again.

"Maybe. Maybe not." He shrugged. "Does knowing the truth change your feelings toward Gavin?"

I mimicked his shrug. "Maybe. Maybe not."

Kenny let out an annoyed sigh. "Yes, Kellyn is alive. I'm not sure about Mike. He wasn't looking his usual badass self when I left." He narrowed his eyes. "Now you."

I shoved away another rush of fear and focused on staying calm. "I've been unconscious for most of the time since I found out, so I haven't really had a chance to process the news." I gave him a tight smile. "And now I'm focused on you."

He brightened at the statement. "Good answer."

Taking advantage of his improved mood, I rose tentatively to my feet. "What do you plan to do with me?" I asked. "What's your goal?"

Kenny studied me for a few beats, unmoving. "As I told you before, you are the yin to my yang. We began on opposite sides—and we obviously still are—but eventually you'll realize how well we complement each other. Alone, we are each great, yes, but together we can be greater. Stronger. More powerful. Unstoppable." His expression softened and eyes glazed over, as if he were imagining all the destruction we would wreak. "Once you see that, we will accomplish so much."

"Like what?"

The sound of my voice jolted him back to reality, and he let out a delicate sigh. "You'll find out soon enough." He smiled pleasantly. "My turn."

Clamping my mouth shut, I shifted to the other foot, adding a few inches to the distance between us—and bringing me a few inches closer to the closed door. I gave an exaggerated wave to cover up the movement. "Of course. Go ahead."

"If you somehow manage to escape me, who would you choose—Mike or Gavin?"

Again, I answered without thinking. "Mike. I told you, I don't love Gavin anymore."

Kenny's eyebrows arched. "Even if Mike cheated on you?"

I tried to keep my face blank. "Are you implying that he slept with Sardelis?"

"That's exactly what I'm implying."

My stomach turned, and I swallowed hard. "Do you have proof?"

"Do I need it?" he shot back.

"Do we need to review your track record again?"

His eyes flashed. "It doesn't matter if you believe me. The seed is planted."

"What difference does it make?" I exclaimed, throwing my arms in the air and taking another tiny step away. "If you're planning on holding me hostage until one of us kills the other, none of this means a damn thing!"

The corners of his mouth lifted into a smug smile. "There it is," he said in a singsong voice. "Your fire. One of many reasons I chose you."

"And what happens if I refuse?"

"I realize it's going to take some time to bring you around, but ultimately, if you refuse..." Voice trailing off, he shrugged. "Then I was wrong about you, and I'll have to start over." He shook his head ruefully. "I really hate wasting time, almost as much as I hate being wrong."

"Get used to it." I glared at him defiantly. "I will never be your partner."

"Even if it means you'll cause the deaths of more people—including your own?" He paused, and when I didn't answer, he smiled smugly. "You have two options. One, you can continue to resist and make the rest of your life a living hell. Or two, you can come to terms with the situation and make the best of it." He crossed his arms over his chest. "Your choice."

I shook my head. "You're forgetting the third option." I pivoted away from the bed and began inching backwards. He followed me with his eyes but otherwise remained still. "That's the one where you go to death row, and I live happily ever after."

He snorted. "Happily ever after? You think you can be happy after this?"

"Why wouldn't I be?" I retorted. "You'd spend the rest of your life in a six-by-six metal box until they put a needle in your arm, and I would never think of you again."

Eyes flashing, he took a step closer to me, and I compensated by stepping backward. "You will never forget me," he seethed. "Free or imprisoned, dead or alive, I'll always be there." Another step. "Lurking in the back of your mind." And another. "Haunting your dreams." He closed the distance between us, backing me up against the cold cinderblock wall. "Controlling your thoughts, your actions, *your entire life*." He shouted the last three words, sending flecks of saliva across my face, and I flinched. "After all, haven't I been doing it for the past seven years?"

I shook my head automatically, but I wasn't certain he was wrong. As if sensing my trepidation, Kenny smiled again, but this time it wasn't the carefree, harmless smile he'd been using up until now. This smile was ominous, made colder by his icy eyes and flat expression.

"You don't have to admit it to me, or even yourself, but you know deep down I'm right." He took a few steps backward and held his arms out wide. "And now I'm going to give you the chance to prove it."

"I don't think it would be a fair fight," I said, trying to keep my voice from shaking. "You've got at least fifty pounds and six inches on me, plus a clear head. You're setting me up for failure."

"As usual, you are right."

"So what do you propose?"

"As a show of good faith, I'll give you a sixty-second head start." He gestured to something behind me, and I glanced over my shoulder to see I was pressed up against a door. "It's unlocked. If you can make it outside in a minute or less, you'll be free."

I stared at him, my body motionless as my mind raced to find the loophole. He sighed and pulled his cellphone out of his pocket, tapped it a few times, and turned it around to show me.

"Sixty seconds," he said, his finger hovering over the start button of the timer. "Go."

I didn't need to be told twice. Heart pounding, I whirled and yanked on the door handle, relieved to find it unlocked. I propelled myself through and slammed it closed, glancing around as my eyes readjusted. The room was dark but for a narrow shaft of moonlight filtering through a pair of high windows to my right, and I realized I was in a basement.

I dashed up half a dozen creaky stairs, finding myself in a small foyer on the landing, with a front door to my right and more stairs to my left. I paused with my hand on the doorknob as my mind raced to catch up with my heart.

This was too easy. Something was wrong.

That's when I heard it—a muffled scream from just beyond the top of the stairs.

Shit. There was someone else here.

Fighting against every instinct screaming at me to save myself, I stumbled up the rest of the stairs and into the dark room before I could change my mind. My eyes had adjusted to the darkness enough that I could make out the form of a body writhing on the carpet. As I approached, the screams grew more hysterical, and I realized it was Kellyn.

"Omigod, Kell." I dropped to the floor next to her and ripped the tape off her mouth. "Are you hurt?"

"I think I'm okay." I felt around for her hands and, when I found them, yanked hard at the bindings. "I'll get the rest," she hissed as the rope fell away. "Go find something to use as a weapon. *Hurry.*"

Holding my arms straight out zombie style, I bolted into the next room and promptly rammed my hip into the corner of something—a countertop. Biting back a curse, I ran my shaky hands along the surface, finding it empty but a microwave set against the side of a refrigerator, followed by a wall.

I spun around and ran my fingers along the wall until I bumped into another countertop. I followed it, trailing my hands across a stovetop, over a sink, and finally, across the smooth wood of a fully stocked knife block.

Just as I seized a butcher knife, the door in the basement creaked open. My heart plunged into my stomach, and I tiptoed back to the other side of the kitchen, where I could use the cabinets as cover.

A few seconds later, a stair let out a soft groan. I flattened myself against the wall that separated the kitchen from the stairs. Me from Kenny.

I tightened my grip on the knife.

A pair of feet shuffled across the landing, and I mentally kicked myself for not opening the door and leaving it ajar.

A second later, another creak. I drew in a shallow breath and held it, straining my ears to listen.

There was a long silence, followed by a swish of fabric and a blur of solid black. Kenny bolted across the room, and Kellyn let out a shriek. Crouching down on the floor, he pulled her into a sitting position and clapped a hand over her mouth.

"Come out, come out, wherever you are," he called softly. The dark shadow of his body shifted. "You know I can see you, right?" I hesitated, and he let out an irritated sigh. "You're up against the kitchen wall like paint."

I let out the air I was holding. "I think I'll stay right here until you step away from Kellyn."

"I admire your confidence, Jennifer, but you have zero bargaining power right now."

"And if you kill her," I said, "neither will you."

"That's true." He made another quick movement, but in the darkness I couldn't tell what he'd done. Kellyn whimpered. "But I could do a lot of damage."

"All right, Kenny." As I took a baby step out of the kitchen, he released her and straightened to his full height. Gasping in relief, she army crawled backward. "Have it your way."

I lunged forward, leading with the butcher knife. I managed to connect with something solid, and he let out a hiss but quickly recovered, catching my wrist and jerking my arm out to my side.

We tumbled backward several feet until I slammed into the kitchen wall, and before I had a chance to catch my breath, he pressed his forearm across my neck, cutting off my oxygen. He grasped my right wrist so tightly my fingers began to tingle, and the knife dropped to the floor with a clatter.

"I give you props," he said, his breath hot on my face. "That was a courageous effort, but unfortunately you weren't able to escape." He let out a short laugh. "Guess you're staying."

Behind me, blinds crunched against a window pane as I fought ineffectually to free myself. The pressure of his arm against my neck intensified, and I struggled to breathe, the fingers of my free hand desperately roaming the empty air for something to grab on to.

"I told you, if you had just given in—"

A frenzied scream cut off the rest of his sentence, a second before Kellyn slammed into us. The force of her collision caused Kenny's weight to press into me harder, and I choked. Tears sprang to my eyes, my lungs burned, and the edges of my vision darkened. I gagged and squeezed my eyes closed.

This was it.

Suddenly, unexpectedly, he let go of me. My knees gave out, and I sank to the floor, sucking air into my chest. He let out an enraged shout and spun away, and I shimmied across the floor, feeling for the knife.

The relief was short lived.

Kellyn yelped in surprise when Kenny grabbed her and threw her against the wall. My fingers brushed against the cold steel of the knife handle as she fell silent and crumpled to the floor.

Then he was back on top of me, and I let out a strangled scream as he pinned me to the cold tile. He grabbed both of my wrists in one hand and pressed them to the floor above my head. The knife slipped out of my grasp, a second before he dragged its tip lightly down my face. I froze as I stared up at him, wide eyed and barely breathing.

"I wasn't expecting that." His alcohol-laden breath slithered across my skin. "This has been more fun than I had hoped." He pressed the knife into my cheek, and I winced as the blade pierced my skin. "I can't wait until the next stage."

A fresh wave of panic surged through me, and I tried to shift my hips to knock him off, tried to yank my hands out of his, tried to lift my leg to knee him in the groin—but he only crushed down harder against me.

My fingers began to tingle as something dripped down the side of my face; I wasn't sure if it was blood or tears. Maybe both.

Kenny glanced to his right. "It's too bad about Kellyn." I let out a strangled cry and jerked my head away, long enough to see her inert form, a lifeless heap just out of reach. He dropped the knife; it hit the floor with a clang as he grabbed my jaw in his hand, swiveling my face back to him. After staring at me for a long time, he relaxed his grip. "It would have been even more fun if she could've joined us."

"Leave her alone." I whispered the words, afraid my voice would shake and betray my fear. "Haven't you done enough to her?"

The corners of his mouth twitched. "If you wanted me all to yourself," he said, fingers grazing across my cheek, "all you had to do is ask."

I shuddered involuntarily. "You can't win. You won't win. They'll find me—"

A slow, maniacal smile spread across his face. "Oh, I know they will," he said. "But that doesn't mean I won't win."

"You could go now." My fear oozed from my body like blood, and I hated myself for not being able to control it. "You could still get away."

"I don't want to get away—at least not yet." His fingers trailed across my jawline, down my neck to my chest. I swallowed hard as he slid his hand across my belly and under the hem of my shirt, just barely touching my skin. "I've waited too long for this to rush it."

He wasn't afraid of getting caught, I realized. Nothing was more dangerous than a desperate person who didn't care what he lost or what price he had to pay—as long as he got what he wanted.

And that's when what little hope I had left dissipated, and panic consumed me.

"Shh," Kenny murmured as I started shaking uncontrollably. I squeezed my eyes shut when I felt his lips skim across mine, and my stomach rolled nauseatingly. "Everything's going to be okay. You'll see."

Letting go of my hands, he thrust his fingers into the side of my neck, just under my throat. Whimpering, I used my now-free hands to push against him, to scratch his face and arms, to strike anything I could find, but with each passing second, my energy and awareness dwindled exponentially, and I grew weaker.

I had one last thought before I lost consciousness—the sound of my mother's voice, whispering through my memory.

He wants his victims to fight back.

CHAPTER 21

AFTER THAT, EVERYTHING BLURRED TOGETHER.

I didn't remember waking up, or how much time passed. I didn't remember Kenny dragging me back down to the basement, back into his secret lair and locking the door, leaving Kellyn unconscious on the kitchen floor. I didn't remember him tossing me down on the mattress and tearing off my clothes.

But I remembered sheer panic flooding my veins when I became aware of it.

I remembered his eyes, cold and unblinking and triumphant. His hands roaming across my trembling body, his weight crushing against me so I couldn't move, could barely breathe.

I remembered my mother's words as I struggled against every cell in my being that wanted me to fight and shriek and claw his eyes out.

I remembered him screaming at me to fight back. Taunting me and calling me vulgar names. Slapping me or pressing his forearm across my neck or sliding the tip of the knife across my skin when I didn't comply.

I remembered wondering if ignoring my instincts would prove to be fatal. If my refusal to play his game would make him so angry that he'd slit my throat in a fit of rage and storm off to find someone else to torture. If he'd leave me here to rot in a dark, secret room where no one would ever find me.

I remembered the trickle of tears sliding down my face as pain ripped through me, spreading across my nerves, from my core to the tips of my fingers and toes, and bleeding into my soul.

I remembered letting my vision go fuzzy, so Kenny's face blurred around the edges and his icy blue eyes deepened into bright cerulean. When he turned into Mike, summoning images that flashed unbidden through my mind: The look in his eyes just before he kissed me for the first time. The feel of his fingers brushing across my face to tuck my hair behind my ear. The sound of his easy laughter when we stayed in bed late on Sunday mornings.

I remembered the cry of agony ripping from my throat when I realized it wasn't him. Realized I might never see him again. Realized he was probably dead. Realized maybe I would be soon, too.

I remembered when the nausea took over. When my eyes slid shut, leaving me in darkness. When seeing nothing became preferable to seeing the evil around me.

I remembered the afterimage of Kenny's face shifting against my eyelids until it resembled Gavin's: Cold blue eyes warming into dark brown, smug sneer softening into a reverent half smile.

I remembered how he ripped me back to reality, shattering my short reprieve, when he whispered in my ear: *You can never be with either one of them, now that you know the truth.*

I remembered the shock of comprehension, of knowing that he was right. The way it took my breath away, squeezing my chest tighter and tighter—the physical sensation of my metaphorical heart and soul breaking apart.

I remembered when the realization hit me, when it finally dawned on me that I was going to die.

I remembered welcoming death. Pleading with it to take me. Now, before it was too late, before my soul dissolved into nothing, before I stopped existing.

I remembered not caring.

Only then did my mind dissociate from my body and my surroundings fade away, and I finally went numb.

《》

THE SOUND OF EAR-PIERCING SCREAMS jolted me back into consciousness. Sucking in a gasp, I sat up straight, a corpse coming back to life, as my eyes darted around trying to find Kellyn, trying to find Kenny. Everything around me was shrouded in a too-bright fog.

That's when I realized I had no idea where I was, and the panic intensified.

There was a shuffle to my left, and I whirled in the direction of the sound. Kenny was closing in, his face blurry and unrecognizable as he pushed me back down onto the bed. I squeezed my eyes shut and thrashed against him, my guttural shrieks diluting the sound of his voice as he pressed firmly against my shoulders.

I *should have fought before*. The words circled my mind in an endless loop, mingling with the knowledge that now it was too late. Someone pressed a mask over my mouth and nose, and the terror intensified. I tried to kick my legs, swing my fists, but something held me down. I couldn't move.

And then, as my muscles relaxed and my body melted into the thin mattress, I finally heard the words, repeated over and over and over—hollow and far away, but becoming clearer.

You're safe.

My eyes flew open, and I blinked up at a young man, his light brown eyes wide with concern, sandy hair ringed in a halo of bright white light. It slowly dawned on me that the screams were the sirens of an ambulance; this man was a paramedic who wanted to help me. With this epiphany, my mind allowed my body to slacken and succumb to the unexpected relief.

"You're safe," he said again, his voice softer. When I stopped struggling, he let go of my shoulders and picked up my hand, giving it a tight squeeze. "It's over."

I stared at him, unblinking, afraid that if I closed my eyes, it would all fade away into a dream. Hot tears streamed down my face until my eyes stung, and I couldn't keep them open any longer.

I didn't understand then that the nightmare wasn't over. It had only just begun.

《》

AN EERIE CALM HAD DESCENDED on me by the time the special victims detective arrived in the cold, sterile hospital exam room. The E.R. doctor sent her a brief glance as she finished dressing the cuts on my face and offered me a mild painkiller—just strong enough to take the edge off, but not so strong that I would be unaware of what happened next.

As if being alert would be reassuring.

To my relief, I didn't recognize the detective, whose name dissipated as soon as she began explaining why I should consent to a sexual assault exam, wherein a specialized nurse would gather evidence that could help identify and prosecute my attacker.

My laugh barely came out, the sound of it dry and throaty as I slid my eyes away from her to stare blindly at a small chip in the pale green wall. I wanted to ask her what the point was—I knew damn well who my attacker was; the sight of his face above me, the feel of his body pressing against mine, the sweat that dripped from his forehead onto my face would be burned in my memory until the day I died—but I couldn't form the words. My throat was raw and aching, and I could feel phantom hands wrapping around my neck.

The detective gave me a minute to compose myself. "I know you're not supposed to talk right now," she said, and I briefly wondered why but said nothing. "For now, just nod to consent to the exam. We can talk about what happened later, when the swelling in your throat goes down."

I didn't want to nod, but I did anyway.

The detective faded into the background when a solemn nurse, her black hair tightly bound in tiny braids that grazed her shoulders, shuffled into my room with a tall, kind-faced woman whose wrinkles belied how many times she had done this.

The nurse introduced herself as Naomi—or was it Nina?—before busying herself with exam prep. Margie, the older woman, told me she was a victim advocate, and my stomach turned at the term. As she explained what her role in the process was, she handed me a styrofoam cup of water with a thin straw and wrapped her hands around mine as I shakily lifted it to my lips.

Naomi-Nina sat down on a stool to take my medical history. Because I couldn't speak, she gave me the forms where I could disclose my own and my family's disease history, any drugs I was taking, my recent sexual activity, and number of partners prior to the incident. She asked me to place X's on a two-dimensional outline of a woman's body wherever there might be any evidence. I stared at the page for a few long beats, tears blurring my vision as I marked both sides of the body with two large X's.

Then Naomi-Nina drew a curtain separating us from the detective and gave me a hospital gown to put on. She and Margie looked away as I undressed atop an oversized square of white paper, meant to capture any stray hairs or skin cells. I caught sight of my right hand and noticed numbly that my ring finger was bare.

Another piece of my heart cracked off.

When I eased myself back onto the gurney, Margie folded my chilled hand into her warm one. She murmured meaningless words of comfort in a soft, sympathetic voice as the nurse gave me the most thorough exam I'd ever had. She swabbed inside and outside my body, yanked out hairs, scraped under my nails, took blood and urine samples and immediately sent them off to the lab. She photographed every scratch, every cut, every bruise, every square inch of skin.

Time disappeared along with whatever dignity I had left as she asked me questions that made me cringe and avert my gaze in shame. Somehow I answered every one of them. With each question, each poke or prod, each flash of the camera, another little piece of me chipped away and died. But still I felt nothing.

Hours or days or years later, Naomi-Nina packed everything she'd gathered into a cardboard box and sealed it with a long sticker. She patted my hand, her black eyes glistening and sympathetic as she told me she'd be back soon. Margie squeezed my hand again and asked if I was hungry. I wasn't. She went to refill my cup with water, and I barely noticed she was gone.

Some time later, the doctor came back in and dropped onto the stool Naomi-Nina had occupied earlier. She gave me the results of my blood and urine tests, which I promptly forgot. Then she talked to me about my risks of contracting STIs, about post-exposure prophylaxis to prevent them, about emergency contraception to prevent pregnancy, about follow-up care.

I swallowed hard against the vomit that bubbled on the edge of my throat, signed the consent forms, and somehow managed to choke down the array of pills she presented me.

When Naomi-Nina returned, she brought with her a pair of navy blue scrubs, an oversized gray hoodie, a pair of thin socks, and some cheap cotton underwear. She and Margie tiptoed to the other side of the curtain, promising to return with the last round of paperwork.

And then I would be able to go home.

I sat on the thin mattress for a few minutes, ears ringing in the sudden silence, as I contemplated what came next. Home? My home was destroyed, and I had no idea how I'd ever be able to go back.

Finally, I slid off the gurney and pressed my bare feet onto the cold tiled floor as I shakily straightened my legs. My head spun sickeningly, my vision darkened, my body transformed into lead, and I began to fall.

Once again, I welcomed unconsciousness.

CHAPTER 22

THE NEXT TIME I WOKE, I was in a different hospital room, dark but for a puddle of yellow light streaming in from beyond the cracked door and the red and green lights of the machines ticking next to me. On one wrist, I wore a plastic bracelet printed with my name and blood type; in the other, an IV connected to a bag of clear liquid hanging above me.

I hadn't wanted to go home so badly that I'd passed out and gotten myself admitted to the hospital. I almost laughed.

Too tired to sit up on my own, I fumbled at the buttons on the bed's handrail, pressing a few before I found the lift. By the time I got myself comfortable, a nurse breezed in, features flat in the darkness.

"Good, you're awake." Her shoes squeaked softly on the floor as she strode up to me, and she reached behind my bed to flip on a dim overhead light. "How are you feeling?"

Blinking to clear the film over my eyes, I considered this, ultimately deciding it was too complicated to figure out right now. "Exhausted and sore," I croaked. "What time is it?"

She glanced at her wristwatch. "Just after three in the morning."

"Um—what day is it?"

"Friday." At my confusion, she frowned. "What day do you remember it being?"

"Wednesday, I think."

"I'm going to go find the on-call doctor," she said. "In the mean time, there's someone who wants to see you."

"At three in the morning?"

"He arrived shortly after you did yesterday and paced the halls until one of the other nurses convinced him to go home and get some sleep," she explained. "He made us swear on all we hold dear to call him immediately when you woke up." She raised her thick brows in question. "So, are you feeling up to a visit?"

I blew out a breath. "How bad do I look?"

She smiled ruefully. "You look alive."

Closing my eyes, I dropped my head back against the pillow. "Okay." Without another word, she patted my hand and left, and I concentrated on breathing.

And realized I was scared.

A few minutes later, the on-call doctor arrived and checked my vitals. He explained that they'd kept me overnight because I was severely dehydrated, and my blood pressure and temperature had been borderline dangerous. He expected everything to stabilize as the ketamine worked its way out of my system over the next few hours and assured me that memory loss was normal.

"You may remember what happened," he said gently, "but there's a good chance you won't."

On his way to the door, he flicked off the overhead light, leaving me in semi-darkness. I closed my eyes and prayed I never did.

《》

WHEN I HEARD THE DOOR open and close—so quietly that I wouldn't have heard it if my fight-or-flight senses weren't on overdrive—I took a few seconds to steel myself, knowing that when I opened my eyes, I would have to confront a new reality.

Mike leaned against the door frame, the light from the hallway barely touching him. I blinked a few times while my eyes adjusted, trying to make out his face.

"Hey," I whispered, so he wouldn't hear how terrible my voice sounded.

He let out a deep sigh. "Hey."

I held out a hand toward him. "Come here."

His shoes were silent on the tile floor as he closed the distance between us, his hands warm as he grasped mine. He bent down to kiss each of my knuckles before folding my hand into both of his and staring at me for a few long beats. The knot in my belly loosened as I clutched onto him, the buoy I'd been desperately searching for.

"How do you feel?" he asked finally.

I shook my head. "I don't know."

He let out a harsh breath. "God, Jennifer, I'm so sorry."

I felt an unexpected prickle behind my eyes, and I drew in a shaky breath. "It's not your fault. I shouldn't have confronted him."

Mike sank down into a chair next to my bed, still firmly holding my hand. "Maybe. But if you hadn't, he might have killed Kellyn."

"Is she okay?"

He nodded once. "She went home with your parents last night."

I swallowed the lump in my throat before choking out the words: "Did he rape her?"

"No."

I let out the air I'd been holding. "And Gavin?"

"He's fine." He let out a short humorless laugh. "Mad as hell, but physically fine."

"And you?"

"About the same."

Unconvinced, I shifted onto my left side and studied him. There were dark circles under his eyes, a gash on his forehead held together with butterfly bandages, a bruise along his jawline—and I suspected there was more I couldn't see. "You don't look fine."

"Don't worry about me." He lifted a hand to brush away a strand of hair that had fallen across my face, and I bit down hard on my cheek as an unwelcome image flashed through my mind. "I'm fine. I'm more concerned about you."

I squeezed my eyes shut and lifted my free hand to my rub my forehead, barely registering the uncomfortable pull of the IV. "I thought you—" Afraid I would cry if I continued, I cut myself off and pressed my fingers against my eyes. "He led me to believe you were dead."

"Honey, I told you, I'm fine." He pulled my other hand into his grasp, careful not to press against the IV. "But you—"

"Where is he?" I interrupted, no longer whispering. Mike grimaced at the sound of my voice, rough and strained. "He got away, didn't he?"

He shook his head vehemently. "No, we've got him. He's at the detention center awaiting trial. Judge denied bail at arraignment."

My body went slack with relief. "What about Natasha?"

"She's in custody, too—thanks to your stupidly brilliant idea of planting a GPS tracker in her duffel bag." Mike gave me a weak smile that quickly faded. "Soon as he found out what happened, Orlando marched into the precinct with the information. We were able to get a location and followed it directly to you, then were able to narrow down her location before the battery died." His eyes drifted downward to our clasped hands. "I don't want to think about how long it would've taken us to find you if you hadn't done that."

"Did they confess?"

"He did not, though we eventually broke her." He shook his head. "We didn't need his confession. There was more than enough evidence to charge him, even without the fact that he was caught in the middle of—" He stopped abruptly when he saw my stricken expression and studied me for a few beats. "You don't remember."

"No," I said, my voice cracking. "I remember bits and pieces, but—" I drew in a long, shaky breath and let it out slowly. "Where were we? Who found me? What was he—"

"We've got him, and you're safe." He leaned his forehead against mine. "It's over. That's all that matters."

I wasn't sure if I wanted answers to those questions, so I didn't press him. But we both knew his statement was a blatant lie.

We just didn't know how big of a lie it was.

«»

AFTER I WAS RELEASED LATER that day, I went home with my parents. Even if I'd wanted to go back to my condo, Mike had barred me from going home until it had been cleaned by professionals who were used to scrubbing blood out of carpet and patching holes left by bullets, without asking questions.

Or that was the reason he gave out loud. It was true, but more likely, he meant until the fear softened. For him, the fear—of how helpless we'd been, of failing, of losing me—would become memory within a couple of months. Once our physical wounds healed and scarred over, once we both went back to work, once Kenny was convicted and sent to prison...That was when he would relax, and the fear would finally fade into memory.

But I knew for me, it would last much, much longer.

Over the next week, I spent most of my time in my old room, where I felt like a stranger amongst framed photos of me and Christine on my dresser, posters of Muse and the Chicago skyline tacked to the aqua-painted walls, thriller novels and old A.P. stylebooks neatly lined up in my bookshelf. In between the two daily meals my mother forced me to eat, I drew the blackout curtains and lay face-up on my bed, staring at the faint glow-in-the-dark stars stuck to the ceiling, until my eyes glazed over and I finally fell into a fitful sleep.

Until I inevitably woke consumed by unmitigated panic—heart pounding, gasping for air, cold despite the sweat-dampened sheets around me.

One afternoon when I opened my eyes, sucking in oxygen and blinking in the unexpected light of day, I found Gavin sitting in an overstuffed armchair he'd dragged over to my bedside from the other side of the room. He waited for me to catch my breath, while observing me with a heartbreakingly sad expression.

I rolled over onto my back, instead watching inkblots of red and purple spill across my lids as I rubbed my eyes. "How long have you been sitting there?" I asked, my voice hoarse from disuse. When I was released from the hospital, the doctor had warned me to keep the talking to a minimum until the swelling went down. Once it did, I realized it wasn't so much that I couldn't talk as I just didn't want to.

He didn't answer. "How are you feeling?"

A short humorless laugh slipped from the base of my throat. "Terrible." I let my arms fall to the bed, and I blinked up at the ceiling. "Or something fifty times worse."

Gavin blew out a breath. "Goddammit," he said. "I knew it was bad, but you're not even trying to deflect."

I bit the inside of my cheek until the prickle at the back of my eyes was replaced by the metallic taste of blood, then swiveled toward him. He was bent over with his arms resting on his legs, head in his hands.

"How are you feeling?" I asked, in little more than a whisper.

He scrubbed his face with his palms before lifting his head. "Terrible," he said, and I noticed his eyes were bloodshot and rimmed in dark circles. "Powerless. Worthless. Disgusted." He shook his head. "Guilty."

Summoning what little energy I had, I hauled myself into a sitting position and threw back the covers. "This isn't your fault," I said, wincing at my body's aching protest as I rotated to face him. "There's nothing you could have done—"

"Of course there is," he blurted out, fury flashing across his face. "I could have told you the truth three years ago. I could have reported the threats to the police. I could have not broken your heart and sent you off alone with no idea of what you were facing." His shoulders dropped, and he sank back against the chair in defeat. "You were right. I was lying, and if I'd just told you what was really going on, we could have figured it out together."

Suddenly nauseated, I bit back a flood of questions and dropped my eyes. Having the answers wouldn't make a difference. I'd spent three years trying to answer other equally difficult questions, and now that I had those answers, they didn't mean anything. They didn't change a damn thing.

"It doesn't matter now," I said, staring down at the carpet. "Don't beat yourself up anymore."

"You mean like you are?"

I slid my eyes up to his and blinked a few times to clear my vision. "What?"

"This isn't your fault, either," he said. "None of it—not then and not now. You know that, right?"

"Sure," I said, lifting one shoulder in a half shrug.

Gavin leaned forward and tentatively picked up my hands, folding them into his. My body went rigid, and my feet twitched with an inexplicable need to run. I swallowed hard and squeezed my eyes shut, trying to focus all my energy on just breathing. When I didn't pull away, he gave me a few beats to adjust to being touched, but he didn't let go.

"Look at me, Jennifer," he said firmly. I clenched my jaw and opened my eyes, feeling the knife in my heart twist a little more when I saw his earnest expression. "You are not to blame. Kenny and Kenny alone is responsible for this." At the sound of his name, I sucked in a shallow breath and held it, my muscles tensing to the point of pain. Gavin squeezed my hands harder. "You did everything you could, okay? You saved Kellyn and God knows how many other women. You brought a killer to justice and gave the victims' families some peace. And you did exactly what you were supposed to." At my blank face, he gave me a small smile. "You survived."

Later, after Gavin finally left, I closed my door, drew the curtains again, and lay back down on the bed, pulling the blankets up to my chin to stave off the persistent chill. I stared up at the ceiling, but I couldn't see the stars anymore. Their light had burned out.

Had I really survived?

I hadn't let myself consciously review what had happened to me, but it was all I could visualize when I closed my eyes. Every time sheer exhaustion took over my body and I drifted into sleep, the nightmare replayed through my mind in visceral detail. The things he said. The things he did. The absolute fear and helplessness. The feel of the knife tip as he dragged it across my skin, his fingers as they gripped my arm or thigh, the weight of his body pressing down on mine and making it harder to breathe.

The marks he left on my body would eventually heal and scar over, but they would always, always be there.

Too many other women had endured the same torment as he razed a path to me. They had died terrible, torturous deaths—in excruciating pain, completely alone. Their bodies had been abused and desecrated, laid out on display like a freak show, photographed for their killer's sick game. And they all died because I had let Baratti convince me he'd had an affair.

Because I hadn't listened to my gut.

Everyone on the planet could tell me that wasn't my fault, every minute of every hour of every day for the rest of my life, and it still wouldn't be true. Maybe I hadn't been the one wielding the weapon, but if it weren't for me, none of this would have happened. If it weren't for me, they would all still be alive. And that was precisely the definition of fault.

Although I wished with every fiber of my being that they hadn't died, part of me was envious of them. They'd experienced the same fear, the same pain, the same humiliation and powerlessness and despair that I had. But unlike me, they didn't have to feel it anymore. They didn't have to be haunted by the memories and guilt and resentment for the rest of their lives. They didn't have to live knowing that they had caused so much suffering, so much death.

Yes, I had survived. Yes, I was alive. But it wasn't because of anything I'd done. It was because Kenny had let me survive.

And I hated him for it.

TO BE CONTINUED

ACKNOWLEDGMENTS

WRITING IS OFTEN THOUGHT OF as a solitary pursuit, but I wouldn't be where I am now without the help and support of so many people:

My husband Josh, whose borderline unhealthy fascination with true crime mirrors my own and whose twisted brain helps me plot horrific (fictional) murders.

My late grandmother, whose love of reading inspired me more than I realized at the time.

My family and friends, who believed in me, encouraged me, supported me, and never once made me feel like writing fiction was a waste of time.

The community of writers in The Write Practice's 100 Day Book program, for giving me constructive feedback and, more importantly, confidence in myself.

Book coach Rochelle Sangabriel, whose enthusiasm and support gave me confidence and motivated me to keep going when I felt like giving up.

And to you, my friend, for taking a chance on an unknown writer. Of all the imaginary worlds you could have traveled to, I am honored you chose to spend time in mine.

AUTHOR'S NOTE

Every sixty-eight seconds, one American is sexually assaulted. If you or someone you know is a victim of sexual assault, you are not alone.

Please visit the Rape, Abuse & Incest National Network (RAINN) at www.rainn.org to access resources and support.

ABOUT THE AUTHOR

 KRYSTEN BENNETT is a lifelong reader, writer, and animal lover. In addition to being a self-published author, she is a communications and design director for a state association. She holds a bachelor's degree in journalism with a minor in English and psychology and is a self-taught graphic and web designer. In her free time, she enjoys listening to true crime podcasts, practicing her wine tasting skills with friends and family, and spoiling her niece. A lifelong Buckeye, she lives in Columbus, Ohio, with her husband and their furbabies.

LET'S STAY CONNECTED!

Sign up for Krysten's monthly newsletter to get a sneak peek at the next Breaking News mystery! Visit **www.krystenbennettwrites.com** to subscribe, and follow her on social media at:

 @krystenbennettwrites   @krystenbennettwrites

 @kbennettwrites   @krystenbennett

THANKS FOR READING!

AUTHORS LOVE TO HEAR FROM readers! Please take a few minutes to submit a rating and review on Goodreads and wherever you purchased this book. In a crowded and competitive industry, reviews boost indie authors' visibility and help their books get discovered by more readers. Even a brief review will go a long way in making that happen!

Printed in Great Britain
by Amazon

75314200R00201